Thomas Masters Markoe

A Treatise on Diseases of the Bones

Thomas Masters Markoe

A Treatise on Diseases of the Bones

ISBN/EAN: 9783337035150

Printed in Europe, USA, Canada, Australia, Japan

Cover: Foto ©Andreas Hilbeck / pixelio.de

More available books at **www.hansebooks.com**

A TREATISE

ON

DISEASES OF THE BONES.

BY

THOMAS M. MARKOE, M. D.,

PROFESSOR OF SURGERY IN THE COLLEGE OF PHYSICIANS AND SURGEONS. SURGEON OF THE
NEW YORK HOSPITAL, SURGEON OF BELLEVUE HOSPITAL, SURGEON OF THE ROOSE-
VELT HOSPITAL, CONSULTING SURGEON OF THE MOUNT SINAI HOSPITAL,
OF THE STRANGERS' HOSPITAL, OF THE STATE WOMAN'S
HOSPITAL, AND OF THE NURSERY AND CHILD'S
HOSPITAL, ETC., ETC.

NEW YORK:

D. APPLETON & COMPANY,

549 & 551 BROADWAY.

1872.

DEDICATION.

PREFACE.

THE book which I now offer to my professional brethren contains the substance of the lectures which I have delivered during the past twelve years at the College of Physicians and Surgeons of this city. It does not claim to be a complete compendium of all that is known on the subjects of which it treats; for so much has been learned in bone-pathology since Stanley's work was published, now nearly a quarter of a century ago, that I have not had the leisure, and certainly not the ability, to write such a treatise. I have, therefore, in the arrangement of the different parts of my work, followed rather the leadings of my own studies and observations, dwelling more on those branches where I had seen and studied most, and perhaps too much neglecting others where my own experience was more barren, and therefore to me less interesting. I have endeavored, however, to make up the deficiencies of my own knowledge by the free use of the materials scattered so richly through our periodical literature, which scattered leaves it is the right and the duty of the systematic writer to collect and to embody in any account he may offer of the state of our science at any given period. In all cases where I have thus made use of the labors of others, I have given credit in the text to the authors from whom I have quoted.

The study of Diseases of the Bones has had for me a life-long interest, and my opportunities for its cultivation

have been ample. I can only regret now that these excellent advantages have not been turned to better account, and
that my industry and perseverance have been so far below
my privileges. For this, my apology, not my excuse, must
be, a life somewhat actively devoted to the practice of my
profession and to its public teaching, leaving me less time
to devote to scientific studies, than those studies, for their
successful prosecution, imperatively demand.

In illustrating the work, I have not hesitated to borrow
largely from my friends. By the kind permission of the
publishers, I have availed myself of a large number of admirable woodcuts from Paget's work on Surgical Pathology,
and from Billroth's work on the same subject, translated by
Hackley. All the original illustrations, mainly taken from
specimens in the cabinet of the New York Hospital, were
made for me by Mr. Joseph Harley, of this city, and are, 1
think, remarkably fine examples of his beautiful art. The
photographs, on which so much of the success of a woodcut
depends, were made by Mr. O. G. Mason, the accomplished
photographer of Bellevue Hospital.

I cannot too warmly express my thanks to my professional friends, who have in every possible way encouraged
and assisted me in my work. I can only say that, if there
be any merit in the book, it is largely the result of their
kind and active coöperation, and that a good share of the
most valuable observations have been contributed by their
generous friendship.

If the reading of my book should afford as much profit
as the preparing of it has given me pleasure, I shall have
reason to be abundantly satisfied with what I have done.

NEW YORK, *March* 6, 1872.

CONTENTS.

CONTENTS.

PART III.

MALIGNANT DISEASES OF BONE.

DISEASES OF THE BONES.

INTRODUCTION.

THE office of the skeleton in the animal economy may be said to be threefold, viz.: 1. To afford that support to the softer tissues that is needful to maintain the shape of the individual; 2. To give the protection to some of the more important organs which the delicacy of their structure demands; and, 3. To supply the necessary levers by which locomotion is to be accomplished. In the lowest classes of animals, whose functions are simple and few, and whose vital activities are moderate, the skeleton seems to be designed sometimes for mere support, and sometimes mainly for protection: in the higher and more complex animal, where the tissues are beginning to arrange themselves into distinct organs with specific functions, we need both support and protection; while, in the highest classes, including man, the increasing diversity of organs and functions requiring varied and precise movements, we have the skeleton divided into many distinct parts, articulated with one another in such a way as to be capable of an infinite variety of movements, upon the strength and precision of which the perfection of the varied functions depends, while the offices of support and protection have become secondary ones, almost lost sight of in the more prominent and more important relations of the skeleton to locomotion.

Thus, the coral animal supports its position on the rock on

1

which it grows by slowly calcifying its oldest and deepest layers until they become part of the stony structure itself, while its younger and softer parts are sprouting and growing, to repeat, in their turn, the same process of solidification, till reefs, and islands, and continents, are upreared by their marvellous multiplication. Thus, too, in some of the other of the lowest zoophytes, whose whole body is little more than a mass of jelly, and whose almost only function is nutrition of the simplest and most direct character, we can only regard its silicious or calcareous covering as bestowed upon it for protection against the rude agencies to which, in the ever-moving waters of the ocean, it is constantly exposed, and without which protection even its incalculable fertility might not be able to save its species from extinction. In the higher classes of the Radiata, when distinct digestive, respiratory, and generative systems begin to show themselves with some definite powers of locomotion, we find a framework which is designed not merely for protection, but evidently also for preserving form, and for giving effectiveness to the limited movements which the animal is capable of making. In the Mollusca, where the vegetative or organic is developed so greatly in excess of the animal or locomotive system, we find the shell serving the purpose almost exclusively of protection, neither support nor locomotion depending on it in any very marked degree; while in the Articulata, which as a class present a preponderating development of the locomotive system, we find their hard calcareous or horny casing so arranged as not only to preserve their perfect shape, but to give variety and power to the complicated movements by which they are characterized, and upon which their vital functions in a great measure depend. In the Mammalia, some of the more delicate organs, as the brain and lungs, require the protection of a bony envelope like the skull and the thorax; all parts require the support necessary to maintain their shape; and the same support is necessary for the action of the muscles on the unyielding levers supplied by the bones.

The mechanical necessities of the case, then, are threefold: 1. Firmness of tissue sufficient to afford the requisite support and protection; 2. Mobility of one part upon another, such as to permit the movements of which the muscular system is capable; and 3. A power of increase and change which will adapt it to the increasing size or changing shape of the animal. These mechanical requirements are, in the lowest classes of animals, easily answered by a silicious or calcareous covering, which increases in extent as the animal inhabiting it increases in dimensions. This increase, however, it must be noted, is one merely of superaddition to the edges or surfaces of the original shell, which, once hardened, is no longer under the influence of vital action in any such sense that it can undergo any change either in its consistence or in its size. It must be evident, however, that such an arrangement can only be efficient in the simplest shapes that animal life assumes, and that the moment complexity of form is assumed, and variety of locomotive action exhibited, a new element is added to the problem of the skeleton, and that this new element is the power, not merely to increase, but to change its form, in obedience to the changes which each part of the more complex animal is liable to present, as each part grows to a greater size, and usually to a greater power. Thus, in the cell-like protozoa, already alluded to, we can readily conceive that the rounded or elongated form, partly roofed in by a rounded or elongated shell, may, as it increases in size, be still covered by a simple increase of size of its protecting case, and the difficulty is not much increased in the Radiata, whose form is merely a repetition of simple elements round a common centre. But, among the Articulata, as the Crustacea and the Insecta, the growth of the animal in all the segments of its body, and in all the complex subdivisions of limbs and antennæ, must be accommodated by a provision for something more than a mere superaddition at the edges of the original-simple formed shell.

This part of the problem is differently solved in different classes of animals. In the gasteropod Mollusca, for example, it is evaded rather than solved. As the animal grows it leaves the narrow quarters of its original dwelling, and finds better accommodation in the larger segment of shell which, as it grows, it adds to the old homestead, from which it usually shuts itself off by a partition-wall, which completely isolates the old chambers from the new. In this way many of our most beautiful shells are produced, their form and size depending on the successive additions and alterations which the increasing size, and often the changing form, of the animal has obliged it to make to its original construction. In the oyster, each degree of growth of the animal is provided for by an entire new layer of shell-growth, which, being internal and larger than the preceding one, takes its place; and thus we have produced the peculiar lamination and the very thick, heavy shell by which these valuable animals are protected.

In many of the Crustacea, some of whom, as the crab and the lobster, are entirely encased in a calcareous envelope, the difficulty is met by a process of throwing off the skeleton entirely, and providing a new and larger one, proportionate to the increase in size of the animal. A similar action is observed in some of the changes which take place, during the development of several species of the Insecta. This process of the periodical shedding of the shell is a very curious and interesting one, and it may enable us to appreciate somewhat better the difficulty of the problem we are now studying, to watch the tedious, difficult, and one would think painful exertions which these animals have to undergo, in order to free themselves from a covering which has simply become too small for them, and has by this clumsy process to be got rid of, to make way for a larger one. The imperfection, if we may so speak, of the mode is still more strikingly shown by the unprotected and helpless condition in which the unhappy animal is left after casting off its old coat, and before the new one is firm enough to be available.

In some of these species, and also in some of the Vertebrata, which have a partial external skeleton, another arrangement is sometimes found, by which the growth of the excrementitious skeleton is provided for. It is composed of numerous plates, fitting more or less closely together, but separated from one another by a portion of the foundation membrane of the shell, which is not calcified, and which therefore allows a certain degree of mobility among the plates. This provides, to some extent, for the increasing size of the animal, but the change is still further accompanied by an actual increase in size of each separate piece, by deposition at its edges. By this method form is maintained, and mobility secured, without the necessity of the uncomfortable and expensive process of shedding.

In the Vertebrata, where great complexity of structure and function demanded great variety and precision of muscular movement, and where the importance of the life of external relation required something more sensitive than a calcareous shell, the skeleton becomes more complex in its form, greatly multiplied in the number of its pieces, and either mainly or entirely internal in its position. And now we find, in obedience to its higher requirements, that the skeleton is no longer a mere dead, unchanging, excrementitious substance, entirely removed from the actions of the living organism, and incapable, except by bare addition to its mass, of changing with the changing necessities of the body. It has now become a living part of a living body; it is capable, by its own nutritive capacities, of growing and changing with the increasing size or varying necessities of the part which it supports. In short, it is endowed with all the powers of adaptation which the most favored tissues possess, and exhibits in a high degree the presence and action of that formative force and nutritive energy by which the integrity of all parts of the living body tends to be preserved, both under the demands of health and the pressure of disease.

And here the vital problem is superadded to the mechanical. How to endow with all the attributes of life a tissue that shall be hard enough, and therefore strong enough, to answer the mechanical purposes of an internal skeleton, was the question to be answered, and most admirably has it been solved. The unabsorbing and impenetrable bone-tissue forbade the imbibition of the nutritive juices into its substance, by which imbibition, indeed, the very strength of the structure must necessarily be compromised, and therefore we find its nutrition carried on on a plan entirely peculiar to itself. Not only are the vessels introduced into every part even of the hardest bone, but its tissue is studded everywhere with minute centres of cell-life in the form of the bone-corpuscles, which are, in fact, nothing more than bone-spaces containing cells. These spaces are far too numerous, and much too minute, to have any direct relation to the bone-capillaries, but they are brought into such relation by a series of fine tubes, or canaliculi, which permeate all the interspace between the bone-cells and the capillaries, opening a communication between them, by which the plasma of the blood, exuded from its vessels, finds its way easily and abundantly to the most distant bone-corpuscles, and thus permeates the bone to its minutest elemental particle. This beautiful and perfect system of pores, traversing all the territories between the Haversian canal and the bone-corpuscle, secures all the advantages to the bone which imbibition gives in the nutrition of the softer tissues, and yet, by the fineness of its arrangement, it does not interfere with the solidity and strength of the hard and intractable substance for whose nutrition it so perfectly provides.

By these peculiar and admirable arrangements of its nutritive supply, bone becomes endowed with a grade of vitality equal to that of the most favored tissues of the body. It is not only a living part, capable of growing with the growth and changing with the change of the growing and changing frame, but it is endowed with all the highest attributes of vitality, not only in its power, first, *of Growth*, but second, *of Development;* third, *of Regeneration;* fourth, *of Repair;* and, fifth, *of Disease.*

1. *Of Growth.*—The increase of size of the shell of the oyster or of the crab is, as we have seen, one of mere super-addition to parts already formed, and which in themselves are incapable of any other change. Bone grows by an inherent vital power, by which it accommodates itself to the increasing size of the animal to which it belongs, and this by a series of interstitial changes in its particles as complete as, though probably much less rapid than, those with which we are familiar in the soft parts. This growth, of course, is mostly observed in the younger and softer bone, which is in the process of attaining its final and adult size; but it is, nevertheless, true, that the process of true interstitial growth can be demonstrated on the mature and firmly-ossified bone of young adults; and it is altogether probable that, even in the most solid and mature

bones of later life, the interstitial and molecular changes, which we know to characterize the life of the softer tissues, are the constant conditions of the life of the bone.

2. *Development.*—No phases of development are more beautiful or more interesting in their study than those of the skeleton from its first rudimentary trace up to its perfect form. None afford better opportunities for observation, and none better illustrate the laws which regulate the process. But, besides this original development, by which the properties of mature bone are assumed, after its passage through many intermediate, less perfect, and gradually improving stages, we have the fact daily verified that the mature adult skeleton will develop itself not merely in general robustness, but in the actual increase of its bony processes, by virtue of the law that every part grows in size and strength by increased exercise of its function. Exercise and labor will develop the bones just in the same manner, and precisely for the same reason, that they develop the muscles themselves; and, moreover, though it may be a slower result, yet, if the increased exercise be maintained sufficiently long, the development of the bones will be precisely proportioned to the increase in size and power of the muscles which move them.

3. *Regeneration.*—M. Ollier, of Lyons, and others who, with him, have been engaged in showing how large a share the periosteum takes in the formation of bone, have, in the course of their numerous experiments, fully demonstrated how complete is the regenerating power of bone if only care have been taken to leave the periosteum uninjured, and that, under favorable circumstances, the periosteum, thus left, will generate a new bone almost as perfect as the one which has been removed. But, still further, when the whole bone, periosteum included, has been removed, a certain amount of regenerative power remains, and instances are on record where the lower jaw, the clavicle, the ulna, and several other bones, have been removed by operation in the human subject, with the result of a reproduction, imperfect, it is true, but, nevertheless, a regeneration of the removed bone, sufficient to maintain in part the shape,

and in some degree to supply the loss of the original. Similar partial regenerations have been observed in animals when, in experimental operations, entire bones, with their periosteum, have been removed.

4. *Repair.*—Each of these processes of growth, development, and regeneration, is abundantly provided for in the skeletons of those lower animals to which allusion has been made in former paragraphs. Of repair, however, in the proper sense of the term, they are not capable. A fractured coral stem is a hopeless severance; a crushed shell, in that portion from which the animal has retired, is an unchangeable injury. Even in that part which it still inhabits, no proper repair of the injury to the shell takes place, though the animal protects its body from the effects of exposure by forming a new calcareous layer opposite the damaged spot, by which the mischief is rather compensated for than healed. The same is true of the Crustacea. In a lobster whose claw had evidently been broken by contact with some sharp, hard edge, I recently observed the mode by which the serious wound was closed. The injury was evidently an old one, and still remained—a gash, as it were, in the upper edge of one of the large claws, nearly an inch in depth. The opening was thoroughly and neatly closed by calcareous matter, which had been deposited by the vascular membrane which secretes the shell, and the injured part was thus separated from its old relations to the surface of the animal. No deposit was found on the broken edges, but by time, through the attrition against the gravelly or stony bottoms in which they live, the sharpness of the edge was smoothed off so perfectly that it was only by examining somewhat carefully that the scar could be distinguished from that left by a proper healing of the tissue. In all such cases, and in similar instances among the Insecta, the absence of repair does not at all depend on the want of reparative power in the animal, but simply on the excrementitious nature of the skeleton, which is, in that sense, no longer a living part of the body, and cannot, therefore, in its injuries, profit by the immense reparative capacities of the animal. The same animal, and by a law evidently of compensation, which cannot repair

a compound fracture of its shell, can reproduce, it may be, the entire limb, if the injury happen to be severe enough to tear it from its body.

Contrasted with these imperfect efforts in the lower animals, we find in the higher Mammalia, and particularly in man, that the repair of injured bone is among the most beautiful and perfect of all the reparative actions: 1. Its most striking feature is that it is intrinsic; that is, it depends for its perfection on the perfect life and high vital organization of the bone-structure itself. 2. It is reliable. Under all circumstances of age and condition, and under all degrees of injury which do not compromise the life of the injured part, it may be so surely counted on, that occasional failures excite our surprise, and can in most instances be explained by some mechanical interference with the process, rather than by any want of inherent power of repair. 3. The repair is economical. No more material is employed than necessary, and this material is so perfectly transformed into bone-tissue, that the microscope cannot distinguish between the old and the new formation. 4. The repair is complete. Although, in the highest Vertebrata, the repairing material is thus carefully economized, the result of the process is that the bone is, at the point of injury, as strong as, and usually stronger than, it was before, so that, after the healing process is perfected, a fracture would be more likely to occur at some other point than at the seat of the perfectly-mended original break. Finally, the process is so arranged that its result is shapely. No deformity is left beyond what is the necessary result of the displacement of the broken fragments. The uniting medium is so proportioned, and so arranged between the parts it is intended to heal, that, after the process is completed, no superabundance remains, and, if the broken ends have been maintained in perfect apposition, so shapely and so perfect is the result, that it is oftentimes difficult to decide that a bone has been broken, when it is examined long after the injury, or, if the fact of fracture is known, to point out the precise spot at which the fracture was situated.

It is true that, in some of the Vertebrata below man, the union of broken bones is accompanied by a superabundance of the ossific material of repair, and that hence the union in these animals is accomplished with a deforming prominence of the callus at the seat of the fracture. But this apparent imperfection in the process is so evidently in obedience to certain mechanical conditions of the injured part, connected with the impossibility of securing its absolute rest, that it should rather be regarded as an admirable illustration of adaptability to circumstances of the reparative force, than any impugnment of the power and perfection of that force itself.

5. *Disease.*—I have classed the liability to disease as one of the evidences of the high vital endowments of bone-tissue; and while I am not prepared to maintain that there is in the capacity for varied and serious disease any direct indication of high organization, yet it must be acknowledged that, under our present dispensation of sorrow, such liability is in fact always associated with those tissues, and, indeed, with those animals who hold the highest place in the scale of complex organization and varied function. Comparative pathology has not yet been studied so carefully as its importance in illustrating human disease would seem to warrant, but enough has been learned to give us some valuable hints. Thus, as a general law, I think it may be stated that the reparative power increases as perfection and complexity of organization diminish. I know that this law is not by any means uniform in its application to the different classes into which we divide the animal kingdom, but, for our present purpose, it is quite safe to accept it as a general fact that reparative power increases as we descend in the animal series, and that, while in the higher animals moderate injuries are often followed by fatal consequences, in the Mollusca and the Articulata we find species in which whole limbs may be reformed after detachment, and, in the Radiata, some that can reproduce an entire and perfect body out of each of the fragments to which accident or design may have reduced it. This reparative force, thus readily called forth by injury, we may be pretty sure, I think, is also ever present as an antagonist to disease; and that, by the ever-present virtue of this powerful controlling agency, disease in many of the lowest animals is either altogether prevented or is only allowed

to assume its lowest, simplest, and least dangerous manifestations.

Thus, I believe it might be maintained that the proneness to disease is in an inverse ratio to the reparative power, and that therefore the animals highest in the scale are those most likely to show varieties of severe and complicated disorder. The same principle seems to me applicable to the relative liability of the different tissues of the same individual. Those, for example, of the lowest class, enjoying a mere vegetative life, as tendon, aponeurosis, and cartilage, we find but rarely the subjects of disease, and, when diseased, their affections are commonly of the simplest character. Disintegration from the effects of inflammation is almost the only morbid process we know of in the tendon, and ulceration in its varied forms is the chief disease of cartilage. It is in the higher, more vascular, more actively living tissues, that the most varied, the most frequent, the most interesting, and in all respects the most important, morbid changes are observed to take place, the careful study of the minuter shades of which is the difficult and laborious task of the modern student of pathology.

Among these higher tissues, bone, as we have seen, holds, by right of its elaborate vital provisions, a very high position, and this position it abundantly vindicates by the immense variety of the shades of its morbid actions, as well as the frequency and severity of its diseases. We shall find no morbid condition of the soft parts of which a counterpart may not be found in the bones, and few of the tissues present so large and varied a catalogue of diseases as this same apparently insensible, and, to the careless eye, lowly-organized, bone-substance. It is liable to every form of nutritive change, as in hypertrophy and atrophy; it is subject to its own peculiar constitutional disorders, as in rickets and malacosteon. It is prone to inflammation in all its forms, and illustrates most admirably its every variety and every grade, and at the same time sympathizes so keenly with every constitutional taint that a large chapter in the history of syphilis and scrofula must be taken from the behavior of these poisons toward the bones. Its softer portions are invaded by caries and tubercle, while every part is liable to the insidious visitation of morbid growths of all forms, both benignant and cancerous. In short, it is a microcosm in which the whole story of disease is to be traced, and yet which presents many phases of morbid action, so entirely peculiar to itself as to entitle its study to be ranked among the most interesting and fruitful provinces of the great domain of Pathology.

PART I.

DISEASES OF BONE.

CHAPTER I.

Bones, like the soft parts, are liable to hypertrophy from two classes of causes: 1. Those which are morbid in their action; 2. Those which are unconnected with any appreciable diseased condition. Of the morbid conditions of bone, terminating in an increase of their dimensions, we shall have very frequent occasion to speak hereafter, and we shall find it to be one of the commonest results of long-continued inflammatory disease in all its forms; so much so, that an experienced eye can pronounce, with much accuracy, that chronic inflammation has existed in a bone, from an inspection only of its enlarged size—an enlargement which, in the hypertrophy from disease, is usually accompanied with more or less distortion and deformity.

In the cases of hypertrophy of bone which occur without apparent morbid cause, we find the condition usually limited to a single bone, as the femur or the tibia, which, by its undue growth, makes such a disproportion between the length of the limbs that serious lameness is sometimes thus produced; and it is always well for surgeons to take into account the possibility of such a condition in measuring the length of the two limbs, to clear up doubtful points of diagnosis. Such embarrassment in the study of obscure cases is spoken of by several authors; and in the New York Hospital an instance presented itself, where only the history of a previous elongation of the femur explained a discrepancy in the symptoms which we could not otherwise comprehend.

Mr. Stanley speaks of several of these cases of simple hy-

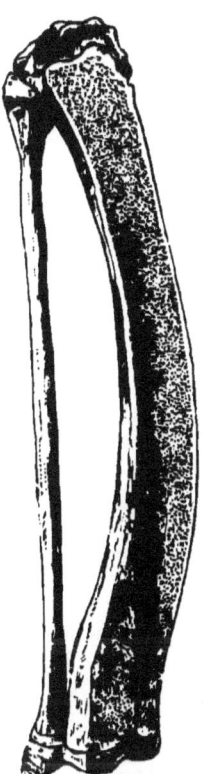

pertrophy where the affected bones had become curved, and Mr. Paget gives a curious instance. from St. Bartholomew's Hospital Museum, where, the tibia having become hypertrophied while the fibula remained unchanged, the tibia had become curved outward in order to accommodate its increase to the unaltered fibula, to which it was tied by its ligamentous attachments above and below. Fig. 1, taken from Mr. Paget's work on "Surgical Pathology," gives a very good idea of the deformity.

Hypertrophy of bone may, however, be the result of increase in the duty which a given bone is called on to perform. Of this compensatory hypertrophy the best example with which I am acquainted is shown in a specimen in the museum of the College of Physicians and Surgeons. The young lad from whom it was taken suffered from an acute necrosis of one of his tibiæ, involving almost the whole length of the shaft. For some reason, the reparative actions were very imperfect, and almost no involucrum was formed, so that, when the sequestrum

Fig. 1.—(From Paget.)

became loose and was removed, no new bone replaced the loss; and, though the wound healed, and ho was able to go about, yet the tibia was represented, for several inches, by a mere fibrous band, in which but little bone-deposit could be detected, and which gave no support whatever to the limb. Under these circumstances, he was advised to use the limb as much as possible, which he did, and gradually found that it began to be stronger, so that before his death, which took place within two years of the operation, he could bear considerable weight upon it. The bones of both legs are preserved, and show the tibia of the diseased side replaced in its middle portion by a mere fibrous cord, with some nodules of bone continuous with the sound bone above and below, but not fused together in the middle; so that the supporting power

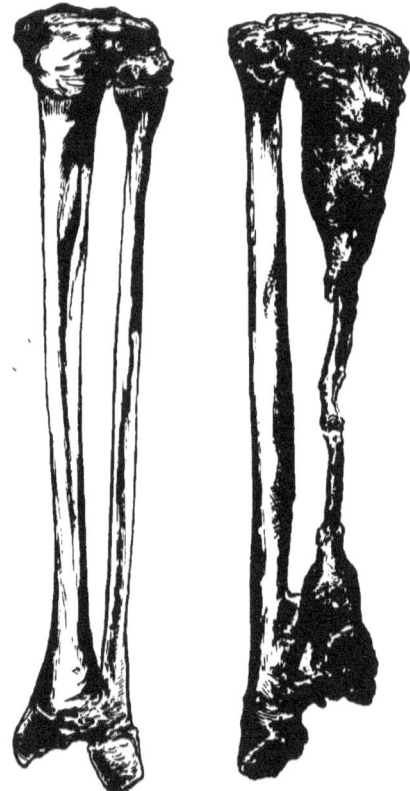

FIG. 2.—(From New York Hospital Museum.)

of the tibia is as completely abrogated as if it had suffered a fracture which had not united. The fibula of that side, however, has undergone hypertrophy, most marked opposite the deficiency in the tibia, and so considerable that, on comparing it with its fellow of the opposite side, it is at least three times its superior in thickness and strength. A more perfect illustration of simple compensatory hypertrophy, and a more beautiful manifestation of the intelligent action of the laws of nutritive reparation, can hardly be found. (Fig. 2.)

Another form of hypertrophy of bone is that which affects the bones of the face, and is commonly spoken of as the ivory exostosis.   It consists of a very dense and solid growth, which slowly involves the bones of one side of the face, more commonly in the neighborhood of the orbit, and which gradually converts them into a tumor of great size, which projects from the surface of the face, and which encroaches on the cavities of the nose, eye, antrum, and mouth, in such a way as to produce the most serious and sometimes the most dangerous deformity.   A large number of cases of this curious form of hypertrophy have been collected by Mr. Heath, in his admirable essay on the "Injuries and Diseases of the Jaws."   The disease is usually painless throughout its entire course, except where it inflicts pain by its encroachment, and it is unaccompanied by any evidences of inflammatory action.   It seems to affect adults of middle age, and is not traceable to any injury or connected with any constitutional taint.   The progress of the disease is extremely slow, and presents ordinarily no other features but those of simple increase.   This form of hypertrophy, however, is so much allied to the tumors which affect the bones of the face, that its more particular description may be conveniently reserved for a future chapter.

Atrophy of bone most commonly presents itself as the consequence of long‑continued disuse; but several other causes sometimes produce it.   Thus, Mr. Curling has shown that, in certain cases of fracture, where the injury involves the trunk of the nutritious artery, the fragment of bone which is deprived of its vascular supply from that source will sometimes undergo a process of atrophy, and that in this way non-union is sometimes produced.   Atrophy of bone is likewise seen in those cases of localized paralysis under which the whole limb wastes away, and in young children never attains its proper development.   Disuse, however, may, I think, be said to be by far the most common cause of atrophy of bone; and, inasmuch as a certain amount of diminished activity accompanies the action of all other causes, it is difficult to prove that any one of them is sufficient to produce the condition without the assistance of some degree of diminished functional activity.

Two forms of atrophy present themselves: one in which

there is simply a diminution in the amount of bone material; and one in which there is at the same time an excessive development of fat. These two forms correspond to the two conditions of atrophy met with in the soft parts; and, while it is not possible to define precisely the circumstances under which each occurs, yet I think it would be correct to say that, generally, the simple atrophy is best seen in cases where the change takes place very gradually, and from simple disuse, while the fatty degeneration is most striking where the affection is somewhat acute in character, particularly if it be associated with some inflammatory action about the part diseased. Thus, the most striking example of simple atrophy that I have seen, is in a stump of a tibia, where the end of the limb below the knee had not been used for support for many years. Here the bone is rarefied, its cavities enlarged, its walls thinned; but, in other respects, it is normal. On the other hand, the most marked instance of fatty change is in the bones of the leg of a lad upon whom Dr. Stevens performed exsection and wiring of the fragments of an ununited compound fracture. After giving the poor boy a long and faithful trial, the limb was amputated. The bones are small and light, and almost pliable, but they are so much imbued with fat that, though the specimen has been in the cabinet of the New York Hospital for about twenty-five years, it still, in warm weather, distils oil enough each season to destroy the varnish, and run down on the stand upon which the specimen is placed.

The occurrence of atrophy from disuse has some important practical relations. First, a bone in a condition of progressive atrophy must be very liable to undergo other changes, in obedience to mechanical influences acting upon it. I have now under my care a lady who had rigidity and a vicious position of abduction of the hip-joint, following a delivery, accompanied by convulsions. For many months she has not been able to use the limb, and, though there is no marked shortening, yet the trochanter of the affected side has fallen in so much as to leave no doubt that interstitial absorption of the neck and head of the bone has taken place to a very marked extent. Similar changes we see in old luxations; and in atrophied limbs, where unfavorable positions have been assumed, we see the bone be-

2

coming absorbed under the influence of the pressure, or bent by the gradual action of the force exerted, to a degree which we would not expect in sound, healthy bone. But perhaps the most important practical deduction from the history of atrophy is that which inculcates extreme care in manipulations with bones which have long been disused. The fact that disuse for a few months, or even for a few weeks, will reduce the resisting power of bone, should never be forgotten, and was impressed upon my recollection, in the most emphatic but unpleasant manner, by the following case:

Patrick Barry, aged forty-two, was admitted to the New York Hospital, October 28, 1854, with a dislocation of left femur, of seven weeks' standing. The symptoms were unequivocal, and the head of the bone could be felt on the dorsum of the ilium. The man was of good muscular development, but the limb was flabby and wasted from inaction. Attempts were made to reduce it by Reid's method of manipulation, and, being unsuccessful, were abandoned for the ordinary method of Sir Astley Cooper. Extension was made by pulleys, and, while a strong movement of adduction was being made by my own hand, a crack was heard, and it immediately became evident that the neck of the femur had broken. On taking off the pulleys, the crepitus, the form, and all the symptoms, made the diagnosis clear. In the original minute of the case, the remark is made: " With regard to the fracture of the cervix, we were all surprised at the slight amount of force which was competent to produce such a mortifying accident." A similar accident occurred to one of my colleagues in attempting to reduce an old dislocation of the elbow-joint. While making extension, and at the same time trying to flex the forearm on the arm, the humerus gave way, and a very oblique fracture was found to have occurred about a hand's breadth above the joint. These unfortunate occurrences (and most surgeons have had a similar experience) should lead to the greatest care in using bones, which have long been disused, as levers in reducing displacements, remembering that great power is developed by the lever-action, and that the bone-tissue is not so strong to resist as it is in an unchanged bone.

CHAPTER II.

INFLAMMATION OF BONE.

THE process of inflammation in bone presents many modifications, due to the peculiar structure in which it occurs. Its essential character is the same, however, and the laws which govern it in the soft parts are those which regulate it in the bones, due allowance being made for the density and intractability of the tissue involved. As in the softer tissues, so in the bones, we may conveniently arrange our study of inflammation into divisions embracing the various effects of the morbid process, as shown at each stage of its progress; for, while it is well understood that no absolute line separates one stage from another, and that one stage is constantly mingled with another during its progress, yet, for practical purposes, we shall recognize that each case assumes its importance from the prominence of one or more features which give it its individual character, which features are those of some particular stage or effect of inflammation. Thus we may include under one head all those inflammations of bone which are attended with organization of the exuded products. A second class may embrace those in which the exudation goes on to purulent formation. A third will include all those cases in which ulceration and destruction of tissue by molecular disintegration take place, embracing most of the cases called caries; and a last will embrace that large class in which death of tissue is the consequence of the inflammation, as in necrosis.

Inflammation of Bone with Organization of the Inflammatory Products.—The cases coming under this head are, almost uniformly, of a chronic character, and of a moderate degree. Their causes are habitual exposure to wet and cold, injuries of moderate severity, and sometimes a constitutional vice, either acquired, as syphilis or scurvy, or original, as scrofula and its numerous allied taints of the blood. Their pathological anatomy seems to be a low grade of inflammation pervading a certain part or the whole of a bone, and which, after it has been fully developed, presents microscopical characters which have now been pretty thoroughly investigated. To the unaided eye, the bone is of distinctly pinkish or ruddy hue, usually in patches of irregular extent and shape, and differing among themselves in depth of color. The compact tissue, as well as the spongy, shows this inflammatory redness, though, of course, in a less degree, and, when thus reddened by inflammation, has usually lost some of its apparent density. The periosteum and the medulla usually participate, in a marked degree, in this vascular change, as they do in all the morbid actions of bone. Indeed, writers are generally agreed that they are both of them intrinsic parts of bone, and that the study of their diseases cannot be and ought not to be dissociated from the diseases of the bone-tissue itself. Sometimes, it is true, the inflammatory actions are mainly confined to the periosteum, and more rarely to the medulla, but the neighboring bone is always more or less implicated, and must necessarily be so, because its vessels are derived from, and form part of, the circulation of the membranes by which it is covered. After the inflammation has existed for some time, the bone begins to be enlarged, showing the addition of new bony matter to its original substance. This enlargement shows itself in two principal ways: first, by increase of size, and, secondly, by increase of density—two conditions which, though usually associated, are not by any means constantly so; and hence, among the numerous specimens of inflamed bone which encumber every pathological museum, we find some which are merely enlarged, in all their dimensions, about the seat of inflammation, without any manifest consolidation of tissue, and others where the bulk has not undergone any marked change, while the increased weight and solidity show that abundant interstitial deposit has been taking place.

Under the microscope the first noticeable feature is the enlargement of the Haversian canals. This takes place in obedience to the requirements of the increasing vessels, for in a condition of health the canal is so nearly filled by the vessel which traverses it, that little or no enlargement of the latter can take place without some yielding of the former. So true is this, that it is believed by most pathologists that this impossibility, in

bone, of yielding to the pressure of a suddenly-increasing circulation, is one principal reason why acute inflammation of
bone is so liable to produce necrosis. In more chronic and
moderate attacks, there is time afforded for the bony canals to
enlarge by absorption, and thus allow the gradual expansion
of capillary vessels ; and hence there is usually little or no liability to necrosis where the inflammatory process assumes this
deliberate and sometimes extremely tedious course. Besides
this enlargement of the Haversian canals, the lacunæ also
undergo a change both in size and shape, and the same is observed in the canaliculi. Mr. Barwell, in his admirable account of these changes, says: " The lacunæ have increased still
more in size and breadth ; even those of the Haversian systems are very broad, oval, or are rudely circular ; their interior,
instead of remaining dark, has, as it were, opened out into a
light space, marked by light-colored round spots, surrounded
by dark lines, or *vice versa*, according to the focus and direction
of the light. Some of them are very granular ; others, more
rare, are crowded with round, cell-like bodies, forming a mul-
berry mass, which appears to stand out above the bone-surface.
The canaliculi, remaining large in number, have increased in
size chiefly at their commencement in the lacuna, so that they
appear to open into that space by a broad mouth like an estu-
ary. They are throughout more marked than the normal
tube ; they branch also in many instances into three or four
channels, and, sometimes, at the spot whence these branches
diverge, a considerable enlargement in the main trunk is
perceptible, as if at that point a new lacuna were being
formed. While these changes are going on in the lacunæ and
canaliculi, a change is also noticeable in the granular substance of the bone-tissue itself. The granular character
becomes more distinctly marked, as if a partial disintegration were about to take place, and the bone were about to
break up into its original particles. What is the precise meaning of this change, has not been, so far as I know, positively
determined, but Mr. Follin does not hesitate to attribute the
general granular appearance of an inflamed bone to an enlargement of the orifices of the canaliculi, such as has been
above described, which, when the bone is macerated, gives a

dotted or granular appearance of the surfaces on which they open. The further microscopical changes in inflamed bone are merely the more advanced stages of what has already been described; the bone-structure gradually disintegrates and dissolves away, and this to an extent and in a manner which vary considerably, according to the characters of the inflammation and the tendency which it develops. Consequent, however upon these merely destructive actions, we soon begin to see some attempts at reparation, and, in the moderate form of inflammation we are now studying, these actions soon assume the prominence. Into the natural cavities of the bone now enlarged by the processes we have been studying, we soon have poured out the plastic exudations which are the results of the inflammation, and which begin to show organization. This organization leads by a strong and almost unvarying tendency to the development into bone, so that we soon begin to find new bone deposited in all the vacancies and porosities of the old. By means of these two processes, the first one of absorption, and the second one of deposit, we have two conditions of bone produced, which are spoken of by writers as respectively rarefaction and condensation of bone. When in any given case the absorbent actions are in excess, and more particles are removed than are replaced, then we may have an expansion with rarefaction of tissue, or, as it has been termed, osteoporosis. When, on the other hand, the destruction is more than compensated by the deposit of new bone, then we have an expansion with consolidation of the inflamed bone, so that it becomes harder and heavier than natural. The enlargement of bone, with expansion or rarefaction of tissue, is the rarer of the two, though Mr. Stanley says, "I have learned that the simple swelling of bone, from expansion of its tissue, is one of the most frequent alterations to which it is liable." We have, in the cabinet of the New York Hospital, a specimen which shows this condition in a remarkable degree. It consists of the bones of the knee-joint taken from a patient, a young adult, whose limb was amputated for long-continued disease of the joint. The whole bone is enlarged, without marked deformity, but every part has undergone a sort of atrophic change, by which the external lamina, the plates of the cancelli, indeed every separate layer of bone, has become reduced down to the thinnest possible dimensions; so that, while every thing seems to be present that originally constituted the bone, yet it is so refined and so rarefied as to look as if some process of corrosion had been adopted which had begun to act upon the surfaces of the bone, but had been arrested before any lamina had been completely destroyed. The weight of these bones cannot much exceed half of what it originally was. Some degree of this . expansion is very commonly seen in the neighborhood of caries, and I suspect most often in those cases which depend on scrofula.

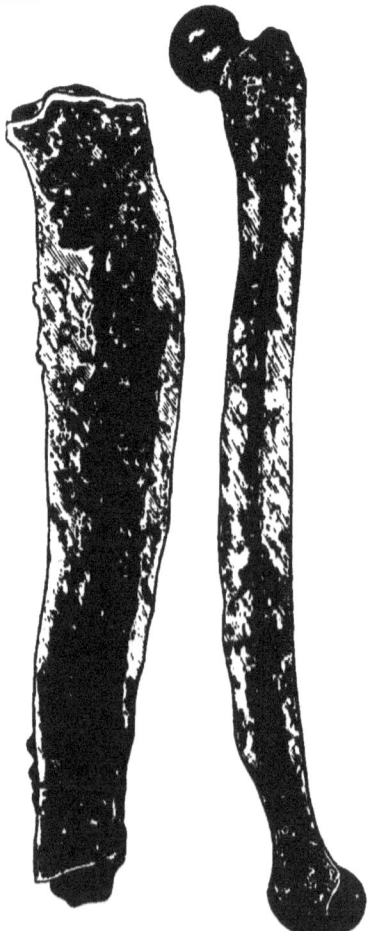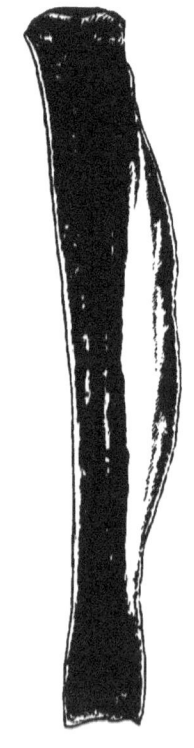

Fig. 3.—(From Billroth.)   Fig. 4.—(New York Hospital)

The other condition, viz., enlargement with consolidation of tissue, is certainly the most frequent of all the changes produced by inflammation in bone. It presents itself under three distinct forms: 1. Mere enlargement, by which all parts of the bone seem to have increased so equally that the apparent structure is not altered, except perhaps by exaggeration; 2. An enlargement in which the tissue is condensed in such a manner that the original cavities of the bone are encroached

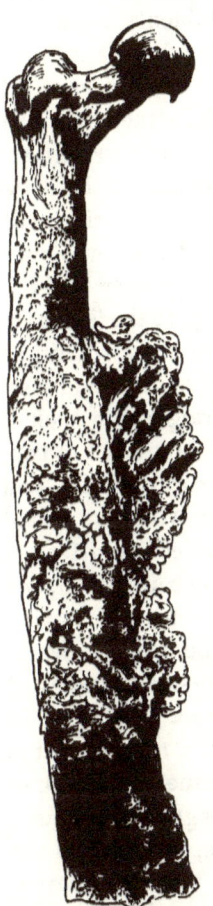

Fig. 5.—(Museum of College of Physicians and Surgeons.)

upon by the new deposit; 3. One in which the action seems to be confined to the periosteal surface, and where we have sometimes the most abundant deposits on that surface, with perhaps little or no change in the bone itself. Fig. 4 is an example of remarkable thickening and induration of the anterior wall of the tibia, and also of the femur. The thickened portion is as hard as ivory, which it much resembles in appearance. This change probably originated in periosteal inflammation. Of these three conditions, I think the latter is the more common, but in all pathological collections each of these forms abounds, sometimes existing separately, and very often all combined in the same specimen (Fig. 3). The tendency of the periosteum to inflammation is recognized by all pathologists; and it is this inflammation of the periosteum, rather than of the bone itself, which leads to the formation of the surface-deposits, which often present themselves in such abundant masses and with such varied and sometimes fantastic shapes (Fig. 5). This affection is one of the forms of tertiary syphilis, but it is also met with where no such disease exists. It sometimes presents itself as one of those vague forms of disease which are loosely classed as rheumatism or neuralgia. The following is a good illustration of one of its most common manifestations. A gentleman, of about forty years, came under my care, many years ago, for a severe attack of neuralgia, as he called it, in one of his legs. The pain was seated along the anterior aspect of the tibia, and was accompanied by great tenderness of the bone, so much so that he could hardly bear it to be touched. He was a man ordinarily in good health, and attributed his attack to exposure to wet and cold, and informed me that several times within a few years he had had similar seizures. The attack had come on rather suddenly a few days before my seeing him. The pain was paroxysmal, and, as he described it, intolerable, when at its height. I found some difficulty in procuring him relief, but finally the attack subsided, and then I discovered, when the tenderness would permit the examination, that the tibia was enlarged, apparently by a deposit of bone on its whole anterior surface. On pressing with some firmness, it could be perceived that the deposit was quite abundant, and, though distributed pretty evenly over the surface, was itself very irregular and rough, giving to the finger the idea of the skin being stretched over a mass of coral. This, he informed me, was the seat of habitual tenderness, and had been for years subject to occasional attacks of neuralgic pain such as above described. These attacks laid him up for a week or two, and, for some time after his recovery, walking was painful, and in fact he was gradually falling into a state in which he would have to consider himself as permanently disabled. I attended him in one or two other attacks similar to the one described, and found them becoming more frequent and severe, and leaving the bone each time less free from soreness and pain in the intervals. I put him on the constant use of moderate doses of the iodide of potassium, which seemed to have a good effect in relieving and diminishing the frequency of the attacks, but it was not until I had established a nitric-acid issue, on the upper part of the side of the leg, that the paroxysms gradually ceased altogether. He has worn this issue ever since, and, though the bone-deposit on the tibia has undergone no material diminution, it is no longer any source of annoyance to him, and he walks on the diseased leg almost as well as upon the other. Mr. Stanley thinks that, when once bone has become enlarged, no medicines have any effect in reducing it. At the same time he is a warm advocate of the efficacy of the iodide in reducing inflammation of bone, for which, indeed, he regards the remedy as almost a specific.

The other conditions of enlargement, in which the bone-tissue itself is more especially implicated, may be studied to great advantage in the actions which go on around a seques-trum in an advanced case of central necrosis. There we shall find, if the case be a recent one, and the processes active, that all the original bone, around the central dead piece, takes on an involucral action, and thickens and strengthens, so as to compensate for the loss sustained. This condition may be re-garded almost as a physiological one, in which Nature adopts this method of providing for the danger inflicted by the separa-tion of the dead piece. This presents as good an illustration as we can have of simple hypertrophy from inflammation, and shows the bone-tissue merely increased in quantity, without any marked change in structure. If, however, these actions are prolonged by the continued residence of the sequestrum within the cavity of the bone, then we have a gradual thicken-ing and condensation of the hitherto merely enlarged involu-cral portion, which in old cases seems to attain to the density of the hardest ivory. Besides these cases of necrosis, there are many others whose clinical history has not, so far as I know, been very thoroughly studied, where after years of rheumatic and neuralgic pain in one or more of the bones, perhaps with a syphilitic or scrofulous taint of the system, and a life of habitual privation and exposure, we find after death several of the bones presenting marks of inflammation in their increased size and density, indicating processes which have been going on for years, and yet without any marked point in the history at which we can say that osteitis, as a distinct affection, commenced.

The treatment of chronic inflammations of bone is not very satisfactory. Much can be accomplished, however, in the ear-lier stages, by local bloodletting, blisters, and the careful use of mercury, and, in the later stages, by issues and derivatives. The cases, whose pathological anatomy we have been studying, are apt to be so vague and indistinct in their outlines during life that systematic treatment for osteitis is generally either not instituted at all, or is so mingled with other therapeutic indications as to be very much lost sight of in summing up the results of the whole case. We can, however, accomplish much in relieving the paroxysms or attacks of acuter inflammation to which these chronic cases are always liable, and, by the iodide of potash, with issues and counter-irritation, we can so far arrest the progress of the inflammatory actions that the patient no longer suffers any inconvenience from his disease, except that arising from the weight or deformity of the affected limb. As for the influence of remedies on the deposits of bone from inflammation, authorities are pretty well agreed that nothing is to be expected. Mr. Stanley says: "Upon enlarged and indurated bone, medicines have no effect; its condition will be permanent. . . . But, against the tenderness and irritation of the periosteum, which precede and accompany the morbid changes in the bones, treatment may be directed with the best effect, particularly the local application of mercury to the limb, with the administration of iodide of potassium and sarsaparilla."

CHAPTER III.

SUPPURATION IN BONE.

As in every other part of the body, so in bone, suppuration presents itself under two distinct forms, viz.: 1. Where the action is circumscribed, and the pus, as it forms, is contained in a cavity, and called an abscess; and, 2. Where the action is not circumscribed, but spreads extensively through the affected part, and the resultant pus is infiltrated through the substance of the bone. These two forms have so great differences in their pathological characters, as well as in their clinical significance, that they will be conveniently studied as separate affections. And, first, for abscess of bone. Here, it will be understood, that we do not now include in our study those various collections of matter which form so important a part in the pathological progress of caries and necrosis. These must be considered hereafter, and thus our field is narrowed down to the comparatively small number of cases in which the ab-

scess character is not only the primary but the only feature of
the disease throughout its whole course. Such abscesses present themselves in three situations: 1. In the cancellous structure; 2. In the medulla; and, 3. Between the periosteum and
the bone. As a general fact, it may be stated that all of these
abscesses are of a chronic character, or perhaps it would be
more accurate to say, that they are made up of a series of successive attacks of acute or subacute inflammation, each of
which subsides to a certain extent, but, by their constant recurrence, finally lead to the formation of the abscess, and thus give
to the whole case a chronic course, though made up in part of
acute elements. Thus, to take one case as an example: Bernard
Riley, aged twenty-one, was admitted to the New York Hospital, June 16, 1857, with a diseased condition of the lower half of
the left tibia, of which he gave the following history: About
seven years previous, he had, without any assignable cause, a
sudden attack of acute inflammation in the upper part of this leg,
which was attended with severe pain, rapid and considerable
swelling, and suppuration, which discharged itself on the anterior part of the limb at the end of about three weeks. The
inflammatory symptoms subsided, but the abscess continued
open for about a year, when a small piece of bone came away,
and it soon healed up. He had been much reduced in health
by this attack, and was not yet able to walk about, when, as
the abscess above healed up, pain and swelling gradually came
on in the lower part of the leg, and, after nine weeks, an abscess formed and opened, a piece of bone came away, and soon
after the sore healed soundly. Several other abscesses formed,
in the same way, during the next four years, though they were
not all accompanied with a discharge of bone. Since this
time, say, for the last three years, he had been improving in
health and strength, but the lower half of the tibia had been
the seat of frequent attacks of pain, lasting for a few days, not
attributable to any particular cause, and usually relieved by
hot fomentations. The tibia is now very much enlarged in its
lower half, but there is no evidence of any formation of matter,
and, during the intervals between his attacks of pain, he is
able to walk about, and to use the limb freely. The pains are
always most severe at night. There is no suspicion of a syphi-

litic cause. He left Ireland quite well on the 17th of the previous month, and on the 1st of April he received a pretty hard blow from a rope, across the diseased tibia, which produced a very bad attack of pain, with some swelling, which, however, soon subsided, and, when he landed, he was as well as usual. By walking about the streets another attack was produced, and, altogether, he found himself so much annoyed with these repeated attacks of pain that he became very anxious to have something done for his relief. The lower half of the tibia was much enlarged, very hard, slightly tender to the touch, and of a constant temperature sensibly above that of the surrounding parts. There was no point more sensitive than the rest, nor any evidence of matter seeking the surface. He says that his pains, even at their worst, are not very severe, and it is rather on account of their constant recurrence that they have become so very distressing to him. From this history of localized pain, enlargement, and increased heat, abscess was suspected, and, after he had been in the house a few days, an operation was performed, which it was hoped would have a good effect on the chronic osteitis, even if no matter should be found. The tibia was exposed on its anterior surface, and a trephine was carried deeply into its substance, about the middle of the greatest enlargement. When the instrument had reached the centre of the bone, pus began to ooze from the saw-cut, and, on removing the disk, we found we had opened into the cavity of an abscess, from which two or three drachms of pus flowed out. The walls of the cavity were smooth and even, and no dead nor bare bone could be discovered. The wound was dressed lightly with lint. No unfavorable symptom occurred. The suppuration gradually diminished, the wound filled up from the bottom with healthy granulations, and he was discharged from the hospital, August 25th, without any return of pain, and with the wound almost entirely healed. This case is a fair specimen of the ordinary form of the disease, though some patients suffer much more acute pain, and in many the disease is prolonged through a much greater period of time. The seat of the affection is commonly the expanded articular extremity of the bone, and, not unfrequently, the abscess is situated so near the joint that its increase tends to involve the joint-cavity, and its rupture to take place into it (Fig. 6). Of this, numerous examples are on record, and it need hardly be said that

this relation to the joint becomes, in such instances, the important feature of the case, demanding an early recognition and a prompt evacuation, if any hope is to be entertained of saving the limb, and, perhaps, the life of the patient. The clinical features of this disease seem to be mainly those of chronic osteitis, but characterized by the frequent recurrence of attacks of pain, and other evidences of increased inflammation, each of which attacks subsides, leaving the bone gradually enlarging, somewhat tender to the touch, and a little hotter than it should be, as the principal signs

Fig. 6.—(From Erichsen.)

of the condition of chronic inflammation which maintains itself in the intervals between the acute attacks. The diagnosis of abscess cannot in all cases be made with certainty, but with such a history of frequently-recurring attacks of acute inflammation, supervening on a condition of permanent osteitis, we shall rarely be wrong in suspecting the existence of pus. Occasionally the pus makes its way through its bony encasement, and approaches the surface, as in the following instance:

Pierce Doheny, aged twenty-four, was admitted into the New York Hospital, March 28, 1860, with an affection of the upper part of the left tibia, of which he gives this account: When he was about nine years old, he had an attack of inflammation in this leg, which terminated in abscess, with the discharge of a small fragment of bone. This process lasted two years before the wounds were all healed, and left the limb tender, but without any new attacks, until he was twenty years old, when another attack came on, which was relieved by two blisters. This left the bone considerably enlarged, and more tender than ever to the slightest injury. Three months before his admission, he had another attack in the upper part of the bone, which had never entirely ceased, being better and worse at times, but on the whole gradually increasing in severity. At the time of admission the swelling occupied the upper third of the tibia, approaching the knee-joint—which, however, is not involved. He suffered a good deal of pain, which was so aggravated by exercise that he was obliged to keep his bed. There was a general inflammatory thickening of the soft parts, but it could easily be distinguished that a solid enlargement of the bone made up the bulk of the tumor. Fluctuation could be perceived on the central most prominent part of the swelling. The limb, on measurement, was one inch longer than its fellow, which was found to be due to hypertrophy of the entire tibia, the result doubtless of the long-continued afflux of blood, from the frequent inflammatory attacks of which the bone had been the subject. His general condition was good. The diagnosis here was clear, and on the 17th of March an operation was performed, by raising the integuments by a crucial incision and exposing the surface of the enlarged tibia. In doing this, a small quantity of pus was found between the skin and the bone. On wiping this pus off, it was found to have exuded from an irregular opening in the bone about three lines in diameter, into which a probe being passed entered into a considerable cavity filled with pus. It was an abscess in the cancellous substance of the head of the bone, which, having perforated the external compact shell, was making its way to the surface. By the chisel and trephine, the anterior wall of the bony cavity was largely opened. It was found of sufficient size to contain a large hickory-nut, and no sequestrum could be discovered. As there had been no external discharge, its entire independence of necrosis was demonstrated. His recovery was perfect and without accident. He was discharged from the hospital, cured, September 19, 1860.

The treatment of these cases consists in a free opening of the abscess, and, happily, it is a treatment which is usually entirely successful. Mr. Brodie was the first to call attention to these abscesses and to their treatment, and he has published the details of seven cases in which he established the diagnosis of abscess. All his cases were in the head of the tibia, and in all but the first he had the happiness of curing his patient by opening the abscess. In the first case the limb was amputated, and the patient died; and it was by the careful study of this unfortunate case that he was led to recommend the treatment afterward adopted, with such satisfactory results, in the six successful cases. The operation consists in exposing the bone at the proper point, and introducing a small trephine, burying it deeply enough in the enlarged bone to reach the matter. The selection of the exact spot for making the opening is a point of much moment, for a few lines' deviation might lead to a disappointment in finding matter; and Mr. Brodie speaks of one such case as occurring under his observation, where "a very experienced hospital-surgeon applied the trephine for a supposed abscess in the head of the tibia. No abscess, however, was discovered, and in consequence the limb was amputated. On the parts being examined afterward, the abscess was discovered at a small distance from the perforation made in the operation; and it was plain that the removal of a small portion more of the bone would have preserved the patient's limb." In such a case it would be proper to make another opening, or what is, I think, better, to search for the abscess by cutting away the bone at the bottom of the trephine-cut by a small gouge-chisel. In this way it can rarely happen that matter will escape detection if it really exists, accumulated in an abscess, though on this point Mr. Stanley makes this very sensible remark: "At the same time it must be recollected that the smallest quantity of purulent fluid confined

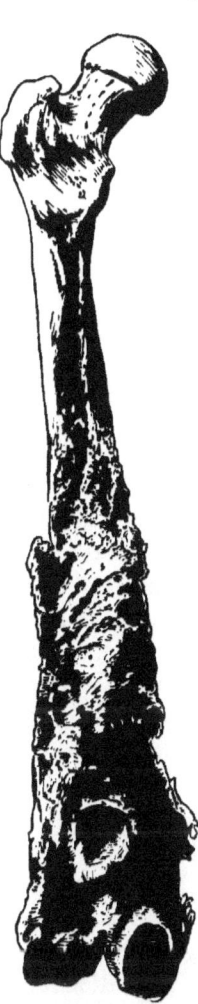

FIG. 7.—(New York Hospital.)

within a bone has been the source of very severe suffering; and that when mixed with the blood, which in general freely escapes from the inflamed cancellous texture around the abscess, the purulent fluid might not be distinctly recognized. The character of the fluid escaping from the bone should therefore be closely scrutinized." Fig. 7, taken from a specimen in the New York Hospital Museum, shows the changes produced by an old abscess in the lower end of the femur. The bone is much thickened, the surface covered by periosteal growths, and an oblique opening on the posterior part shows where the abscess had discharged into the popliteal space.

CHAPTER IV.

CHRONIC SINUOUS ABSCESS OF BONE.

BESIDES the cases of abscess of bone which have been discussed in the previous chapter, and which have been so well described by Mr. Brodie, there are a certain number of others, in which, with a similar commencement, a very different progress is observed, and in which the diseased actions, though quite as distressing and perhaps more tedious and intractable under ordinary management, present the features not so much of abscess as of its effects; not so much the characters of the primary disease as of its consequences or sequelæ. I refer to cases in which the inflammation of the bone begins as an acute attack, passing rapidly into suppuration, and in which the abscess, thus rapidly formed, finds its way early to the surface, through the compact external shell of the bone, and is discharged, to the temporary relief of the sufferings of the patient, though, it may be, not greatly to his advancement toward a cure. From this point begins the marked difference in the progress of those cases which Mr. Brodie describes, and those to which I wish now to direct attention. In the former, the abscess, once well open, goes on rapidly to a cure. In the latter, the opening not being free, and probably not being direct, accumulations of matter take place within the cavity, and new inflammations and suppurations are excited in the bone-substance surrounding the original focus of disease. New abscesses are thus formed, which either break into the original cavity, or discharge themselves upon the surface by forcing their way through the compact outer layer of the bone. By the repetition of this process the bone gradually becomes the seat of an inflammatory hypertrophy, and the patient is harassed for months by the constitu-

3

tional disturbance and pain accompanying these repeated suppurations. After a time, varying in different individuals from a few weeks to many months, the disposition to form new abscesses seems to cease, perhaps because all the cancellous tissue of the affected region has become involved, either in suppuration or in hypertrophic induration; and the bone is left perforated in all directions by two, three, four, or more sinuses, generally all communicating with one another and with a central excavation or chamber, which marks the position of the original abscess. From these openings is discharged, often in considerable abundance, a thinnish pus, sometimes offensive, varying in its quantity and quality with the condition of the patient's general health; which discharge, from the shape and position of the channels through which it comes, is indirectly and imperfectly evacuated, and by its retention keeps up and aggravates the chronic inflammation which is early set up in the surrounding bone-tissue.

In this state the parts may continue without alteration for an indefinite period of time, the disease not showing much disposition to make encroachments, but evidencing no tendency whatever toward improvement. The system, gradually accommodating itself to the existence of the disorder, becomes accustomed both to the drain and the irritation, and the general health is often completely reëstablished. The diseased bone becomes entirely a local affection, only troublesome from the amount of pain and soreness experienced—an amount which, in different cases, varies from a slight feeling of tenderness to a constant and severe gnawing pain, both conditions being occasionally interrupted by more or less severe attacks of acute inflammation, generally accompanied by an increase of suppuration and sometimes by severe constitutional disturbance. In this condition, the presence of the disease does not interfere with a certain amount of use of the limb; and thus patients are sometimes willing to endure for an indefinite period the pain and inconvenience which attend it. We have in such cases an opportunity to learn the natural history of the disease, and may appreciate the amount of its tendency toward a cure—a tendency which, existing fifteen years in one of my patients, and about sixteen years in another, had not sufficed, at the time of operation, to leave any evidences of reparation, much less of cure. Among diseases which do not tend to progressive disorganization, this is a rare degree of obstinacy, and the reason of this intractability and indisposition toward a cure I take to exist, not so much in the nature of the diseased actions as in their unfavorable physical conditions. Thus, though the character of inflammation in the bone may be perfectly simple and healthy, yet the resulting abscess has assumed the form of a deep cavity, communicating indirectly and imperfectly with the surface by means of narrow, ill-placed, and often tortuous canals. Such a condition of abscess in the soft parts is recognized as extremely unfavorable for the healing process; how much more so when, as in bone, we have not only an unfavorable shape, but an unyielding wall, which deprives us entirely of the immense advantage which, in the treatment of similar abscesses in the soft parts, we derive from pressure in approximating the walls of the suppurating cavities !

This view of the local cause of the obstinacy of these cases of chronic abscess of bone is still further strengthened by several considerations. In the first place, there seems to be no necessary or usual connection of the inflammatory action with any constitutional vice, as scrofula, syphilis, or any other contamination of the general system. On the contrary, the affection seems to occur by preference in young, vigorous, and robust persons, and generally as the immediate consequence of injury, or of exposure to cold and wet, or some other well-recognized cause of local disease. In the second place, the effect of remedies administered with a view to their constitutional or alterative effect seems usually to be inappreciable in producing any curative change in the diseased part; and, when any such favorable effect is seen in diminishing pain or improving discharge, it is merely temporary, and the power of the remedy for good is soon exhausted. This was abundantly illustrated in three of my patients, in whom the disease had longest existed, from whose previous histories, as well as from my own persevering efforts in the use of remedies, I arrived at the conclusion that the cure was not to be accomplished, nor any important improvement secured, by any form of internal medication. Lastly, and in contrast with the inefficiency of medicine, the effect of the operation, by which the physical conditions alone can be affected, seems to me the strongest proof that it is upon these physical conditions that the difficulty depends, a conviction which I think must force itself upon the mind of any one who has watched the beautiful reparative appearances which the wound presents from the moment of the operation, and the certainty and soundness of the cure which follows its thorough performance.

The following cases will serve to illustrate the main features of what I think may properly be termed *chronic sinuous abscess of bone:*

CASE I.—George Brown, aged nineteen, a German seaman, came to the New York Hospital, November 17, 1857, with a diseased condition of his left tibia. It commenced about fourteen months previously, after severe exposure in going round Cape Horn, and seemed at first of a rheumatic character, attacking first one ankle and then the 'other. He was recovering from the lameness caused by this attack, when, without evident cause, the inflammation concentrated itself upon the lower part of the left leg. He was again confined to his bed, and suffered much from pain and fever. An abscess formed in about three weeks, and broke on the anterior surface, about four inches above the joint. The swelling and inflammation continued, and, during about five months, he was scarcely ever able to leave his bed, except on crutches. During this time, abscesses formed and broke at several points of the swollen limb, and, at different times, ten or twelve minute pieces of bone came away, the largest not bigger than a pea. For the last few months, since the acuter symptoms have subsided, he has been able to go about most of the time, but not without great discomfort and inconvenience. On examination, the lower third of the tibia was found enlarged to more than double its natural size. Over it the tissues were thickened and brawny, and the skin presented the orifices of several sinuses which led down into the substance of the bone, and discharged a moderate quantity of pus. The probe, passed into any of these, goes deeply into the bone, and encounters some rough, exposed, bony points, but no distinct or considerable surface of sequestrum can be recognized. One of the openings on the anterior surface communicates with another near the malleolus internus, as can be shown by passing in two probes, one at either orifice, and making them touch in the middle. The ankle-joint is, and long has been, a little swollen, and somewhat stiff in its movements. His general condition is that of a healthy and vigorous young man. No suspicion of any syphilitic taint.

In the light of our previous experience, the diagnosis here was clearly made out, of sinuous abscess of bone, and the operation for its cure was performed by Dr. Van Buren, on the 19th, as, from the proximity of the disease to the ankle-joint, it was feared that inflammation might at any moment extend to its cavity. By the trephine and chisel, the whole anterior wall of the cavity in the bone was removed, and every sinus freely exposed. They were all found to communicate with a central cavity, as large as a hickory-nut, which lay so near the ankle-' joint, that there appeared to be merely a thin shell of bone between it and the cavity of the joint. The sinuses, which opened on the anterior surface of the bone, were entirely exposed by removing their bony covering. Two sinuses, however, penetrated the bone so deeply, and had their external orifices so far back, that it was not thought best to cut away all their anterior wall, for fear of too seriously weakening the bone. The portions of their track which were nearest the central cavity were therefore freely exposed, while their openings through the compact shell of the tibia were left untouched. The whole of these cavities were lined by a smooth, soft, reddish, and very vascular membrane, which, to the finger, felt very thick, and seemed to be composed of abundant firm granulations. Through this membrane the bone-tissue could be felt, but it was not anywhere extensively exposed, or apparently diseased. The bone cut through in the operation was of moderate firmness, and appeared to be simply hypertrophied. It bled freely when cut. The wound was dressed with a view to its granulating and filling up from the bottom. Although a slight attack of erysipelas occurred on the third day after the operation, every thing went on as favorably as could be desired. Healthy suppuration came on, with good, firm, florid granulations, and the wound filled up rapidly. On the 15th of December, it was noticed that the sinuses whose orifices had been left on the inside of the limb had healed entirely. He is entirely free from pain. No interruption occurred in the progress of his cure, which was complete when he was discharged from the hospital.

CASE II.—Edward Smith, aged nineteen, I saw at Bellevue Hospital, by the kindness of Dr. C. D. Smith, under whose charge the patient was admitted. He had presented himself at the hospital, November 11, 1857, with an enlargement of the lower part of the left tibia, which, he said, had commenced with an acute attack of inflammation of the leg, last July. This attack he attributed to a very prolonged exposure in fishing for oysters while the water was yet quite cold. He went to bed ill that night, and the next morning great pain in the lower portion of the leg announced the commencement of a severe inflammation, which soon terminated in suppuration. It was opened in about two weeks, and a large quantity of offensive matter discharged. Several other abscesses formed at intervals, and from them small fragments of dead bone were discharged, the largest not bigger than the finger-nail. He continued to suffer a great deal of pain and discomfort about the limb, and the irritation was so great, and so easily aggravated by handling or by exercise, that he was confined to his bed during most of the time. When admitted, his general condition, though obviously affected by long-continued suffering, was tolerably good. The lower third of the tibia was much enlarged, and the integuments over it thickened and inflamed. Five orifices were situated on the anterior surface, into each of which a probe could be passed deeply into the substance of the bone. Here and there the probe seemed to grate against bare bone, but no distinct sequestrum could be discovered. The lowest orifice was about two fingers' breadth above the ankle-joint, which was not in any way involved in the disease. The discharge was not large, but was somewhat offensive. The case was pronounced to be one of sinuous abscess, without necrosis, and the operation was performed by Dr. Smith on the 28th of November. By the trephine and chisel, the sinuses were carefully followed through the bone, and their anterior wall removed, thus laying them freely open to the bottom. They were all found to communicate with one another, and at the deepest part of their course, toward the lower part of the bone, the cavity expanded so as to admit the end of the finger, but at no point was there any distinct or considerable chamber; which, in most cases of this disease, indicates the seat of the original abscess. No sequestrum was found in any part of the cavities, but their walls were, in places, rough or granular to the feel, giving the impression of an ulcerated or carious condition of the surrounding bone-tissue. The external aspect of the enlarged part of the bone was rough, and the periosteum over it much thickened. The pieces of bone cut away by the trephine and chisel showed the natural spongy substance of the bone hypertrophied, but not otherwise altered.

The wound was dressed lightly with lint. Some trifling feverish reaction followed the operation, but healthy granulation was soon established, and, on the 10th of December, he was reported as improving rapidly. Dr. Smith since informed me that the further progress of the case was satisfactory, and that the wound healed entirely, and apparently soundly, within a few weeks after the operation.

These two cases are presented, as among those best illustrating the usual characters of chronic sinuous abscess of bone. As deduced from these, and a number of other cases, it appears plain to me that the pathological anatomy of the disease is an inflammation of the cancellous tissue of the ends of the long bones, rapidly terminating in suppuration. The matter thus rapidly formed early approaches the surface of the bone, and soon reaches its compact outer shell, which it perforates, and then, without obstruction, attains the surface of the integument, and is discharged. The deep cavity in the bone, thus communicating with the surface by a narrow and indirect channel, is not properly evacuated, and the lodgment of pus in its most depending portions provokes anew inflammation and suppuration, which extends the original excavation, and often finds its way to the surface by some new channel; and thus, by a repetition of the original morbid process, the disorganization of the bone assumes the extent and severity with which it ultimately comes under our notice. These repeated inflammations cannot occur without exciting vascular action in the surrounding parts, and we have, accordingly, inflammatory hypertrophy induced in the affected portion of the bone, and, later in the disease, induration and eburnation, particularly about the abscesses and their connecting sinuses. With this action in the bone, we have a corresponding chronic inflammation and thickening of the periosteum, with osseous deposits from its inner surface; so that the surfaces of the hypertrophied portions of bone, when stripped of their periosteum, have a rough, irregular, granulated appearance, in all respects similar to the surface of the involucrum in cases of necrosis.

The discharge, during the earlier periods of the complaint, varies in quantity and quality with the varying activity of the inflammation; but, in the later stages, when the tendency to abscess-formation is exhausted, and the parts have become consolidated by chronic inflammation, the discharge is moderate in quantity, and, in quality, generally thin, sometimes sanious, and very rarely offensive. Caries of the walls of the cavities may occur if the constitution be predisposed to scrofula, or contaminated by syphilis; and, in the same way, necrosis of small portions of the original, or of the morbidly-indurated cancellous tissue, may take place, as an accidental complication of the case; but neither caries nor necrosis has any thing to do with the original character of the affection, nor do they usually play any important part in its later history and progress.

A most important feature in the anatomy of these cases is the disposition shown by the abscesses to approach, and to involve the joint near which they are situated. This tendency, in the mere chronic form of the disease, when the abscess has not been able to make its way to the surface, but remains a source of irritation, pent up within the swollen end of the bone, is recognized by Mr. Brodie, and, indeed, by many other observers, as one of the most dangerous features of the disease. The same tendency is observable even in the open abscess we are describing. Though there be no pent-up fluid seeking an outlet through the joint, yet the tendency seems very strong for the excavations to extend toward the nearest synovial surface; and, even when no communication takes place, the inflammation of all the tissues round the abscess easily spreads to the joint, and, rather by its constant recurrence than by its immediate severity, seriously compromises its integrity.

The symptoms of this affection have already been so fully described as not now to require recapitulation, but its resemblance to and its diagnosis from necrosis demand a moment's notice. The resemblance is striking and obvious. The age of the patient; the most common causes of attack; the early symptoms of inflammation of the bone, terminating in suppuration; the numerous and successive openings; the enlargement and induration of the affected region; the unchanging and intractable character, and the interminable duration of the disease—are all marks of identity, which, I believe, habitually deceive careless observers, and which require, for a proper discrimination, much care and a thorough knowledge of the two diseases, and their distinctive characteristics. There are, however, some features which are diagnostic.

And, first, we have the situation of the affection. In necrosis, the compact, and, in abscess, the cancellous structure, are respectively the parts implicated. We have, therefore, necrosis ordinarily affecting the middle portion of the long bones, which is mainly compact tissue, while abscess is formed at the enlarged extremities, where the more vascular, and therefore more highly-organized, spongy tissue prevails. How uniformly this law is obeyed I cannot say, but in eight cases which I have seen there has been no exception to it.

Secondly, the actions set up in necrosis, particularly if a large portion of the calibre of the bone has perished, are for the formation of new bone around the dead sequestrum, and, consequently, the enlargement is commonly very great, from the thickness of the involucrum, which, it must be remembered, more than supplies the place, as far as mere bulk is concerned, of the bone destroyed. On the other hand, the actions which go on in connection with abscess are merely those of thickening of the surrounding bone, by a process of inflammatory hypertrophy, strictly analogous to the induration of the tissues round any series of chronic abscesses in the soft parts. The enlargement, therefore, which accompanies necrosis is very great, while that which exists with abscess is comparatively moderate.

Thirdly, the early history of these cases of abscess of bone shows that, with each opening formed, there is usually cast off a small piece of bone, a few days or weeks after the opening has taken place. This does not occur with the abscesses of necrosis; and it appears to me that the explanation of the difference between the two affections, in this respect, is not difficult. Where suppuration occurs within the substance of a bone, it may well be supposed that the rapid course of the matter toward the surface, bursting, as it were, through the outer shell, before the slow action of the osseous vessels can provide by absorption for its quiet transit, will or may, in many cases, produce the death of a small portion of the compact tissue which offered the first resistance to its progress; which small fragment thus killed will separate and make its appearance, in a longer or shorter time, after the opening of the abscess. In necrosis, on the other hand, all the compact tissue implicated dies in mass, suppuration occurs outside of the dead bone and between it and the periosteum, and no separation of fragments usually takes place until the whole mass begins to loosen from its attachments. The pieces which come away in abscess of bone are described as being very small, and are often likened to a finger-nail; and I have so constantly met with them, in the history given me, by the patients, of their earlier symptoms, that I cannot help considering them as very characteristic.

Fourthly, I think that there are, generally, less pain, less inconvenience, less inability, and less discharge produced by the abscess, in its chronic condition, than by necrosis, while the sequestrum is present. So much so is this the case, that it must be extremely rare for a patient with a large sequestrum in his tibia, for example, to be able to be about his ordinary occupations with the same degree of comfort as is often enjoyed by those affected with the chronic abscess.

Lastly, the most important of all the diagnostic signs is derived from the information given by the probe. In necrosis, there is usually no difficulty, if the openings be free, in finding the bare and rough surface of the sequestrum. In the abscess, on the contrary, with openings equally free, no bare bone is discovered, or, if any appears to be touched, it is so slight and so uncertain in its indications as to leave us in doubt whether the sensations may not be produced by the rude use of the probe, rubbing off the granulations from the surface of otherwise healthy bone.

From the view which has been presented, of the anatomical features of this affection, the character of the operation necessary for its cure is directly deducible. If the difficulty lie essentially in the physical conditions of the parts, then these physical conditions must be altered. If the abscess lie deep from the surface, it must be freely exposed to that surface, and made, as nearly as may be, a part of it. If the channels through which it is discharged be narrow and indirect, they should be made large and direct. In short, if the obstinacy of the affection depend upon its character as a sinuous abscess, then that character must be destroyed, as completely as possible, by converting it into an open wound. In carrying out this indication, it must be remembered that it is a cardinal one, and that upon the thoroughness with which it is done will depend the rapidity and completeness of the cure. I am entirely convinced that the failure in one of my earliest cases was due to the fact that, not fully appreciating the importance of thoroughness in the operation, I contented myself with opening the cavity of the abscess by removing a portion of its anterior wall, but did not, as I now think it necessary to do, remove the entire covering of the suppurating cavity, both upward and downward, and convert it into a mere groove or excavation on the surface of the bone. Another case, of abscess of the femur, which occurred to me soon after, presents an illustration of the same principle, and leads me somewhat to doubt the general applicability of the operation to abscesses in the femur. The diseased bone is so much more inaccessible, covered as it is with the thick, muscular mass of the thigh, and the operation necessary for fully exposing it is so serious and extensive, that I fear, in most cases, it would be left incomplete, and therefore ineffectual. Besides, even if the operation be well and thoroughly done, the suppurating cavity in the bone is so covered in by thick, soft parts that, by their healing, it in a very short time approaches again to the character of a cavity with narrow outlets, and tends to reassume the appearance and behavior of a sinuous abscess. When, however, the operation can be thoroughly done, as in the tibia, and in most of the other long bones, and when, in addition, all the fistulous tracks can be also freely laid open, the cure will be speedy and complete.

It is usually best to commence the operation with the trephine, and particularly in old cases where the osseous tissue is apt to be much consolidated from long-continued and frequent inflammation. After exposing the main cavity by the trephine, then with the gouge the whole of its anterior wall, and such other parts as may seem necessary in following up the fistulous tracks, may be chiselled away. It is very desirable to have the tourniquet applied to the limb above, not so much for the saving of blood, of which there is usually but little lost, but with the view of keeping the cut-bone surfaces clean and dry, so that we may be able to judge correctly of the course and condition of the various tracks which it may be necessary to follow. As far as practicable, there is no doubt that it is best to follow up and lay open each of the sinuses which lead from the central cavity to the surface. That this is not absolutely necessary, however, is shown by the satisfactory result reported in Case I., where two sinuses, which penetrated the bone quite far back, were from motives of prudence left untouched, and nevertheless healed rapidly and soundly as the rest of the wound began to fill up. If the principal part of the operation be thoroughly done, this will, I think, be usually the case with any sinuses which may be allowed to remain. In any case where it seems necessary, no hesitation need be felt in making deep and extensive chisellings of the bone, for the repair is abundant and certain. We have here to deal with original bone-tissue, thickened and hypertrophied from long-continued inflammatory action, it is true, but with all its original reparative capacity unexhausted and unimpaired. The case is very different from the involucral covering of necrosis, where we are dealing with an entirely new formation, one which is itself the product of surprising vital and reparative energy, which energy may be supposed to have, at least in a great degree, exhausted itself in the formation of the involucrum, leaving no excess to be available in a process of reformation after its destruction. At the same time, it is well to avoid weakening the bone by unnecessarily cutting away its substance, as we never can be certain but that, by some mischance or misbehavior of the wound, or of the constitution, the reparative actions may be delayed or imperfect.

The after-treatment is usually the simplest possible. By light dressings of the wound, which is of course left wide open, it granulates from the bottom, and generally begins to heal at its edges before the excavation is filled up. No tents or sponges or deep dressings with lint will be required, and time only is necessary to complete the cure. As soon as the wound has begun fairly to fill up and to contract, if it be otherwise in a healthy condition, the patient should be allowed to go about with a roller-bandage to support the limb, that he may secure the benefit of air and exercise. If an unhealthy condition of the sores should persist, or if caries of the bone should be suspected, constitutional treatment will of course not be neglected; but, in a large proportion of the cases where the operation has been well done and thoroughly done, nothing further will be required to restore the patient to perfect health.

CHAPTER V.

DIFFUSE SUPPURATION.—OSTEO-MYELITIS.

In strong contrast with abscess of bone, we have that form of inflammation in which the suppurative action is not limited by a wall of fibrine, but is diffused throughout the whole substance of the bone. This form of disease has long been recognized by surgical writers, but particular attention has of late been drawn to it, by observations made in the Crimean and Italian campaigns, and in our own late war of the Rebellion. It seems to be, in a very eminent degree, a disease of crowded military hospitals, where, from the necessity of the case, the hygienic conditions are often extremely unfavorable, and it is comparatively unknown in civil practice. It is a condition induced, almost exclusively, by injuries of the bones, and is a very serious and fatal complication, both of amputations and of resections. From the fact that its most prominent features are developed in the medullary cavities, it has received the name of osteo-myelitis, or inflammation of the marrow of the bone, though it must be understood that its effects are by no

means confined to the medulla, but very often involve all the
component parts of the bone affected.   The clinical history of
the disease seems to be that, after some injury or operation on
a bone, which has involved its medullary cavity, symptoms of
inflammation of the bone begin to show themselves.   These
symptoms are usually a dull, heavy, aching pain in the bone,
great tenderness on moving or handling the part, and very soon
some swelling of the surrounding soft parts.   With the super-
vention of these symptoms, there is usually noticed a change in
the appearance of the wound.   The discharge diminishes, and
for a time dries up ; the granulations lose their reparative aspect, and present a dry, sometimes a sloughy appearance; the
whole group of symptoms indicating that some serious disturbing cause has arrested favorable progress of the wound toward
healing.   With these, constitutional symptoms, usually of a
very formidable character, are developed.   Sometimes a chill
may announce the invasion of the disease, and very commonly
irregular rigors are present during its course.   Fever soon
comes on ; at first, of the inflammatory type, soon changing to
the typhoid character.   Delirium is often an early sign, and in
all cases the nervous power seems to be rapidly exhausted, and
the patient soon presents those signs of prostration which so
commonly accompany the severer forms of constitutional irritation.   Very often the symptoms merge into those of pyæmia,
with severe rigors, followed by slight fever, and very profuse,
exhaustive sweats, rapid emaciation and loss of strength, shrivelling, blueness, and maceration of the surface, low, muttering
delirium and death, often as early as the third or fourth day.
If, while these symptoms are in progress, the diseased bone can
be watched, it will be seen to present an inflammatory redness
of the exposed medulla, which, however, soon begins to be
specked with purulent dots ; and a thin, ill-looking pus, in a
very short space of time, begins to ooze from the opened medullary cavity.   At the same time, the periosteal surface shows
that it participates in the morbid action, and the membrane is
soon detached from the bone by a layer of exudation which
rapidly becomes purulent.   Examination of the part after
death, or after amputation, reveals the fact that these changes
reach far into the medullary cavity, in fact usually involving

the whole of it, and often extending more or less into the cancellous tissue both above and below. Dr. Lidell, who observed
the disease in our military hospitals during the war, has found
three conditions of the marrow which he regards as stages of
the disease, and which he denominates—1. Carnification, or
hepatization; 2. Suppuration; 3. Mortification. The first
stage, or that of carnification, Dr. Lidell describes as characterized by a reddening, and increase of density and tenacity,
of the medullary substance. The color, he says, varies from
coppery-red to crimson, to brown, and almost to black. In this
stage, the normal proportion of fat in the medulla is diminished, and the cellular elements of the medullary substance, viz.,
the marrow-cells, are increased in quantity, and become granular in appearance. Of course, the quantity of blood in the
part is much increased, and it is observed that the inflamed
medulla bleeds easily when injured. The second stage, or that
of suppuration, supervenes on the former, and is the characteristic condition of the disease. In acute osteo-myelitis proper,
the suppurative action is not limited by the surrounding carnification, but all the tissue tends to break down rapidly, and in
fact simultaneously, into the purulent state; just as, in diffuse
inflammation of the subcutaneous cellular planes, the whole
affected region is in a state of induration to-day, and to-morrow
the whole indurated district has become softened and infiltrated
with pus. This suppurative softening is more or less complete
in different cases, and goes sometimes to so great an extent
that the semi-fluid marrow slowly oozes from the bone, a turbid
mixture of pus, oil, and disintegrated marrow-cells. In that
more healthy form of simple inflammation of the medulla,
which we sometimes meet with in civil practice, it is not uncommon for the suppurative action to be circumscribed by the
limiting induration in the form of a perfect abscess, but in this
adynamic form of the disease we are now considering, and to
which specially the name of osteo-myelitis has been given, we
find the characteristic behavior of the non-limited, diffuse, or
infiltrated suppuration. This peculiar tendency of the pus to
diffuse itself rapidly over all the affected region of the bone
seems to be only another evidence of that depressed vital power
which disarms and defeats healthful constitutional reaction, and

makes the disease so dreaded and so fatal. The third stage, or that of mortification, is only another step in the process of destruction. The inflamed tissue has not vitality enough to disintegrate by the slow process even of diffuse suppuration, but gives up the contest and yields in mass to complete, and often very rapid, death.

The above outline of the clinical history and pathological appearance in osteo-myelitis is drawn from cases in which gunshot or other injury of the bone has been the cause of the disease. The following case is an excellent example of that form of the affection where the whole bone, including the medulla, takes on acute suppurative inflammation from causes apparently too trivial to explain the occurrence of such severe consequences. The case was reported by Dr. Sands to the Pathological Society, and I condense it from the account published in the *Medical Record*, May 15, 1871 :

" The patient was an active, healthy boy, nine years old, who was attacked, February 12th, with severe pain in the knee. Some tenderness was observed about the knee, though it could be moved without pain. This pain and tenderness continued for a day or two, but were soon accompanied with fever and an elevation of temperature to 103. On the fourth day he was delirious at night, with a pulse of 140, and feeble, the tongue dry, and every thing indicating serious disease. The tenderness had now diffused itself along the whole thigh, deep pressure upon which gave great pain. There was no effusion into the knee-joint, and now no tenderness about it. There was no swelling of the thigh, and he was able to move it with some freedom. Careful measurement showed the left thigh to be an inch larger in circumference than the right. The pain was paroxysmal and very severe. On the fifth day he was much worse, delirium incessant, pulse failing, temperature rising. The thigh was now considerably swollen, but not œdematous. He died on the morning of the sixth day.

" At the autopsy, the only part of the body examined was the femur, but the appearances of this bone sufficiently explained the nature of the trouble. The left thigh was not measured just before death, but after death it was found to be two inches more in circumference than its fellow. The dissection was made by an incision on the outer aspect of the limb. The muscles were somewhat infiltrated, but otherwise healthy. There were no appearances of inflammation, until the periosteum was reached. The outer surface of this membrane, throughout nearly the entire length of the shaft of the femur, was surrounded with pus, accumulated in greatest quantity at a point below and a point above, on the outer aspect, and behind the superior extremity of the bone, underneath the quadriceps femoris. So far as could be ascertained, there was no perforation of the periosteum. This membrane was the seat of an acute œdema, and separated more readily from the subjacent bone than it should. On raising it from the bone, there were small deposits of pus here and there, lying between the attached surface and the bone, but these deposits were not so much in quantity as those on the external aspect of the membrane. The hip and knee joints were perfectly healthy.

" On section of the bone, it was at once seen that the focus of the disease was the interior. The whole of the marrow was found to be hyperæmic. In some places it appeared very soft, and intermingled with patches of a whitish-yellow color, which were due to diffluent purulent material. It appears that this infiltration extended up toward the epiphysis, though it was not traced through the epiphyseal line in either direction. There is no evidence to show that the extension of the disease from within outward has been one of continuity. There are no openings in the bone or periosteum. So far as I have examined, the inflammation seemed to have occurred by contiguity."

Dr. Edward Curtis, who made the microscopical examination of the specimen, gives the following account of the appearances presented:

" On section of the bone, the marrow, throughout its whole extent, appeared redder than normal; that in the medullary canal of the shaft being of a darker shade than the marrow of the cancellated tissue of the extremities. In the medulla of the shaft, especially in the upper half, were numerous foci, where the substance was of a pale cream-yellow color, like pus. This material, on microscopic examination, was found to be mainly composed of closely-aggregated, small, roundish cells,

4

smaller than pus-corpuscles, pale, and very finely granular,
without visible nuclei, embedded in an extremely viscid granular substance. Very little of the usual fat of the medulla
was present in this yellow material. The bright-red pulp of
the marrow of the shaft presented a much smaller proportion
of similar cells to those just described—a greater amount of
fat and granular matter—and was gorged with blood. In the
cancellated tissue of the extremities, the marrow was hyperæmic, but the examination failed to detect any abnormal cellular elements."

Dr. Sands considered that, in this case, the medulla was the
starting-point of the inflammation, though the *post-mortem*
appearances indicated that the disease was rather further
advanced in the periosteum than in the medulla. I do not
think such a distinction can often be made in these acute bone-
inflammations; to my mind the case affords a classical illustration of the great pathological law that, in such inflammations,
the whole bone, both periosteum and medulla, is involved; if
not in all parts equally and simultaneously, yet sufficiently so
to show that the mischief developed in each part is the result
of a process of diseased·action pervading the whole bone, and.
really belonging to it as an entirety, even although it may seem
to commence at one point and spread to the rest. That this
was the course of the disease in this particular case, would
seem to be shown by the fact that, at the end of six days, all
parts of the bone were so nearly equally implicated. It seems
to me extremely probable that, if this little fellow had been
able to maintain himself under the first onslaught of the inflammation, the case would have terminated as an ordinary
example of complete necrosis of the central parts, if not the
whole, of the shaft of the femur.

· The recognized causes of osteo-myelitis are usually connected with some injury of the bone, as in contusion, fracture,
amputation, or resection, injuries which seem much more
liable to be followed by the disease, if air has admission to the
wounded bone. In military practice, it is thought that the
transportation of the wounded is a fertile cause of inflammation of the bone, as we know it to be of the soft parts which
lie round it. The jolting of compound fractures, or of resected

joints, over rough military roads, must necessarily induce a rubbing of the wounded bones against one another, whereby inflammation would be produced, and even in stumps the contusion of the flaps against the bone may very well be supposed to set up inflammatory actions, which may involve the bone as well as the soft parts. Dr. Lidell has particularly noticed this point, and alludes to the corroboration his views have received from several surgeons who have directed their observations toward this matter.

But, of all the causes which may produce this disease, none is so efficient as the impure air generated in over-crowded military hospitals. The disease may be said essentially to depend upon bad hygienic conditions, and it is because these bad conditions are particularly liable to be found in large hospitals, that it is in these establishments we find it almost exclusively present. Dr. Lidell observes: "Observation has shown that, other things being equal, the wards of a hospital that are most impure in respect to their atmospheric condition generally furnish the largest proportion of fatal cases of osteo-myelitis. Observation has also shown that surgical patients—for example, those who have sustained gunshot-fracture, or amputation, and are treated in the portion of the ward where the air is most likely to stagnate, for example, the corners—are considerably more likely to become affected with destructive osteo-myelitis than those who are treated in other portions of the same ward where the air is more free from impurities. Observation has further shown that surgical patients treated in hospital-tents, if they are properly pitched and policed, are much less liable to be seized with fatal osteo-myelitis than a similar class of patients treated in the wards of a hospital building." These views are amply confirmed by the more limited experience of civil practice, where the few cases that do present themselves can always be traced to the same vitiation of atmosphere, which at the same time shows its ill influence by the production of erysipelas, pyæmia, gangrene, and typhoid, to all which osteo-myelitis has undoubtedly many close relations.

The treatment of this dangerous affection might perhaps properly be said to consist in its prevention, and it is certain that, in this direction, much may be accomplished by carefully regulating the hygienic conditions of the wounded man. These hygienic precautions are undoubtedly the first and most important features in the management of osteo-myelitis, and, even when the disease has already declared itself in a given individual, his chances for life would mainly depend upon what could be done to improve his hygienic surroundings. Removal from the place of original infection, separation from others suffering from similar disease, change of bedding and of clothing, scrupulous cleanliness, and abundance of pure air, will often modify most favorably an attack which threatened to be fatal; and, in the absence of this kind of care, military surgeons are often obliged to witness the utter inefficiency and even worthlessness of every other species of management whether medicinal or surgical. Nevertheless, there is something left to be done by both general and local treatment. The character of the general treatment must be mainly that which supports the strength of the patient through a disease in which that strength is sorely taxed. The best food which the stomach will receive, offered in such form as to be most easily digested and assimilated, with such stimulants as will not exaggerate the acuter symptoms of inflammation, together with the exhibition of such tonic medicines as will help to sustain the nervous power, or prevent, as far as may be, the rapid disintegration of the tissues; these seem to be the main indications of general treatment. With regard to local treatment it must always be borne in mind that, in all forms of bone-inflammation, the imprisonment of the inflammatory products within the unyielding bone or the scarcely less tractable periosteum, forms one of the most important elements of suffering and of danger, and that therefore the first consideration of the surgeon should be, as far as possible, and as early as possible, to give the freest issue to any such inflammatory secretions as, by retention, would be likely to be injurious. For this reason, wounds in the soft parts should be freely and unhesitatingly opened, in such a way that gravity will assist in keeping the discharges free, and, if necessary, free incisions should expose the bone to our view. The tense and inflamed periosteum may often be incised longitudinally, so as to remove its pressure on the bone beneath, and in some instances it has been recommended, if there be not free exit of the contained fluids, to perforate the bone with a trephine, in order to afford an easy route by which the injurious fluids may find the surface. These somewhat summary proceedings are justified by two considerations: First, the immediate effect of the retention, under pressure, of the fluids within the bone is, to enlarge the area of disease, and intensify its severity; and, secondly, the continuance of the pressure soon leads to disintegration and death of the bone-tissue involved; and, if the patient should happily recover from his primary disease, he has still to encounter its dreadful secondary consequences, in the shape of pyæmia, caries, and necrosis. Again (and this is the really practical question in the treatment of osteo-myelitis), what are the chances which the removal of the diseased bone affords? The first efforts made in this direction were made by amputation or exsection of the affected bones, and with a very unsatisfactory success. Vallette, in the Crimean War, and Jules Roux, in the Italian campaigns, discouraged by these ill results, adopted the plan of exarticulation, thereby removing the whole of the affected bone, with a success which they report as extremely marked. Mr. Thomas Longmore, in a paper read before the Royal Medical and Chirurgical Society, February 8, 1865, combats these views of Drs. Vallette and Roux, and insists that a great many of these cases may be saved by allowing the disease to go on to its full development, and then, by removing the sequestrum, he says the stump may be saved. These views of Mr. Longmore I consider unsound and founded on an erroneous pathology. The tubular sequestra of which he speaks, and which he regards as always the result of osteo-myelitis, have in fact no connection whatever, in most cases, with this formidable disease. It is a fact which I think the carefully-recorded experience of any practical surgeon will verify, that the cases in which these tubular sequestra are found are the very cases which, perhaps, have done the best in their earliest stages, and that the first symptoms have been after the wounds have nearly closed, when gradually-increasing pain and soreness of the stump, with an increasing instead of a diminishing discharge, have led to the discovery of a thickened bulbous condition of the end of the bone, which after a certain time has been found to contain a tubular sequestrum. This is not the history of osteo-myelitis, and I confidently believe that, in most cases, no form or degree of medullary inflammation has preceded their formation. They are dependent upon the cutting off, in the amputation, of the nutritious artery of the medulla, whereby death of the inner shell of the bone, which receives its supply from this artery, is produced, which dead shell only announces its presence by the irritation and discharge which it excites, after it is separated from the living tissue, and has become a foreign body, and by the involucral thickening which it produces around the sequestrum, giving the enlarged bulbous feeling to the end of the bone in the stump. I have given, in the chapter on Necrosis, a full exposition of my views on this matter (see page 119), and I think a right idea of the pathology of this troublesome form of necrosis is in no respect more necessary than as it bears upon these practical questions of osteo-myelitis.

In my judgment, therefore, the conclusions of Drs. Vallette and Roux are not invalidated by the reasonings of Mr. Longmore, and the recommendation of these gentlemen, who had seen so much of the real disease in its earliest stages, to amputate always, by removal of the whole affected bone, remains a sound maxim in surgery, and one which is fortified by a gratifying success in its performance.* .

CHAPTER VI.

RICKETS.

RICKETS is a disease so rarely seen in our country that I have no experience which would entitle me to speak of it authoritatively from my own observation. In the Old World, and particularly in the large cities, it would seem to be common, and our best accounts of it are pictures of the disease as it exists in Paris and London. Many writers have given excellent de-

---

* See, also, a valuable paper by H. Allen, M. D., U. S. A., on Osteo-myelitis, in *American Journal of Medical Sciences*, January, 1865.

scriptions of the affection, and its different features have been most carefully investigated by very able observers, so that there is perhaps no disease more thoroughly studied and better understood. I know of no better account of what is know non the subject than that which is contained in the admirable lectures of Dr. William Jenner, published in the *Medical Times and Gazette*, of London, during the year 1860. These lectures are the more valuable, inasmuch as they are not a mere *résumé* of other men's ideas, but are founded on the author's large experience in the Hospital for Sick Children.

Rickets, evidently, is not to be regarded as in any proper sense a primary disease of the bones. It is a peculiar condition of the general system, showing itself by many striking symptoms, of which one very important class present themselves in the bones. So important, however, and so characteristic, and so constant, are these bone-changes, that the affection very naturally ranges itself among bone-diseases, and systematic writers have agreed to give it a place among these disorders. The first symptoms of the disease show themselves usually from the third month to the beginning of the third year of age ; not commonly much later, and very rarely earlier than these dates. Some writers speak of congenital rickets, but the best authorities deny its occurrence. At first, there are usually some vague and undefined symptoms of deranged digestion and vascular action, which perhaps, at first, are not characteristic, but their continuance, or perhaps their recurrence, soon shows that something more than mere temporary disorder is present. Dr. Jenner points out three symptoms which, even in the earlier stages, are characteristic of rickets : The first is an unnatural and profuse perspiration about the head and neck, and upper part of the chest. This sweating is out of all proportion to the heat of the room, or the exercise the child may have taken, and also out of proportion to the same action on all the rest of the surface ; for it constantly happens that the abundant perspiration will be seen on the upper parts of the body, while the rest of the skin is perfectly dry. It is mostly in sleep that these drenching sweats are observed, but they may occur at any time from the most trivial causes. A second symptom of approaching rickets is the desire of the child to be cool at night, leading it to throw off the bedclothes, and lie exposed, even during cold weather, and when other children are disposed to be well covered. This symptom, it is true, is so common among children otherwise perfectly well, that it cannot be considered as by itself characteristic, but yet Dr. Jenner insists that its prominence and constancy are so decided as to distinguish the rickety children, as a class, from others, in a ward where all are sleeping together. A third symptom, and I suspect a more characteristic one than either of the preceding, is a general tenderness to the touch of the whole body. The child seems to shrink from even the gentlest pressure, or the most careful handling. Not only this, but his own movements seem to give him pain. Dr. Jenner says : " The child suffering severely from the general cachexia which precedes and accompanies the progressive stages of the bone-disease, ceases its gambols ; it lies with outstretched limbs as quietly as possible, for voluntary movements produce pain. Its unwillingness to be moved is so great that, as Stiebel has observed, it will cry at the approach of those who have been accustomed to dance it—of those at the sight of whom it previously manifested extreme pleasure. As the disease progresses, the child gets a peculiar staid and steady appearance; its natural lively expression is replaced by a pensive, aged, languid aspect; its face grows broad and square, and, when placed upright on its mother's arm, it sits, as she says, ' all of a heap.' Its spine bends, and its muscles are too weak to keep it erect. Its head seems to sink between its shoulders ; its face is turned a little upward."

These indications of constitutional cachexia may be more or less distinctly developed in individual cases, and may occupy a longer or shorter space of time. But soon the peculiar feature of the disease begins to show itself, namely, a change in the condition of the bones. Sometimes, we are assured, that this change in the bones shows itself at the same time with the constitutional symptoms above described, and sometimes even before their appearance. In some cases, too, there is little or no constitutional suffering from the beginning to the end of the disease. These, however, are the exceptions to a rule and mode of progress which are tolerably regular and constant. Dr. Jenner classifies the most striking anatomical lesions in rickets under seven heads, of which five have reference to changes in the bones, and two to alterations in the soft parts. Thus, he says we have: ◢

1. Enlargement of the ends of the long bones.
2. Softening of all the bones.
3. Thickening of the flat bones.
4. Deformities which follow from mechanical causes acting on the softened bones.
5. Arrest of growth of the bones, muscles, etc.
6. Certain lesions of the pericardium, lungs, and spleen, the direct consequence of the thoracic deformity.
7. Less constant but highly-important changes affecting the nutrition of the brain, spleen, liver, lymphatic glands, and other organs.

1. *The Enlargement of the Ends of the Long Bones.*—This seems to be one of the earliest and most distinctive features of the disease. It is observed in all the bones, but is most striking in the wrist, the ankle, the elbow, the knee, and the articular extremities of the ribs. The change seems to be one in which the cartilaginous substance of the ends of the bone is developed in excess, without, however, any increase in the ossific action, so that the end of the bone grows larger than it should be at the given age, while ossification is retarded, and hence we have the joint-end of the bone not only enlarged but softer than natural from the absence of calcareous deposit in the exaggerated cartilaginous tissue. The periosteum is also very considerably thickened over this enlarged end of the bone, thus adding very materially to the deformity which is so characteristic of the early stages of rickets.

2. *The Softening of all the Bones.*—This is the most peculiar and most interesting, and in many respects the most important feature of rickets. It has accordingly been very carefully studied by all the writers on this subject. It is pretty certainly ascertained that this softening of the bones depends in most cases upon a want of a due proportion of earthy salts in their composition. Thus, as a general statement, it may be said that, while in healthy bone we have one part of organic, and two parts of inorganic matter, in rickety bone the proportion is exactly reversed, and we have, in a given weight of bone, two

parts of organic, and only one part of inorganic constituents. Besides this, however, there is a rarefaction of the bone-tissue which may or may not coexist with the changes in its chemical composition. Of these two conditions of the bone, Rokitansky says : " The texture of the bones is affected in two ways, of which sometimes one preponderates, and sometimes the other. In the first case, the bone is rarefied and increased in size, expanded, in fact. A pale, yellowish-red jelly is effused into its enlarged canals and cells, into the medullary cavity, and even under the periosteum. The bone itself is abundantly supplied with vessels, and full of blood, and its color is, therefore, darker than natural, and red. Occasionally this change reaches to such a degree that the cells of spongy bones, and those in the interior of medullary tubes, become excessively distended, and, as their walls disappear, are merged in larger cavities : medullary cavities at last become single, spacious chambers, and the bones uncommonly soft and fragile. In the second case, in addition, it is deprived more or less of its mineral constituents ; and sometimes it is completely reduced to its cartilaginous element, and appears like a bone that has been steeped in acid. The bony corpuscles are empty, and their rays have disappeared, and, when this is the case, the lamellar structure is here and there obliterated ; at other parts the lamellæ appear, as it were, to have fallen asunder, and the corpuscles are seen quite distinctly interposed between them. It is upon this condition that the softness, the flexibility, etc., of rickety bones depend. These two conditions exist together, as has been remarked, and sometimes one preponderates, and sometimes the other ; it is, however, remarkable that, in cases of general rickets, the reduction of a bone to its cartilaginous elements so preponderates in some bones as to go on even to completion without any trace of rarefaction." He gives, also, the following analysis of a scapula and a humerus affected by rickets :

Scapula—specific gravity..........0.612

Cartilage, vessels, and fat 81.12	organic constituents.	
Basal phosphate of lime and of magnesia 15.60		
Carbonate of lime............. 2.66	18.88 inorganic constituents.	
Salts, soluble in water......... 0.62		

The humerus contained 10.54 per cent. of fat.

This may be compared with an analysis which he gives further on of a simple induration of the skull of a lunatic:

Specific gravity...................1.911
Cartilage and vessels.................33.41 organic constituents.
Basal phosphate of lime, etc....54.10 ⎫
Carbonate of lime..............10.45 ⎪
Phosphate of magnesia......... 1.00 ⎬ 66.59 inorganic constituents.
Salts, soluble in water.......... 1.04 ⎭

Or with the following, taken from Carpenter, of the healthy bone of a man twenty-five years of age:

Cartilage and fat.....................31.03 organic constituents.
Phosphate of lime, etc.........59.63 ⎫
Carbonate of lime... .... 7.33 ⎪
Phosphate of magnesia......... 1.32 ⎬ 68.97 inorganic constituents.
Salts, soluble in water.......... .69 ⎭

Besides these changes in the chemical composition of bone, there is another less distinctly noticeable, but perhaps not less important, which exists in the animal matter of the bone, whereby it is so altered that, on boiling, it does not yield either chondrin or gelatin, as is the case in healthy cartilage and healthy bone. What precise relation this change may have to the softened condition of the bone-substance has not yet been clearly ascertained.

3. The *thickening of the flat bones* of the cranium seems to be another illustration of the irregular nutritive behavior of the bone-substance in rickets. The thickening is associated with the other changes noted above, and is sometimes very great. It is usually just at the growing margin of the bone, and least at the centres of ossification, obeying thus the same general law by which the earliest and most marked changes in the long bones are found at their extremities, where growth is most active.

In contrast with this excess of deposit, we have, in some cases, as an early rachitical symptom, a deficiency of bony matter in certain points of the cranial bones, which has been called craniotabes. This curious affection is most frequently seen in quite young children, and affects the posterior parts of the cranium rather than the lateral or anterior. It consists of a deficiency, probably from absorption, of the earthy constituents of the bone, in circumscribed, irregular, and sometimes numerous spots; these deficient points not being found at the ossifying edges, but rather in the central districts of the bone where ossification has been longest complete. The following case is reported by Dr. A. Jacobi, in the *New York Medical Journal* for November, 1865: "A child aged five months died after having suffered from frequent convulsions during a fortnight preceding its death. The convulsion was usually announced by an attack of laryngismus stridulus, but no other cerebral symptoms were manifest. In other respects, it had seemed to be a tolerably healthy child, though it presented the enlarged epiphyseal extremities of the long bones so characteristic of rickets.

"On examination after death, the dura mater was found tightly adherent in the situation of the lambdoidal suture. The upper portion of the occipital bone and the lower portion of the parietal bones have been removed, and, on holding them to the light, there are evidently a great many places in which there is apparently no osseous tissue whatever—especially is this the case on the right side. I forgot to state that the occiput of the child appeared at one portion to be flattened; this condition can now be appreciated in the general configuration of the bones. The right parietal is evidently the one which is most affected; the left parietal bone shows a number of very distinct, softened spots, in which there is no appearance of bony tissue. Through one spot, where I had previously removed the pericranium, I was enabled to-day to see a large letter. There was softening of the cerebral substance, and there was further some effusion in the arachnoid sac, which, judging from the symptoms, must have occurred during the last days of life. There was a little effusion in the spinal canal, which would flow down into the cranium when the child was turned over." All the other organs were healthy. The periosteum was very easily stripped off the parietal bones.

In the *American Journal of Obstetrics*, published in New York, in the number for November, 1870, Dr. Jacobi has published a very full and very able paper on the subject of craniotabes, and its relations to the other better-known rachitical changes. He says that the peculiar change we are considering is apt to commence at about the age of three or four months, when the rachitical condition of the cranium can usually be appreciated by the finger gently pressed upon the softened spots. Dr. Jacobi considers that "the clinical cause of the predilection of rachitical absorption for the occipital portion of the head must be sought for in the recumbent posture of the infant. The whole cranium gets softened, more or less; the side on which the patient is mostly resting gets flattened, and the corresponding oblique diameter shortened, but absorption will take place at a number of spots which fulfil the following conditions:

"1. Rachitical deposits must have taken place very copiously.

"2. The weight of the brain must fall on the softened spot.

"3. The pressure of the pillow must form a third factor.

"Thus, in every instance, one of the sides is flattened—mostly the right—and the majority of the softened spots are found on that flattened right side."

Dr. Jacobi considers the prognosis of craniotabes as no more unfavorable than that of the other signs of the rachitical disease, provided there be no complication on the part of the brain or its membranes. The liability to this complication gives a somewhat grave character to the prognosis.

4. The importance attached to the *softened condition of the bones* in this disease is derived from the fact that this altered condition leads to *deformities* from mechanical causes acting upon the skeleton, and that these deformities become permanently impressed upon the bone as the original disease disappears, thus leaving its life-long and ineffaceable traces behind it; traces which mark themselves as the causes of some of the most serious diseases and dangers to which the frame is liable. These changes have been very carefully studied, and occur most distinctly and most commonly in the spine, in the thorax, in the pelvis, and in the long bones of the extremities. The spine presents an increase in its natural curvatures, and the change is therefore usually confined to the antero-posterior directions. A lateral curve of the spine is sometimes associated with other more marked antero-posterior curves, but, as a primary or a

principal change, lateral curvature is rare. The cervical vertebræ are so softened that they can no longer support the great weight of the head, which therefore falls either backward or forward. Dr. Jenner explains its falling most commonly backward by the desire of the child to see what is going on around it, which it can do more easily with the head thrown back than when it is allowed to fall forward on the sternum. There is also a curve developed in the dorsal and lumbar region, which, in the dorsal region particularly, is sometimes extreme, and

forms a very important element in the accompanying deformity of the chest. The femur becomes curved outward and forward (Fig. 8), the tibia outward, and these curves become much increased as the child begins to walk. The radius and ulna are also somewhat bent, according to the muscular actions they have been subjected to, and are not unfrequently twisted as well as bent. The humerus usually bends about the insertion of the deltoid, and the clavicle, from transmitting all the forces which act upon the body, through the upper extremity, is often bent at several points, and at a very considerable

FIG. 8.—(Bellevue Hospital angle.
     Collection.)

The deformity of the thorax is very marked, and exercises, no doubt, a great influence on the health of the child, by the imperfect manner in which, both from its shape and its softness, it performs its part in the respiratory acts. Dr. Jenner believes that this is a very important element in the mortality of rickety children, who may be attacked with any pulmonary inflammation ; the disease demanding increased play of a chest which cannot fully respond to the demand, and, therefore, cannot lend to the little sufferer that aid which the increased expansion of the cavity brings to healthy children suffering in the same way. In regard to the change of shape, Dr. Jenner says: "The back is flattened. The ribs are bent at an acute angle, where the dorsal and lateral regions unite. At that part, the lateral diameter of the thorax is the greatest. From it the ribs pass forward and inward to the point where they unite with their cartilages; on that line the lateral diameter of the thorax is the least, the cartilages curving outward before turning in to unite themselves to the sternum. The sternum is thrown forward, and the antero-posterior diameter of the thorax is abnormally great. The consequence of the direction of the ribs being inward, and of the cartilages outward, is that the thorax is grooved, from above downward, on its antero-lateral face, from the first to the ninth or tenth rib; the deepest part of the furrow being 'just outside the nodes formed where the ribs and cartilages meet. This groove extends lower on the left than on the right side, but it is deeper on the fifth and sixth ribs on the right than on the left side; the heart and liver respectively supporting, to some extent, their corresponding ribs. The points of maximum recession correspond to the fifth, sixth, and seventh ribs. A little below the level of the nipple the chest expands considerably, the chest-walls being borne outward by the liver, stomach, and spleen. If we examine the thoracic walls from the inside, the appearance is most remarkable: where the ribs join with the cartilages there are much greater projections than on the outside; but the eleventh and twelfths ribs, which are not inflexed, have the same enlargement on the inside as on the outside." Add to these statements as to shape the fact that the bones are yielding from their softness, and add still further the fact that the muscles are weakened in their tone as well as their texture, and I think it is not difficult to understand how much below the normal standard of healthy children the respiratory power of rickety children falls, and how little it is suited to meet the increased respiratory necessities of severe disease.

The pelvis, in rickets, undergoes changes, not less marked, but perhaps less constant, in their effect upon the shape of the structure. These consequences are due to the weight of the body being transmitted through the pelvis, and received upon the heads of the femora, and as this weight is very varying in its action, according as the child walks, or creeps, or sits, or lies, or as either of these motions preponderates over the others, so it must necessarily be with the resulting deformity, it showing the effects of pressure in that direction in which the pressure is most frequently and most forcibly made, and varying there-

fore with the habitual muscular actions, as well as with the
habitual attitudes and positions he tends to assume. The interest attac he to these changes in the rickety pelvis depends
mainly upon the effect of the resulting deformity, in so changing the size and form of the outlets that the process of parturition, in after-life, may become difficult or impossible. It
is mostly to these changes that are due those dreadful cases
in which the obstetric practitioner is obliged to resort to his
most fearful, and, unfortunately, most doubtful 'expedients, to
terminate a process, which is only impeded by the mechanical
disproportion between the head of the child and the openings
it must traverse. These terrible deformities are produced
mainly by rickets, but sometimes also by the disease of the
bones known as malacosteon, a disease which has this in common with rickets, that in it the texture of the bone is softened,
and yields to pressure. This pressure is considered to act differently on the pelvis in these two diseases, so that it is thought
that the deformity of the pelvis produced by rickets and that
by malacosteon differ so much that, by mere inspection of the
bones, the diseases can generally be distinguished from one
another. In general terms, the difference can be expressed by
stating that, in rickets, the pressure acts from before backward,
so that the promontory of the sacrum approaches the pubis,
thereby narrowing the antero-posterior diameter of the outlet,
while the transverse diameters are increased; while in malacosteon it seems that the pressure of the femora, on each side,
tends to thrusting in of the sides of the pelvis, so that the lateral
diameters are diminished, while the antero-posterior are lengthened, giving the outlet what Dr. Tyler Smith calls a rostrated
form. Besides these two modes of deformity there is a third,
more rare than either, in which the pelvis is obliquely distorted,
the pubis being thrust either to one side or the other of the
median line, so that the pelvis has a twisted appearance, and
the lines of the outlet differ on the two sides, according as the
pelvis is pushed to one side or the other of the promontory of
the sacrum. Of this oblique distortion, Naëgelé was the first
to give a description, in a special memoir which he published
on this subject, in which he details, most accurately and carefully, the features presented by thirty-seven obliquely-distorted

pelves, which, he had the opportunity to study. Writers do not seem to agree that this peculiar deformity is ever the sole result of rickets, or of malacosteon. Naögelé believes that it is an original failure in the process of development, and he gives many reasons for his belief. Of the proper rickety pelvis, Dr. Tyler Smith says : " The sacrum, in such cases, is placed more horizontally than natural ; the promontory projects forward, and sinks, as it were, into the cavity of the pelvis, so as to bring the fourth or fifth lumbar vertebra into the position naturally occupied by itself. The sacrum is somewhat diminished in depth, though not so much so as in the case of malacosteon distortion ; its vertical and lateral curvatures are both diminished, and the bone is consequently very much flattened. The apex of the sacrum and the coccyx are bent acutely forward and inward. The wings of the iliac bones are somewhat flattened, and everted, and carried bodily forward toward the anterior part of the pelvis. The symphysis pubis is sometimes projected inward, so as to give the inlet of the pelvis an hour-glass shape. The tuberosities of the ischia are separated, so as to increase both the transverse diameter of the outlet and the width of the sub-pubic arch."

5. It is only, however, when we add to these statements the fact that *arrest of growth* always accompanies the distortions of rickets, in a greater or less degree, that we can form a proper idea of the actual change produced by the disease, and the amount of impediment which the two conditions combined may produce to the passage of the fœtal head through the outlets. On this point, Dr. Alexander Shaw, in his admirable essays on rickets, in the *Medico-Chirurgical Transactions*, vol. xxvi., says, in a foot-note : " To ascertain the average amount of this deficiency, and thus judge of the share which the consequent smallness of the pelvis has in impeding the passage of the child in parturition, and causing difficult labor, I took the measurements of twenty-nine deformed pelves, from patients of the female sex, and compared them with those of the natural female pelvis. The result was, that the deformed pelves fell short of their normal dimensions by nearly one-quarter of their proper size. So that, in women distorted from rickets, two distinct causes give rise to difficult

5

labor : First, the distorted condition of the pelvis, consequent
on the softened state of the bones, and the compression to
which they have been subjected. Secondly, the general smallness of the bones depending on the pelvis having been originally, at childhood, of remarkably diminutive size, and on its
growth having been interrupted by the attack of rickets."

The changes which rickets produces on the shape of the
head have been particularly studied by Mr. Shaw; and the
results of his numerous observations lead him to several interesting conclusions : First, that the size of the whole head in
rickety persons is below the standard dimensions. Secondly,
that the degree of deficiency is greater in the face than in the
cranium ; and that therefore, thirdly, the apparent great size
of the head in these persons is due, not to the actual size of the
cranium, but to its disproportion to the size of the face. The
mode in which this disproportion is produced seems to be by a
failure on the part of the rickety skeleton to obey that law of
development which Mr. Shaw, in his most ingenious papers,
has shown to be a universal one in the healthy individual. He
shows, very clearly, that the head and upper part of the body
are, in the fœtus, developed much in advance of the pelvis and
lower extremities, and this, for obvious reasons connected with
the well-being of the fœtus and of the young infant, and that
from the time of birth this unequal development of the upper
over the lower parts of the body is gradually disappearing by
the increased rapidity of growth of the lower half. In rickets,
he is satisfied that this accelerated rate of development of the
lower parts of the body is checked, and upon this theory he
explains the changes which rickets impresses upon the skeleton.
It retains its infantile proportions rather than those of adult
age, and this he proves to be a fact by numerous and very
careful measurement statistics. The same law, which he shows
to guide the development of the whole body, governs also the
development of head and face. The cranium of the fœtus bears
a much larger proportion to the face than does that of the
adult. In rickets, this disproportion more or less remains, and
the face does not gain on the cranium as, in the healthy individual, it should do, and therefore, as all the parts grow together toward adult size, the face is, like the lower extremities,

left behind in the progress of development, and the adult presents some of the features of infantile proportion, while, perhaps, the whole frame may have attained a fair average size. In speaking of this effect of rickets, Mr. Shaw says : " Besides causing a general smallness of the head, it will occasion a disproportion between the parts of which it consists. As the two divisions, the face and the cranium, grow respectively at different rates of activity, it must follow that, when the whole process is interrupted for a certain time, the stoppage will have a more decided effect upon the one than upon the other ; upon the division which grows at a rapid rate than upon that which grows at a more moderate rate. Hence, as it is the face which is developed in the most active manner, and the cranium which increases at a slow rate, we may expect to find that there will be a very considerable defect in the size of the face, and only a trifling defect in that of the cranium. In other words, in persons whose growth has been interrupted by rickets the face will appear extraordinarily diminutive, while the cranium will retain about its natural dimensions." The effect of these changes is, as a general rule, to give, not only the appearance of undue size to the head, but, from the smallness of the face, the forehead appears broad and square, and often so prominent that the facial angle is very conspicuously increased. This prominence of the forehead, when associated with the precocity in the mental faculties, so common a characteristic of rickety children, gives the impression of a finely-developed head, and, consequently, of great intellectual promise. Too much stress will not be laid upon these delusive appearances, when it is remembered that the actual development of the head is below the normal standard, and that precocity is apt to show itself in nervous, excitable, delicate children, from whatever cause this bodily state may arise. One curious result of Mr. Shaw's careful measurements relates to the size of the orbital cavities. These he found unvarying in their dimensions, whatever might be the size of the skull. In speaking of a table, in which he gives numerous measurements of their size, he says : " If this list be examined, by running the eye along the line of figures which shows the measurements of the orbits, it will be perceived that there is scarcely an appreciable difference between the dimensions of these parts in any of the skulls. Whether we take the rickety skulls, those of standard size, or the skull of the giant, the diameters of the orbits measure the same in all. As they are not below the standard dimensions in the rickety specimens, so they are not above them in the giant."

Fig. 9 is a drawing of a specimen, recently deposited by Prof. Humphry in the Anatomical Museum of the University of Cambridge, and gives a good idea of most of the changes

Fig. 9.

produced in the various parts of the skeleton by this disease. Prof. Humphry publishes a full account of this case in the *Journal of Anatomy and Physiology*, for November, 1867.

In this connection, it is proper to notice the effects produced by rickets on the process of dentition. All the actions connected with this process seem to be imperfectly accomplished. The evolution of the teeth begins late, it is slow in being completed, and the life of the teeth is apt to terminate early, either by their falling out, or by a rapidly-destructive caries. These effects seem to be produced by the constitutional weakness, which elaborates, slowly and imperfectly, the complex phases of dentition, but perhaps also, in a very great degree, they are determined by the want of proportion between the teeth and the jaw in which they grow. The teeth have their normal size, the jaw has not, and that gradual change by which, in a healthy individual, the relative proportion between the teeth and the jaw is constantly being maintained is, in the rickety, materially checked, so that, as the teeth push forward to the surface, room is not afforded them, by the proper expansion of the jaw-bones, for their emergence in the regular and orderly manner on which so much of their usefulness depends. Hence, we have the teeth crowded, irregular, and imperfect, appearing above the jaw late and slowly, giving rise to many painful and sometimes serious symptoms, arising from the mechanical obstructions against which they have to contend, and doing poor and painful service while they last, to be lost early, either from decay or from want of a well-developed alveolar base, on which they might be maintained.

We have now remaining two classes of anatomical lesions characteristic of rickets, which show themselves, not in the bones, but in the soft parts. These are—

6. *Certain Lesions of the Lungs, Pericardium, and Spleen, the Direct Consequence of the Thoracic Deformity.*—Of the lungs, we have two conditions which are abnormal, viz. : 1. Emphysema. 2. Collapse. These two conditions of the lung-substance are both of them evidently due to the unequal pressure exerted on the lungs by the deformity of the thorax, and by the imperfect action of such a thorax, in accommodating itself to the varied necessities of respiration. Of the emphysema, Dr. Jenner says it is " that variety which has been termed insufflation. It is mere over-distention with air of the vesicular tissue of the lung. It invariably occupies the same situation in the lungs of the rickety child, viz., the whole length of the

anterior border of both lungs, extending backward for about three-quarters of an inch from the free margins. The emphysematous portion is separated from the healthy part of the lung by a groove formed by collapsed lung. The groove of collapsed tissue corresponds to those projections of the ribs inward which are situated at the points where they unite with their cartilages." The collapse is sometimes confined to this border or groove above noticed, but it is extremely common to find large portions of the posterior and inferior parts of the lungs in a state of collapse, which sometimes extends to the superior lobes. Thus it is a pathological fact of much importance that, in rickety children, not only do we have imperfect formation, and diminished power of action on the part of the thorax, but we have an imperfect condition, more or less extensively pervading the lung-substance itself, a fact which has much significance when, through stress of disease, unusual demands are made upon both thorax and lung, to meet the requirements of increased aëration, which the affection of the lungs imperiously calls for. Besides these anatomical lesions of the lungs, authors notice certain white spots or patches on the surface of the pericardium, and on the surface of the spleen, which would seem to have excited more attention than their importance entitles them to. They correspond with the points where the pressure of the deformed thorax is most constantly felt by the organs affected, and are doubtless produced by the constant attrition of the projecting bone against their serous surface.

7. *Important Changes affecting the Nutrition of the Brain, Spleen, Liver, Lymphatic Glands, and some other Organs.*— These changes occur gradually, and without any signs of inflammation, and are the evident expression of a constitutional cachexia which they in their turn tend very materially to aggravate.

Their most common seat is in the lymphatic glands, which are apt to be extensively, often universally, diseased, and with them the spleen is almost certain to be more or less implicated. The other organs enumerated are less frequently the seat of this peculiar change. The pathological state seems to be one in which an infiltration of what Dr. Jenner calls an albuminoid exudation, throughout the substance of the organ, slowly takes place, much after the manner of infiltrated tubercle, which so thoroughly incorporates itself with the substance of the affected tissue that its original texture is entirely lost, it assumes a fatty or waxy appearance, and loses, more or less completely, its functional power. After stating that the lymphatic glands thus affected are considerably enlarged, Dr. Jenner thus describes their appearance: "The cut surface of the glands is singularly pale and transparent, compact, smooth, tolerably moist, and, to the unaided eye, uniform in appearance. The substance is tough, and the gland heavy in proportion to its size. In rare cases, instead of being pale, the glands may be purplish in color." Of the spleen he says: "It is increased in size: the increase may be either trifling or extreme. Thus I have seen it little larger than in health, and I have seen it measure as much as eight inches from above downward over its convex surface, and four inches from side to side. It is never adherent to the parts adjacent, as a spleen containing tubercles often is, and its capsule generally is scarcely, if at all, thickened. Its anterior border is pretty sharp; it is firm to the touch, and smooth on the surface; its weight, regard being had to its size, strikes one as considerable. The substance is tough but elastic, and the thinnest sections can be cut with facility. The cut surface is remarkably smooth and transparent. It is not unlike what one might suppose would be its appearance if the whole organ were infiltrated with glue. Only a little pale blood can be expressed from the cut surface. Usually, the organ is pale red, but occasionally it is dark purple. The more transparent any given part is, the paler it is; the most transparent parts are almost colorless. The splenic corpuscles are sometimes more readily seen than in a healthy spleen; they may be mistaken for gray tubercles. I have never seen in the spleen of rickety children the sago-like little masses, so often present in the spleens of those who die of phthisis."

With this anatomical change in these organs, and very much in proportion to its extent, we have the constitutional cachexia becoming more marked and more distinctly progressive. Emaciation is sometimes extreme, muscular power grows gradually less and less, the derangements of digestion become more and more constant, and the little patient either wastes gradually away, or succumbs to the attack of bronchial or intestinal inflammation, whose effects his weakened organization is not able to contend with. Dr. Jenner thinks that the most common cause of death in rickets is acute bronchitis, and explains its fatality by the imperfect action of the soft and yielding walls of the thorax. He also says what seems very astonishing, that to rickets is due, in London, directly or indirectly, a larger percentage of infantile mortality than can be credited to any other single disease.

With regard to the causes of rickets, nothing very positive has been ascertained. It is very certain that it prevails principally among the poor, though it is sometimes seen in the children of the rich. Its prevalence is certainly favored by bad hygienic surroundings, but the same may be said of every diathetic disease; and why these unfavorable conditions should produce in one region rickets, and in another scrofula, as a preponderating disease among the infantile population, does not seem clear. It has been pretty distinctly shown that it is not hereditary, and yet, when one child in a family has the disease, those born afterward are extremely apt to show traces of it. Dr. Jenner thinks that the state of health of the mother has much to do with the occurrence of rickets in the children; if she be feeble, delicate, ill nourished, and ill cared for, she will be much more likely to have rickets in her children than if she were strong and robust in her own health. Phthisis and rickets have no necessary connection. Statistics show that phthisical parents are no more liable to have rickety offspring than those who are not phthisical; and it appears that scrofula, the twin-sister of tuberculosis, is not by any means commonly associated with rickets in the same individual. Bad food, bad air, bad clothing, bad habits of life, and exposure—in short, all those circumstances which are generally combined in the miserable, crowded, filthy habitations of the poor, and which so manifestly affect the general mortality of the districts where these habitations are crowded together—all these have an undoubted influence in producing the disease; and this is more practically interesting because it is in this direction that we must look for our principal means of controlling and curing it. In fact, the treatment of rickets, as such, is entirely unsatisfactory; and the very natural idea, that, by supplying an excess

of earthy matter to the stomach, we should cure a disease characterized mainly by its deficiency, has not proved in practice
to be well founded. Not only is there no specific for rickets,
but there is no specific treatment. Every case must be studied
by itself, and managed on the general principles of constitutional treatment. The first cares are hygienic. Improve as far
as may be the home and the habits; and, of these, none are so
important as the habits with regard to food. The children of
the poor are always fed improperly. Even with those who are
industrious and thriving, and who, therefore, have the means
of supplying a sufficiency of good food to their families, we
constantly find the younger children, particularly the infants
of from one to two years of age, fed on food too stimulating
for their stomachs. There seems to be in the minds of these
people a kind of pride in seeing their babies sitting at the
table with them, and, even before they are weaned, partaking
of the strong food which makes their parents' ordinary fare.
It requires some time, much care, and some trouble, to prepare
the milk-food which should be the principal food of every
child under two years of age. From these two considerations
arises the habit, almost universal, of giving the children whatever they like to eat, and rather letting them feed themselves,
than taking any pains to provide or prepare for them food such
as shall be suitable for the digestive power of their tender
stomachs. This is undoubtedly a common cause of disease
among the poor. The strong bear it, while the feeble die
under it. In rickets there is so marked a tendency to derangement of the digestive organs, that it would seem that the
regulation of the food was a point of even more than usual
importance, and its proper quantity and quality a prime subject for the watchfulness of the physician. After the care of
the food comes that of the air, the exercise, the clothing, the
cleanliness, and the hundred other things which go toward the
making of good blood and strong muscle. In the regulation
of many of these points much can be done, for it must be
remembered that a large proportion of the errors committed
in these respects arise much more from ignorance and inatten-
tion than from actual poverty.

In regard to medication, the main indication is to improve

nutrition. Tonics, such as iron, and cod-liver oil, are most commonly useful, and spoliative and depressing treatment, such as is usually called the antiphlogistic, is badly borne. Particular caution is required in managing the acute affections, which so frequently supervene in the course of rickets, that too much reduction of the powers of life be not produced by the very remedies we use to save it. Mercury and bloodletting are both reprobated as dangerous by the best authorities, and the care of the practitioner should be to accomplish his ends with the mildest means compatible with success. Each case and each complication must be judged by itself, and treated both hygienically and medicinally, according to its own indications; but, in all, the one main fact must be constantly kept in view, that we are dealing with a diathetic disease, and one whose tendencies are all toward a feeble reaction, and a diminished reparative power.

CHAPTER VII.

MOLLITIES OSSIUM—MALACOSTEON.

A CERTAIN number of cases present themselves in the adult, in which a softening of the bones takes place somewhat like the softening of rickets, but in which the accompanying features do not warrant us in placing the disorder in that class. These cases are quite rare, and are scattered over the records as individual cases by single observers, few writers having had an opportunity of observing any number of them, and none, therefore, having had that kind of experience which can only arise from a comparison of many examples of a given disease. From these recorded cases the general history of the disease may be gleaned, and yet, so considerable are the diversities of character among the individual cases, that it is difficult to present a clear picture of the affection, such as can be recognized by its own characteristics, and distinguished easily from other disorders to which it is closely related.

The cases thus far observed have occurred in young or

middle-aged adults, a little more frequently among females than among males, and so often in connection with the puerperal state as to warrant the opinion that this state is at least a strong predisposing cause of the disease. In a few instances it has seemed to be transmitted from parent to child. With these exceptions very little is known of the cause of the disease.

The changes that take place in the bone seem to vary considerably, both in their nature and in their extent, in different cases. In all, however, a gradual diminution, and in some an entire disappearance of the earthy salts of the bone, takes place; a change upon which, of course, the main features of the disease depend. This change takes place gradually, and invades more or less completely all the bones of the skeleton. In some cases this loss of the earthy constituents seems to be almost the only change which takes place, the remaining animal substance not having undergone any very marked alteration. In other, and much the larger number of instances, marked degeneration of all the component elements of the bone-tissue is found. Thus the original structures are often replaced by fat or free oil, and this is so common a feature that Mr. Paget is inclined to regard the affection as essentially a fatty degeneration. This fatty change involves the whole bony substance, and, when excessive, converts the bone into a bag of soft, oily substance, enclosed in the periosteum, which itself may not be materially altered from the healthy condition. That it is not a fatty degeneration in all cases, however, is shown by certain examples where the replacing material is of a gelatinous nature and presents few or no traces of fat, and certain others where the amount of fat in the bone does not vary from its normal proportion. The change in the bone sometimes involves the compact and the cancellous structures equally in its progress, and when this is the case there is a gradual diminution of the firmness of its texture, which permits it to bend instead of sustaining mechanical force. This flexile condition of bone is sometimes found to the most marvellous degree, and in all the bones of the skeleton, and it seems to depend for its production upon the evenness of the process in all parts of the bone at once. Sometimes, however, it happens that the central cancellous portions are far advanced in the degenerative changes, while the external compact shell, yielding more slowly, is only thinned and weakened, but not yet disorganized. In this condition the bone does not bend so readily as it breaks, and we have produced sometimes one and sometimes many fractures, arising from so slight a force as almost to seem spontaneous.

The microscopic study of the altered bone shows so very different appearances in different cases that it can hardly be said that any thing distinctive has been discovered which characterizes osteomalacia as contrasted with rickets. Still the general features of this disease, as displayed by the microscope, are not the same as those of rickets. Follin says: "The alterations in this case are very different from those which are established as belonging to the rickets of children. Thus, in the osseous layers of recent formation, we find an alteration in the bone-corpuscles, which have become elongated, fusiform, and without regular borders, and have taken on the character of the elements of fibrous tissue. More deeply we observe bone-cells which have become irregular, enlarged, with shining outline, and with a disappearance of their canaliculi; they contain sometimes small drops of oil, and sometimes granulations grouped together. The fundamental substance of the bone presents an infiltration of fatty granulations, which impairs its transparency and gradually invades the surrounding parts. The Haversian canals are also infiltrated. Thus, when we examine by the microscope a section of one of these Haversian canals, we see in the centre a darkish part formed by a mass of blood-globules, and around this mass a cavity with distinct borders, filled with little drops of oil, with fatty granulations, and with marrow-cells in process of formation. In the medullary tissue we find hypertrophy of the marrow-cells and an increase in their number, as is also the case with the fatty cells." Mr. Dalrymple, in a case which he examined, found some peculiar caudate cells, which induced him to regard the disease as malignant in its essential characters, and other observers have given accounts varying in many points from those given above. It would seem, therefore, that the microscopical appearances vary with the other peculiarities of each case, and that thus far no features can be said to be absolutely characteristic.

The symptoms of this disease seem to be more uniform than the pathological appearances. In the earlier stages, the patients complain of vague, wandering pains, at first not severe, increased very much by exercise, and accompanied by a distressing sense of weariness, which is but little relieved by rest. These pains are sometimes periodical, and often accompanied, particularly after exercise, with severe cramps. Writers speak also of a tenderness and soreness to the touch which much aggravates the sufferings of the patient. As these symptoms advance, the general state of the patient deteriorates. He becomes feeble, emaciates, and begins to have irregular fever, followed by very copious and exhausting sweats. The digestive power begins to fail, a change very much hastened by the condition of the teeth, which soon become so loose in their sockets, from the softening of the alveolar processes, that they either drop out, or give infinite inconvenience and discomfort in the attempt to masticate. Of course, when the softening of the thorax has reached an extreme degree, the function of respiration must be imperfectly performed, and another serious embarrassment is added to the load already pressing so heavily on the powers of life. The termination of much the largest number of cases is fatal, after a longer or shorter course of suffering; but a certain number of recoveries are reported by various authors, and in particular Naëgelé cites a case in which the Cæsarean section was performed on a woman whose pelvis was so deformed by an attack of osteomalacia that natural delivery was impossible. Other recoveries are also spoken of, in which the deformities produced by the softened state of the bone remained permanently impressed upon them.

During the course of this disease, the most striking symptoms are due to the mechanical results of the yielding of the softened bones. The lower extremities are bent and twisted in the most remarkable manner, and, after the patients are bedrid, the upper extremities, upon which they now have to depend for movements of all kinds, begin also to be distorted. The cranial vault sometimes undergoes a change, being either flattened by compression, or rounded by the weight of the brain; but these changes are pronounced to be very rare. The spine is deformed mainly by an increase of its natural curves, and the changes in the thorax are due mainly to the position of the patient in the bed. If he lie constantly on his back, the antero-posterior diameters are diminished, and the chest-cavity becomes broader laterally and shallower from before backward. If, on the other hand, he lie habitually on his side, the change in the form of the chest becomes marked by an antero-posterior increase, and a lateral diminution in diameters, together with such other deformity as the twisted position of the spine may impress upon it. In the pelvis, these changes are very marked, and have been particularly studied. We have already seen how the form of the pelvis is affected by rickets. In malacosteon, the deformity presents features so different that writers contend that the disease can be distinguished by the deformity; rickets exercising its effects mainly by a diminution of the antero-posterior diameters, while osteomalacia usually produces a contraction of the pelvic circles in a lateral direction. This distinction, however, is not to be relied on too implicitly, for several authors speak of cases in which rickets produced a lateral deformity precisely similar to that ordinarily resulting from osteomalacia. The general fact, however, remains, that in malacosteon the deformity is produced by the yielding of the sides of the pelvis. Dr. Tyler Smith thus sums up these changes: "The general effects produced in malacosteon are: narrowing of all the diameters of the pelvis, but especially of the transverse, whether of the brim, cavity, or outlet. The antero-posterior diameter of the brim, or rather, the distance from the promontory of the sacrum to the symphysis pubis, is, relatively to the transverse diameter, very much increased; absolutely it is somewhat less than natural. The pubic arch is very much narrowed; the tuberosities of the ischia are approximated; the sacrum is very much incurvated, and the acetabula are much closer together than in the normal pelvis; the ilia, instead of being carried bodily forward, as in the rickety pelvis, are folded up, and the iliac fossa is made to resemble an oblique furrow, running from above downward." Dr. Matthews Duncan, in a paper published in the *Edinburgh Monthly Journal* for April, 1855, has very carefully compared these deformities with one another, and gives a series of ingenious diagrams, by which he illustrates, by accurate measurement, the difference produced on the absolute and relative diameters by the two diseases. His demonstrations are very full and clear, and minutely establish the difference in the effect of the two diseases on the form of the pelvis—a difference, the general features of which are sufficiently expressed in the statements made above.

The urine, in malacosteon, has sometimes presented marked alterations in quality and appearance, and several of the earliest writers have recorded cases where it deposited a copious sediment of a white, chalk-like substance, sometimes described as a mortar-like material on cooling, or after·evaporation. Later and more thorough observations have shown this substance to be mainly phosphate of lime, and the idea was naturally suggested that this might, therefore, throw some light on the pathology of the disease; the waste of the bone-earths through the kidneys explaining very satisfactorily their disappearance from the bones where they properly belong. This renal view of the pathology of malacosteon, though so promising, has not borne the test of larger experience; and it is found that, in a certain proportion of the cases, there is at no time any change in the urine which will in any way correspond to the changes in the bones; in fact, that there is, in some cases, .no deviation whatever from the healthy constitution and appearance of the renal secretion. Still, though the urine may not have supplied a key to the real pathology of malacosteon, its changes in this disease are certainly worthy of careful consideration, and we can hardly regard as merely accidental, phenomena which present themselves in certainly the larger proportion of cases thus far recorded. Besides the more numerous cases in which an excess of phosphates has been found in the urine, there are some where other substances have been discovered which did not belong to its healthy condition. Thus Mr. Dalrymple reports a case on which Dr. Bence Jones made some observations in the "Philosophical Transactions," vol. lxvi., in which he shows that the peculiar matter in the urine which Mr. Dalrymple had described was, in fact, a deutoxide of albumen, combined with water so as to form a hydrate. Dr. Jones says: "There was as much of this peculiar albuminous substance in the urine as there is of ordinary albumen in the blood. So far, then, as the albumen is concerned, each ounce of urine passed was equivalent to an ounce of blood lost. The peculiar characteristic of this hydrated deutoxide of albumen was its solubility in boiling water, and the precipitate with nitric acid being dissolved by heat, and reformed when cold; by this reaction, a similar substance in small quantities may be detected in pus, and in the secretion from the vesiculæ seminales. This substance must be again looked for in acute cases of mollities ossium. The reddening of the urine on the addition of nitric acid might, perhaps, lead to the rediscovery of it. When found, the presence of chlorine in the urine (of which there was a suspicion in the above case) should be a special subject of investigation, as it may lead not only to the explanation of the formation of this substance, but to the comprehension of the nature of the disease which affects the bones." Mr. Erichsen refers to the analysis of the urine, in a case of Dr. McIntyre's, published in the "Medico-Chirurgical Transactions," vol. xxxiii., in which an animal substance, differing in most of its chemical reactions from albumen, was found in the urine in great abundance.

In illustration of the general features and course of this singular disease, I add a sketch of the famous case of Madame Supiot, one of the most remarkable, and probably the best known, of any on record:

Elizabeth Querian—afterward Supiot—came under observation in the year 1752. She was then thirty-six years of age. She had had three children and one miscarriage, without any serious accident. She had twice had falls, which produced more than usual swelling and lameness of the limb injured, but no fracture. She had had, however, much aching pain in her extremities, and of late had not been able to sustain herself on her feet without suffering. She had now been bedrid from this cause about two years. About a year before—that is, in 1751—she had commenced to observe a milky sediment in the urine, and about the same time the bones began to show some evidences of softening, and the legs to assume a distorted position from the retraction of the muscles. This was accompanied by a very great increase of the pains in the limbs, which at times were intolerable. At first sight, the

woman, as she lay in bed, seemed to have neither feet nor legs
nor hands. It seemed that the body terminated at the pubis.
The thigh-bone had curved so as to allow the foot and the leg
to turn up by the side of the body, so that the left leg inclined
to be under the back, and she could on this side lay her head
on her foot. The right thigh-bone was similarly bent, and the
whole extremity drawn forcibly against the right side of the
body. The patient could not move herself in bed. Defecation
and urination were not interfered with. This violent separation and twisting of the thighs, however, caused sufficient
pressure on the crural vessels to interfere in some degree with
their free circulation of the blood, and consequently some
œdematous swelling of both limbs existed. The thorax, sinking down at certain points upon the lungs, interfered with respiration, and at times she spat some blood. The upper part of
the sternum was prominent, the lower part sunken in. The
clavicles were more than usually prominent at their sternal extremity. The humerus was curved about its middle from within outward, as well as the forearm, so that the middle part of
the right arm was habitually applied against the internal malleolus of that side, while the middle of the left arm rested on
the upper part of the tibia, just below the patella. She could
make no use whatever of her limbs, being able to move only
her head and the left arm. She could also separate some of
her fingers slightly, but could not bend any of them in the
slightest degree. The right hand much atrophied. Her teeth
were discolored and loose, and the gums swollen and ulcerated.
When an attack of pain came on, she often had severe fever,
followed by profuse sweats, which were apt to be followed by
the eruption of papules or pimples, which caused very distressing itching. Her menstruation was regular, but was exceedingly apt to be accompanied by very serious exaggeration of
her other disorders and sufferings.

6

CHAPTER VIII.

FRAGILITAS OSSIUM.

A WEAKENING of the texture of the bones, rendering them more than usually liable to be broken from slight causes, is found to occur in the course of several very different diseases of the bone-tissue. Thus we have seen that certain conditions of malacosteon present great fragility of the bones, while it is well known that carcinomatous infiltration will sometimes so weaken them that fracture occurs on the slightest possible provocation. Several instances are recorded where, both in malacosteon, and in cancer, the thigh-bone has snapped asunder from turning in bed, and the arm-bone from an attempt to raise the body in bed on the elbow. But, besides these cases, there are certain individuals in whom, with all the evidences of good health, we have a degree of brittleness of the bones which exposes them in a remarkable degree to the occurrence of fracture, and in whom fractures take place from the most trivial causes. I had under my care, some years ago, a gentleman, then in middle life, who had from various accidents seven times fractured one or both bones of the forearm, and on one of these occasions the fracture was produced by somewhat too cordial a shake of the hand. This gentleman was rather slender in his formation, with small hands and feet, and delicate limbs, but was always a healthy and active man, and the father of a large family of well-formed children, none of whom presented any trace of this peculiarity of their parent. A gentleman of our profession, who has practised many years in this city, has twice fractured his leg by a slight stumble in passing along the street. He also has the slight frame and delicate formation which characterize the female, but he was, at the time of receiving his injuries, in excellent health. He has since suffered severely from rheumatism. Mr. Stanley alludes to a case under the care of Mr. Arnott, in the Middlesex Hospital, where, "in a female, aged fourteen, the first fracture occurred at the age of three years; altogether there were thirty-one fractures in different bones, and in some of them the fracture was many times repeated. Many of the fractures occurred from the slightest effort, and there was no difficulty in obtaining their union. In a sister of this patient, six years of age, there was the same condition of the bones, favoring the occurrence of fractures. She had suffered nine fractures since the age of eight months." Other writers speak of this peculiarity as belonging to several members of the same family, and there are certain cases in which its hereditary character is unquestionable. An instance is mentioned by Dr. Pauli, of Leipsic, in which, for three generations, certain individuals of a family have suffered from extraordinary fragility of the bones.

These cases are such as appear to be unconnected with any disease of the bone, or any constitutional disorder, the patient enjoying a good degree of health, and capable, ordinarily, of fulfilling the duties of life in a satisfactory manner. There are others, however, in which some symptoms precede the condition of fragility, and these symptoms are generally rather vaguely spoken of as chronic rheumatism. Thus Mr. Stanley reports the case of a woman, aged twenty-six, who was admitted into St. Bartholomew's Hospital, with a fracture of the left femur. "She stated that she had suffered rheumatism in this limb, and that, three days previously, the fracture occurred as she was crossing a road. She was placed on her back, with a straight splint on the outside of the limb. When she had been in the hospital about two months, while lying perfectly quiet in bed, she suddenly cried out that she felt a severe pain in the other thigh, and that the bone had broken. The house-surgeon happening to be in the ward, found the right femur fractured in its centre. At subsequent and distant periods, while confined in bed, a second fracture of the left femur occurred, a little above the knee, and fractures of both tibiæ, immediately below their tuberosities. She remained in the hospital above two years, during which every effort was made to obtain the union of the fractures. Throughout her general health was unimpaired, the appetite good, bowels regular, and the urine perfectly natural. At the expiration of two years from the occurrence of the first fracture, the patient left the hospital, both lower limbs being powerless, and, when moved, severely painful. None of the fractures had united, and both limbs were shortened to the extent of several inches, with considerable distortion." In another case mentioned by Mr. Stanley, the symptoms were very similar, excepting that the patient's health gradually broke down, and she suffered constantly with general weariness and aching in the bones. She died about four months after the first fracture. "A portion of the recently-fractured femur exhibits a thinning of its walls from the absorption of its inner laminæ, but without softening of its texture; it retains the hardness of healthy bone." A man was received into the New York Hospital a few years ago who had received a fracture of the clavicle from a very trivial cause. He told us that he had been suffering for some weeks with rheumatic pain, and great tenderness about the bone, for which he could give no explanation. His general health was good, and he had no syphilitic history. The bone was found broken near its middle, and was exceedingly sensitive to the touch. This was not confined to the point of fracture, but extended along the whole clavicle, which was manifestly thickened through all its middle portions. The limb was dressed in the usual way, and the only uncommon feature noticed during the progress of the cure was that an unusual amount of bony matter seemed to be thrown out, forming apparently a thick ferule of callus around the fractured ends. He was put upon the use of full doses of the iodide of potassium, and, when he left the hospital, the fracture was united, but the bone remained considerably enlarged, and very tender upon pressure.

With regard to the result of fracture in these cases of fragility of the bones, it seems to be different in the two classes of cases. In those where no disease exists, and where, therefore, the pathology of the case may be considered to be a mere delicacy and slenderness of construction of the bone, it seems to be generally conceded that we may hope for a very rapid and very perfect cure. Indeed, it would seem that the ease of the cure bore some proportion to the facility of the fracture; many of these patients being reported as having much less suffering and trouble during the union of their fractures than occur in ordinary cases. In many of the cases, however, when the rheumatic pains, showing diseased action about the bones, had existed in a marked degree and for a considerable period of time, the sufferings inflicted by the fracture were very great, and the union slow or imperfect, sometimes failing altogether, and in some instances inducing so much constitutional irritation as finally to wear out the powers of life. The prognosis, therefore, seems to depend more upon the sound condition of the bone at the time of fracture, than upon the degree of mere fragility.

With regard to treatment, it would hardly seem probable that what may be regarded as a mere peculiarity, such as obtains in simple fragility, could be influenced in any important degree by medicines or regimen. Still, I can conceive, in cases where the peculiarity shows itself in early life, that, by a robust regimen, and careful attention to all the details of hygiene, something may be done to strengthen slender bones as well as to improve a slender constitution. In those cases where some inflammatory action has given rise to the pains called rheumatic, of which some of these patients complain for a long period before the first fracture, I am in hopes the iodide of potassium may prove of benefit; though my own experience is limited to the case mentioned above, and in that the result was not very definite. Finally, I fear there are a number of cases where the disease is general, where it is severe, and particularly where it has been long continued, in which nothing can be accomplished but the palliation of suffering.

CHAPTER IX.

TUBERCULAR DISEASE OF BONE.

That true tubercle may exist in bone, I believe is denied by few pathologists; that it is a common affection of bone, is denied by many of the most eminent. In the earlier days of the revival of pathological anatomy, before the microscope had revealed its immense multitude of facts, leading us to reconsider and to change all our generalizations on the nature of morbid products, pathologists easily found tubercle in bone, and gave it a prominent position in bone pathology. Nélaton took the lead in this department of study, and his chapters on tubercle in bone were among the earliest, and have ever since been recognized as among the best of the publications on this subject. He accepts and describes every form of tubercle from the minute gray granulation up to the most extensive infiltration of crude yellow tubercle, and has no hesitation in bringing them all under the tubercular category. Later writers, among whom is Mr. Barwell, whose careful and conscientious studies entitle his opinions to great weight, have been disposed to limit very much the use of the term tubercle to those instances in which the normal history of tubercle can be distinctly made out in all its stages, and to exclude from the list a large number of those affections of bone in which a plastic or degenerating lymph assumes the form, and sometimes rather closely imitates the behavior, of true tubercle. In fact, when we reflect how close this resemblance is between tubercle and degenerating lymph in the soft parts of the body, where the difficult problems of structure are so much more easily unravelled than they can be in the hard and unmanageable tissue of the bones, we can easily find reason for being particularly cautious in pronouncing a judgment on changes which we cannot always satisfactorily appreciate, a judgment which therefore we are apt to found upon imperfect analogies rather than upon careful observations. It is acknowledged by all that there is here a debatable land, in which it is impossible to decide on each individual instance as belonging either to one category or the other, and it is therefore eminently wise not by any violent generalization to throw all cases under either head, reserving opinions as to the tuberculous or non-tuberculous nature of the various deposits, until our knowledge shall be more extensive, or at least more accurate.

With these reservations we may say that tubercle in bone presents itself under the two forms usually described, of gray granulation and of crude yellow tubercle. The first is commonly regarded as the elementary form of the disease, or at least the form most characteristic and unequivocal, and therefore, in settling the question of tubercle in bone, it has been sought for with particular anxiety. It is in this search that the hardness of the bone-substance interposes such great difficulties, and it is only by the most tedious and careful dissection that we can arrive at any clear view of the pathological conditions we are studying. Nélaton, however, persevering in his investigations, claims to have several times succeeded in demonstrating the presence of the gray granulation. He says, in describing one of his dissections : " In the centre of the spongy tissue which occupies the base of the great trochanter was found a mass, of six or seven lines in extent in all directions, formed by the aggregation of small pearly granulations, of a half a line in diameter, and of an opaline-white color. Many of these granulations, and particularly those which were placed near the periphery, were surrounded by a little osseous shell, so thin and transparent that at first sight it could not be recognized ; in fact, its presence could only be demonstrated by the resistance it offered to any attempt to pierce it with the point of a needle. Some of these granulations presented, in their centre, a yellow opaque point, evidently the indication of commencing transformation." This seems a distinct observation of the gray granulation, and there are several others on record. The crude form of tubercle, or that in which larger masses of the opaque yellow material are found variously disseminated through the bone, is not only more easily recognizable, but is much the more common form of the deposit in the bone-tissue. Both these forms of tubercle are usually found in masses more or less isolated ; often so distinctly separated from the surrounding tissues that some authors have described them as encysted. Both forms are recognized in the soft parts, and particularly in the lungs, as sometimes assuming the character of infiltrations, and undoubtedly the same is true in bone ; but it must be acknowledged that, for the gray, transparent form, the demonstration in bone must be difficult and uncertain. Nélaton, with his usual careful minuteness, describes this infiltration, and gives a case most particularly and thoroughly studied out, in which this infiltration existed at a number of points in the sacrum and pubis. The case seems a clear one, but the want of microscopic examinations must always cause it to be received with some doubt as to its real nature.

The crude yellow tubercle is not uncommonly infiltrated through the spongy substance of the bone. The normal tissue does not seem to be displaced by the deposit; simply its interstices are occupied by it, and its cavities filled up by it. Sometimes the deposit is firm and solid, sometimes softer and cheesy in its consistence, and sometimes it is not easy to pronounce whether we have under view an infiltration of soft tubercle, or of inspissated lymph. In its microscopic characters, the tubercle of bone has no different features from those of tubercle elsewhere, and, in its behavior after it is deposited in the tissues, it obeys the same laws and goes through the same transformations as in the lungs or in the lymphatic glands. Clinically, these changes have some peculiarities impressed upon them by the peculiarities of the tissue in which they are developed, but, in all essential particulars, tubercle in bone presents the same history as tubercle in the soft parts. The first change noticed is that by which the gray tubercle changes to the yellow. This change commences in the central parts of the tubercle, and gradually proceeds until the whole is transformed. While this process is going on, we usually have an increase in number and size of the deposits, so that, when the change is completed, we have large crude tubercles replacing what were at first small and scattered gray granulations. That this change does occur, most of the best authorities agree; but, that it is the invariable law of progress, is more than doubtful. That some gray granulations, by aggregation and the yellow change, become crude yellow tubercle, may be considered as certain; but it is equally certain that many, and perhaps most, of the crude tubercles we encounter, have never had any previous stage of gray granulation. Once having reached, however, the stage of crude tubercle, the changes are more distinct and more constant. The tubercle itself tends usually toward softening (Fig. 10). This change also commences in the centre, and spreads to the circumference. While it is going on, inflammatory action begins to be developed in the surrounding soft parts, the products of which, mingling with the softening tubercle, favor its disintegration; while, being retained, they add to the local irritation. Soon, a process of ulceration begins, and the cancellous tissue slowly breaks down, forming irregular cavities, which at first contain, mingled together, the substance of the softened tubercle and the purulent results of the surrounding inflammation. The rate at which the changes go on is very vari-ous. In the circumscribed tu-bercles it is said to be more slug-gish than in the infiltrated form, and again, the harder deposits change more slowly than those originally of a softer consistence. In all cases, a wider and wider area is involved, and the disease finally makes its way to the outer compact shell, which, either by a process of necrosis, or by a con-tinuation of the process of ulcer-ation, is finally perforated, and the matter comes in contact with the soft parts surrounding the diseased region of bone. These have been already involved more or less in the inflammatory ac-tions which, for so long a time, have been going on in the bone,

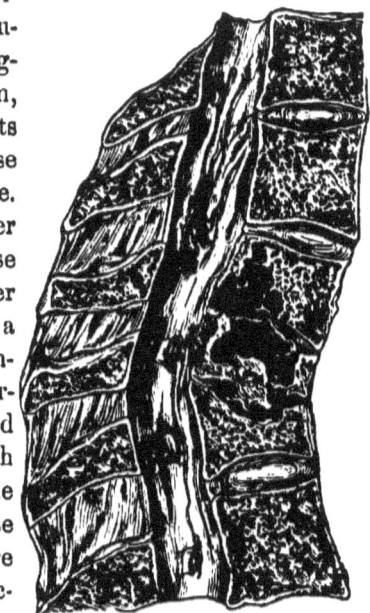

Fig. 10.—(From Billroth.)

and they are ready to contribute their share to the mixed, semi-fluid mass which is struggling slowly toward the surface; and thus we have formed the tubercular abscess, which finally opens on the integument, and discharges a fluid composed of softened tubercle, mingled with the pus derived from the inflamed tis-sues which have been traversed, and also the detritus of these tissues as they have yielded to ulceration and molecular disin-tegration. From this point the changes vary in different cases. Sometimes this seems to be the termination of the tubercular action, and reparative dispositions begin to show themselves as soon as the evacuation of the morbid products is completed. Healthy granulation begins, the cavities in the bone and the soft parts are gradually filled up, and a perfect cicatrization terminates the disease. This favorable behavior is, however, the rare exception, and, though ultimately we may hope, in perhaps a large number of cases, that a cure will take place, it is not commonly realized without a period of protracted local disease, which gives to the tubercular morbid processes their peculiar character of obstinacy and of danger. These traits they well deserve, and are exemplified in two ways: First, we may have in the tissues, immediately surrounding the original focus of disease, a new deposit of tubercular matter. This is now usually of the crude yellow variety, and of the softer form. It is more commonly infiltrated in the surrounding tissues, bringing larger and larger districts under its baneful influence, and going through the same destructive processes above described, the whole series of changes being repeated indefinitely, until the local ravages and the constitutional cachexia together bring either limb or life into a hopeless condition. Secondly, even if true tubercular deposits can no longer be found to take place, we constantly have the ulcerative actions slowly going on, forming new excavations, reaching into new regions, keeping up foul and profuse discharges, and, in short, presenting all the well-known and much-dreaded features of tubercular caries, so hopeless in treatment, and so fatal to the joint upon which it is slowly making its destructive invasion. Through all their course these changes are slow and deliberate, characterized by acute inflammation only as an occasional accident, and accompanied by a condition of the general system of which the local behavior is merely the expression, and which in its turn is constantly deteriorating from the irritation reflected upon it from the local disease.

The suppuration which accompanies this process presents often some peculiar features. Sometimes the amount of pus formed is very small, never collecting into abscesses, but, remaining infiltrated among the degenerating tissues, seems to take no further active part in the process. Thus we have not unfrequently extensive tuberculous destruction of the bodies of the vertebræ, and yet no abscess may ever make its appearance. It would seem as if the absorbents were able to dispose of all the dying particles of tissue, as well as all the pus formations, so rapidly that no accumulation could take place, and it is well known that these cases often go through their whole course, and arrive finally at a complete cure, without the formation (certainly without the appearance) of any abscess whatever. But, though extensive tubercular disease may thus occasionally exist without the formation of distinct abscess, yet the general fact is that, some time during the course of the disease, abscesses do form, and it is their course and behavior which give their peculiar character to all the later stages of the affection. Sometimes these abscesses slowly reach a certain size, and then seem to remain stationary, and even to retrograde. Such are occasionally seen on the front of the dorsal vertebræ, where caries is arrested and a cure beginning. Sometimes forming slowly, they grow out from the diseased point, and receiving from the tissues around them very firm walls, they gradually extend in various directions, and, with curious, fantastic shapes, insinuate themselves between and among the muscles and the bones and the organs, until they reach into regions perhaps far distant from their point of origin, "and hang like huge leeches," as Nélaton expresses it, "on the sides of the vertebral column." He gives a drawing of a specimen in which these bags have been dissected out from the surrounding tissues and left hanging from their points of attachment, and their appearance as thus seen certainly justifies his simile. But again, without appropriating to itself any such distinct sac, the matter may gradually push its way, without inflammation, without pain, often without any symptom marking its travels, until it comes to the surface at a point far distant from its source. This is most familiarly illustrated in the psoas abscess, accompanying disease of the bodies of the dorsal vertebræ; and there are on record numerous examples where the pus has wandered to the most wonderful distances, and showed itself in the most extraordinary situations. The ordinary course of psoas abscess is very slow and very painless, and often it happens that the matter announces its presence by a fluctuating tumor below Poupart's ligament, while its course along the sheath of the muscle has not been attended with sufficient inflammatory action to give rise to any pain or tenderness that might serve as a warning of the mischief that was in progress. In these cases there seems to be a mere burrowing of the matter along the areolar interstices, almost without limiting inflammatory deposit, and therefore without the distinct,

firm, and well-developed cyst which in other cases encloses
the pus, and very much restrains its distant wanderings.   A
somewhat similar history may be given of the abscesses which
form in connection with tubercular caries of the joints.   Sometimes they form with much evidence of inflammatory activity,
break early, and discharge good healthy pus, and soon put on
a reparative aspect, which may result in their prompt healing.
Often, however (and this is particularly the case with the hip-
joint), they form slowly and travel quietly to a considerable
distance along the intermuscular spaces, and then bulge out,
forming a painless, cold, fluctuating tumor, whose only vital
activity during months, and even years, may be displayed in a
gradual and often extremely slow increase in size.   This concealed suppuration, escaping our notice during the earlier part
of the disease, sometimes adds suddenly to the gravity, both
of our prognosis and of our diagnosis, and the possibility of its
latent existence should always be recognized and carefully
watched.

After opening, these abscesses usually continue to behave
as their previous demeanor would lead us to expect.   The cavities show but little elasticity or tendency to contract, and it
is only after a long time that the abscess contracts into a
proper fistula, and, even when this has occurred, we are never
quite sure that some deeper parts of the original cavity may
not remain uncontracted, and may yet be burrowing in some new
direction, to surprise us with a new opening in some distant
spot.   The fistulæ thus formed discharge a matter which varies
in its quality according to the condition of the diseased bone
on which they depend.   It is very apt to present the appearances characteristic of caries in its ordinary forms.   It is thin,
sometimes curdy, often acrid, excoriating to the surface over
which it flows, and particularly, if the tubercular caries be in
active progress, it is fetid.   The further clinical history of these
abscesses depends on the course of the disease of which they
are symptomatic.   If this be healing, the abscesses will also
gradually heal, leaving deep-seamed and purple-colored scars,
usually adherent to the bones over which they have been situated, apt to reulcerate from trifling causes, and only after many
months becoming sound and white, and free from tenderness.

The tendency of these scars to contract in every direction was strikingly shown in the case of a young girl, who recovered from what seemed to be a case of strumous disease, probably tuberculous, of the hip-joint, during the course of which, many abscesses formed, leaving many sinuses running from the diseased joint, and opening at various points on the surface. After all the sores healed, and her health became reëstablished, she grew fat. The scars of the healed sinuses had contracted down so firmly as to make deep fossæ at the point where each of them presented at the surface, and the wall of fat round each of them gave them the appearance of a very deep umbilicus, at the bottom of which was the scar. These, scattered, to the number of six or seven, over the buttock and hip, gave it a most extraordinary appearance. If, on the other hand, the disease of bone, on which the abscess primarily depends, be progressive or even stationary, the abscesses remain, sometimes the source of a good deal of irritation and annoyance, and sometimes so quiescent that the patient has no care for them except the daily dressing they require. As a general rule, their further history and course are intimately associated with the primary bone-disease, though occasionally it will happen that, as said above, they will show a disposition to accumulate the pus in some of their irregular cavities, which pus, thus prevented from a ready outflow, sometimes burrows silently and extensively into regions where we do not expect to find it.

The disease thus described is most frequently found to affect the cancellous rather than the hard portion of the bones, such as the vertebral bodies, the carpus, the tarsus, and the articular extremities of the long bones. Mr. Paget makes the important observation that, " when it affects bones that are arranged in a group or series, it is usually found in many of them at once. Thus several vertebræ, or several carpal or tarsal bones, are commonly at the same time tuberculous; yet not often so equally but that one of them appears first and chiefly diseased; while, in those gradually more distant from it on either side, the tuberculous deposits are gradually less abundant. In like manner, the parts of bones that act together in a joint are, usually, at the same time tuberculous."

The treatment of tuberculous disease of the bones is, as far

as its constitutional character is concerned, no different from
the treatment of tuberculous disease elsewhere, and it seems
scarcely worth while to repeat here what has been so well said
by systematic writers on tuberculosis. The local management,
however, presents many features of individual importance, and
demands our most careful study. So much of this local treatment depends more on the effects than on the nature of the
affection, and so much of it is included in the history of the
treatment of caries, in its various forms, that I reserve all that
I have to say on the subject till we have discussed the latter
disease, to which nearly all the cases of tuberculosis are so
naturally related.

CHAPTER X.

CARIES.

CARIES is a condition of bone in which suppuration and
ulceration are combined, but in a proportion so varying that it
has been found somewhat difficult to give a concise definition
of the disease. Different authors, looking at the prominence
of one or the other of these processes, have described it either
as a suppuration or an ulceration, as one or other action seemed
to them most important, and hence, perhaps, there is no disease
in which there is more apparent discrepancy of view and of
statement than in this. Without attempting, therefore, to define caries, I will content myself with describing it as a disease
of the cancellous structure of bone, characterized by a chronic
or subacute inflammation, terminating in suppuration, which
is partly infiltrated, and partly collected into abscesses, the
cavities of which abscesses, after they have discharged their
contents, have a tendency to ulceration, whereby sometimes
extensive destruction of bone-tissue results. With this there
are usually to be marked some abortive attempts at reparation,
such as large, flabby granulations protruding into the ulcerated
cavities, and irregular and ineffectual depositions of new bone
in and about the diseased parts. It is essentially chronic in

its character, showing very little disposition toward healing, and it is generally associated with some constitutional cachexia, or local unfavorable condition, on which its existence seems to depend

Commencing our studies with this general description, we shall further find that caries sometimes presents itself as a disorder arising from some slight exciting cause, and running its course without any evident connection with or dependence upon any other disease or injury ; while sometimes it is manifestly dependent on some disease or injury of which it seems to be the consequence and effect. This seems to me to justify a distinction into primary or idiopathic and secondary or symptomatic caries, a distinction which I think is found in Nature, and will be useful in practice.

Taking, now, a case of primary or idiopathic caries as a type of the disease, we shall find that in a young person, who has probably already presented some of the evidences of a strumous disposition, a slight swelling, with some pain and tenderness, presents itself in, we will say, a wrist- or an ankle-joint. This is at first attributed to some sprain or other injury, and then to rheumatism. The inconvenience caused by the affection at this stage may be very slight, and the patient may continue to use the limb without distress; but soon stiffness after exercise, and more or less pain on motion, begin to show themselves, and the joint gradually grows more disabled as the disease advances. The affection becomes more and more markedly inflammatory, involving the surrounding parts in its increase, but evidently centring its effects on the bones of the tarsus or carpus, rather than on the ankle- or wrist-joint. Gradually, and generally very slowly, the motion of the parts gets to be so painful that the limb becomes entirely disabled, and sometimes constant pain is experienced independent of any movement, pain which is worse at night, and aggravated by damp and changeable weather. Soon the inflammatory signs begin to concentrate themselves at one point, and a fluctuation and a pointing announce the formation of abscess. These abscesses are not usually large, and, when they break, discharge a moderate amount of thin, flaky pus. Little or no disposition is shown toward any healing action in the abscess, the discharge from which continues, generally consisting of a thin, acrid irritating, and bad-smelling pus in moderate quantities. No relief of the symptoms, but rather an exaggeration of suffering, occurs after the abscess has broken, and, if not before, now certainly, constitutional sympathy begins to declare itself. Fever of a hectic character develops itself, emaciation is marked, and the patient becomes a confirmed invalid. The progress of the constitutional symptoms varies very much in different individuals, the general deterioration progressing very rapidly in some, and in others so slowly as scarcely to be marked, even when local destruction has made extensive progress. Of course, the size and importance of the joint, and the extent of the disease will have much to do with the gravity of the general affection. New abscesses now form at various points round the diseased centre, deformity increases, and sometimes, as in the knee, displacement of the joint-surfaces takes place, owing to the loss of tone in the ligaments, which may proceed so far as to simulate a real luxation. These

FIG. 11.—(From Erichsen.)

abscesses, particularly those accompanying caries of the vertebræ, are often of the cold variety, and extend sometimes to a great distance from the original seat of the disease. The psoas abscess is an example of this pathological fact, and we often find the matter travelling into very distant and unexpected regions before it approaches the surface. Fig. 11, copied from Erichsen's work on Surgery, shows the extensive wanderings of an abscess originally developed on the anterior surface of the bodies of the lumbar vertebræ. The soft parts, in these confirmed conditions of caries, are extensively implicated, being thickened and consolidated by the inflammatory exudations, and traversed in various directions by sinuses, which lead, often indirectly, from the diseased bone to the surface. This condition, once established, may last for an indefinite period, and may have one of two terminations: It may either settle down into an inactive and unchanging condition, lasting for months, and even years, without any manifest progress; or it may go on through a process of local disorganization and general depreciation, which brings the patient to the point where both life and limb are imperilled, and where the interference of art is imperatively demanded. If, on the other hand, a favorable change is to take place, we have again one of two results to hope for: First, an improvement in all the conditions of the part, and a gradual restoration to health, with such an impairment of the joints affected as shall not entirely interfere with the usefulness of the limb; or, secondly, in the more advanced cases, we have to hope that, if the destructive actions be arrested, a gradual consolidation shall take place, such as will permit a return of soundness to the diseased tissues, though at the expense of an anchylosis either partial or complete—an anchylosis, the ill-effects of which mechanical ingenuity can often very much neutralize, and which in some instances surgical art can measurably improve.

Symptomatic or secondary caries has, of course, no such distinct history of its own, but is developed in connection with some injury or disease of the surrounding soft parts, upon which it depends. Long-continued destructive inflammations of joints very often produce this carious condition of the bones which compose them. Thus, we often find, in white swelling of the knee, that the disease has involved the head of the tibia, and sometimes the condyles of the femur so far that the bone-disease has assumed the prominence both in prognosis and in the indications of treatment. This is sometimes particularly well marked in the conditions of joints which have been destroyed by inflammation following penetrating wounds. In these cases it is well known that the cartilage rapidly disappears under the influence of the inflammatory actions set up by

7

the wound, and the articular lamella is early exposed. From this the inflammation gains ready access to the cancellous tissue underneath, and we have infiltrated suppuration and caries as the common consequence.

The symptoms indicating secondary caries are usually so mingled with those of the original disease that it is not easy to separate them. The extension of the joint swelling so as manifestly to embrace the joint ends of the bones; the tenderness and pain in the heads of the bones; abscesses breaking at a distance from the joint and over enlargements such as above described, and the detection of carious bone by the probe—these are the most striking and unequivocal symptoms of this form of caries; but it may be stated that the long continuance and destructive behavior of joint-affections generally may lead to the suspicion that caries of the articular extremities of the bones has taken place.

From this sketch of the clinical features of the two varieties of caries we may now proceed to a study of its pathological anatomy. Beyond a doubt, the first morbid conditions which would be found in a bone which was falling into caries would be those of inflammatory excitement. Increased vascularity throughout the cancellous tissue is, however, a pathological fact sometimes difficult to verify. The violence caused by the saw leaves a surface which always seems too red to be healthy, and in young people the circulation in the heads of the long bones is so active that in the most healthy specimens we find what seem to be the evidences of great and irregular congestion. Much care, therefore, must be exercised in deciding upon the existence of diseased states of the circulation in these cases, and conclusions should not be too positive. The increased action is soon accompanied by exudation. This exudation—at first a reddish serum—is infiltrated through the bone, and tends very soon to be converted into pus—a pus, however, which does not assume a very perfect form, and which at first seems disposed to remain disseminated rather than to collect in the form of abscesses. This imperfect suppuration has no doubt often been mistaken for true tubercular infiltration of bone, which is certainly a rare condition, but it should be remembered that the lines between true tubercle and imperfect suppuration are not very cleanly drawn, and that, though it is extremely rare to find in bone a deposit which answers the description and obeys the laws of tubercle, yet we do often find, in this imperfectly-developed suppuration, in scrofulous subjects, something which, histologically and pathologically, very closely assimilates to it. As the disease progresses, it takes on more and more distinctly the characters of disseminated suppuration, and collections of matter, gradually accumulating, begin to show themselves, at various points, forming abscesses. Some increase in activity accompanies the formation of these abscesses, and they seek the surface with some signs of acute inflammation. They point and break, or are opened by the surgeon, and discharge a small quantity of matter, which, according to the activity of the inflammation, has more or less of the character of healthy pus. Frequently it presents the thin curdy or flaky character which is considered characteristic of struma. These abscesses show no tendency to heal, and yet a reparative disposition is evinced by large granulations, soft, flabby, which spring up and usually fill to a great extent the suppurating cavities. Instead of being truly re-

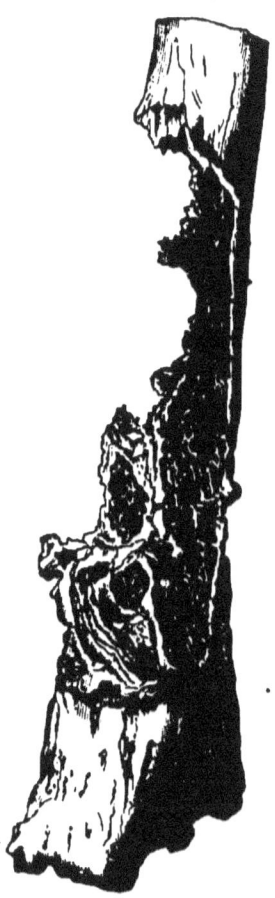

Fig. 12.—(From Billroth.)

parative, however, the presence of these granulations is not incompatible with an ulcerative action by which the cavities are being slowly enlarged, and the cancellous tissue more and more extensively broken down. This destruction of the bone-tissue is a complicated process, and seems to be made up of two kinds of action, one where the bone-substance undergoes a change in which its earthy element is absorbed, and the other a true pro-

cess of ulcerative absorption whereby the altered bone is removed (Fig. 12). The changes which go on in bone during
this process are extremely interesting, and have been fully
investigated by many recent observers. Mr. Barwell, in his
work on "Diseases of the Joints," gives a very full account
of his observations on this subject, which seem to have been
made with great care and thoroughness. He considers the
first change to be an enlargement of the lacunæ and their
canaliculi. The lacunæ gradually lose the elongated shape
and approach to circular or broad oval. The canaliculi are
larger and more numerous, and seem to open into the lacunæ
by broad mouths. Where the canaliculi intersect each other,
there seem to be new spaces formed, which assume the characters of new lacunæ. Thus there is a positive increase in the
number as well as the size both of the lacunæ and canaliculi.
During this change, the bone-substance itself undergoes a
transformation, which commences nearest to the Haversian
canal or cancellus and spreads outward. The bony substance becomes granular; that is to say, it looks as if it
were composed of dark and light dots placed close together.
As this change spreads from the Haversian canal or cancellus
outward, the margins of the cavity lose their distinctness of
outline and become very irregular; in parts the edge is gone,
the cavity is therefore on that side increased; in other parts
the spotted bone-tissue appears to mingle, or to be continuous
with some granular contents of the cavity. It is quite evident
that, in these places, the bone-tissue is softened; one can trace
the gradual completion of the process, from some point which
is only slightly spotted, to the part next the cavity, which is
a mere pultaceous granular mass, in which many of the dots
have the appearance of nuclei.

"Another change in the cell forms part of this softening
process, viz.: that as the dotted or granular condition reaches
a certain stage, so do the canaliculi disappear; therefore, of
course, from that side first, which is turned toward the cavity
(Haversian or cancellar), they vanish by simple shortening, by
recession from the entirely softened bone, until they are reduced to mere little rudimentary projections on the surface of
the cell. At this time the cell itself is visible, as a granulated

dark bag, more or less transparent, and very highly refracting, which projects from the wall of the scarcely-resistant bone, and is of large size ; it bulges out and seems swollen, projects more and more, and at last breaks away from its attachment, and lies among the softened *débris* in the cavity, still retaining its dark color. In breaking away, however, it often leaves behind those of its canaliculi which were turned away from the cavity, and which may often be seen on the edge, but which soon disappear as softening goes on, spreading outward. Frequently several smaller cells come out of the lacuna, instead of one large one. In this way a lamina between two cancellous cavities very soon disappears, from softening on both sides : in this way, also, circlet after circlet of cells around an Haversian canal caves into the cavity, and thus the system melts away and leaves around the vessel only a soft granular and cellular

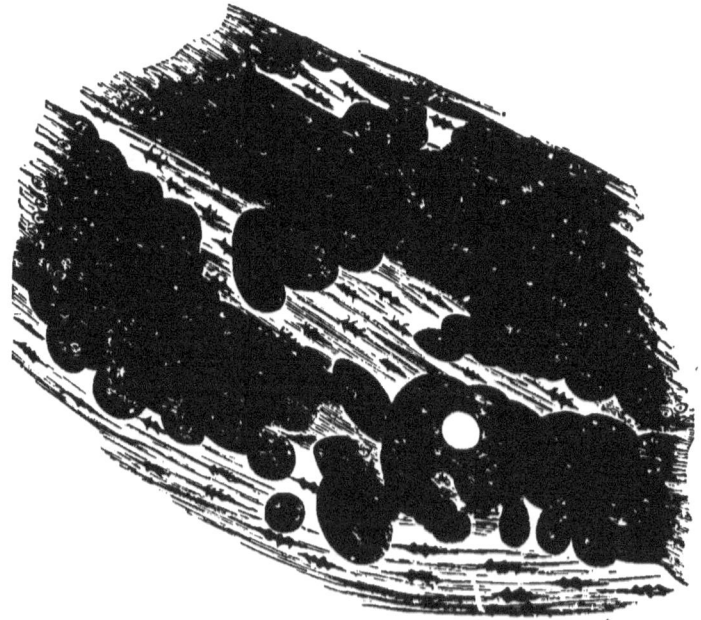

Fig. 13.—(From Billroth.)

mass." Fig. 13 shows the worm-eaten appearance of carious bone under the microscope.

By these processes, the bone-substance becomes gradually

disintegrated, so that, before actual ulceration has taken place, it is so softened that the scalpel or even the probe can be readily pushed through it. In some points the bone-elements seem to disappear entirely; in most, however, some of the original framework remains so as to maintain the shape of the part. Not unfrequently, from this softened condition of the joint-ends, great deformity results from unequal yielding to pressure—a circumstance which, the vertebræ excepted, I have more frequently noticed in the knee than in any other joint, and one which, if a favorable change takes place in the original disease, leaves behind a distortion which is permanent and irremediable. As the process of ulceration goes on, some parts of the bone-substance are apt to die, giving rise to small sequestra, generally upon the ulcerated surfaces, which thus attract less attention, because easily cast out with the discharges. These sequestra which accompany caries, however, are occasionally of considerable size, and assume great importance when, as is sometimes the case, they involve the articular lamella, and fall into the joint-cavity; thus forming a complication which renders the destruction of the joint almost a certainty. Where much of this necrotic action accompanies caries, the disease is spoken of as caries necrotica.

While these destructive actions are going on, reparative dispositions show themselves unequivocally, though ineffectually, in the diseased parts. We have already noticed the luxuriant granulations which fill the cavities of the abscesses; the bone-tissue shows the same tendency. Mr. Barwell thinks he has ascertained that, in the early period of the disease, the bony lamellæ become thickened and indurated, as one stage of the inflammatory process. This must be a pathological fact extremely difficult to verify, but, be it as it may, it is certain that later in the disease new bony deposit is seen around the central points of carious bone, as almost a universal fact. Sometimes this is only noticed to the extent of some slight surface incrustations round the diseased spots, but commonly there are considerable thickening and consolidation through the substance, and often a very great amount of stalagmitic deposit on the whole of the neighboring surfaces, and sometimes extending to the nearest bones, which may themselves be entirely free from other signs of disease (Fig. 14). In the caries, so common, of the bodies of the vertebræ, this deposit is often seen to be very extensive, forming bridges of bone between

Fig. 14.—(From Billroth.)

Fig. 15.—(From New York Hospital Museum.)

neighboring vertebræ, as if to strengthen the column, while the disease is still progressing; and as favorable changes begin to take place in the carious parts, fresh and stronger developments of new bone are observed, which finally fuse together in one solid anchylosis the vertebræ whose bodies have been more or less completely destroyed by the ulceration (Fig. 15).

When a cure is about to take place in ordinary cases of caries, the ulcerative action ceases; the granulation-substance assumes a healthier and firmer character, and gradually organizes itself into tissue. The suppuration ceases, and the inflammatory congestion diminishes. New bone-deposit, formerly confined to the outskirts of the disease, now is deposited so as in part to restore the deficiencies which have occurred. Sometimes this action is a prominent one, the granulations springing from opposite bones coalescing and ossifying; and in this way we have true anchylosis as one of the methods of cure in

bones which have been long and extensively carious (Fig. 16).
A modification of this conservative action is sometimes observed in carious bones which have formed part of an articula-

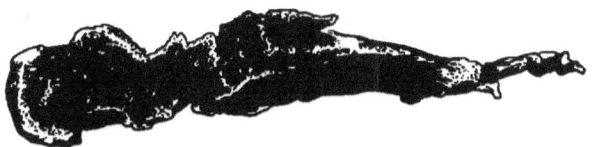

FIG. 16.—(From New York Hospital Museum.)

tion; that the opposed surfaces, from which, perhaps, cartilage
has long been removed, as healthy action is resumed, become hard
and smooth, so as to allow of a certain amount and freedom of
motion, which tolerably preserve the usefulness of the member.   This induration of the surfaces is sometimes so complete
as to assume the appearance of ivory or porcelain, and hence
it is often spoken of as the porcellanous or ivory-like change.
Finally, in cases where the ravages of the disease have not
been so extensive as to disorganize the neighboring joint, we
may have a recovery so perfect as to leave no impairment of
function, and no traces other than the cicatrices both in the
bone and in the surrounding soft parts, which must necessarily
follow the ulcerative actions which have been going on.
     Caries, in all its forms, is emphatically a disease of the
cancellous tissue; indeed, it would be somewhat difficult to
comprehend how the compact substance could take on the
actions of primary caries.   A secondary invasion of the compact substance in the neighborhood of active caries, whereby
it is gradually changed in its structure by a process of osteoporosis, and then invaded by the ulcerative actions proper to
caries, is not at all uncommon ; but any such action developed
as a primary affection must be regarded as exceedingly rare.
The bones most commonly affected by primary caries are the
the bodies of the vertebræ, the tarsal and carpal bones.   The
joint-ends of the tibia and humerus are, among the long bones,
the most frequently attacked, but no bone is entirely exempt.
Fig. 17, from the New York Hospital Cabinet, shows the extent to which carious destruction will sometimes proceed.
The specimen here represented is from " a mulatto seaman,

who suffered from excruciating pain in the left ear, with deafness and swelling, for several months, at the end of which time
he died comatose. Patient had nodes and other symptoms of
syphilis. On examination, the disease was found to have destroyed almost the whole of the petrous portion of the tempo-

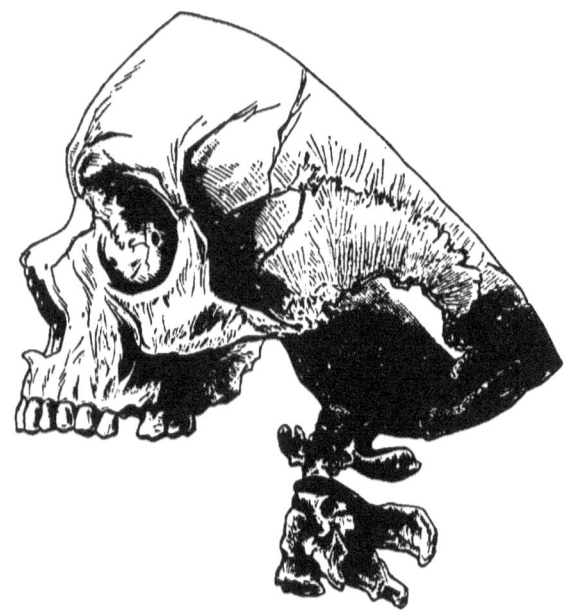

FIG. 17.—(From New York Hospital Museum.)

ral bone. The dura mater had been either absorbed or decomposed, and an immense collection of pus extended along the
whole of the base of the brain. After maceration, the remainder of the temporal and a large part of the left half of the
occipital bone, extending into the foramen magnum, the left
portion of the body of the sphenoid, and a part of the arch of
the atlas, were found to have crumbled to pieces, thus leaving
a hole admitting the closed fist."

The disease is almost entirely confined to persons below
the age of puberty; though a few cases of caries occur in
highly-scrofulous young adults. The caries of the vertebræ,
independent of injury, is almost unknown after puberty, while
the disease in the tarsus and carpus is occasionally seen in the

adult. In general, it may be stated that primary caries is an
affection of childhood and early maturity, while, strange to
say, secondary caries is of comparatively rare occurrence in
childhood, but frequent in the injuries of bone and inflammations of joints which occur in adult life. It would seem as if
the abundant vitality of the child protected him against secondary caries, as a consequence of injury; but that that very
abundant vitality, if tainted with constitutional vice, tends to
crop out in primary caries and its allied diseases in early life :
while, if the individual survive these early perils, the constitutional taint seems often to disappear in a vigorous maturity,
and with it disappear the peculiar tendencies to disease which
characterized and imperilled his childhood. It need hardly be
added that no bone and no age are entirely protected against
secondary caries.

The prognosis of caries is always bad; that is to say,
wherever the disease has fully developed itself, serious consequences are sure to follow. These consequences may be limited to some local destruction of bone-tissue, which may be
repaired to such a degree that the form and usefulness of the
bone may not be lost; or they may be so severe that destruction of joints and peril to life may become imminent—peril
from which amputation or exsection alone can extricate the
sufferer; or, finally, in not a few cases, either in spite of the
resources of surgical art, or because we cannot bring them to
bear, death will be the result. In primary caries, every thing
seems to me to depend on the condition of the constitution.
If this be deeply tainted with scrofula, the case is almost hopeless from the beginning. If, on the contrary, the scrofulous
manifestations are not marked; if the system be in a tolerably
vigorous condition ; if the remedies and the regimen employed
have the effect to invigorate and improve the general health ;
then we have a good ground for hope that the local disorder
will prove tractable, and particularly if our remedies are
brought to bear early in the case. Indeed, I think this an element in prognosis second only to the constitutional state; viz.,
the stages at which the disease falls under surgical care. If
remedies, and particularly regimen, can be wisely employed in
the earlier and forming stages of carious disease, I do not

hesitate to class it among the manageable affections. If they are not afforded till the destructive features of the disease are developed, we can do little to avert its consequences. Youth does not seem to modify the prognosis so favorably as in other diseases, as the strumous taint of young subjects seems to be more distinct and more disastrous than in those somewhat older; but, nevertheless, I think it may be safely said that, other things being apparently equal, young children do better with carious disease than those in the neighborhood of puberty. One other element in prognosis should not be overlooked, viz., social condition. Those who from wealth and intelligence can command, and will use with steadiness and perseverance, all the best resources of art, have a vastly better chance in this disease of securing a favorable result, than can be looked for in those whose circumstances will not permit them, and whose intelligence will not guide them, in the wise use of means whose careful application may have to be continued through long and weary months, and perhaps years, of doubtful and anxious care.

That the treatment of caries is, as a general thing, extremely unsatisfactory, I suppose no surgeon of any experience would be disposed to deny. And yet, most good surgeons do not hesitate to acknowledge the efficacy of certain remedies, and certain modes of management, in particular stages and in particular conditions of the disease. The study of treatment may here be advantageously divided into two stages or periods; one which represents the commencing or inflammatory stage, and the other which has to do with the consequences and effects of the inflammation. It is manifest that these periods cannot be defined with accuracy, and that they must vary in different individuals, and yet in most cases there can be distinguished a period where the inflammation is going through its stages of congestion and effusion of serum, of lymph, and of pus, when the inflammation itself is the main feature of the disease, and requires to be the main object of attack in the treatment. Again, when the results of this inflammation have developed themselves into abscess, ulceration, necrosis, and extended disorganization, it is no longer so much the inflammation, as its results, that we have to do with, and these consequences now have become the main features of the case, while the inflammatory action itself may have ceased to be an object of special consideration. In the first stage, then, we have to deal with an inflammation which is essentially subacute, and will hardly bear active depletion. Nevertheless, a few leeches over the affected part, perhaps repeated at intervals, will certainly control the tenderness and pain, and seem to have a good effect in preparing the way for other remedies. I have sometimes employed this treatment in the earliest stages of hip-disease, depending on osteitis, with a good effect in quelling the nocturnal attacks of pain, with which the first stages of this affection are sometimes accompanied. Two or three leeches behind the trochanter in these cases have seemed to me to do good, particularly if repeated at intervals of ten days or two weeks. At the same time free local depletion is not allowable. The local actions are too sluggish, and too much dependent on constitutional causes, to be favorably modified by considerable losses of blood; and it should always be remembered that the vital powers of the part are to be taxed heavily for many weeks and months, and it would be very poor preparation for such effort, to weaken the part by too much or too frequent local bleeding. Blisters may also be of service in relieving pain, and it is reasonable to believe that a positive advantage may be derived from counter-irritation, particularly if periosteal surfaces are the seat of the inflammation. We are cautioned by most writers against applying blisters too near the seat of an inflammation, a caution which probably in acute synovial affections of the joints is a wise one. In cases of osteitis, which we fear will prove to be caries, however, I have never hesitated to apply my blister immediately over the affected part, and have always felt that its action was useful in proportion to the precision with which it could be brought to bear on the threatened locality, and I have never realized any injury which seemed to me attributable to transmission of the surface irritation to the parts beneath. In the use of blisters in these, and indeed in all cases, I have the conviction that it is their primary effect which is the valuable one, and that they are very poor and very uncomfortable derivatives. If any such permanent drain is desired, it is much better attained by an issue or seton, and I never now keep my blisters sore.

The more powerful derivatives, the issue, the seton, etc., have in former times been very generally regarded with high favor in the treatment of caries; but whether their importance has not been exaggerated, admits, I think, of a question. Mr. Brodie speaks unhesitatingly; he says: "I much doubt whether setons and issues are ever useful, except in some cases in which the disease has its seat in the hip-joint." Mr. Barwell gives them credit for doing some good in the earlier or inflammatory stage, but denies them all value in the second or destructive condition of the bone; while he acknowledges that their application, and particularly in the form of the actual cautery, has a marked effect in arresting the pain of the disease—an arrest which he insists is always very temporary. Both from reasoning and experience, I have been disposed to accord a higher value to these remedies than is given them by these distinguished writers, but every thing, I think, depends on the character of the individual case to which they are applied. In those sluggish, painless, slowly-progressing disorganizations of the bone which are found in connection with what we call white swelling of the joints, where every local action seems the expression and result of a constitutional cachexia, and when the ordinary demeanor of inflammation is entirely masked by that cachexia, I acknowledge that little or no benefit is to be derived from this class of remedies. But in all those, perhaps more numerous cases, where the inflammatory processes show some of their normal activity, and where it is rather the apprehension that the vital actions will be modified by strumous sluggishness, than that they actually indicate the presence of that unfortunate taint, and where great sensitiveness on motion or use shows that more acute action could be easily lighted up, and when particularly the case is complicated with, and, as it were, interrupted by, attacks of acute inflammations from no very obvious causes, then I conceive that we have in permanent derivation a very important means of controlling and often of curing the disease. In these cases the seton or issue (and I greatly prefer the issue), placed a little distance above the affected bone, and so arranged as not to interfere with the apparatus which is to be applied, nor with the motion which by-and-by will have to be made, and kept running with issue-peas

until the actions begin to indicate clearly that the tendencies
are toward cure, and then allowed to diminish in amount
of suppuration, and gradually to dry up, is, as I believe, a
very positive agent in promoting the cure. In this respect,
the actual cautery holds a high position. Its primary action
is so peculiar and energetic that it controls with great certainty the symptoms of the disease for a time, and its resultant issue is the best that can be made. In the most acute
cases, when much pain is an early and prominent symptom, I
consider it peculiarly valuable.

The use of mercury in osteitis tending to caries has also
been the subject of much difference of opinion among good
surgeons. My own experience is unequivocal, and has impressed me strongly with its value in appropriate cases. And
these will embrace the early stage of a large proportion of the
whole; all, indeed, excepting those of very feeble constitution
and irritable fibre. Two ways of using mercury are commonly
employed with entirely different indications, one as a purgative and the other as an alterative. The purgative action is
supposed to clear the intestines of such vitiated secretions as
oppose their proper action upon the alimentary mass, and in
this way indirectly improve the character of the nutritive actions, while the alterative effect, obtained by the continuous
administration of small doses, is supposed to show itself not
only in an improvement of these nutritive actions, but also and
principally in a direct effect upon the course of the inflammatory disease which it is supposed to affect favorably. Both
these modes of using mercury are useful in this disease. In
the forming stage of such cases as occur in patients of tolerable
vigor, and with inflammatory symptoms of some activity, mercurial purgatives occasionally administered have the happiest
effect in improving the general condition of the system, and
often in directly relieving some of the most distressing of the
local symptoms. Mr. Barwell very happily illustrates this effect by the well-known influence of mercurial cathartics in certain cases of strumous ophthalmia, where such surprising relief
is often found to accompany their proper employment.

The alterative method also has its value in cases where the
progress of inflammation seems steadily onward, increasing its

area and accompanied by distressing pain and startings at night, with fever, more or less distinctly developed, at irregular intervals. In these cases the careful use of calomel, combined with opium in small doses, has seemed to me in many instances to have had the happiest effect, both on the sufferings of the patient and on the progress of the disease. In more chronic, less distinctly inflammatory cases, I have much confidence in the controlling power of the bichloride, used in exceedingly small doses, say the twenty-fourth or thirty-second part of a grain twice or thrice a day, combined with tonics, and perseveringly employed for weeks or even months. I need hardly say that in all the methods of employing mercury its injurious effects should be carefully guarded against—hypercatharsis on the one hand, and salivation on the other, being likely to inflict more mischief than the happiest influence of the drug can compensate for.

In regard to the necessity for rest of the diseased part during the earlier stages of caries, all authors are agreed, and their judgment is in accordance with the instinctive feelings of the patient. Much, however, depends upon the thoroughness with which absolute rest is not only insisted on, but by appropriate arrangements secured. In the acute cases, when the disease is in the lower limbs, the bed is the only security against injurious and painful motion; and even in bed it is often necessary to apply some apparatus to the limb to secure it against involuntary and accidental movements. As almost all cases of caries occur in immediate proximity to joints, the treatment of the bone-disease involves, in all its stages, the proper management of the joint, and here the indication is to keep the joint immovable in order to give rest to the inflamed bone in its neighborhood; and much comfort, and I am sure much advantage, is secured to the patient by splints so arranged as to secure him against the painful movements to which accident or muscular spasm makes him continually liable. About these points there can be but little diversity of opinion or practice, but the more important question presents itself: How long shall absolute rest be maintained, and how soon and to what extent may use be allowed? I believe there is no more important practical point in the history of these diseases, and I

am sure there is none requiring more careful and enlightened
judgment.

The importance of this point arises out of the fact that disuse of a limb is certain to be followed by atrophy, and atrophy
means degeneration. Now, where this degeneration of all the
tissues of a limb has been going on through months of disuse,
it seems to me to be certain that the reparative powers of the
part must be depreciated in a proportional degree, and I have
long been of opinion that many cases of chronic surgical disease are prolonged indefinitely, and sometimes brought to an
unfavorable issue, by this loss of reparative vitality, from too
long-continued disuse. It is confessedly a difficult point to
decide when passive motion and when active use should be
allowed in these cases, and I do not feel competent to lay down
distinct rules by which practice should here be guided. The
general principles of action are that, as soon as active inflammation has sufficiently subsided, the use of the limb will promote the vital activities which have been held in abeyance by
disuse; and that, therefore, we should endeavor to seize the
moment when inflammation will not be aggravated, and when,
therefore, nutritive activity will be increased by appropriate
exercise of the limb. In judging of this, we must be guided
principally by two symptoms, viz., the heat and the tenderness
of the part. If heat have steadily and permanently subsided,
until the ordinary condition of the diseased part is one of natural temperature, as appreciated by the hand or by the thermom-
eter, and if at the same time tenderness have so far diminished
that moderate pressure is no longer painful—always provided
that the other morbid signs have also been undergoing a favorable change—we may suppose that the time for considering the
question of passive motion has arrived. And perhaps there is
no better way of ascertaining the fact than by cautiously making the experiment. When, therefore, circumstances seem to
indicate that the proper time has come, careful and very slight
movements of the joint should be made by the surgeon's own
hands, for this is a thing that should never be committed to
the patient or his attendants, repeated daily or at such intervals as may seem best. Undoubtedly all local symptoms will
be increased for the time by such a procedure, which in its

performance will give the patient much pain. This need not
necessarily forbid its repetition, and by no means indicates that
it is not judicious, and it is only by its ulterior effect that the
wisdom of the manipulation can be vindicated. One practical
precept, for the clinical enforcement of which we were all indebted to Dr. Alexander H. Stevens, then Surgeon of the New
York Hospital as well as Professor of Surgery in the College
of Physicians and Surgeons, seems to me a safe and useful
guide in this matter, viz.: if the pain and tenderness produced
by passive motion last more than twenty-four hours, we have
done too much; if, on the other hand, how much soever pain
we may give in the manipulation, its effects have entirely
passed away by the same hour of the next day, we may be
encouraged to proceed. Without claiming this rule to be a
positive guide, I can say that I have found it a very useful
assistant in my own cases, and one which has very rarely seriously misled me. Another and an important point is still to
be decided, as to when the use of the limb may be advantageously permitted. This question will no doubt generally decide itself, as the results of passive motion are developed, but
still cases present themselves where passive motion has been
sometimes employed without manifest injury, and yet, where
no improvement follows, and where the general atrophy of the
limb is so decided as to lead to the belief that nothing but the
stimulus of use will bring about a healthier reparative condition. In these cases careful but courageous use, perseveringly
and judiciously insisted upon, seems the only way of solving
the problem—a solution which is sometimes among the happiest and most satisfactory of surgical therapeutical results.

In securing the complete rest, so necessary in the earlier
stages of caries, position is most carefully to be attended to.
The limb will usually have assumed, if the disease have been
long in existence, a position to which the patient has been in-
stinctively led by finding it most comfortable. This position is
usually one of moderate flexion of the joint implicated, if it be
a large joint, as the knee or elbow, while the wrist or ankle
will be kept nearly midway between flexion and extension,
which will be for the wrist nearly a straight position, and for
the ankle about a right angle of the foot with the leg. It often

8

happens, however, that this position has been allowed to become a vicious one, and one which, if maintained till a cure is
accomplished, would leave the limb in a more or less deformed
and useless condition. These faulty positions may be almost
invariably rectified by gradual and very careful extension which
may be applied by the apparatus used for securing the rest of
the limb. Our instrument-makers make a very excellent light
frame, well padded with soft leather, which, moving on a hinge
at the situation of the joint, can be flexed or extended by a
screw. This screw is moved by a key, which is retained by the
surgeon or the nurse, so that in unruly children no letting up
of the pressure can be accomplished without proper advice.
By the steady and gradual application of a gentle force, the
rectification of position can usually be accomplished without
division of tendons. With some surgeons this division of tendons and contracted muscles is much resorted to, and much advantage is reported as being gained in the treatment, in relieving both the spasmodic and the permanent contraction of the
muscles. My own experience does not entitle me to pronounce
on its value, as I have rarely had occasion to resort to it.

If the case have been under our care from the onset, then
there is a mode of securing rest to the limb, the most complete
and comfortable that can be attained, which prevents any possibility of a faulty position, and which is attended with the
very great advantage of relieving the pressure of the joint
surfaces against one another, produced by the tonic contraction
of the muscles surrounding the joint. I allude to what is now
commonly spoken of as elastic extension. Extension is applied
to the limbs by means of the adhesive bands, and the weight and
pulley, as is now universal in the treatment of fractured thigh,
and this, in the case of the knee or hip, is. made while the
patient is lying on the back, and at other joints in varying
positions according to the part involved. Somewhere between
the pulley and the limb, a band of India-rubber is introduced
through which all the traction passes, and this by its elasticity
so equalizes the extension that it is always in uniform action,
and can be borne without the least inconvenience. The
advantages of this mode of managing the earliest stages of
joint affections are incontestable ; and in caries it cannot be

less important, both to the comfort and to the cure of the patient.

When caries, as is too often the case, proves unmanageable by all the remedies employed to check its progress, we have often presented to us a surgical problem which deals with the results of the carious disorganization, and in which the main question is, What shall be done with the hopelessly-diseased bone, and in what way can it best be prevented from inflicting injury on the surrounding healthy tissues, and on the patient's general health? This problem embraces the destruction or the removal of the diseased bone, and must, of course, in its full decision, depend upon all the particular circumstances of situation, degree, age, general condition, etc., which give individual character to the case. Some general considerations, applicable to all cases, however, will help us in the solution of each particular problem. The destruction of the diseased tissue may be effected either by the stronger escharotics, or by the actual cautery. The difficulty of limiting the action of a caustic, and the uncertainty of its effects, have been, I suppose, the reasons why they have not usually been employed for this purpose; while the completeness of the destruction, and the certainty with which we can calculate upon its extent, are good reasons for preferring the hot iron. The most favorable cases for the use of this method of treatment must be those where the disease is either not extensive, or is mainly situated over a surface which can be easily reached by the application. To such cases the iron is applied at a full red heat, holding it on the diseased part until its full effect is produced. Of course, a careful preparatory exposure of the bone will be made, and the soft parts drawn aside, and carefully protected against the heat. The destruction of tissue thus produced is usually not so deep as would at first sight appear, but it is perfect, and the whole burnt substance now occupies the wound only as a sequestrum, which soon separates and is cast off, leaving either a healthy granulating surface, or one which indicates that the diseased tissue is not all removed. If this be found to be the case, then the application must be repeated at proper intervals as often as may be necessary. The older writers speak very highly of this method of attacking caries, but it seems to have lost credit with the more modern surgeons; perhaps, because the various operations for removal of diseased bone have attracted so much of their attention, and are, after all, the only operations to be relied on when the carious disease has involved the greater part or the whole of a bone, or of several contiguous bones.

The operation of exsection or excision of bone is comparatively a modern one—Mr. White, of Manchester, being commonly regarded as the first who, by a defined and purposed procedure, undertook the removal of carious bone, he having removed the head of the humerus for caries in the year 1768. Since his time, surgeons have been gradually growing to the appreciation of the important step thus indicated, and no operation has, during the last fifty years, commanded more universal interest than that of excision of carious bone, particularly in connection with the diseases and injuries of joints. The principle of the operation is founded on the fact that the caries is localized in its action, and that, when the diseased parts are removed, healthy reparative processes may be expected to begin, and the success of the operations founded upon this principle may be properly said to have inaugurated a new era in the treatment of diseased conditions of the joints. Exsection has now been practised on almost every bone in the body; and while the value of the procedure varies much according to the locality affected, yet no doubt remains of the great value and importance of the operation itself.

The operation consists in exposing the diseased bone by appropriate incisions, and then, with the saw, or the bone-forceps, removing all that portion which is implicated in the disorder. As this operation is so commonly performed for caries as a part of joint disorganization, it is usually performed in such manner as to expose and remove both of the opposed joint surfaces, and it is this operation which is meant when we speak of exsection or excision of the joints. In operating thus, great care is to be taken not to interfere any further than is necessary with tendinous insertions, in order not to impair the efficiency of the muscular actions of the joint, and also not to remove any more of the bone than disease makes necessary. It is true that Nature has wonderful resources in repairing the mutilation of this procedure, and surgeons have not hesitated to remove several inches of each bone where it has been clearly necessary, but the rule of saving all that may be saved is none the less imperative, and the success of the procedure will, in a good degree, depend upen the amount of bone which is taken away. Where the operation is successful, one of two results is realized: first, the wounded surfaces take on a healthy action, and the bone granulates, and a uniting medium thus forms which ultimately becomes firm enough to produce an anchylosis between the opposing bones; while, at the same time, all diseased action ceases, and the soft parts cicatrize soundly. This is the result most commonly aimed at, and, probably, always most desirable in the lower extremity. In the upper extremity, however, a certain amount of motion is hoped for, and quite frequently a useful degree of it is attained. The uniting medium does not completely solidify, but remains sufficiently yielding to imitate some of the movements of the original joint; while, if the tendinous insertions have not been too extensively disturbed, the muscles resume their power, and an amount of voluntary motion is regained which is often extremely valuable in the shoulder, the elbow, and the wrist joint. In realizing these two different results, of course, much will depend upon the management of the limb after operation. If firm anchylosis is desired, absolute rest will be most carefully maintained during all the cure; while, if motion is sought for, properly conducted passive motion will be the principal means of arriving at the result desired.

The success of these operations has been extremely satisfactory, and, when we consider that the alternative presented is amputation, we can hardly accord too high a position to this great conservative triumph of modern surgery. Two modifications of the operation of excision for caries have lately been presented to the surgical world, by men of eminent repute, both claiming superiority over the rival proposal, as well as over the old operation. These are brought forward respectively by M. Ollier, of Lyons, and by M. Sedillot, of Paris; both are fortified by a considerable number of cases, and both are reasoned out with great scientific ability. M. Ollier claims that the true method of excision is what he calls the sub-periosteal section; that is, one in which the diseased bone is removed, leaving behind its periosteal covering. According to his views, which indeed are those generally received, the periosteum is the great bone-producer, very greatly superior in this power to any of the surrounding tissues, or even to the bone itself. If, therefore, in any exsections of bone, we leave the periosteum behind, we have the element of reproduction of the bone to help us in the reparative processes which we are anticipating; so that, if every thing proceeds favorably, we accomplish, by sub-periosteal resection, not merely the removal of the disease, but the regeneration of the bone removed, so perfectly and to such an extent as makes the result more perfect and more complete than can in any other way be accomplished. M. Sedillot contends that the periosteum cannot be relied upon to do its full regenerative duty in these cases, and that the only way to secure a complete reformation of the bone to be removed, is so to proceed as to leave a thin shell of bone attached to the periosteum, from which shell he says there will be the most perfect possible regeneration of the bone removed. His operation consists, therefore, in scooping out all the diseased bone-tissue, leaving behind a thin layer of bone, attached, of course, to the periosteum, and forming thus a thin shell which maintains the shape and size of the bone removed, thus preventing, according to M. Sedillot, the deformity which necessarily follows the other operation, and which, M. Sedillot believes, will not in any material degree be prevented by M. Ollier's sub-periosteal method. Much has been said, and many cases have been published in the journals, by some of the most eminent surgeons of Europe, on this subject, and the result of all the discussion seems to be that neither operation is entitled to exclusive preference; but that, while the old operation is the only one which can be performed in perhaps the greater number of cases, yet there are a certain number in which the new operations will realize many of the advantages claimed by their enthusiastic originators. Active minds are industriously employed on this interesting subject in every country, and the appreciation of the various operative methods bids fair to be soon practically settled. Mr. Hancock, in London, has done more than any other man to illustrate and enforce M. Sedillot's views, and very numerous experimenters in Europe and in this country have proved the value of M. Ollier's important suggestions. While, therefore, some features of the operation of exsection of bones may still be considered as not yet fully and finally decided upon, the general value of the operation and its estimation as a surgical resource are gaining daily, and it now ranks as one of the most valuable contributions of modern science to conservative surgery.

CHAPTER XI.

NECROSIS.

THE death of bone, so common in its occurrence, either as a primary and essential, or as a secondary and accidental circumstance, is one of the most extensive and interesting subjects which bone pathology presents. For the frequency of its occurrence two circumstances, connected with its vascular supply, present themselves in explanation: First, the periosteum contains a larger part of the vessels whose small branches pass inward to supply the superficial or sub-periosteal layers of bone-tissue, and upon the integrity of this membrane, and upon its close adhesion to the bone, depends the continuance of this supply of blood. Now, it so happens that the periosteum is liable to injury or inflammation, which may either destroy it *in situ*, or, what is more common, may cause an effusion between it and the bone, which, separating it from the bone, destroys the continuity of circulation between the vessels of the periosteum and of the adjacent bone which these vessels should nourish. In this way, there is no doubt, many superficial necroses take place, and a considerable proportion of the thin exfoliations we so often see after slight injuries are thus produced.

But, in the second place, there is, in the expansibility of bone-tissue, another and more widely operating cause of necrosis. All the circulation in the substance of bone is through vessels traversing bony canals which they entirely fill, and which canals, therefore, compress and support the vessels on all sides. Under the first stimulus of inflammation in the soft parts, it is well known that the vessels are crowded with blood so as to be largely dilated in their calibre. This dilatation would seem to be a necessary mechanical result of the increased quantity of blood forced into tubes whose walls are capable of yielding, and it would also seem to be a necessary vital action whereby the yielding vessel grows more capable of transmitting the increased current of blood, which, without this relief, would be dammed up and stagnate in the capillaries of the part, thus arresting entirely the circulation, which, if life is to continue, should only be retarded, not stopped entirely. Of this yielding to dilating force, of course, the vessels of the bone are by their position entirely incapable. In bone inflammation, therefore, the blood, attracted by the new stimulus, crowds the unyielding capillaries so urgently that transmission of the current becomes slower and slower, the thinner parts of the blood move on, while the corpuscles become more and more jammed and packed in the channel now relatively too small to receive their increased number, until presently the current is arrested altogether, and the circulation ceases.

Thus it would appear that one essential element of acute inflammation of bone is such a mechanical condition of the affected part as directly tends to the destruction of life—a destruction, the certainty of which depends probably more on the acuteness of the attack than on its severity or extent. That this is so we are instructed by observing that the deliberate actions of chronic inflammation, though extensive and severe, are very little liable to produce necrosis, whatever other disastrous accidents they may entail, apparently because the vascular movements are of such a character as to give time for the vessels and their bony canals to accommodate themselves to changes which, in the acute inflammations, hurry on the bone to death. These considerations may also serve to explain the fact that the compact tissue of bone is more liable to necrosis than the cancellous. In the cancellous tissue a large part of the circulation is distributed through the medulla, the terminal capillaries alone entering the bony channels, and hence any increased hydraulic pressure is received, in great part, upon vessels which have the space in which to expand. In the compact tissue, on the other hand, the whole vascular system of the part is contained within the rigid Haversian canals, and the pressure is resisted equally by the capillaries and the vessels from which they spring. Hence, doubtless, the comparative frequency in the one and the rarity in the other tissue of an accident, which has, in its nature, no elements of difference besides the mechanical one upon which we are now insisting.

From the study of these intrinsic predisposing conditions, we may deduce the most important exciting cause of necrosis, namely, inflammation; or, in other words, we may appreciate the reason of the acknowledged fact that inflammation is the great producing cause of necrosis. All those accidents and exposures which are likely to induce, and all those conditions of the system which favor, the occurrence of inflammation in any of the component tissues of the bone, may be regarded as the exciting and predisposing causes of necrosis.

Of the predisposing causes, we have those that are local and those that are general or constitutional. Thus the superficial situation of the tibia, and its consequent exposure to the vicissitudes of temperature, are thought by some to be the explanation of its greater liability to necrosis; an explanation which will certainly stand, in those cases where the disease follows injury, to which the bone is more liable from its exposed situation. Again, the condition of the circulation in the lower extremities, as influenced by standing, exercise, etc., is, doubtless, often a predisposing cause of bone inflammation, and, therefore, sometimes of necrosis. But the most unequivocal of the predisposing causes are those which may be termed constitutional. In the scrofulous and in the syphilitic there is manifested a tendency to bone-disease; in fact, a predisposition to necrosis, which only requires a slight exciting cause for its development. Besides these, there are certain slender, delicate, feeble persons in whom no syphillis and no scrofula can be detected, and yet who show a proclivity to necrosis, which is evidenced by the repeated attacks, perhaps at far-distant periods, of the disease in various situations, and provoked by exciting causes so insignificant as often to leave us in doubt whether the affection might not be regarded as spontaneous. To these ought to be added those enfeebled conditions of the system which are understood to favor mortification, such as the condition induced by long exposure, privation, and hardship, and particularly the condition following severe and exhaustive diseases, as scurvy, typhoid fevers, and such other disorders as may be presumed to diminish the power of the circulation to maintain itself against the sudden assault of inflammation.

With these predispositions, both local and general, the exciting causes of necrosis may be enumerated as—

1. *Exposure to Wet and Cold.*—I believe this to be a very common cause of the disease. It would seem as if exposure to mere cold, while it has great influence in producing superficial mortification, did not especially compromise the bones; while the combination of wet and cold is one of the most common causes of inflammation in the osseous structures. The *modus operandi*, on the bones, of this particular exposure is not more easily explained than the action of the same cause in producing catarrh, bronchitis, or rheumatism. All that can be said is, that it seems to be an analogous process in the case of the bones, intensified by the fact that the bones most liable to suffer are those most liable to direct exposure to the injurious cause, as the bones of the feet and the shaft of the tibia. It would seem, also, that the exposure must be prolonged in order to produce its effect, for we find that most patients report their attack as having come on after long tramping through snow and slush, or after bathing too long in rather cold water, or some such exposure as has been prolonged sufficiently to act as an exhauster of the general power of resistance, as well as a depressor of the local circulation of the part about to be affected.

2. *Injury.*—In a variety of ways injury may serve as the starting-point of a bone-inflammation, which shall terminate in necrosis. Contusions, lacerations, punctures, detachments of periosteum; fractures, strains, bendings, and crushing of the bone itself; lacerations and exposures of the medulla are all causes of inflammation of bone, which may take any one of the many courses which in such cases is determined by the constitution and the surroundings of the patient. As a direct and immediate cause of death, injury does not often act. It is, rather, by setting up of inflammatory actions, which, by un-

favorable influences, shall be so modified as ultimately to produce a fatal effect that injury acts; and thus we may consider
violence as rather the indirect and secondary, than as the
direct and immediate, cause of necrosis. The inflammations
which follow injury to bones are generally localized about the
injured parts, and are moderate in their accession, so that it is
not till suppuration has taken place, or exposure to the air has
occurred, that we find, as an ultimate result, that a limited
necrosis has taken place. This is well illustrated in certain
compound and comminuted fractures, where the injury to the
bone is about as severe as it can be, and yet where, if the fracture behave otherwise well, we expect no necrosis to occur;
and it is only after long suppuration, and perhaps denudation
of periosteum, and exposure of the bone to the air, and to the
putrefying discharges of the wound, that we find a small portion of the end of the broken fragments has fallen into necrosis. But besides these cases which may represent the behavior
of bone after injury in a healthy condition of the system, and
under favorable circumstances, there are a certain number in
which—a strong predisposition to bone disease existing—a moderate injury will be the starting-point of severe and destructive
inflammation, rapidly terminating in necrosis. Here the exciting plays so much less important a part than the predisposing cause, that it is often difficult, as before remarked, to
be sure that the injury has had any thing to do with the production of the mischief.

3. *Mercury.*—The stomatitis resulting from the use of mercury sometimes involves the bones of the jaws in its progress.
The action here is more frequently that of caries than of necrosis, mainly because the alveolar, rather than the compact
tissue of the bone, is attacked. We do, however, occasionally
find that the inflammation creeps along the periosteum, separating that membrane from the bone, and producing actual
necrosis, generally of a limited portion of the jaw-bones. I
do not know that I have seen a general or even an extensive
necrosis from this cause, the most considerable having been
observed in cases where cancrum oris has existed as the primary disease, whose dependence on the influence of mercury
has been more than questionable.

4. *Phosphorus.*—Dr. Heyfelder, of Nüremberg, first called attention to the fact that the operatives in match-factories were liable to a peculiar form of necrosis of the lower jaw. His observations were published in 1845, and since that time the disorder has attracted the attention of surgeons in all parts of the world, and much recorded experience has accumulated, giving us a tolerably complete idea of its pathological as well as its clinical history. It is undoubtedly produced by the prevalence, in the air which the sufferers have long been breathing, of the fumes of phosphorus. These fumes are mostly in the shape of phosphorous acid, which is generated when phosphorus is burnt in atmospheric air. How this vapor acts—whether by being absorbed into the system, and acting through the general circulation, or whether its action is local, producing its effects by coming in direct contact with the parts liable to be poisoned by it—is a question upon which much difference of opinion has existed. It is possible that both modes of action may be combined; but one fact, which points very strongly to the local character of the cause, is found in the statement that those operatives who have sound teeth are rarely affected with the disease, while those who have unsound, carious teeth, or spongy gums, are extremely liable to be attacked, and, in particular, it is stated than any who are exposed to the phosphorus-fumes soon after the extraction of a tooth are almost certain to suffer. This would seem to render it probable that phosphorus, or rather, perhaps, phosphorous acid, has a direct poisonous effect upon the jaw-bones, and this poisonous effect must be much increased by the solubility of the gas in the fluids of the mouth, by which the poison is not only concentrated, but brought into easy contact with all parts of the buccal mucous membrane, acting therefore with peculiar intensity wherever the protection of the epithelium is removed by ulceration, or where any breach of surface lets the poisoned fluid into contact with the bone-tissues to which it holds so mortal an enmity. Why the Schneiderian membrane, which, in the same manner, and at least to an equal degree, is exposed to the poisonous fumes, is not liable to equal injury, it is not easy to explain.

5. *Syphilis.*—Many of the secondary and tertiary symp-

toms of syphilis manifest themselves on the periosteum, producing often a separation between that membrane and the bone, which is followed by a necrosis. There are also cases where, in the progress of the dreadful ulceration which syphilis sometimes produces in the facial, buccal, palatine, and nasal regions, large portions of the subjacent bone die, and are separated *en masse*. Still further, there is a form of syphilitic disease of the skull-bones where the action terminates in the death of a portion of the bone, and this death creeps slowly and gradually over such extensive districts of the skull, that in some instances almost the whole vault of the cranium is finally involved in the destruction. In these, and in some other less marked cases, the poison of syphilis seems to be directly responsible for the destruction of the bone, and this is made more evident by the fact, hereafter to be more particularly studied, that most of these cases of syphilitic necrosis have, in their history, features which are quite different from the ordinary manifestations of the disease, and which are entirely characteristic of the action of a specific poison.

6. *Fevers.*—It is popularly believed that fevers do frequently produce necrosis, and hence one popular name of the disease, viz., fever-sore. It certainly is observed that, after an attack of fever, necrosis declares itself; and it must be acknowledged that the depressed condition of the system, which exists during and after long-continued and severe fever, is a predisposing cause strongly favoring the occurrence of the disease. I am not, however, prepared to say that it is a common result of the idiopathic or of the specific fevers. In my own experience, I have been a little surprised that I have been so rarely able to trace necrosis as a sequel to any regular form of fever, as typhus or scarlatina, the history of which has been distinct and unequivocal. Rather, I am inclined to believe that, in most cases, where this disease has been said to have followed a fever, it has been one affection from the beginning, and that affection has been an osteitis terminating in necrosis; the earlier stages of the disease being characterized by fever, more or less continued in type, during which the local symptoms were either unusually slight, or were overlooked, and in which, the fever abating when the abscess had discharged itself, the local disease

came to be considered as the consequence of the fever of which it was in reality the cause. That this is the case in a large majority of so-called fever-sores, I feel very confident; that it is uniformly so, I will not positively assert.

The seat of necrosis varies very greatly. Mostly confined to the compact tissue of the long bones, it may affect the cancellous in any part of the skeleton. Of the cases in which the cancellous tissue is the seat of proper necrosis, I think the greater part will be found to be instances in which the affection has been associated with caries, and in which, therefore, the necrosis is a secondary rather than a primary feature of the disease. This is the fact with a great many cases of those ulcerations of the bone, with necrosis, which accompany the advanced stage of joint destruction, and it is sometimes observed that a small sequestrum of the cancellous tissue of the articular end of a bone is a fatal element of a joint disease, which might otherwise prove manageable. There are, however, a certain number of cases in which the death of the spongy tissue is the primary element of the disorder, and in which necrosis, commencing thus, presents all the pathological history of the disease as it occurs in the compact tissue. Of this, I have seen two examples in the os calcis, which I have had an opportunity to verify by operation. We have, in the New York Hospital Museum, one specimen illustrating this fact, in the upper end of the humerus, and one, a syphilitic specimen, in the lower end of the tibia. Again, it is often observed that the cancellous is involved with the compact tissue in extensive examples of the disease, as in the necrosis of the shaft of the long bones, involving some of the expanded extremity; and, in the spreading form of necrosis of the bones of the cranium, the diploe does not seem to offer any material check to the progress of the necrosis, becoming itself affected almost as rapidly and nearly to the same extent as the external table, which seems to be the primary seat of the malady. These, however, it must be noted, are only offered as exceptional facts, and in contrast to them it should be stated that, in many cases the compact tissue dies, while the cancellous in immediate contact with it lives; and thus we have produced those tubular sequestra in which the outer compact shell of the bone only has died, leaving a living centre or axis of cancellous tissue which has been able to maintain its vitality. This I have several times observed in those cases where necrosis declares itself after compound fracture, and I have been much disconcerted to find that, after I had removed the most superficial and accessible layer of dead bone, a similar layer surrounded the whole shaft, the extraction of which necessitated a long and difficult operation. In this way are produced the varieties we notice in the *extent* of necrosis. These varieties may be classified as—1. The superficial. 2. The internal or central. 3. The complete, where the whole thickness but not the whole length of the shaft is involved. 4. The total, where the entire bone has perished.

It is interesting to observe, in this connection, that certain bones are more liable than others to the disease. Thus we have, according to Mr. Stanley, the tibia suffering much more frequently than any other bone. The femur is next in order, but at a great distance from the tibia. Then we have the humerus, flat cranial bones, lower jaw, last phalanx of finger, clavicle, ulna, radius, fibula, scapula, upper jaw, pelvic bones, sternum, ribs. This peculiarity of the tibia, disposing it in so eminent a degree to necrosis, seems to be most marked in its upper expanded portion, where not only do we see necrosis occurring very frequently, but many forms of inflammation and abscess, and a large proportion of the malignant as well as other tumors of the bone, find their favorite seat in this portion of the tibia. M. Ollier has thrown some light upon this subject, by the general law which he has discovered, that the extremities, both of the femur and tibia, which form the knee-joint, have in themselves a much greater amount of power of growth and development than the other extremities of these bones, which form respectively the hip- and ankle-joints. This interesting observation has many practical relations, and, among others, it seems to explain how it is that the head of the tibia plays so important a part in the diseases of the skeleton ; being more highly vitalized, it is more active in all the processes of health, and therefore probably of disease, than other portions of the skeleton, lower in the scale of vital activity.

In proceeding now with the further study of necrosis, it
will be convenient to take a typical example of the disease, say
a case occurring in a young healthy person, in the shaft of the
tibia, and of moderate extent, and make it the basis of systematic study.   In pursuance of this study we shall have to notice
—1. The pathological conditions and changes which the case
presents.   2. The symptoms accompanying and characterizing
these conditions.   3. The treatment appropriate to each stage.

1. *The Pathological Conditions.*—The first condition which
can be recognized in a case of commencing necrosis is, without
doubt, one of inflammation, involving, we will suppose, the
greater part of the shaft.   I do not know of any observations
which have thrown any light on this point in the human subject, but, reasoning from what is observed in experiments upon
animals, it seems probable that the whole bone partakes more
or less of the inflammatory congestion, of which the central
part of the shaft is to be the principal seat.   This inflammatory
congestion probably is manifested most distinctly by the vessels of the periosteum, and by those of the medulla.   Whether
any increased vascularity can be appreciated by the eye in the
compact substance of the bone, I cannot affirm.   In the portion
which dies under this inflammatory effort, no further obvious
change occurs.   The circulation ceases, and the section of bone
is no longer associated in any of the vital changes which go on
about it.   The dead portion of bone, or sequestrum, as it is
called, very shortly becomes of a uniform, pale, waxy, yellow-
ish-white color, differing very slightly and yet distinctly from
the color of living bone; a difference which, I think, is somewhat exaggerated by maceration and drying of the bone, under
which condition we most commonly see it.   During all the
further changes of the disease, the sequestrum undergoes no
change of appearance, except that it may be accidentally
tinged by exposure to the various fluids and gases developed
about it.   The most common of these accidental colorations of
the sequestrum is the brownish black which it sometimes presents, where it has long been exposed to the air, in such a way
that the surface shall be alternately wet and dry.   This, mainly
a surface color, stops abruptly at the point where the sequestrum is constantly covered over by soft parts, and is so abiding

that prolonged maceration will scarcely remove it. What the chemical nature of the change is I do not know; but one would naturally suspect the hydrosulphuric acid, generated in the decomposition of the pus, to be the active agent in its production.

The actions which accompany this death of a portion of a bone in the surrounding living textures are more interesting, more distinct, and more important. The outline separating the dead from the living bone is extremely irregular, made so by the fact, probably, that each vascular twig does not fail to maintain itself at precisely the same level, some sustaining life a little further or a little longer than their neighbors. The unevenness of outline thus produced is rather more marked in the cancellous than in the compact substance of the bone, and gives to the extremities of the sequestrum, where they encroach upon the cancellous tissue, a particularly irregular, fissured, and branched outline. When the separation takes place through hard bone, it is sometimes quite smooth and even in its outline. The part of the bone covered by periosteum presents usually a more even and natural surface. Here the line of separation is accurately between the periosteum and the bone, so that the sequestrum is just as smooth and regular as the natural bone would have been if macerated; while, at the points where dead and living bone have separated, it is, as stated before, extremely irregular and uneven.

The action of separation is accomplished by a process of molecular death, and the removal of the particles of living tissue next in contact with those which have died. These particles are removed by the vessels of the living part, by a process of absorption, which, in healthy and young subjects, goes on with considerable rapidity. Much doubt formerly existed on this subject, whether the line of separation was at the expense of the living or dead bone; a doubt that had this practical importance, that it left unsettled the question as to whether the sequestrum is capable of removal by absorption. Mr. Hunter showed clearly that the action took place on living particles only, the dead taking no part in the process; and this view, so entirely in consonance with our ideas of pathological action in other tissues, is now universally accepted. Whether all the bone-matter is removed by absorption, or

9

whether some portion of it is cast off in the discharges, is another question of some interest, perhaps more pathological than practical. Mr. Bransby Cooper's observations go to show very distinctly that pus, in the neighborhood of diseased and exfoliating bone, contains much more than its usual proportion of phosphate and carbonate of lime, leading to the inference that a portion at least of the bone-matter was thrown off by the pus. These observations of Mr. Cooper's, which have been much quoted, are not published in full detail, the paper in the *Medical Gazette,* for the year 1845, being merely a sketch of a lecture given by Mr. Cooper on these subjects, and are imperfect, as far as relates to our point, in not specifying the nature of the diseases of the bones on which the observations were made. While, therefore, they prove that pus from diseased bone contains an unusual proportion of the elements of bone, there is nothing in these observations to show that exfoliation is accomplished by any other than a process of absorption. Indeed, the microscope makes it pretty clear that it is a pure act of absorption; for all observers agree that the first step in the process is a removal of the earthy matters from the bone-tissue, which is about to be the seat of the change; and subsequently to that removal, while the bone is in the condition of fibrous tissue, the real ulcerative or absorptive process goes on. This being the case, it would hardly seem likely that, as the ulceration is progressing in a tissue deprived of its earthy constituents, any of those earthy constituents could be found in the discharges. The act of separation begins at the surface of the bone, and proceeds in depth, till the whole interval between the dead and living tissue presents a space, generally of one or two lines in width, so that, when the process is complete and the dead bone separated, it is found to be lying loose in a space or cavity which is considerably too large for it, and in which, therefore, it can be moved about sufficiently to indicate to the surgeon, by this mobility, that it is entirely separated from its connections.

The surface of the living bone, looking toward and forming the wall of the cavity in which the sequestrum lies, corresponds pretty accurately with the general outline of the dead portion; and, probably, if the bone were macerated immediately after separation was accomplished, this correspondence would be still more perfect; but, as has been remarked above, the cavity is larger than the sequestrum by all the space in which absorption of tissue has proceeded. This space is not always maintained without change; for it is noticed in old cases that the cavity is sometimes much larger than the sequestrum, though no bone has been discharged; and our present views forbid us to believe that the dead bone can undergo any alteration in size. It would, therefore, seem pretty certain that this enlargement is caused by absorption, provoked, probably, by the movements of the sequestrum, or by its pressure at particular points, a view which is strengthened by the fact that the enlargement is not constant nor uniform, in some cases being only at limited portions of the cavity, while the rest embraces the sequestrum so tightly as to prevent its moving freely, even in the macerated specimen.

This space between the living and the dead bone is not a vacuum during life, though it appears so when the bone is dried. It is occupied, and usually pretty accurately filled, by soft, luxuriant granulations, which, springing up from the living bone on all sides, form a bed in which the sequestrum lies, and by which its injurious contact with the living bone-tissue is prevented. This layer of granulation-substance, in a healthy subject, is of a firm, ruddy appearance, and represents Nature's endeavors to repair the mischief which has occurred; which endeavors are of course ineffectual, on account of the presence of what has now become a foreign body. Nevertheless, though the main object for which they are thrown out fails to be accomplished, yet the secondary purpose of protection and support to the loose sequestrum is scarcely of less importance for the comfort of the individual; and it is worthy of remark, and I think of special admiration, that this admirable cushion fulfils its duties so well, that the patient may carry a large and rough sequestrum for many years, without ever being sensible of its motions, and without the least sensation of suffering from its contact with its living tissues. This arises from the fact that Nature not only provides this soft layer of protecting granulations, but makes them so firm and so callous in their endowments that they are entirely insensible to any painful contact, while they are sufficiently consistent to secure the immobility of the otherwise loose sequestrum.

The granulations thus lining the cavity secrete a moderate quantity of pus, which finds its way out of some of the openings in the surrounding bone. In a healthy person this discharge is exceedingly small in quantity, amounting, even from a large cavity, to only a few drops in twenty-four hours. This, however, is liable to the greatest variations, both in quantity and quality. In some cases the discharge is so constant and profuse as to be in itself an element of danger to the patient's life; and there are others where, temporarily at least, it ceases altogether. It may always be accepted as a favorable sign, when this discharge is small in quantity and healthy in appearance; and it should always excite apprehension of progressive local disease when it is ill-conditioned and profuse. Mingled with this pus, blood is sometimes seen, doubtless from the friction of the rough sequestrum against the granulations; and, when it is from this source, it is usually in very moderate quantities. Large quantities of blood, issuing rapidly from a case of necrosis, indicate a different source and a much more serious danger, as will be hereafter particularly explained.

While this process of separation has been going on, other changes have been taking place in the surrounding soft parts, which we must now study. Nature, as if anticipating the result which must follow the separation between the dead and living bone, summons up her reparative activities to supply that support to the limb which is about to be destroyed by her own hands; and, long before the actual solution of continuity has taken place in the shaft of the bone, we find that the compensatory strengthening process has made sufficient progress to prevent any evil consequences from the break. This process consists essentially in an ossification, springing from the parts surrounding the dead bone, which, reaching from the living bone above to the living bone below, bridges over the breach, and forms a sort of ferule of new bone, which, by its abundance and perfect organization, more than supplies the wanting support. Out of this important and very interesting process grow many of the most striking features of the disease we are studying, both clinical and pathological; and it may even be affirmed that most of the indications for and the success of any treatment that may be instituted for the cure of the mischief, must be founded on a careful consideration of this action of Nature, and that upon its perfection or imperfection will necessarily depend the future usefulness of the member.

It is now generally conceded that the new bone is derived from four different sources, viz., the periosteum, the medulla, the old bone in immediate proximity, and the nearest surrounding soft parts. These are all believed to contribute their share in supplying the new material, but under very varying circumstances; and there are few questions upon which opinions have been more fluctuating and contradictory than upon the relative efficiency of each source of supply. From the time of Duhamel, whose first memoir was published in 1739, the opinions of most of those who have made this a subject of study, has been unequivocal in favor of the periosteum as the principal agent in this ossification; and more recently M. Ollier, of Lyons, has demonstrated, by a series of careful and well-conducted experiments, fortified by abundant observation on the human subject under various conditions of disease, that not only is the periosteum the principal source of ossific supply, where bone has been removed by disease or operation, but that, in fact, the other parts mentioned play a very subordinate and insignificant part in the process. M. Ollier conducted his experimental observations on dogs, cats, rabbits, lambs, pigeons, etc., and carefully studied to make the necessary operations in such a manner as to interfere with his results as little as possible. In this, by practice, he became very skilful, and hence his operations deserve more confidence and illustrate more distinctly the points he wishes to make, than those of most of the experimenters who have preceded him. Some of the most important deductions of M. Ollier are—1. That the periosteum is the great source of reproduction of bone under all ordinary circumstances. 2. That the periosteum presents two layers, an inner and an outer one, of which the inner alone is endowed with the bone-producing power. 3. That the medulla is not, under ordinary circumstances, disposed to the formation of new bone; but that it is, under conditions of irritation, capable, to a certain extent, of such production, but always in a much

inferior degree to the periosteum.   4. That the bone-substance
itself may also give rise to a growth of new bone, but that its
powers are much more limited than those of the medulla.
5. That though in certain exceptional cases the surrounding
soft parts can accomplish a partial bony reproduction, yet,
practically speaking, such reproduction is not to be expected,
when the whole, or a portion of a bone, with its periosteum, is
removed. These views of M. Ollier are so nearly in accordance with the opinions of the best observers who have preceded him, and are so well defended in his work, that I think
they may be accepted as expressing the view most generally
received on this subject, and as being as near the truth as the
present state of science permits us to arrive. Nevertheless,
there are not wanting those who differ from him *toto cœlo*. Of
recent observers, Marmy, of Lyons, quoted by M. Ollier, asserts
that in his experiments he has succeeded better in procuring a
reproduction of lost bone by removing than by preserving the
periosteum ; and Hein, of Dantzic, though he does not deny
the utility of the periosteum, thinks that the surrounding tissues may very well replace it.

In the case of necrosis, which we are now studying, we
will suppose that the whole of the middle portion of the shaft
has perished. In such a case, the dead portion is immediately
surrounded by its periosteum, and in contact above and below
with the living portions of the shaft, the medulla being supposed to have perished with the bone. We have here, therefore, only two sources from which the supply of new bone can
be derived, viz., the periosteum and the adjacent old bone. It
is observed of the periosteum that it soon begins to vascular-
ize, and take on granulation action by its internal surface,
which surface is separated by these granulations from contact
with the sequestrum. We have already seen that, at the
point where the dead separates from the living bone, the surface of the living bone becomes also covered with a layer of
granulations. It is in these, probably, that the further changes
occur. It was formerly held that these granulations were the
forming stage of an exudation or plasma, thrown out in a fluid
state, which, coagulating, developed itself into the new bone.
Virchow has shown that, at least in many examples, such ex-

udation does not occur, and his theory is, that there is no such thing as spontaneous organization of living forms in any exuded fluid, but that such actions are to be referred to a growth or proliferation, as he terms it, of germs which, already existing in the tissue, assume the actions of increase and development under certain conditions of excitation. Whether Virchow's views are to be accepted in all their extent, or, indeed, whether they are applicable to the question before us, need not now be insisted on; but it is somewhat interesting to observe that, after the lapse of more than a century, Duhamel's original idea, that the periosteum itself is converted into the new bone, is so nearly identical with that which the distinguished Berlin professor now so strongly and so ably advocates.

The periosteum then gradually becomes thickened and vascularized, and on its internal aspect begin to be seen the first traces of ossification. This action, it must be remembered, begins very early in the case, and may be considered to be complete generally in the same space of time that is occupied by the separation of the dead from the living bone. Large quantities of new bone are deposited thus round the sequestrum, until finally it becomes enclosed in a casing of new bone which is in reality much more bulky and much stronger than the original bone, whose loss it is intended to replace (Fig. 18). The pus which is secreted from the granulation surface finds its way out through fistulous openings, at various points in the periosteum; and, as new bone is not deposited at these openings, they remain as outlets through the bony casing by which, through fistulæ reaching to the cutaneous surface, the pus finds exit. These openings are termed cloacæ (Fig. 19).

While this action is taking place in the periosteum, the bone-tissue, which borders on the cavity containing the sequestrum, is presenting analogous phenomena. It is becoming vascularized, and giving origin to granulations which have a tendency, when the sequestrum is removed, to be converted into bone, and thus assist in filling up the vacuity which has occurred. It is noticed, however, that this action is extremely limited, and by itself constitutes a very unreliable source of supply. In cases where the periosteum is not preserved, the amount of new growth, from the ends of the living bone, will

not serve even to unite the extremities of the gap, much less
to fill it up.   In cases, again, where the periosteum is preserved
and contributes its usual share to the filling up of the cavity,

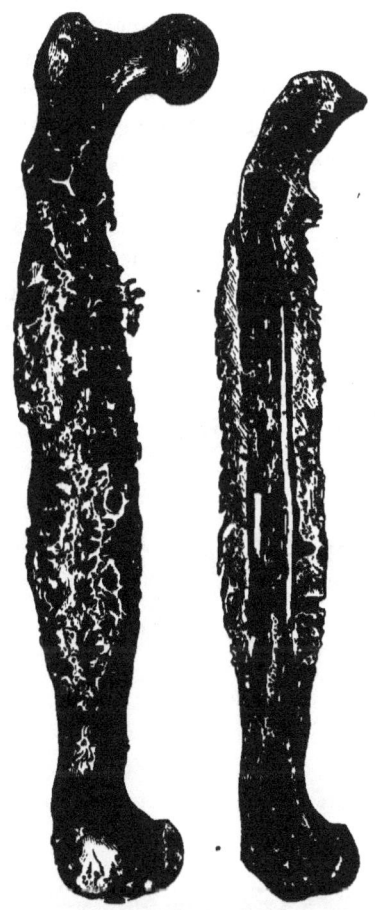

Fig. 18.—(From Billroth.)   Fig. 19.—(From Erichsen.)

the new bone which it deposits, and that which comes from the
ends of the old bone, are so amalgamated together, that the
share of each cannot be recognized, and it is only by observing
those cases in which the periosteum does not enter into the
reparative action, that we can distinctly see how very limited
a power of producing new bone is exhibited by the old bone in
its neighborhood.

The sequestrum being thus separated, and the loss being repaired, or rather compensated for, by the growth of new bone, the getting rid of the sequestrum is the next point which demands our attention. In those forms of necrosis where the dead portion is small and superficial, there is usually no enclosure of the sequestrum within the involucrum in such manner as to prevent its extrusion; so that no mechanical obstruction prevents its being cast out. We usually observe, therefore, in such cases, that, as soon as it is entirely loose, the sequestrum begins to make its way to the surface, in obedience to a law by which foreign bodies, lodged in the tissues, find their way toward the nearest surface by which they can conveniently be discharged. The process seems to be one in which the granulations press on it behind, and are absorbed before it

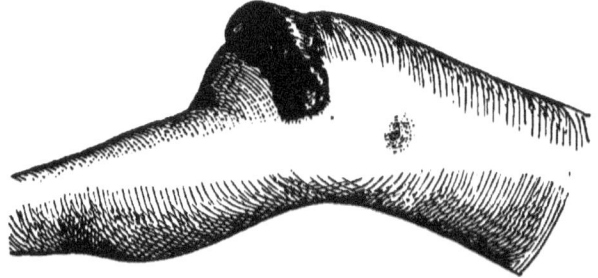

FIG. 20.—(From Billroth.)

in such a way that it gradually works toward the surface, and finally projects at one of the fistulous openings, whence it is easily withdrawn (Figs. 20 and 21). This disposition of these small sequestra may serve to indicate to us the intentions of

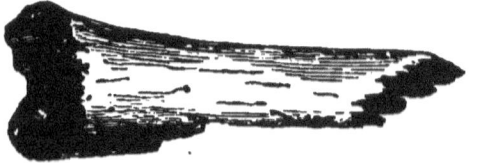

FIG. 21.—(From Billroth.)

Nature with regard to the larger ones, which we are now particularly studying. The intention undoubtedly is to extrude the larger as well as the smaller sequestra, and the extrusion

would, I doubt not, be more often accomplished if it were not
for the mechanical obstacle which is presented by the unyielding involucrum in which the dead bone is imprisoned.   Examples are not unfrequent in our museums of large sequestra
which are gradually liberating themselves from imprisonment,
and projecting themselves toward the surface.   This course is,
perhaps, sometimes determined by a large and favorably-situ-
ated cloaca, or possibly by a partial absence of involucrum
at a certain point; but while it may not often serve to free the
patient from his encumbrance, it does certainly show that there
is probably in all cases a tendency, more or less decided as it is
more or less resisted, to the spontaneous extrusion of sequestra.
This action, though conservative in its intention, is not without its dangers and inconveniences.   We have, in our museum
at the college, a specimen in which such a sequestrum, thus
partially extruded, has eroded the popliteal artery, causing the
death of the patient from hæmorrhage ; and I have seen
another case in which destruction of the knee-joint, with com-
pete bony anchylosis, was produced by a similar cause.   While,
therefore, it is important to recognize the fact that there is a
tendency toward the throwing off of these foreign masses, by
Nature's spontaneous actions, yet it will be found that in
practice not much can be expected from her efforts ; and, as a
general rule, it may be stated that, where the sequestrum is
enclosed in a bony involucrum, surgical assistance is required
to remove the mechanical resistance to its expulsion.   Where
this assistance is withheld, the case will pass on for years, even
for a long lifetime, without any material change either in the
condition or the position of the sequestrum, which has now become the mere mechanical cause of the symptoms under which
the patient will thus long continue to suffer.   Of this imprisonment of the sequestrum within the involucrum, Fig. 19, taken
from Erichsen's surgery, is a good example, though the cloacæ
are commonly much smaller, and the imprisonment therefore
more complete, than here exhibited.

    The symptoms which characterize these different stages of
necrosis may be studied as belonging to the three periods in the
pathological changes, which we may mark as—1. The period
of inflammation, by which the necrosis is originally produced ;

2. The period of sequestration, during which the separation is proceeding and the involucrum being formed ; and 3. The period of retention, during which the sequestrum remains as a foreign body within the involucrum.

1. The inflammation which produces such a necrosis as we have chosen for our type of the disease is almost invariably an acute attack. At a certain period, after the action of some of the causes we have noticed above, pain and swelling attack the limb, which soon becomes the seat of severe and manifest phlegmonous inflammation. The whole limb (the leg, for example) is involved in this inflammation, which indeed often extends to the foot below, and to the thigh above. For this reason it is often difficult, in the early stages, to decide accurately where the effects of this violent and extensive action are to concentrate themselves. It is in this stage that most of the mistakes are made by practitioners of limited experience, and the disease is looked upon as erysipelas, simple phlegmon, or rheumatism, until the progress of the case throws light upon its nature. No man can with certainty pronounce a positive diagnosis, in all cases of inflammation, which are to terminate in necrosis; but the possibility of such a chain of symptoms, depending on osteitis, leading to necrosis, being borne in mind, it is not likely that the careful observer will long be deceived. This inflammation occurring, as it does, in young and sometimes vigorous subjects, passes through its stages rapidly, and soon terminates in suppuration. We have seen that the first exudations probably take place between the periosteum and the bone. It is here, also, that suppuration begins, and, separating the periosteum from the bone, distends that membrane as far as its unyielding nature will permit. This is the period which is accompanied by the most urgent symptoms of fever and pain ; and when the periosteum gives way, and the matter escapes into the surrounding soft parts, the severity of the suffering is somewhat relieved. Through these soft parts, which participate in the general inflammation, the matter makes its way to the surface, sometimes only after having accumulated to a very large extent. Naturally or artificially the pus is finally evacuated, and the first stage may be regarded as terminated. This stage is marked by very severe constitutional

disturbance, very high inflammatory fever, and active delirium, sometimes existing during all the earlier days of the attack. This fever with delirium is often mistaken for typhoid fever— the delirium masking the local complaint, so that attention is not called to the suffering limb, till inflammation has made extensive progress. When the pus is evacuated, a sensible improvement occurs in the general symptoms, as well as in the local sufferings. The fever abates rapidly, the pains cease in a great degree, the great swelling subsides, and every thing seems rapidly returning to a condition of health. Here, again, a false hope is apt to be entertained that the cure of the abscess will be the cure of the disease, and the patient is flattered that he will soon be entirely well. Instead of this, however, it is found that the abscess does not heal. Fistulous openings continue to discharge pus, the limb remains swollen and tender, and it is liable to occasional recurrences of inflammation, which are sometimes almost as severe as the original attack, and are attended by the formation of new suppurative tracks, which at new points communicate with the cavity of the involucrum. On examining the limb at this time, it is found that the swelling and induration of the soft parts are gradually disappearing, while a deeper and firmer enlargement is taking their place, which is manifestly due to the gradual formation of the involucrum. This is the condition of the limb during the process of sequestration.

When the sequestrum is fully detached, and after the involucrum is completely formed, no marked change takes place in the symptoms. The abscesses have gradually contracted down to fistulæ, the orifices of which present a few large, soft, pouting granulations, which are characteristic of the presence of a foreign body at the bottom of the fistula. The soft parts have resumed their natural condition, and the deep involucral swelling has become of a bony hardness and almost insensible to pressure. The discharge continues constant, but usually small, from the fistulous tracks, and the patient, having recovered his general health, begins to use the limb with more and more freedom. This state of things may continue indefinitely with but little variation. If the fistulæ show a disposition to heal, the matter accumulates and gives rise to a renewal of some of the old sufferings until it again finds its way to the surface. As a rule, the fistulæ do not heal even for a short time, and I believe never permanently, while the sequestrum continues unremoved.

I have thus presented an outline of the ordinary course of one of the most characteristic and common forms of necrosis. During the course of this disease the patient is exposed to several sources of danger which are worthy of being separately noticed. In the first place, when the death of bone has involved the tissues near the joints, these may become implicated directly or indirectly in the consequences of the disease. It is always noticed that, when the sequestrum is near the joint, the surrounding inflammation reaches to the fibrous structures of the joint, which gradually grows stiffer and stiffer, until the use of the joint is seriously impaired, and often till complete immobility is established. This is particularly marked in cases of necrosis of the lower end of the femur, where the knee-joint is apt to become the seat of a false anchylosis, which is often complete enough to entirely abolish its movements. This is a condition which is a necessary consequence of the proximity of the disease, and one which therefore cannot be entirely prevented. Something may be done, however, by encouraging the patient to practise the movements of the rigid joint systematically and regularly, and thus in some degree obviate the increase of the trouble. But, the most important practical indication to be deduced from this well-known tendency to impairment of a neighboring joint is, to remove the cause of the impairment as soon as possible, by getting rid of the sequestrum. If for no other reason an operation is required, this is always a good one. I had under my care, a few years ago, a member of our medical class, who had suffered for years with necrosis of a limited extent in the lower end of his femur. For some reason he had not been advised to have it operated on, and he had submitted to its annoyances, and had attended lectures regularly, until he began to find that the knee, which had long been getting stiff, was fast becoming useless. He then consulted me, and I advised an operation, which was performed, and a considerable sequestrum, of the compact layer of the condyles just above the joint, was removed. The wound

healed rapidly and perfectly, but the stiffness of the joint was
no more tractable than it had been before.   Under these circumstances, anxious to fill a hospital appointment which his
merit had secured him, and ambitious to distinguish himself in
his profession, he begged me to try forced flexion of the joint.
The original wound made in the operation being several months
healed, and there being no evidence of any disease about the
joint, I thought it a favorable case for this proceeding, which
I accordingly adopted.   Placing him under ether, and having
arranged a couch with reference to the leverage of the leg, I
made the most powerful efforts to break up the adhesions, but
with only a partial success, which, though it procured him some
increase in the movement of the joint, did not satisfy him.   At
his urgent request, and sympathizing with his brave determi-
nation to fit himself for life's duties, I made, a few weeks after,
another attempt, and, being better prepared with my mechanical arrangements, and perhaps being more determined to succeed, I made more strenuous efforts to move the obstinately-
rigid joint, when all at once, while I was trying to force flexion
as far as I could, something gave way with a snap, and the
joint yielded in the most satisfactory manner.   I was shocked
to find, however, that this success had been secured at the expense of a considerable laceration of the integuments of the
anterior aspect of the joint at a point where there had been
some cicatricial adhesion of the skin to the bone, from long-past
inflammation, and still more alarmed to find that this laceration, of some inch and a half long, admitted the finger into
the cavity of the knee-joint.   I instantly closed the wound,
and placed the joint at perfect rest, and had the good fortune
to secure immediate union, without a bad symptom on the part
of the joint, and I had the satisfaction to find that I had gained
a degree of flexion which was amply sufficient for the ordinary
use of the limb, and which he not only retained, but by persevering effort considerably improved upon.

Another mode in which the joints become involved by
necrosis, and fortunately a rare one, is by death of cancellous
tissue reaching to the articular surface itself.   When this occurs, there is sometimes a protective inflammation which shuts
off the general cavity of the joint from the effects of the sepa-

ration of and suppuration round the sequestrum, and the dead piece may be removed without really opening the synovial cavity ; or this protective inflammation may be wanting, or of an unhealthy character, allowing contact of the morbid fluids with the synovial cavity, and thus producing a general arthritis which is apt to be destructive in its tendencies, the more so from the constant presence of the exciting cause. Of this we had a good exemplification in a syphilitic patient in the New York Hospital, who had been long suffering from disease of the lower end of the tibia, embracing the internal malleolus. This falling into necrosis, involved the joint in acute attack of inflammation, which soon rendered amputation necessary. The specimen, when macerated, showed a considerable disk of the cartilaginous surface forming part of the sequestrum, which was almost ready to separate. Similar facts have been reported in many instances ; and the whole subject of the danger to joints from their proximity to sequestra is most important, as suggesting the early removal of the dead portion of bone, before the evils apprehended have had time to occur.

A second danger in necrosis is hæmorrhage. We have seen that the sequestrum when separated has a tendency to work its way toward the surface, and that, when it is not resisted by the imprisoning involucrum, a large sequestrum will sometimes be thus extruded. In working its way thus among the tissues, it is liable to encounter some artery of importance which may be eroded by its pressure. In vessels of moderate size, and sometimes, doubtless, in the main trunks themselves, Nature institutes a protective process against such erosion, and the vessel is closed by fibrine before its coats are perforated, and hæmorrhage is thereby prevented. Unfortunately, however, it does sometimes happen either that the protective action is imperfect, or that the destructive effect of the sharp edge of the bone is too sudden and rapid for the calibre of the vessel to be entirely sealed, and hæmorrhage takes place. This accident, as far as I have observed it, always takes place in the largest trunks, small vessels being so much more likely to be safely plugged than large ones, and this pathological fact has, I think, great practical significance ; for, if we can confidently pronounce that the hæmorrhage, in a given case of necrosis, has its source in the erosion of a large trunk, and not of a small branch, it is evident that the case from that fact assumes an importance which is immediate and pressing. And it is the more necessary that this should be fully appreciated, because these hæmorrhages are sometimes exceedingly deceptive in their behavior, and some of those which first occur, even from the largest trunks, are quite trivial in amount, and are easily checked, or stop spontaneously. This is extremely apt to deceive the surgeon into the belief that the bleeding vessel is not large, and that the danger is not great. It may be a fatal mistake.

We have, in the college museum, a beautiful preparation taken from a medical gentleman of this city, who had been suffering from necrosis of the femur for many years. On a sudden, without assignable cause, he was attacked with hæmorrhage, the blood flowing quite freely for a time from the fistulous openings, and then ceasing of its own accord. Once or twice bleeding recurred, always stopping in a short time spontaneously, but nevertheless reducing him considerably by the whole amount of blood lost. Finding the bleeding so moderate and so controllable, neither he nor his medical advisers took serious alarm until a day or two after, when a rapid and profuse hæmorrhage brought him almost to death's door. In this unpromising state amputation was performed, but too late to save the unfortunate gentleman from a death clearly due to a non-appreciation of the pathological condition which the specimen most sadly illustrates. It shows a large, sharp-edged sequestrum, which, having partially emerged from its bed, had worked its way down toward the popliteal space, and there, by erosion, opened the popliteal artery. By contrast, another case occurred to my colleague, Dr. Gurdon Buck, who had under his care a boy of about twelve or fourteen years of age, with a very extensive necrosis of the femur. As it was during the hot season, and, as the patient was much reduced by his disease, an operation was postponed, and the boy was allowed to go about, hoping that his health would improve as the cooler season arrived. In fact, he was improving very greatly, when, after a moderate walk, he found his pantaloons and shoe of the diseased side filled with blood. This bleeding stopped of itself, but, from its extent and rapidity, Dr. Buck believed it to be from a main trunk, and stood ready on the occasion of its recurrence, which soon took place, to amputate the limb, which he did quite high up, and the boy's life was saved. Dissection showed that the upper sharp point of the sequestrum had opened the femoral artery not far from the origin of the profunda. This specimen is preserved in the New York Hospital Museum.

I have examined carefully, during the last twenty years, thirteen cases of necrosis in which hæmorrhage occurred of sufficient severity to require surgical interference. In every one of these it was the main artery of the region which was the source of the hæmorrhage, except in one case, and then it was the vertebral which had been eroded by a fragment of dead bone, from a pistol-wound, which was in a favorable state of healing when the fatal hæmorrhage occurred. In each case the coats of the artery were eroded evidently by the direct contact of a sharp edge of the sequestrum, with one exception, and then, though the main artery was opened, and a sharp sequestrum was quite near, we could not pronounce positively that the hole observed in the side of the artery was actually due to the pressure of the sharp edge of bone. The number of observations is too small to decide the point that small vessels never bleed from the cause we are studying; but the testimony of these few is so nearly uniform that I think it may safely be accepted as a pathological law, and I am quite sure it affords our soundest practical indication. Precisely what that indication is, must be settled by the features presented by each case; but it is hardly necessary to say that the remedy does not consist in the mere removal of the cause of the mischief, that is, the sharp edge of the dead bone. When that is removed, there remains the opened artery to be cared for, and, if my position is correct, that this opened artery is a main trunk, very little hope can be entertained that Nature will be able to close the wounded vessel without assistance from art.

Two courses present themselves to the surgeon in this serious emergency: The first is, to make an attempt to reach and tie the wounded vessel; and the second is, to amputate if the ligature cannot safely or successfully be undertaken. The

10

point of urgent importance, however, is, in my judgment, not to delay till a sudden gush of blood places your patient beyond the hope of benefit from any operation, be it ever so clearly indicated, or ever so skilfully performed.

The two following cases, which have recently come under my observation, illustrate extremely well the points of practice I have here dwelt upon :

Martin Clancy, aged twenty-four, an oysterman, was admitted into Bellevue Hospital, October 29, 1869. He was extremely feeble and exsanguine, and stated that he had been bleeding for five days from an ulcer in his thigh. This bleeding had occurred suddenly, without obvious cause, and had stopped spontaneously for a time. It had recurred several times in the same unprovoked manner; and by the frequency of these bleedings, some of them very large, he had been reduced to his present alarming condition. He had worn a tourniquet for many hours before his arrival at the hospital, put on by his surgical attendant out-of-doors. It was clear, from the examination of his case, and from its previous history, that he had had necrosis of the lower part of the femur, dating back seven years, and several openings existed in the popliteal region, from which the blood had issued. The probe detected a large sequestrum, lying loose and quite superficial; and the question in consultation was, What was the vessel opened? From the amount of blood lost, from the spontaneous character of the bleedings, and their persistent recurrence, and from the situation of the sequestrum, we had no hesitation in deciding that it was the popliteal trunk that was injured, and in determining to cut down and remove the sequestrum, and, if possible, apply a ligature to the artery. The operation was performed by Dr. A. B. Mott, and was truly a difficult and delicate one. An incision, seven inches long, was made over the course of the artery, embracing as many of the fistulous orifices as possible, and soon a large cavity was exposed, occupying most of the popliteal space above the knee, in which lay loose a large, flat, sharp-edged sequestrum, evidently formed by the death of the compact layer of the posterior surface of the femur, just above the condyles. This removed, left a bed of granulations, in which it had rested; but no hæmorrhage could, at the moment, be induced, by which a clew to the injured artery might be gained. The operator was obliged, therefore, by a most tedious and cautious dissection, among parts consolidated by long-continued inflammation, to search for the artery, guided by a pulsation, which, in this indurated condition of parts, and in the feeble state of the circulation, was of very little assistance. After a long search at the upper part of the cavity, the artery was exposed, and carefully traced downward, until we arrived at a ragged opening on its side, from which, on loosening the tourniquet, the blood now spurted freely. A ligature was applied above and below the opening, the two ligatures being about an inch apart. The wound was only partly closed, leaving its central portion open, and was dressed lightly. Every thing went on favorably. No hæmorrhage occurred, and the man gained rapidly in appearance and in strength. The wound granulated well, and filled up so rapidly, that, by the 19th of December, it was almost healed, and on the 31st he was discharged from the hospital. He could then, about nine weeks after the operation, walk quite well, though he could not flex the foot. No pulsation in anterior or posterior tibials. His health seemed to be perfectly reëstablished.

The second case was not so fortunate in its results, and is a noteworthy illustration of the formidable nature of the accident we are studying, because the gravity of the situation was fully appreciated from the moment the accident occurred, and every thing that science and skill could do was done, and done promptly, without achieving the saving of the patient's life. The case occurred in the practice of my friend Dr. George A. Peters, of this city, and by his kindness I had the opportunity to study the specimens in their recent state. The patient was a gentleman about forty-five years of age, of ordinarily good health and active habits. He had had several attacks of inflammation about his knee, the earliest one occurring in childhood; and on one occasion he had had a slight exfoliation of bone from the lower part of the femur. He had of late years entirely recovered from the effects of these attacks; and, with the exception of a slight stiffness and lameness of the joint, he considered himself a well man. Dr. Peters was summoned to him at his residence, out of town, one Sunday morning in September, 1869, and found that he had had that morning, while making some slight movement in bed, a severe hæmorrhage. which had reduced him to an alarming point of prostration. The history given was, that about two months previously, an inflammation had declared itself in the old seat of disease in the ham, and had gone on slowly to suppuration, and had been opened by his attending surgeon in two places. The inflammation subsided somewhat, but the abscess did not heal; and, though he was able to keep about his business, he suffered more or less constant inconvenience from his disease. He had only been confined to the house a few days; and, beyond a slight increase in local suffering, no new features had developed themselves when the hæmorrhage took place, as above stated.

The bleeding had been so severe, that, although no recurrence had taken place, his alarming condition warranted the most extreme measures to prevent a renewal of it. The wound was therefore opened freely, and a large cavity exposed, occupying the popliteal space, the bottom of which cavity was the posterior surface of the lower end of the femur, in a condition of extensive disease, with a bare and very rough surface extending several inches up the bone and downward, so as to involve the knee-joint, into which, through the ulcerated ligamentum Winslowi, the finger could easily be passed. A small, thin, and very sharp detached fragment of bone lay loose in the cavity. The condition of extensive disease of the femur, the opened knee-joint, with the almost certainty of the popliteal artery being eroded, seemed to justify and to demand amputation of the limb, which was performed without delay, almost without loss of blood. So great was the depression of the system, that no proper reaction took place, and he died during the night following the operation.

On examination immediately after the operation, the large cavity, mentioned as occupying the popliteal space, was found to extend far round the femur on each side; and into it, therefore, the whole posterior and lateral surfaces of the end of the femur formed a sort of projection. All the bone-surface thus exposed was bare, rough, irregularly eroded, presenting only here and there a granulating surface. The knee-joint was filled with pus, and rapidly disorganizing. The popliteal artery ran along the superficial wall of this cavity, but very close to the exposed bone-surface, and, at about the centre of the popliteal space, was opened by a clean oblique cut, just such as is usually made in the operation of venesection. No other detached sequestrum was found. After maceration, the end of the femur was found to be light, porous, and spongy; the medullary cavity very large, and the cancellous tissue very open. Both the posterior and lateral, and some of the anterior surfaces of the bone, were irregularly eroded, the posterior much the more deeply. Almost all the compact portion of

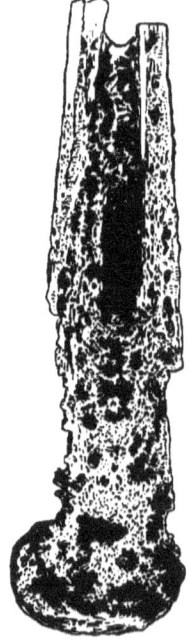
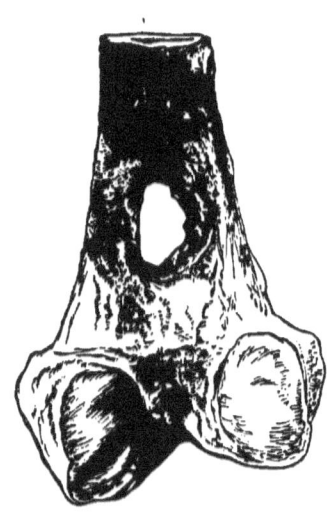

Fig. 22.—(From N. Y. Hospital Museum.)   Fig. 23.—(From N. Y. Hospital Museum.)

the shaft, where it is not destroyed by erosion, has become porous as well as thin. At several points, where this compact lamina still remains undestroyed, a dull, white, opaque appearance of the surface indicates that it has suffered necrosis. Such a necrosed plate, separating from the posterior surface, was undoubtedly the cause of the wound in the artery. The

same necrosed appearance penetrated at points into the substance of the cancellous tissue, which had evidently been extensively infiltrated with pus. In some points small cavities
existed, which doubtless had contained pus, and which did not
communicate with the surface. No loose sequestra were to be
found. At the point of amputation the bone has become
harder than natural, with some small exostotic growths on the
outskirts of the inflamed region.

That the danger from hæmorrhage in necrosis is a real and
a formidable one, even in circumstances most favorable for
prompt surgical assistance, will perhaps more clearly appear
from the statement that, of eleven cases which I have met
with, mostly occurring in the New York Hospital, six have
died. In ten of these every thing was promising well when
the hæmorrhage occurred; and in every case but that of the
vertebral the injured vessel was accessible to ligature, or the
limb might have been removed by amputation. These things
taken into consideration, my recommendation of promptness
in operation receives an emphatic indorsement. Delay in
hope of saving the limb is fatal to life.

Fig. 23 represents the lower end of a femur where amputation was performed for hæmorrhage from the popliteal artery,
which had been opened by a sharp sequestrum detached from
the posterior surface of the femur. The specimen is curious
from the peculiar manner in which the bone is perforated by
the actions going on round the bed from which the sequestrum
came. It is in the New York Hospital Museum.

The last danger to which I shall allude is exhaustion. In
a feeble subject, with extensive necrosis, we sometimes have
thrown upon the powers of Nature more than they can bear.
The reparative actions, which should be promptly and health-
fully excited as soon as the inflammatory stage is passed, are
replaced by the continuance of inflammation in a subacute
form, accompanied with a profuse secretion of pus. No proper
involucrum is formed. The tissues are largely infiltrated with
inflammatory products. The tenderness and pain do not disappear. The line of separation forms slowly and imperfectly.
In short, the whole process is a morbid instead of a healthy
one; and the patient's condition corresponds, in an excited,

irritable pulse, irregular hectic fever, want of appetite, emaciation, and all those numerous evidences that inflammation
rather than reparation is going on about the seat of disease.
Here, every thing depends upon the surroundings of the
patient, and the assiduity with which wholesome and proper
regimen is brought to bear upon the overtaxed powers. The
best of air, the best of food, tonics, invigorants, stimulants, will,
happily, in most cases, carry the patient through the period of
danger; but, if the condition do not soon improve, if the exhaustion be gaining upon you rather than yielding to your
efforts, remember that this very condition is reacting upon the
local state, and making bad conditions daily worse, and it is
well to be very circumspect lest, in the anxiety to save a limb,
you sacrifice a life. This form of danger from exhaustion belongs to the early stages of the disease, and depends very much
upon original weakness of constitution. When once an involucrum has formed, and the patient has recovered a partial use of
his limb, the danger of exhaustion from continued drain by the
suppuration, in my own observation, is confined to those in
whom some other accidental complications have conspired with
the original disease to depress the vital powers, and in such
cases the source of danger belongs more to the complication
than to the primary disorder.

Having thus passed in review the principal features of a
case of necrosis which has been selected as a type of the disease, we must now look at some classes of cases in which important deviations from this standard course present themselves. Among these varieties of necrosis entitled to special
study we have—1. Superficial necrosis or exfoliation. 2. In
heads of bones near joints. 3. In cranial bones. 4. In jawbones. 5. After fractures. 6. After amputations. 7. Without suppuration. 8. Without exfoliation.

1. *Superficial Necrosis, or Exfoliation.*—This simplest and
most common form of necrosis differs from that we have been
studying, mainly in the fact that we trace little or no evidence
of any reparative or compensatory process when the separation is taking or has taken place. Hence we have no involucrum enclosing the sequestrum, which usually lies exposed in

the cavity of the suppurating soft parts. The granulations
which form its bed, after separation is complete, push it without difficulty toward the surface, where it either makes its way
out with the discharge, if it be small, or, if it be large, presents
itself at the opening of one of the fistulæ, whence it can easily
be removed by the surgeon. In this way a large number of
slight necroses, produced by detachments of periosteum, or after
fractures, or after operations on bones, pass through their various stages so easily and with so little disturbance, as scarcely
to constitute a complication of the wound, or materially to re-
tard its healing. There are certain cases, however, where this
superficial necrosis becomes formidable from its shape and extent. It sometimes happens that a considerable portion of the
surface of the bone undergoes necrosis, so that the shaft of a
long bone may present on all sides, and in the greater portion
of its length a necrosis, which is entirely superficial, affecting
only the outer compact layer. As a spontaneous disease this
occurs most often in children, in whom some sudden inflammation of the periosteum has produced the disease, without the
bone itself being seriously implicated. This was well illustrated in the case of a little boy who recently died in the New
York Hospital. He was received in consequence of injuries
from the passage of a rail-car over his right foot. About a
week after, he began to complain of pain in his left tibia, which
was not known to be injured. This was the 19th of July.
Soon phlegmonous inflammation developed itself, occupying
the whole leg, and extending above the knee and below the
ankle. *August 12th.*—The abscess was opened, giving issue
to a very large amount of pus. The matter found vent at
several points, and it soon became evident that the tibia was
extensively diseased. The probe found dead bone at all points,
the integuments were undermined, the discharge fetid, and the
little fellow suffered greatly. He was rapidly sinking from his
disorder, when amputation was proposed to save his life. It
was refused by his friends, and he was soon reduced to a mere
skeleton by his sufferings and the immense discharge from the
cavities. He lingered until the 20th of September, when he
died. The whole tibia was found to be diseased. The external compact shell had died almost in its whole extent, and at

one or two points a partial exfoliation had commenced. Within this outer dead shell the bone-tissue was in a state of inflammation. It was congested with blood, softer than natural, extensively eroded on its epiphyseal extremities, and from several points exuberant growth of layers of new bone, still soft, showed an attempt on the part of Nature to form an involucrum. So soft was the bone-tissue of the head of the tibia that it broke off in removing it, and could be crushed by the fingers. The sequestrum, if removed, would have formed a thin tube, representing all the external layer of the shaft of the tibia.

2. *Necrosis occurring in Heads of Bones near Joints.*— Here the significant feature is, the relation of the disease to the articular cavity. The sequestrum may either extend into the joint, or it may lie near it without involving the articular lamella. In the first case, the danger of destructive inflammation of the joint is very great, and in many instances, I think, I have seen evidence that the presence of a small sequestrum has been the cause of an unfortunate termination of a joint disease, which in other respects might have had a favorable issue. This is the result usually to be anticipated where the sequestrum reaches actually into the joint, but I have seen more than one instance where this condition obtained, and where, nevertheless, the integrity of the joint was not compromised. Thus, I had a young man under my care who had, over the external malleolus, a foul and ill-behaving ulcer, which was probably syphilitic in its origin. It had existed for many months, and, when I saw it, had exposed a considerable portion of the external malleolus, which, dead and dry, formed the bottom of the ulcer. Seeing that in all probability the sequestrum involved or would involve the articular surface, I feared the consequences to the joint when the separation should occur. His general condition was strengthened by appropriate treatment; the character of the sore improved, and very soon the dead piece became movable. It was not disturbed until it had become very loose, and then, being removed, we were agreeably surprised to find that no inflammation occurred in the ankle-joint, though the separated piece showed a considerable portion of the articular surface, which had been

applied against the outer surface of the astragalus. We kept the joint very still for a while, until granulation was well advanced, and then carefully allowed a little movement. It was well borne, and gradually increased, until a very satisfactory amount of motion was gained, the joint all the time remaining free from any indication of inflammation. The only explanation of this interesting fact is, that surrounding adhesive inflammation had closed off the general cavity of the joint from the actions which were going on round the dead bone, which was thus placed practically external to a joint of which really it formed a part. This fortunate termination must be rare. Its occasional occurrence should give us encouragement, and keep us from despairing in similar apparently hopeless cases.

A much more frequent case is that in which the sequestrum does not reach to the joint-surfaces of the bone in which it is situated, but, lying very near these joint-surfaces, involves them in the inflammatory actions of which it is the centre and the cause. Of this, Mr. Stanley gives an interesting example in the case of a young girl of sixteen, who was attacked by an inflammation of the head of the tibia, which was followed by necrosis. Successive attacks of inflammation of the joint occurred at intervals during sixteen years. These attacks finally grew more and more threatening, until the knee-joint became so seriously involved as to render amputation necessary. On examining the limb, there was found " a dead portion of the cancellous tissue, about the size of a hazel-nut, firmly impacted in the interior of the head of the tibia, half an inch below its upper articular surface. . . . The several structures of the joint had undergone the usual changes consequent on long-continued inflammation ; the synovial membrane was thick and pulpy, with lymph adhering to its free surface ; the crucial ligaments were softened, and the articular cartilages were in part absorbed." But, besides these more rare cases where destructive disease of the joint is produced by the proximity of a sequestrum, there are a large number in which, by a slower process, a stiffness of the neighboring joint is produced, which very soon amounts, if the condition be not obviated, to an anchylosis. This is one of the serious consequences of necrosis, and unfortunately it is one which does not cease when the necrosis is cured; for, by the long continuance of the anchylosis, and the consequent disuse of the joint, its constituent parts have become so adherent to one another by organized fibrine, and so changed from disuse, that but little can be done to restore its usefulness. It should be borne in mind that this implication of the neighboring joint may occur in cases where the necrosis is not in the immediate proximity of the joint, but at some little distance from it. I have now under my care a young gentleman in whom necrosis of the femur took place about three years ago. I recently removed the sequestrum, which occupied a very large share of the shaft of the femur, but did not approach within perhaps an inch of the knee-joint, and yet the knee is hopelessly anchylosed, and has been so for many months. I think I have more frequently observed this condition in the knee-joint than in any other, and more frequently as a consequence of necrosis of the lower part of the femur than of the upper part of the tibia. This tendency to the implication of neighboring joints seems to me to offer some practical suggestions in the management of the disease: 1. Where we believe the necrosis not to invade the joint-structures themselves, but merely to affect them by proximity, cannot something be done to obviate the consequences of these successive attacks of inflammation, by rigorously insisting on properly-conducted passive motion, after each attack subsides, and by courageously keeping up such attention to the motions of the joint as shall prevent or diminish its tendency to hopeless rigidity? 2. Let no time be lost in performing the operation and removing the sequestrum. Every day's delay increases the risk of inflammation of the neighboring joint, and adds to the rigidity which is rapidly making it useless.

In connection with these cases, I may here allude to the fact that the cancellous tissue, in some of the short bones, as in those of the tarsus, is sometimes the seat of necrosis, presenting features somewhat peculiar to its situation.

I had, in Bellevue Hospital, a carman, aged thirty-one, in January, 1868, who presented a diseased condition of the os calcis, which at first puzzled me. Ten years ago, he had injured the foot by striking on the heel in jumping from a height. Inflammation followed of the whole region of the heel, which, after several weeks, terminated in the opening of an abscess, and the discharge of matter from the inside of the heel. About a month afterward, a similar opening took place on the outside. The inflammation subsided, but the openings had never healed. He had been able, most of the time, to use the foot without much inconvenience. I examined the foot carefully, on the 19th of February. There was some enlargement and thickening of the whole calcaneal region, and the two original openings remained nearly opposite one another, and communicating, so that a probe could be passed through the bone, from one to the other. The probe distinctly touched dead bone. A surgeon, who had seen him some weeks previously, had passed a seton through the bone, and left it there. It had excited but little action of any kind. The history led me to suspect that it was a case of central necrosis. I proceeded, therefore, to expose the outer surface of the os calcis, and carefully enlarged the opening which led into the substance of the bone. As soon as it was large enough to admit my little finger, I discovered a loose sequestrum, which, as cautiously as possible, I extracted, not without breaking off some of its prominent points. It was of the size and somewhat the shape of a small nutmeg, and was composed of the cancellous texture of the bone. It was shrivelled and apparently partly decomposed, by long exposure to the air and to the foul secretions of the part. After removing the sequestrum, the finger could be introduced into a cavity, the walls of which were covered with thick, firm, and apparently healthy granulations. The patient made a very good recovery. One other case, almost identical in its features, has occurred to me, in a lad of fifteen, in whom a similar operation was followed by a like satisfactory result.

Again, it happens, but I suspect very rarely, that the whole bone dies, and remains enclosed in the bag formed by the periosteum. This condition presented itself in a son of the Rev. Mr. P., whom I saw in consultation with Dr. J. L. Little, in January, 1868. About five weeks previously he had noticed, about the insertion of the tendo Achillis, a swelling which had come on gradually, and which he attributed to a twist of the ankle received some time before. This swelling inflamed and softened, and a very large abscess soon declared itself, involving the whole calcaneal region. This soon broke, and discharged freely from two openings. These openings, which were on the side of the os calcis, had been laid into one, thus exposing the bone to easy exploration with the finger. An abscess was found surrounding the whole of the os calcis, and the finger could be passed around so as to touch the bare and evidently dead bone on all sides. The disease was confined, as far as we could judge, to the os calcis, which was already loosened in its attachments, both to the astragalus and to the cuboid. There was great thickening and induration of the soft parts forming the walls of the abscess, and a very large discharge of pus. He suffered much from pain, and was rapidly depreciating in general health.

Regarding the case as one of entire necrosis of the os calcis, and believing that the destruction was confined to that bone, I heartily concurred in Dr. Little's proposal to remove the dead bone, instead of amputating the limb. It was done by Dr. Little without difficulty, by making a free opening, so as to get control of the bone; and then, carefully separating its ligamentous attachments, it was easily removed. As far as could be ascertained, the parts left behind were in a sound condition. No evil behavior showed itself in the healing of the wound. Granulation took place slowly, and the wound filled up with new material, the shape and size of the heel being in a good degree preserved. This, Dr. Little informed me, finally consolidated by bone, so as to afford a very good instance of regeneration of bone from its periosteum.

3. The third variety of necrosis which I deem worthy of special study is that which occurs *in the cranial bones*. It is not easy to say why the disease should differ in its behavior in these bones from the course it presents elsewhere; but that it does so is abundantly manifest. The most striking peculiarities of necrosis in this situation are mainly two: 1. An indisposition to the separation and casting off of the dead bone. 2. A disposition to spread slowly and gradually, so as to invade large tracts of neighboring healthy bone. These two features render this a formidable disease; and, as they directly interfere

with the reparative action of the diseased part, will explain why it is that necrosis of the cranial bones is so frequently a fatal disorder. It is mostly as a consequence of syphilis that this peculiar form of necrosis arises; but I have reason to believe that in other cachectic conditions of the system, when no syphilitic history can be traced, more or less of the same peculiarities occasionally show themselves. I can best illustrate the disease by giving a typical case, which was undisturbed by surgical treatment. While at Fortress Monroe, in the spring of 1862, McClellan's army then lying before Yorktown, I was asked to see an officer of the regular army, who was suffering from syphilitic rupia. I found a young gentleman covered with large crusts of rupia, and so reduced that he was obliged to keep his bed. He was unable to go on with the army, and finally was sent home, and he came under my care in New York. His case was a most difficult and distressing one, from the extent and severity of the ulceration following the falling of the scabs. He partly recovered under the use of liberal doses of iodide of potassium, and was able to go to his home in the country. I saw him again in the next year, greatly improved, but not well. I lost sight of him then for several years, when my old friend turned up in the wards of the New York Hospital, in June, 1868. I was shocked to see him covered with sores and scabs and scars, emaciated to a skeleton, his voice altered by the destruction of part of the palate, and it was long before I could believe him to be the same man. He was in a deplorable condition; but the most alarming feature to me was the condition of his head. The scalp presented at several points large ulcerations, covering altogether one-half of its surface. The bottom of these ulcers was constituted by the bare, dead, and blackened surface of the cranium, which was manifestly in a condition of necrosis over at least one-half of the vault. Exuberant but pale granulations surrounded these very irregular patches of necrosis, and an abundant fetid discharge flowed from their surface. Some of this discharge, however, came from beneath the bone, where there were several irregular, worm-eaten looking perforations through the dead layer. On pushing back the granulations, healthy living bone could easily be brought into view, and a line somewhat distinct could be traced between the dead and living parts, which at some points showed a disposition to separation, so that at one or two points along this edge considerable excavations, of a very irregular outline and of varying depth, could be seen, some of them penetrating the skull, and giving issue to pus, which evidently came from beneath the bone. In all the rest of the line no distinct evidence could be traced of any attempt at separation of the dead from the living tissue. The bone in the immediate neighborhood of the dead tissue showed, at some points, an increased vascularity, but no other change. This condition had been brought about by a series of morbid actions, commencing a little more than a year ago. The first thing noticed was a small, painful, and tender swelling, several others showing themselves nearly at the same time. These increased, soon suppurated and ulcerated, and at a very early period presented dead bone on their floor. A great deal of pain attended these ulcerations, and made it difficult for him to place his head on his pillow without suffering. His general feebleness, and the long continuance and inveterate behavior of his disease, made his case so hopeless that nothing could be done except by a cordial and invigorating regimen, with anodynes in full doses, to try to rouse up his failing powers. But little was accomplished, however, and he left the hospital in the latter part of August for his home, to die a few days after he reached it, with symptoms of inflammation of the brain or its meninges.

Here no surgical operation was at any time practicable, and the disease followed, therefore, an undisturbed course. In the following cases removal of the dead bone was practised, with a result which, though varying a little in different cases, is, on the whole, far from encouraging :

Sarah Atwood, aged twenty-four, was admitted to the New York Hospital, June 14, 1859, with a diseased condition of the bones of the forehead. Six years before she had had syphilis, not followed by any secondary symptoms. About a year afterward she suffered much from headache, followed by the appearance of painful swellings on the front part of the head, which, after about six months, softened and suppurated. New openings have since formed, and all have continued to discharge, showing no inclination to heal. Her general condition is good, and she has no other secondary manifestations. Five fistulous openings now exist on the anterior part of the os frontis, at the bottom of each of which the probe detects bare and rough bone. On the 18th of June the late Dr. John Watson, then in attendance, made an incision through the line of ulcers, and laid up a flap exposing the diseased surface, which occupied at least six square inches. The periosteum was so easily stripped off from the bone that it was evident it could have had no vital connection with it. The surface of the diseased bone was rough and irregular, and raised from its proper level by elevations and bosses, which showed that a process of thickening had been going on. Several openings presented themselves in the midst of the diseased region, from which pus flowed out, evidently from a space between the bone and the dura mater. It seemed, from the altered color and the bloodlessness of the part, that it was entirely dead; and when the periosteum was still further stripped up, so as to expose the surrounding healthy bone, the contrast was very marked. No line of separation, however, showed itself at any point; and this seemed the more remarkable, as there was reason to believe that the death of the bone had occurred at least three years previously. It was determined to remove all the dead bone, and this was done, after long and patient perseverance, in chiselling and gouging and gnawing the dead bone until living bone was reached. In this way the whole dead portion was removed, sometimes consisting of a superficial layer, not involving the inner table; at other points involving the whole thickness of the skull, and leaving exposed the granulating surface of the dura mater.

The behavior of the wound was very satisfactory. Granulations sprung up freely from the dura mater and from the gnawed surface of the bone. Toward the close of July two firm and hard swellings occurred on the parietal bone, near the wound, one of which suppurated and discharged through the wound, and the other disappeared without suppuration. No necrosis followed at this time. About the 8th of September two sequestra, of an irregular form, and together larger than a quarter of a dollar, separated from under the still-open edge of the wound. These pieces, on examination, proved to be from the margin of the surface left after the operation, as they showed the marks of the *rongeur*. This must have been, there-fore, a spread of the necrosis after the operation; but it is well worthy of remark that Nature had been able, under the altered conditions induced by the operation, to effect a separation in a few weeks, which she had not been able to accomplish during the previous three years. No sign of cerebral disturbance showed itself after the operation at any time. *November 1st.*— All has gone on favorably; the cavities left in the operation being filled up and nearly healed. Unfortunately, however, there is too much reason to fear that the original disease is progressing, and thus far it is not controlled by remedies. New districts of bone were being invaded by the disease when she was discharged, January 9, 1860.

This was the first case of the kind I had studied, and I was much disappointed at its treacherous behavior. The first favorable progress had not led me to expect that its ravages would be resumed, even during the apparently healthful heal-ing of the wound. I was not so much surprised, therefore, when in the next case which occurred I found a similar dispo-sition.

James Hughes, aged twenty-seven, was admitted into the New York Hospital, January 25, 1865, with necrosis of the bones of the cranium. He had had chancre and bubo eight years before, the bubo suppurating. No evident symptoms of secondary syphilis followed, though at various times he had suffered much from pains in the bones. Some months previous to his admission, he found a painful swelling on his forehead, and soon after another on the vertex, and another on the right side behind the ear. These sluggishly enlarged, and, after about six months, opened and discharged pus. The wounds have never healed. The orifices were pouting, and the probe detected dead bone over a considerable surface, covered by un-dermined integument. An operation was performed on the vertex, which was the point most extensively diseased, in the latter part of 1865. The bone was exposed, and the diseased area was found to embrace about two square inches, of an oval form. This was bare of periosteum, of a brownish color, and

11

evidently dead. The living was separated from the dead bone by a line of demarcation, which was tolerably distinct, but which showed no evidence at any point that separation had commenced. With the *rongeur* the dead bone was thoroughly gnawed away, till, at all points, living, bleeding bone was reached. The wound was dressed lightly. Imperfect attempts at granulation were observed for a time, but it soon became evident that the whole surface of the wound was dead, and that the necrosis was extending. He left the hospital in December, 1865, and soon after entered Bellevue Hospital. After he had been in Bellevue about a year, the disease having, in the mean time, spread very extensively, Dr. F. H. Hamilton

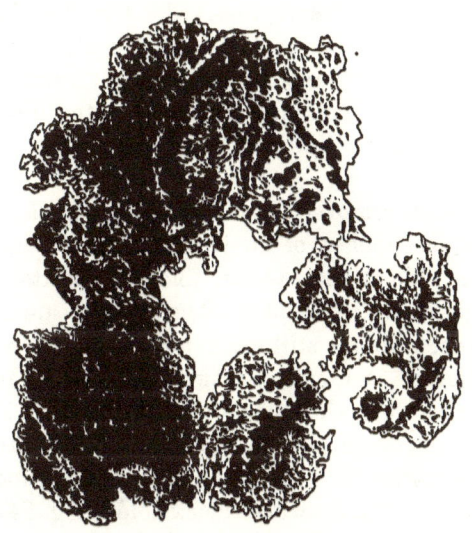

Fig. 24.—(Bellevue Hospital Museum.)

performed an operation, November 26, 1866, for the removal of the dead bone, hoping that by this time, nearly two years having elapsed since the commencement of the disease, separation would have taken place. To some extent his anticipations proved correct; and one large piece, including the whole vertex, came away almost without difficulty. At some points, however, even of this piece, the separation was not complete, and the bone had to be broken in order to remove it. At several other periods similar operations were performed, removing larger or smaller pieces of partially-separated dead bone, a great part of the bone removed embracing both tables of the skull.

His present condition, July, 1868, shows all the central part of the crown of the head occupied by a depressed scar, as large as the palm of the hand. Of this scar, a portion about two inches by three evidently has no bone underneath it, the whole thickness of the cranium having here been removed. The movements of the brain can be felt and seen at this point. Some irregular ossification has taken place in this central space; but, where this is found, some hair is growing, showing that at these points the integuments, and therefore probably the pericranium, had been preserved. On the right side of this central scar, which seems soundly healed, are numerous openings, which lead down to dead bone, showing that, after the lapse of four years, the progress of the disease is not arrested. His general health is good. No signs of syphilitic disease.

The portions removed in the two largest pieces embrace about ten square inches, of an irregular square shape, extending on either side of the median line, the sagittal suture running through nearly its middle. The surfaces are irregular, as if worm-eaten, which is still more marked on the edges. The largest portion of each of these two pieces shows that the disease has embraced both tables of the skull. The signs of the original gnawing operation are seen in the upper surface of the removed sequestrum, and the external surface around this point is deeply stained of a brownish-black color (Fig. 24).

A third case occurred in the hospital service of Dr. Gurdon Buck. John Roberts, aged thirty-three, was admitted into the New York Hospital, January 18, 1868, with extensive necrosis of the skull. Twelve years before, he had had a chancre, followed by a non-suppurating bubo. Secondary symptoms ensued, eruptions on the skin, sore throat, loss of uvula, and pains in the bones. About ten months before his admission, a reddish swelling commenced on his forehead, which suppurated slowly, breaking and discharging pus about eight months after its commencement. Similar sores have since appeared at inter-

vals, scattered on the top of the head. His general health has
been good. On admission there were numerous undermined
ulcers scattered over the front and upper part of the head,
varying in size from that of a pea to that of a dollar, and all
presenting dead bone more or less exposed to view. The discharge was considerable, and fetid. The surface of the dead
bone has not the smooth, even appearance of a bone which has
died in full health, but gives evidence, by its roughness and
irregular erosions, that some changes, probably inflammatory,
have preceded its actual death. Some of these erosions penetrate the thickness of the skull, and give issue to matter from
beneath the bone. At these points the pulsations of the brain can
be seen. On the 24th of January Dr. Buck proceeded to an
operation in which he proposed to remove all of the dead bone
which could be safely got away. Several of the anterior ulcers
were laid into one by communicating incisions, and the flaps
raised, thus exposing largely the diseased surfaces. It was found
that the whole surface was dead ; but, though a line of demarcation could be distinctly traced, separation had taken place at but
few points. The bone in the immediate neighborhood seemed
perfectly healthy. With the *rongeur* principally, by a mixed
process of breaking and cutting, the whole of the cranial portion of the frontal half of each parietal, and a portion of each
temporal bone, were removed, exposing the dura mater over the
whole of this extensive surface. This membrane was thickened and granulating. The posterior half of the vault of the
cranium, which was found to be in the same condition, was reserved for a future operation.

For a few days after the operation, all went on well, and
the wound put on a healthy, reparative appearance. On the
1st of February, however, he had a chill, followed by fever.
This was repeated after several days. Gradually headache and
blindness came on, and soon after convulsions, coma, and death
on the 18th of February.

Inflammation of the meninges was found, on *post-mortem*
examination, with numerous small abscesses scattered through
the most superficial portion of the brain-substance. The necrosis was found even more extensive than we had supposed,
occupying the whole of the cranial vault (Fig. 25).

Several other cases of this formidable disease have occurred under my observation, but these seem sufficient to illustrate its clinical features. I have tried to trace the processes preceding death of the bone in several of these cases, but can only say that it seems to be a slow process of inflammation, in which

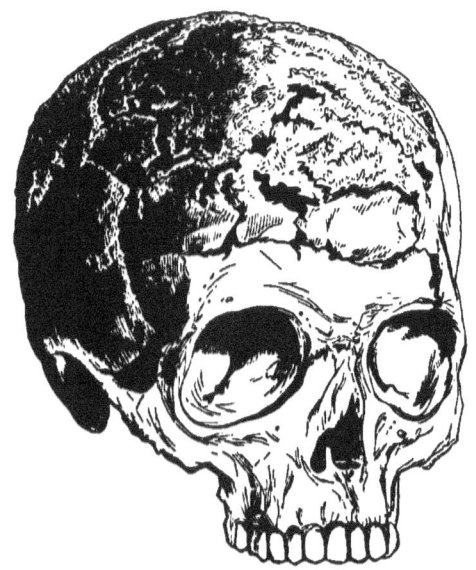

Fig. 25.—(N. Y. Hospital Museum.)

sometimes a mere vascularity of the bone about to die is detected; in other cases the bone is thickened; in others a deposit of a granular, pumice-like appearance takes place on the surface, but whether from the bone before its death or from the living tissues after death, I have not yet been able to detect. Again, erosions and ulcerations of the diseased bone are discovered, which must of course have taken place before actual death has occurred; but the whole process is so gradual that it is not easy to pronounce at any moment what part of the bone is still alive and active, and what is dead and unchanging.

That the peculiarities of the disease now described depend upon some constitutional vice, and not upon the pathological dispositions of the cranial bones, would seem to be clearly shown by the behavior of these same bones under other conditions.   Thus simple traumatic causes produce, in the cranium, a necrosis which differs in none of its clinical features from necrosis occurring elsewhere.   For example: John Murphy, aged twenty-six, in June, 1868, struck the top of his head, in rising from a stooping position, against the iron surface of some machinery he was engaged in oiling.   The contused part inflamed and formed an abscess, which, after discharging, refilled and continued to close and open several times.   He came to the New York Hospital in August, about two months after the injury, with the wound still unhealed.   The probe detected dead bone.   Another opening formed, leaving a considerable space between the two orifices where the undermined integument covered bare bone.   On the 22d of September an incision was made joining the two openings, and then extended so as to expose the dead surface.   It was found nearly round in shape, and about two square inches in size.   A probe introduced under the edge of the sequestrum, which showed clear evidences of separation, loosened the whole piece, and it came away entire.   The main portion of this piece was a thin plate comprising the outer table only, but at several points the whole thickness of the bone was involved at these points.   In the granulating bed, from which it was removed, the pulsations of the brain could be seen.   The wound healed rapidly, and the patient was discharged cured.   In another case, a man was brought to the hospital, wounded by a pistol-ball at the upper and posterior part of the neck.   In trying to trace the ball, it was found to have sunk down deep in the muscular mass between the occiput and atlas, but we could not find it.   Great inflammation and extensive suppuration followed, and, after many weeks, dead bone could be felt by the probe.   In due time an operation was done by Dr. H. B. Sands, by which the occiput was exposed by a long incision, the muscles being partly incised and partly detached.   It was found that the bottom of the wound was formed by the occipital bone in a condition of necrosis, and that the sequestrum was already loose.   By careful manipulation the whole piece was extracted in shape and size much resembling the squamous portion of the temporal bone, and some of it embracing both tables of the skull.   In the centre of the piece removed was found the opening made by the ball, which was also found lying loose in the wound. The man made a rapid recovery.

Again, as illustrating another form of necrosis of the skull, a man was struck at the battle of New Orleans by a glancing ball which bruised the vertex without breaking the skin. Abscess formed at the injured point and remained unhealed. Some months after, I saw him, and, finding dead bone, made an incision and removed several pieces, embracing the whole thickness of the bone, which, from the cleanness of their edges, were undoubtedly fragments which had been broken by the original blow and had subsequently died.

· With regard to treatment, these simple traumatic cases are satisfactory enough; but in the constitutional form my own experience is not encouraging. None of the usual remedies employed have seemed to exert any influence on its course, and surgical interference is apparently able to effect only the removal of the consequences of the disease, without arresting its progress. It is true, perhaps, that in the hopes of spontaneous separation we have wasted time and abated effort in the administration of remedies; and it is much to be hoped that something may yet be discovered that will at least control the march of this obstinate and dangerous disorder; but thus far I have no evidence that any remedy has any positive influence in arresting its fatal march.

The following case I condense from Dr. Agnew's report, who kindly sent me the specimens from which the figures are taken: W. C., aged thirty-eight, had suffered with otitis media of both ears from the age of six years. He retained his hearing partially until about three years before Dr. Agnew saw him, when an acute attack of deep-seated and very severe inflammation in the right ear terminated in complete deafness, accompanied with paralysis of the portio dura of that side.

"The patient came under my observation for the first time on the 16th of April, 1862, presenting evidences of great suffering and debility. He had suffered greatly for months from gnawing pain in the ear, insomnia, loss of appetite, and dizziness. An examination of the external ear was effected with great difficulty, on account of its excessive tenderness. The concha, swollen and inflamed, was elevated by a dense inflammatory tumefaction, circumscribing the external meatus, extending backward over the mastoid process, and forward along the zygoma. Projecting from the meatus was a large pear-shaped polypus of a dense fibrous character, bathed by a constant flow of stinking pus. Desiring to get to the bottom of the case, I placed the patient under chloroform, and removed the polypoid mass by means of a wire snare. In attempting to push the snare to the bottom of the meatus, I encountered a solid obstacle in the region of the middle ear, which subsequently proved to be the sequestrum, represented by the accompanying woodcut. The calibre of the external meatus had been much reduced by boggy swelling of its soft parts, so that I was compelled to make as free an incision as possible to enable me to reach the sequestrum with a pair of small dressing-forceps. Having got the body in the grasp of the forceps, a slight rocking motion with traction enabled me to extract it.

Fig. 26.

"It will be observed that the sequestrum includes the wreck of the labyrinth. The cochlea is shown laid open by caries, and two of the semicircular canals are seen in part. The loss of hearing and paralysis of the seventh pair were explained. Two views in fac-simile are given of the sequestrum in the woodcut, and an attempt has been made by the artist to represent the eroded appearances. The remains of the anterior semicircular canal are indicated by the letter C; and the cochlea B, opened by caries, shows the lamina spiralis. The vestibule is bereft of its furniture and almost obliterated.

"After the operation the patient rapidly regained his health, and by the 3d of January, 1863, the external meatus had become closed by cicatrization. The paralysis still remains."

The patient was subsequently seized with an acute otitis interna of the left ear, which went on to suppuration, and proved fatal by extension of the inflammation to the brain. On *post mortem* the dura mater covering the petrous portion of the temporal bone was very much thickened, and a small abscess was found in the brain immediately above the diseased bone. Fig. 27 shows the appearance of each external meatus after maceration. Both of them are enlarged and irregular, from carious ulceration, and one of them almost closed by an osseous growth, as large as a pea, springing from the ulcerated margin of the meatus. Smaller exostoses of the same kind are forming at several other points round each meatus.

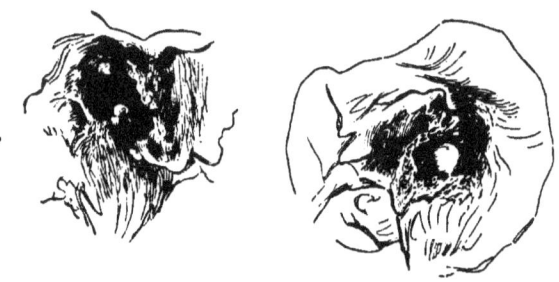

FIG. 27.—(From a specimen in Dr. Agnew's collection.)

A fourth class of cases worthy of special study embraces those which occur in the jawbones. Of the cases of necrosis occurring in these bones we have a great variety, which differ in no important respect from cases of necrosis elsewhere. We have among them, however, two special classes requiring particular mention, and these—1. Those occurring in consequence of the eruptive fevers. 2. Those arising from the poison of phosphorus. The cases occurring after eruptive fevers were first brought to the notice of the profession by S. I. A. Salter, in a paper published in Guy's Hospital Reports. Their dependence as a cause upon the eruptive disease he considers proved by their almost invariable association, and he gives the following account of the symptoms: "A little child has just recovered from one of the eruptive fevers, most probably scarlatina; the case has been in no way unusual as to its severity or its course: within six weeks or two months of the passing off of the acute symptoms, tenderness of the mouth is complained of, and the mother notices fetor of the breath. Upon inspecting the mouth, the gum is seen to be peeling from the edge of the jaw around the neck or necks of some temporary tooth or teeth; pus is discharging, and more or less dead bone is exposed. The denudation of bone progresses rather quickly in depth, but usually not, after the first, in lateral extent; the temporary teeth at the affected part become loose and often fall out. There is no swelling, and no ossifying callus is formed in the region of the necrosed bone. In a few weeks from the first of these symptoms, the sequestrum itself becomes loose, and is easily removed, leaving a large gap and a raw granulating surface which rapidly heals. The necrosis almost always includes the bone which constitutes the loculi containing the developing permanent teeth, as well as the alveoli of the temporary; but it does not go farther, and in the lower jaw the base of the bone is very rarely affected." Mr. Salter further states that this affection occurs only after the eruptive fevers, and that it attacks children from three to eight years of age. He regards it as a self-limiting disorder, requiring only such treatment as local cleanliness and general supporting regimen. The resulting deformity arises principally from the loss of the teeth.

The cases of necrosis of the jaws from exposure to the fumes of phosphorus make a much more interesting and a much more important class, and have during the past few years attracted a great deal of attention. They present themselves, almost exclusively, among the operatives in the match-manufactories, and only in those who have been long exposed to the poisonous emanations. The substance which acts as the producing cause of the mischief is undoubtedly phosphorus-vapor, usually existing as phosphorous and phosphoric acid with probably some free phosphorus. It was at one time thought that arsenic was, in some degree at least, connected with the production of the necrosis, this substance being contained in some ordinary and impure specimens of phosphorus. This suspicion has not been verified, and it is now, after careful investigation, believed that the phosphorus alone is the poisonous agent. The efficient action of the cause seems to depend mainly on two things: first, a long-continued exposure to the poison ; and, secondly, some condition, either of the teeth or gums, which favors the entrance of the poison into direct contact with the tissues. In regard to the first, writers are unanimous as to the fact that it is only after very prolonged exposure that necrosis occurs, so much so that there are scarcely any cases on record in which some years have not elapsed before the disease developed itself. The dangerous exposure takes place in only two departments of the manufacture, viz., the dipping-room, and the counting and packing rooms. In these the patients are subjected to an atmosphere constantly impregnated with the fumes of phosphorus, and this air is still further contaminated by the frequent catching fire of the matches, which generates a large quantity of phosphorous acid, and that, too, in the immediate neighborhood of the face of the patient, so that it is extremely easy for the poisonous fumes, which are quite soluble in water, to come in direct contact with the mucous membranes of the mouth and nose, and also with the bronchial mucous surface. Why the poison of phosphorus does not affect the Schneiderian and bronchial mucous membrane does not appear; but the fact is stated by Von Bibra and Geist, whose work on this subject is the most complete we have, that there is, among the patients thus exposed, no special tendency to bronchial or nasal catarrh, and no effects are noticed on the bone upon which parts of these membranes are spread. These effects seem to be reserved for the bones of the upper and lower jaw, and in these bones, after a prolonged exposure to the poison, the first symptoms of the disease appear.

But, secondly, it would appear that something besides this exposure is necessary to produce the disease, and this something is a carious condition of the teeth, or an ulcerated condition of the gums. It was early observed that this condition of the mouth was a predisposing cause of the disease, but it was only after long observation of accumulating cases that it was shown to be a uniform and an indispensably exciting cause. None of those whose teeth were perfect, and whose gums were sound, were ever attacked, while soundness was maintained, but if caries attacked the teeth, or ulceration the gums, or, worse than all, if a tooth had been recently extracted, then the persons so affected became liable to the development of the disease. From the slow action of such a cause one would be led to anticipate that some evidence of constitutional vitiation would precede the local manifestation. This does not seem to be so, and those who suffer most are oftentimes the most vigorous and healthy of the workmen, maintaining every indication of constitutional soundness up to the moment when the local disease begins to infect and involve the general system.

The first symptoms of the disease, then, are strictly local. A toothache is generally the first complaint, and this may be intermittent, returning at irregular intervals, until it becomes a constant and very distressing symptom, spreading over the whole side of the face. The gums now begin to inflame and ulcerate, and the parts about the jaw become tumefied. Inflammation of the whole affected part is now active, and soon an abscess forms, usually discharging itself alongside of one of the teeth through the ulcerated alveolus. Now, retraction of the gums from the teeth, and exposure of the bone of the jaw, gradually come on until, in a great many cases, the whole dental arch projects into the cavity of the mouth bare of periosteum, and perfectly dead. Numerous sinuses usually form, some opening into the mouth, and some on the cutaneous surface, and from these escapes in large quantity a fetid pus, which, constantly flowing into the mouth, is one of the most offensive and distressing symptoms of the disease; much of it must be swallowed, and can hardly fail to add to the derangement of the digestive function, already impaired by the progress of the malady. As the disease advances, involving a greater and greater portion of the jawbone, the swelling of the face becomes enormous, and the aspect of the patient, particularly if both sides be involved, is hideous and revolting. Soon the system begins to sympathize, and emaciation and hectic are slowly developed. In this respect a good deal of difference is observed, according to the irritability of the patient's constitution, some being affected earlier in the disease as well as more severely. But one point has been distinctly settled, viz., that the constitutional symptoms do not show themselves until after the local disease has manifested itself; the poison, though acting extremely slowly, not appearing to influence the general health until it does so through the effect of the local ravages of the disease. The constitution, however, once affected, rapidly gives way under the constant suffering and exhausting discharges. The patients become pale and emaciated, the digestive system giving out early; hectic fever is established, the strength fails, and the patient dies worn out by months or even years of painful disease.

In regard to this point, of the constitutional impairment

not depending on the direct action of the poison upon the system, Dr. Geist is very explicit, asserting unequivocally that the health of the operatives, not affected with the local disease, is as good as, if not better than, that of operatives in other manufactories. He goes still further, and states that, although the acid and irritating fumes of the phosphorus are so constantly inhaled, no peculiar prevalence of bronchitis or nasal catarrh has been noticed to occur. These facts, together with the facts above stated, that the disease never occurs in perfectly healthy mouths, but always requires a carious tooth or an ulcerated gum for the starting-point of the inflammation, seem to show very conclusively that the action of the poison is entirely local, a view which becomes more important when we address ourselves to the prophylaxis of the complaint.

The swelling about the necrosed jaw feels very hard, and gives to the touch the idea of an involucrum forming about the dead bone, but, so far as I know, no proper involucrum is ever formed. There is found on dissection a great thickening and induration of the tissues about the bone, but no ossification of them. Between the separated periosteum, however, and the dead bone, there is noticed a material which I believe is not found in any other similar disease. It consists of a grayish powdery deposit, which in varying quantities is found to adhere either to the bone or to the granulating surface of the cavity in which it lies. Sometimes this deposit adheres closely to these granulations, and, having some consistence, forms a tolerably firm layer, which seems very much like an involucrum. It will be noticed, however, that this layer is not a proper ossification of the surrounding tissues, but a mere lamina upon the surface which can, with more or less facility, be peeled off from the granulations on which it lies. On examination this substance is found to possess a chemical constitution and a microscopical structure which is that of true bone, but differing from true bone in the completeness of its development. Von Bibra says: " The Haversian canals exhibit in part a larger diameter than those of normal bone, and are empty. .... They are not parallel with the general direction of the bone, but are placed at right angles to the latter; they interlace with one another, sometimes expanding to form sacs, sometimes contracting and ending with open mouths on the surface. These mouths are more minute in the most recent deposit, and appear larger in older layers. The bone-corpuscles are rounded off or angular, and their circumference is less decided; during the progress of the formation of the deposit they are very large, and their contour proportionally undefined. They appear filled and dark-colored. At first they are lighter, and they have ramifications like those of normal bone, which increase in number with the age of the deposit. . . . The matrix of the new deposit is at first very brittle; after the deposit has been exposed to the process of absorption it shows a powdery appearance, as if sprinkled with a coarse powder."

This deposit seems, therefore, evidently to represent an attempt on the part of Nature to form some new bone to take the place of that which is destroyed; but it is also evident that this attempt falls short of the success which it usually attains in other cases of necrosis. Why this involucral effort should be so imperfect and so unsuccessful, it is not easy to say, but the pathological fact cannot be gainsaid. The following appearances were noted in a case which occurred under the care of Dr. Willard Parker, at the New York Hospital, and give, perhaps, a correct idea of the usual pathological condition, with reference to this pumice-like deposit: In exposing the bone after the first incisions, " it was noticed that in some parts, particularly along the base, the bone was entirely separated from the soft parts by a suppurating and granulating surface, such as is ordinarily seen between an involucrum and a sequestrum, while at other points the flap was peeled up from the bony surface by a process somewhat like that by which the dura mater is peeled from the skull-cap, or like that by which the periosteum can be peeled from the surface of an inflamed bone. This raising of the flap revealed the bone, presenting two different conditions of its surface: one a smooth, natural, evidently dead surface; the other a rough, granular, and irregular surface, to which the soft parts adhered as above stated, and which did not seem to be dead-bone tissue, while at the same time it was not the usual vascular-bone surface of an involucrum. The smooth dead bone was in contact with pus, the other of course was not. After fully exposing the bone a chain-saw was introduced near the symphysis, and the body of the bone was divided and raised from its bed. As with the outside, so with the inner aspect of the bone, some of it was separated from the soft parts by a suppurating surface, and some of it adhered rather strongly to the surrounding parts. So strong was the adhesion that at the upper part of the angle and neck portions of the bony deposit flaked off and were left behind in the bed from which the bone was being removed. This had every appearance of being an involucrum at first sight, and we were in some doubt as to whether it was best to leave it. On using the handle of the scalpel, however, the soft parts were easily peeled from it, and it was enucleated and removed. The jawbone separated as usual at the joint and came away entire, and without any considerable force. The removal of the bone left a bed which was composed in part of suppurating and granulating surface, such as is usually left on the removal of a sequestrum, and in part of a whitish, rough, vascular surface, looking not unlike the surface of the dura mater recently peeled from the skull. This seemed clearly to be the inner surface of the periosteum, which had been adherent to the rough deposit on the surface of the bone, and from which, beyond a doubt, the deposit had been poured out. There was no osseous deposit in the periosteum, and no surrounding ossification, as might be expected around so large a sequestrum; in short, nothing but thickened tissues represented the involucrum. . . . The examination of the jaw showed the whole bone to be dead, but not much altered from its natural appearance. On the outer and inner surfaces of the jaw there was an irregular, granular, stalagmitic deposit of bone, somewhat firmly adherent to the dead surface underneath, and looking better organized and more osseous in its appearance than the pumice-like deposit as it is usually described. The deposit was in laminæ more or less complete, and varied in thickness from a line to nearly half an inch. . . . In the main this deposit was adherent to the dead surface of the bone by a sort of mechanical adhesion, but in some points, particularly at its edges, there was a thin membrane between them, so that, while the whole was wet, some motion could be made between the bone

and its false involucral covering (Fig. 28). Under the microscope, the bony character of the deposit was unmistakable."

It is agreed by all the observers of this disease that the
reparation after the removal of the necrosed lower jaw is very
complete, more so perhaps than in any other bone in the body.
In this respect, therefore, it would seem that Nature plans her
reparative work somewhat differently from the mode she elsewhere adopts. In all ordinary cases of necrosis, the periosteum,

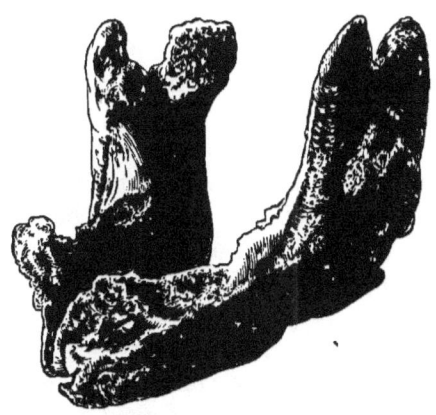

Fig. 28.—(N. Y. Hospital Museum.)

which is the principal agent in forming the new bone, begins
its work before a breach is made in the dying bone, and sur-
rounds the part which is dead and about to separate with a
layer of new bone, so as to be ready to meet the accident of
separation which is about to occur; and before the sequestrum
is removed, or even loose, enough involucrum has been formed
to supply the loss. This admirable provision seems to be intended to prevent the limb from being rendered useless during
the process of separation, by supplying a temporary support
which shall be competent to maintain the functions of the dying
bone throughout the whole process.

In the lower jaw this provision does not seem to be made.
There is no new bone deposited about the sequestrum until it
is got rid of; and it is a curious fact that, however long the
sequestrum may be allowed to remain, the formation of new
bone is still withheld until the foreign body shall be taken out

of the way. After this disturbing cause is removed, however, the process of reparation is very quickly established, and with results which in some instances are truly wonderful. The general shape of the jaw is preserved, the angle is distinct; the coronoid process can be felt, and the muscles seem to have as firm and favorable attachment as ever, while the movements of the jaw are entirely preserved. An excellent illustration of this regeneration was presented in one of our New York Hospital cases, which occurred in Dr. Halsted's care in 1856; the operation of removal of one-half of the jaw was performed in January, 1857, and in December following I have noted: "The half of the jaw removed is replaced by firm bone, in which the angle of the jaw is marked, though not quite as acute as it should be, and the coronoid process is also clear. The whole new bone is a little smaller than the original, but is a remarkable imitation of it. The alveolar border is prominent into the mouth, and he can chew upon it very well." In another case, the one already mentioned, where, at two distinct operations, the whole jaw was removed, I have recorded: "Some months after the operation," referring to the last one, "I saw him and was surprised at the small amount of deformity. An ingenious dentist had adapted a pair of plates with teeth to the absent jaw with great success. The plates rested on a firm cicatricial mass which occupied the place of the removed bone, but it was not certain that any deposit of bony matter had taken place." These two cases present a difference of result which I think has some interest as bearing upon the nature and significance of the pumice-like deposit. In the first there was rapid and complete regeneration by bone; in the latter no bony deposit after the lapse of nearly a year. Now, by referring to the history of the two cases, I find that, in the first, it is explicitly stated that at the time of operation there was no bony involucrum, and no pumice-like deposit; while, in the second, the pumice-like deposit was in very great abundance. In the first, therefore, we find Nature delaying all ossific action until the sequestrum was removed, and then beginning it promptly and carrying it on efficiently to the perfect regeneration of the lost bone; in the second we have a premature, imperfect, and unsuccessful attempt at ossification

12

before the sequestrum is removed, in which the disposition to
form a new bone is frittered away, so that after the operation
there seems no tendency left toward ossification, and a fibro-
cartilage is all that Nature seems willing to undertake. This it
seems to me is a fair view of the significance of this peculiar
deposit—peculiar, I believe, to the phosphorus cases, and I am
therefore disposed to regard it when in great abundance as an
evil sign, and to fear that its presence, before the operation,
indicates the absence of a more healthy and useful ossification
afterward.

An important practical question here arises: What shall the
surgeon do with this layer of imperfect bone-deposit when he encounters it in his operations. Shall it be removed or shall it be
left? If we believe that it is capable of taking part in the regeneration which we hope for, after the removal of the jaw,
then it should be left. If, however, we believe that it is incapable, both from its nature and the situation in which it is found,
of taking on any higher organization, and thus becoming part
of the new bone, then it would be better to remove it. Without having any facts positively bearing on this point, I am inclined to consider it in the light of an excrementitious substance,
not available for regeneration, and therefore to be removed
whenever it adheres to the granulations. Fortunately, this
question is most commonly solved for us by the deposit adhering to the dead bone rather than to the granulations, and being
removed with the sequestrum, to which it is sometimes very

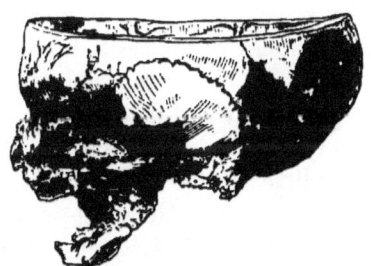

Fig. 29.—(From Bellevue Hospital Museum, operated on by Dr. James R. Wood.)

intimately adherent. Fig. 29 shows almost complete reformation of lower jaw after phosphorous necrosis.

The upper jawbone is also liable to the ravages of the phosphorus-disease. Indeed, the statistics given by several observers show that it is affected nearly if not quite as often as the lower jaw. The disease in the upper jaw presents no features different from those already described, except that all observers agree that very little, if any, bony regeneration takes place. The gap, left by the fall of the sequestrum, is filled by a firm fibrous, or even fibro-cartilaginous substance, which partially obviates the deformity, and also serves by its firmness as a tolerable substitute for the absent bone, but usually no ossification takes place.

The prognosis of this formidable disease is more favorable than would at first sight appear. The disease being so essentially local, and the general system only involved in sympathy with the local disorder, we have usually a prompt recovery when the local cause of irritation is removed. The principal writers on this subject mention very few cases which proved fatal, and in our New York experience of the last twenty years I do not remember one which destroyed life. This favorable prognosis, after the disease has accomplished its destructive mission, must not lead us to expect to find it tractable or manageable in its early stages. It will rather be found that when once the local action of the poison has declared itself, no removal of residence, no cessation of exposure, no surgical treatment, no complete removal of the dead bone, will arrest the progress of the forming disease, or limit its ravages when fully developed. It would rather seem that, when once the local poisoning has been so complete as to produce the initial symptom of the disease, we may count with much confidence that it will proceed through all its stages, not much influenced by the remedies or regimen with which we combat it.

With regard to treatment, from what has been already said, we can hope for but little in the direct control of the disease, but much can be done which shall mitigate suffering, and perhaps shorten its period. And first, as a matter of course, removal from exposure to the fatal fumes must be insisted on. All favorable hygienic conditions must be secured as far as circumstances will permit, and, above all, cleanliness of the diseased parts by frequent ablutions, so that the discharges shall

be kept from becoming decomposed, and in that state finding
their way into the stomach. For this purpose, warm water
freely and frequently used is the most efficient of all detergents;
but, owing to the soreness of the parts and the difficulty of
motion, both of the tongue and the jaws, patients are unwilling
or careless about its use; and it is better, particularly with the
least intelligent, to make some formal prescription which will
be much more likely to receive attention. A weak solution of
tincture of myrrh, perhaps combined with a few drops of Labar-
raque's solution of chloride of soda, makes an excellent and not
disagreeable wash, which gently stimulates the granulating surfaces while it cleanses the mouth. Attention must also be paid
to the diet of the patients. They cannot chew, and the food
must therefore be soft. The condition of the mouth prevents
them from enjoying the taste of what they eat, and this, with
the want of appetite, will lead them to neglect themselves in
this important particular. It is therefore the surgeon's duty
to see that they have the right food, and that they partake of
it in proper quantities and at proper intervals. Milk and
meat-soups, with eggs, will form the most convenient and
nourishing forms of diet, varying the form to suit the changing
taste. Tonics, as iron and quinine, and bitters, will be appropriate as medicines, while, in many cases, stimulants will be
required, either in the milder form of ale or porter, or in the
more decided shape of wine, whiskey, or brandy. This invigorating regimen is called for in almost every case, in the later
and more prolonged period after the first abscesses have broken,
and while the profuse and fetid discharge is creating a constant
drain upon the patient's strength.

The main question, however, remains as to local management; and here two views prevail: One party, fascinated
perhaps by the conservative sub-periosteal surgery of M. Ollier,
is led to devote a great deal of attention to the condition of
the periosteum surrounding the dead bone, and by various
blunt instruments thrust in between the membrane and the
bone to secure its separation and perhaps to hasten the process.
These manipulations are kept up day after day, giving the
patient a great deal of pain, wounding and bruising the tender
surfaces, and exciting sometimes not a little consecutive inflam-

mation. This preliminary treatment, as it is regarded, is intended to prepare the patient for the final separation of the bone, when the time for operation comes, so that the sequestrum shall come away easily, and the periosteum shall not be involved with it. I cannot help believing that this is bad surgery, and I think so for two reasons: First, I do not believe that with any instrument, be it ever so flexile and so delicate, we can follow the line of separation in a bone so irregular as the lower or upper jaw, nor can we accurately appreciate the extent to which the separation is going to take place. We constantly run the risk, therefore, in trying thus to interfere with the process, of wandering from the space which Nature intends to leave between the periosteum and the bone, and also of going farther in the separation than Nature proposes to go. Secondly, we gain nothing by such a course, for Nature will certainly and accurately limit the disease, and the space between the dead and living will be just as perfect and just as distinct as we can make it with our instruments. The operations are useless for the end proposed, and injurious in their effect upon the natural progress of the disease. Their principle, therefore, as well as their practice, is in my judgment equally unsound.

I would recommend, therefore, no interference with the disease, except so far as concerns letting out matter as early and freely as may be, until the time shall come when the removal of the dead mass may be wisely undertaken. And here I fear surgeons are too apt to err on the side of haste. The disease is so distressing, its features so offensive, both to patients and friends, its progress is so unmarked and so slow, that the natural tendency is to operate as soon as possible in order to be rid of so much suffering and annoyance. It is extremely desirable that no operation should be undertaken until separation be so complete that the dead can easily be removed from the living parts. This remark, however, has reference more to the connections of the bone with its articulating cavity, and with the soft parts which environ it, than to any separation which may be looked for in the continuity of the bone. The ligamentous and tendinous attachments of the bone at its articulation will in the course of a few weeks or months become so loosened that, if the whole articular extremity be dead, as is usually the case, it can be torn out of its bed by a sort of twisting motion, by the exercise of a moderate force.   The periosteum will separate from its sides in perhaps a shorter period, so that every part is detachable excepting at the point where the diseased side is continuous with the sound.   Here, Nature seems again to fail in accomplishing her usual task.   Separation either does not take place at all, or takes place so slowly and so imperfectly, that we cannot wait for its completion, and in every case which I have seen it has been necessary to divide the bone at or near the symphysis, so as to get away what was at all other points easily enucleable.   This slowness of separation seems to me characteristic of the jawbones in all their necroses, from whatever cause, where the dead part embraces any thing beyond the alveolar margins.   I have marked the same indisposition to separation in maxillary necrosis after fracture, as well as in the necrosis which occurs from excessive salivation.   In cancrum oris even in very young children the process of bone separation is marked by the same sluggishness and delay.   This general course would lead to the belief that it belonged to the bone itself rather than depended on any particular condition of disease, to undertake the duty of separation slowly and reluctantly.

The operation for the removal of the sequestrum will be modified according to the extent of the disease.   If one entire half, or if the whole bone be dead, then it is necessary to make a free incision along the base of the jaw, from above the angle to near the symphysis, and, cutting directly through the thickened tissues which represent the involucrum, expose the sequestrum freely.   The jaw should next be divided at or near the symphysis by a chain-saw, by which procedure the half we wish to remove becomes manageable.   By now carefully removing the adherent tissues from all sides, and following this dissection up to the articular condyle, we are soon able, by a sort of twisting, tearing movement, to drag the whole mass from all its remaining attachments, and it usually comes away entire.   If both sides are affected, the operation is to be repeated on the remaining half.   If, as is very often the case, the condyle is still living and sound, then no force we can safely use will bring it out of its socket, and the operation should be completed by cutting or sawing off the bone beyond the diseased point, making sure to cut through healthy, living bone-tissue, else some of the sequestrum would be left behind. Very little cutting is required after making the first incision, and there is rarely any considerable hæmorrhage. After making sure that all fragments or flakes of bone are removed, nothing remains but to bring the wound carefully together with fine sutures and dress it lightly. Sometimes it is well to dress the cavity with lint from the inside to keep it in better shape while it is granulating. This is not always necessary, however, as the firmness of the consolidated tissues generally keeps the outline of the jaw tolerably supported. The wound generally behaves extremely well, healing rapidly, and without accident or complications. If the disease be limited to a portion of the body of the jaw, then an incision will have to be made through sound, living bone on both sides of the dead piece, in order to remove it. Sometimes in these more moderate cases, and even in the most extensive, the operation has been practised through the mouth without external incision. This is of course a more tedious process, but wherever it can be done I think it should be attempted, particularly in females, to save the deformity of so extensive a scar.

With regard to recurrence after removal, it is not very unfrequent, even if the patient be not again exposed to the vapors of phosphorus, for the disease to extend beyond the limits of the operation, or to show itself in some new part either of the upper or lower jawbones, and to require a second operation perhaps as formidable as the first. This, however, must be, if the first operation be not too hastily performed, an unusual occurrence.

The upper jaw presents some features in which it differs from the lower jaw in this disease. It is attacked nearly as frequently as the lower jaw, but generally to a more limited extent. The destruction is mostly confined to the alveolar arch, in bad cases, however, involving the bone more extensively. There is but little of the immense brawny swelling which represents the involucrum in the lower jaw, and there seems to be a greater readiness to effect the separation of the sequestrum. The operation is usually simpler, performed more easily

through the mouth than is the case in the lower jaw, and consists mainly in freeing mucous membrane so as to permit of
the pulling out of the loosened dead mass. It is also to be
noticed that no reparation by bone takes place in the upper
jaw, and scarcely any compensating fibrous deposit fills up the
void. The deformity is very great, therefore, and it is fortunate
that the art of the dentist enables him to remedy, in so satisfactory a manner, both the deformity and the disability.

5. *Necrosis after Fractures.*—Nothing is more common
than to find the ends of the broken bone, in compound fractures,
in a state of necrosis. Long exposed to air, in contact with
pus, and with the periosteum perhaps stripped up to a certain
extent by the original injury, it is not surprising that the most
exposed and the most injured bone-fibres should be liable to
die. Accordingly, we find it rather the exception, in compound
fractures in adults, that the wound heals soundly without any
exfoliation of bone. Most commonly the broken end sheds, at
the end of two or more months, a small section of bone, which
finds its way to the surface, and is easily removed without its
presence having in any material degree interfered with the
prompt and complete uniting of the fracture. This necrosis,
however, may be more extensive, more of the bone may be
involved, and thus we have sometimes one or more considerable sequestra lying between the ends of the bone,
interfering with their union and keeping up an excessive
and an unnecessary suppuration. In these cases the earlier
stages of the fracture may not be characterized by any unfavorable symptoms. The wounds may go on favorably toward
healing, and union may occur of the broken bone; but the
wounds do not actually heal, and solid union is delayed. Fistulous openings lead down to bare, dead bone, and the whole
region of the fracture presents an unusual degree of thickening
and induration. This state of things may continue indefinitely;
and, indeed, the patient may be walking about on his limb,
month after month, and yet no bone comes away, and the
wound does not heal. Or it may happen that union is imperfect, or altogether prevented by the presence of some more
important sequestrum between the fragments which have otherwise every disposition toward healthful repair. In one case,

union of a broken femur had been delayed for many months by a fragment of dead bone lying crosswise between the ends; and a feeble bridge of delicate bone is the only attempt which the specimen shows toward the union of the fragments separated, by this foreign body, nearly an inch from one another.

This condition of things is brought about in one of two ways. Either the ends of the fragments die from exposure in the wound, or else original fragments, separated more or less completely from the shaft, die from the same exposure soon after the accident. The difference can be easily recognized in examining the sequestrum, which, in the former case, will always present the irregular worm-eaten surface, which shows where it has been detached by a process of absorption; while the latter shows, on all sides, the evidences of original fractured surfaces.

Fig. 30 shows the ends of each fragment in a compound fracture of tibia in a state of necrosis, with the line of separation well marked, at a little less than an inch from the fracture. Both fragments are affected to about the same extent, and the deposition of callus from the living bone, above and below the line of separation, is hardly begun, though several weeks had elapsed since the injury. This sequestrum, when detached, would have presented one surface of original fracture, and one where it was irregular from detachment by absorption, showing that it was not an original fragment which had died, but a piece separated by Nature long after the injury.

Fig. 31 shows the appearance of a dead, original fragment *in situ*. It was taken from a man, nineteen years old, who suffered a compound fracture from a fall. He struggled for six months to repair his injury, but at the end of that time no union had occurred, and an operation was performed by cutting down at the seat of fracture and removing the large sequestrum which lay between the broken extremities of the bone. Examination showed this to be an original fragment separated at the time of the accident, and dying in consequence of its detachment from the surrounding living tissues. It lay almost transversely between the bones, and, although the young man lingered four months after the removal of the dead piece, yet scarce any union was accomplished, a feeble bridge of bone at the posterior part of the space being all that Nature could accomplish. In the preparation of the specimen the fragment was replaced in its original position, and so appears in the woodcut.

FIG. 30.—(N. Y. Hospital Museum.)   FIG. 31.—(N. Y. Hospital Museum.)

This death of detached fragments is not uncommon in compound, but I think it must be exceedingly rare in simple fractures. The following is an interesting example: A boy entered the New York Hospital in October, 1854, with a simple fracture of both thighs and a fracture of the lower jaw. For about three weeks nothing unfavorable presented itself; but at the end of that time it was observed that the right thigh was a good deal swollen at the seat of fracture, and he had been complaining of pain and tenderness about it for several days. In about a week suppuration was evident, and a large quantity of matter was evacuated by incision. The abscess did not heal, the union of the fracture did not take place, and finally dead bone could be discovered by the probe, while a great deal of solid thickening surrounded the seat of fracture. Several months afterward an operation was performed by cutting down upon the fracture and removing the dead portion of bone. It was found to be a fragment, embracing nearly the whole thickness of the femur, which had been originally separated at the time of the accident and had died entire. Its surfaces showed very distinctly that it had not been separated by any process of absorption. The patient ultimately got a good limb. Whether in this case death of the fragment took place from complete separation, and thus produced the abscess, or whether the suppuration caused the death of the partially-detached fragment, I never was able to determine, but it is so extremely rare that suppuration takes place in a simple fracture that I incline to the first explanation.

Again, there are some cases in which necrosis after fracture involves larger portions of the bone than are either exposed in the wound, or than can be supposed to be affected by the injury. In these cases it must be supposed either that an acute osteitis has spread from the point of injury, or that a suppuration has detached the periosteum from the bone, in either case extending the area of the disease till it sometimes is found to involve the greater part of the shaft (Fig. 32).

The indications of treatment are here very clear. After allowing full time, say an average of three months, for the spontaneous detachment of the sequestrum, it is best to proceed at once to an operation for its removal. A natural unwillingness is felt to interfere with

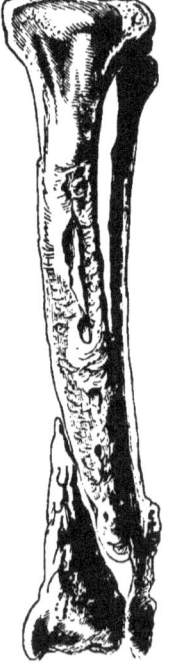

Fig. 32.—(N. Y. Hospital Museum.)

the processes of union of the fracture by a serious and disturbing operation, but this unwillingness will cease if we reflect, first, that the dead bone is itself an obstacle to good union; and,

secondly, that in old compound fractures the effect of free incisions, and free manipulation . with the fragments, is generally
to improve thé sluggish action of the parts, and to insure
a more rapid and solid union. So true is this, that in one
or two doubtful cases, where I have cut down without finding any dead bone, I have found the condition of the fracture improve so much, apparently from the stimulus of the
operation, that I have had no reason to regret my mistaken
diagnosis. Of course no unnecessary violence should be done
which might break up union already secured, and no more
bone-substance should be removed than is absolutely necessary
to insure access to the sequestrum. In one case recently, in
the thigh, I was obliged to break up the union in order to get
at the dead piece which was wedged between the overlapping
fragments. No evil consequences ensued in this case, however,
and I have got an excellent thigh.

Fracture may occur in a bone which is the subject of necrosis, and may involve the involucrum either in its forming or its
completed condition. The fracture of the involucrum during
its forming stage is probably rare, because, though it is the
weakest period of the new formation, yet the limb is usually so
little moved, in the earlier and inflammatory stages of the disease, that it is not very liable to be injured. By the time the
patient is able to use the limb with comfort, Nature has usually
accomplished the solidification of the new bone. After that
period I suppose the bone is usually less liable to fracture
through the involucrum than elsewhere, on account of the
abundant material provided for securing the strength of the
bone at the point of disease. The accident does, however,
occasionally occur, and may happen either before the removal
of the sequestrum or at some period after such removal. The
following case illustrates the fracture of the involucrum while
the sequestrum still remains imprisoned:

Mr. C., aged about thirty, a strong and otherwise healthy
butcher, had been under the care of my friend Dr. James
Fergusson, with necrosis of the left os brachii. A large sequestrum was lying loose in a cavity in the middle portion of the
shaft, and was ready for an operation, which Dr. Fergusson had
repeatedly recommended him to have performed. Mr. C.,

however, had postponed the operation from time to time, as his arm gave him but slight inconvenience, and interfered but little with the prosecution of his business. On one occasion, in trying to lift a heavy piece of meat to hang it on a high hook, he felt a sudden snap in the centre of his diseased arm, which fell helpless to his side. The bone had broken directly through the involucrum, and had torn its way through the integuments, making a bad compound fracture. Between the fragments, in a large cavity which was now quite exposed, could be seen and felt the sequestrum, which itself had not suffered fracture. It was in this condition of things I saw him in consultation. The first thing to be done was evidently to remove the foreign body. This was easily done by rotating the arm so as to separate the fragments and thus more fully expose the sequestrum. Then, by a few touches of the chisel, it was released from its bed and removed. This reduced the injury to a mere compound fracture without complication. The displacement was easily reduced and easily retained, the broad, broken surfaces of the involucrum fitting accurately into one another, and mutually supporting each other. The limb was placed in an angular tin splint, and retained in it during all the time of its union. The cure went on as rapidly as I ever saw in any compound fracture, though the large involucral cavity was somewhat slow in filling up. The wound, however, finally healed, and he had a perfectly sound and strong arm. It is at least eighteen years since the fracture, and Mr. C. has had no trouble with it since. Two other cases of a similar character, and equally fortunate issue, have occurred to me in the New York Hospital.

The next case is one in which fracture took place several months after the sequestrum was removed, and is very interesting in showing some of the remote effects of such an injury, as well as some of the serious emergencies that may arise in endeavoring to obviate them:

Mr. L., a merchant in New York, came under my care in the spring of 1870, for the relief of a deformity of his left femur, of which he gave the following history: At eight years of age he had an attack, resembling acute rheumatism, of the lower part of the left thigh. For about a year the limb continued very painful, and finally an abscess appeared under the knee,

and was opened.   Some time after this a fistulous opening appeared on the outside of the thigh, near the knee, and then a
second fistula formed on the inside.   These openings continued
to discharge, and several small pieces of bone came away at
intervals, until he was about eighteen years old, when he pulled
away a sequestrum as large as his finger.   Soon after this all
the wounds healed.   About eighteen months after, he was
thrown from his horse, and sustained a fracture of the thigh
directly at the point which had been the seat of the necrosis.
The fracture was treated with a long splint, which was kept on
for eight weeks.   During the first few days he was allowed to
move himself about in the bed, but during the rest of the
treatment he was kept quiet.   When he left his bed the limb
was quite straight, but afterward gradually became bent outward, the deformity increasing slowly up to the present time.
Four years ago another abscess appeared on the inside of the
thigh, about a hand's breadth above the knee-joint, followed by
a fistula, which has ever since continued to discharge.   During
the last month the discharge has increased.   Latterly there has
been some inflammatory pain about the knee-joint.   Thinks
that the sensibility of the left foot and ankle has been less
than that of the right.   His present condition is that of vigorous
health, though he thinks it has failed a little in the last few
months.   The thigh is bent at the junction of the lower and
middle third, or a little below this point, so as to make a great
prominence outward, throwing the leg out, so as to make very
serious deformity, and to give him a most ungainly walk.   The
limb, however, is strong, and with a cane he can walk well.
The fistula discharges quite freely, though the probe does not
come in contact with dead bone.   The knee-joint is quite rigid,
and gradually becoming more and more so.   It has on several
occasions been swollen and painful, so as, for a few days at a
time, to prevent his going down to his business.

On the 21st of May, 1870, assisted by Dr. George A. Peters,
Dr. Chamberlain, and Dr. Delafield, I undertook an operation
for the relief of the deformity, and for the removal of any
sequestrum I might find.   An incision was made, beginning at
the fistula and extending upward, by which the surface of the
bone was reached, and, after much labor with the thickened

periostenm, and the consolidated tissues around it, was exposed. No dead bone was seen or felt, nor could we find any cavity which might contain one. Attempts were then made to break the femur, but this could not be accomplished until, by the chisel, the bone had been cut nearly through. After fracturing the bone, and cutting and stretching a few resisting aponeurotic fibres on the inside of the limb, the deformity was easily and completely obviated. The two portions of the femur were nearly in a straight line, and the limb did not appear shorter than its fellow. While pressing the limb inward, so as to straighten it more perfectly, a sudden gush of arterial blood from the wound announced the rupture of a large artery, which, from the situation and the size of the stream, we could not doubt was the popliteal. Pressure was instantly made with the finger on the iliac, and by sponges in the wound, and the flow was stopped, but not till much blood had been lost. The artery was then sought for in the wound, and, after infinite trouble and labor, what were supposed to be the two ends of the lacerated artery were secured by a ligature, and the hæmorrhage ceased. The limb was put up with the extension apparatus, with weight and pulley, in the usual manner. The length and shape of the limb were entirely satisfactory.

He came out from the influence of the ether, and all seemed so well that I left him in charge of Dr. Delafield, taking the precaution to have a tourniquet left loosely round the limb. I had not arrived at my house more than a few minutes when I was summoned with the message that he was bleeding severely. I took Dr. Gurdon Buck and Dr. Peters with me, in consultation, and on our arrival we found that the ligatures, one or both, had slipped off, or that they had not, after all our care, been fairly placed on the vessel; for the gush of blood had been as great and as rapid as at the first, and the patient was in a very alarming state of prostration. The question was between ligature of the femoral artery and amputation. Inasmuch as the ligature could not add materially to the danger of gangrene, the arterial current being already interrupted by the laceration, we concluded to tie the artery low down in Scarpa's triangle, and take what chance there was for saving the limb. This was accordingly done.

From the great loss of blood, the prolonged anæsthesia of

several hours, and the shock of three severe operations, Mr. L. was very much prostrated, and for several days rallied very slowly under careful tonic and stimulant regimen, with the cautious administration of the best food which his stomach would bear. During this critical term, however, while his capillary circulation was so extremely enfeebled, the injured limb was struggling for life. All pressure from the bandages was removed, and, as the surface was white and cold, moderate artificial heat was applied by sand-bags placed around and at some distance from the limb. The result remained several days in suspense, but gradually the circulation failed more and more completely, until June 1st, when the evidences of mortification were so distinct that amputation was performed about the middle of the thigh. The stump did well in every particular, and he rapidly regained his health and strength.

A careful dissection of the amputated limb was made, and the popliteal artery found to be lacerated just opposite the fracture which I had made, the ends of the torn vessel being widely separated; no trace of the original ligatures could be found. The nerve was intact, as was also the vein. All these were very closely bound to the bone, apparently by the condensation of the surrounding areolar tissue, from the inflammatory action which had for so many years been going on in the neighborhood. The edges of the fracture were not particularly sharp, and it seemed to me that the explanation of the accident to the artery was, that it was stretched by the straightening of the bones in such a way as to be pressed upon directly by the ends of the fragments, and, being incorporated with the surrounding consolidated tissues, it had lost its elasticity and its power of eluding pressure, and it gave way. The knee-joint showed traces of recent inflammation, and was extremely rigid. The amputated end of the femur, after maceration, was found to be thicker, harder, and heavier than in a natural state. This was most noticeable immediately about the point of old fracture, where the bone was thickened by involucral action and deposition of callus (Fig. 33). The outline of the old fracture could be distinctly traced. About an inch below the point at which I had broken the bone, a small opening of the size of a pea led into a cavity in the bone about large enough to contain

℥ij of fluid. This cavity extended up to, and was opened partly by the chisel, and partly by the fracture, which extended nearly transversely through the bone, and was without splinters. The bone had separated through the thickest part of the old

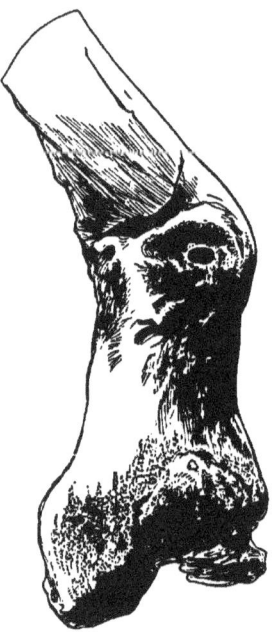

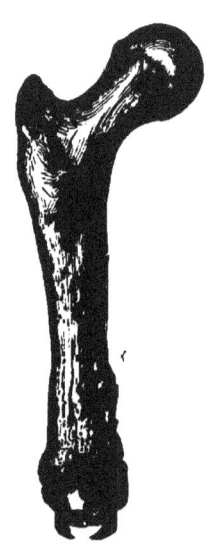

Fig. 33.—(N. Y. Hospital Museum.)   Fig. 34.—(From Billroth.)

union, where the tissue was firm, porous bone, but nowhere cancellous. The cavity was reticulated, but not rough in its surface, not indicating any thing like caries. No sequestrum was found in it, though it doubtless had contained one which had either disintegrated and come away in the discharges, or had been lost in the maceration.

With regard to the prognosis of such fractures of the involucrum, my experience has led me to expect their prompt and firm union, provided the original disease was in a favorable condition, and the sequestrum could be entirely removed.

6. *Necrosis after Amputations.*—It happens after a great many amputations that the healing of the stump is delayed by a small amount of necrosis of the end of the sawed bone. A ring of bone, injured by the violence of the saw, and remain-

13

ing exposed to the air and to the fluids of the suppurating
surface of the stump, dies and separates, usually finding its
way to the surface some weeks after the amputation, without
interfering with the healing of the wound in any other way
than to delay it (Fig. 34). In certain other cases, fortunately
much more rare, the necrosis presents more extensive and more
formidable features, sometimes involving almost the whole
shaft in its destructive results. This form of necrosis is most
commonly seen in the thigh-bone, and always in its compact
portion. I have occasionally observed it in the humerus, and
more rarely in the radius and ulna. The clinical history of
such a case is about as follows : After an amputation of the
thigh, every thing makes a satisfactory progress during the first
few weeks. The wound heals kindly, the ligatures come away,
and both patient and surgeon flatter themselves with the hopes
of an early cure. It is observed, however, that though the
ligatures are all away, and no apparent cause exists to prevent
the healing of the small portions of the wound which still
remain open, yet the wound does not heal, but continues at one
or more points to discharge matter in quantity altogether out of
proportion to the apparent granulating surface. Soon the sores
take on the exuberant pouting appearance of the granulations,
round the orifices from which matter is discharged, which at once
lead to the suspicion that there is dead bone at the bottom of
the sinuses which terminate at these openings. The stump
continues tender, and now, perhaps several weeks after the
amputation, shows more inflammatory disposition than it did
soon after it was made. The stump is also swollen and bulbous
in its appearance ; and this swelling will be found to be due to
an enlargement of the end of the bone, which is most marked
at the sawed end, and diminishes gradually toward the tro-
chanters. A probe, introduced at one of the fistulous openings,
easily recognizes a considerable portion of dead bone, very near
the surface and easily accessible for removal. The patient is
feverish, and suffers a good deal of uneasiness, and perhaps
pain in the stump, which he is very much disappointed in not
finding healed after several months of confinement. If, now,
an incision be made on the face of the stump, and the end of
the bone exposed, there will be found a ring of dead bone,

partly concealed by bony growth, which ring represents the sawed end of the bone. It will be observed, however, that this ring does not represent the whole thickness of the shaft, but rather its inner lamina, which, being dead, is surrounded by living bone, by which it is covered in as by a thick and well-formed involucrum. On seizing this ring of bone, with a strong pair of forceps, it will be found to be movable, but it is only after very powerful traction, combined with twisting and lateral movements, and sometimes after their long and energetic continuance, that the sequestrum starts from its bed, and we draw forth one of those long, irregular tubes of dead bone, of which specimens can now be seen in every museum. These tubes correspond to the inner lamellæ of the femur, or that which looks upon the medullary cavity of the bone, as is shown by the size of the inner cavity of the tube, which is that of the medullary canal; and by the appearance of the surfaces, which on the inside are those of the medullary canal unchanged, while on the outside we have the irregular, worm-eaten surface, which indicates that by a process of absorption it has been separated from the outer lamellæ, which have maintained their vitality. Not only has this outer portion of the bone maintained its life, but it has thickened and enlarged itself so as to cause the bulbous expansion of the end of the bone in which involucral expansion the sequestrum has been enclosed. These sequestra vary in size from two or three to eight or nine inches in length. They are generally more or less complete cylinders, but here and there are sometimes found openings, through which bony granulations from the involucrum may sometimes shoot, thus locking the sequestrum fast in its bed, and making it difficult or impossible to remove it without a considerable operation. The following case illustrates this particular difficulty, as well as the general features of the disease:

James Thompson, aged twenty-six, had his left thigh amputated, May 12, 1855, in the New York Hospital, for an injury to his knee-joint. The stump healed favorably, till only a small ulcer remained, and he rapidly recovered strength and health. In August it was observed that the wound had ceased to contract, that the end of the femur was much enlarged, and a probe, passed in through the ulcer, detected dead bone. The

stump now began to be occasionally painful, the discharge increased, and he was evidently losing ground. About the first of
September 'a small incision was made, and the whole circle of
the cut end of the femur was found necrosed. An attempt was
made to pull out the dead piece, but it was firmly fixed and
was 'left. The mischief in the stump went on increasing.
Abscesses formed, and opened in various directions. The discharge became very profuse, and the patient much reduced by
fever and pain. About the first of October the end of the
stump was again opened, and the sequestrum well exposed and
seized by a pair of powerful forceps. On making very strong
and steady traction it became evident that the piece was loose,
and soon it started from its bed, and was drawn out about
three-quarters of an inch, but beyond that point no force could
move it. It could be pushed back, and it could be moved a
little from side to side, but it could not, with all our force, be
drawn any farther out. Supposing that it was locked in by
bony granulations from the involucrum, it was left drawn out
as far as it would come, and each day traction was made upon
it, hoping thus to cause the absorption of the new bony deposit
which impeded its extrication. This result, however, was not
realized, and at the end of a month the sequestrum was as in-
extricable as ever, and the condition of the stump, as well as
of the patient's general health, was rapidly deteriorating. On
the 2d of November I made a free incision over the anterior
and outer face of the stump, and, exposing the involucrum, I
commenced removing it round the end of the projecting sequestrum. The removal of three-quarters of an inch all around did
not liberate the sequestrum. I then broke up some osseous
matter which had formed a sort of cylinder within the sequestrum, and thus I discovered that from this internal ossification
a spur or process of bone passed through an opening in the
sequestrum, and joined itself to the involucrum without, thus
nailing the loosened bone in its cavity, but permitting it to
move backward and forward about three-fourths of an inch.
This spur being cut by the chisel, it was found that the sequestrum was released, and it was easily drawn out. The stump
improved immediately after the removal of the dead bone, and
healed slowly. He was discharged cured, May 6, 1868. This

operation drew my attention to this inner cylinder of bone, which, as far as I know, has not been noticed by any who have written on this subject. It plays so important a part in this disease, that I present the continuation of the history of the above case, in which the relations of this inner cylinder became more distinct. The man continued well during the summer following his leaving the hospital, but unfortunately had a fall which caused reulceration of the stump. He came back to the hospital, and, as the soft parts had from long-continued disease shrunk away, leaving the thickened end of the bone unduly prominent, this thick bulbous end was exposed by an incision, and one inch and a half of its extremity sawed off. This left the stump in a good condition to heal soundly, which it did without further trouble. On maceration, the removed segment proved to be perfectly sound and healthy bone, but very much changed in size and form. It was twice the diameter of the sound femur, and the expanded extremity had a rougher and more irregular surface. The section showed its structure to be that of a double cylinder, the outer one being very thick, the inner one being quite thin. Within the inner cylinder the medullary canal existed of a size and appearance quite natural. Between the outer and the inner cylinder, a narrow, cylindrical, vacant space existed, from which it was evident that the sequestrum had been removed. The substance of both cylinders was spongy and porous, indicating clearly that the changes were of recent occurrence. Figs. 35 and 36 show these appearances very distinctly.

The explanation of the occurrence of these sequestra, and the reason of their peculiar configuration, have not attracted much attention from surgical writers. Mr. Syme alludes to them as produced by injury done to the medullary membrane, whereby the inner lamina of bone nourished by that membrane dies and exfoliates in a tubular form, an explanation which, as far as it goes, seems to me correct; but what the nature of that injury is, and how it is brought about, are questions which yet remain to be answered. If we admit that the necrosis is of the inner lamellæ next to the medulla, and this seems to be undeniable, then, inasmuch as these inner lamellæ receive their nourishment from the medullary arteries, it would seem certain that the mischief must be due to some action in the medullary circulation, whereby this particular portion of the bone loses its vascular supply. Now, this may be produced in various ways. It may be, for example,

that the medulla is killed by the direct violence of the saw, as we often see lacerated and contused wounds elsewhere mortify on their surface. That this is often the case, and that such a death may explain the narrow ring of bone which often exfoliates from the sawed end, I am not disposed to deny; but that such violence could extend so far as eight or nine inches up into the stump, and produce its effects without entirely destroying the medulla itself, it does not seem to me reasonable to believe. Again, it might be supposed that inflammation attacking the medulla, and suppuration occurring, might separate the bone from the vascular substance of the medulla, and thus produce its necrosis. But such an inflammation would be accompanied, we may well suppose, with very marked and probably very serious symptoms, both local and general, such as accompany osteo-myelitis, wherever it occurs, under other circumstances. No such symptoms are present,

Fig. 35.—(N. Y. Hospital Museum.)

however, in cases where the most extensive sequestrum is found; in fact, the cases presenting this trouble are usually most favorable in their demeanor during all the early period of their healing, many of them not presenting a bad symptom

until the evidences of necrosis begin to show themselves, and even then these evidences accumulate slowly from day to day, not being preceded by any thing which can stand for an apparent cause. We are, therefore, it seems to me, debarred from assuming either direct injury of the medulla, or suppurative inflammation of it, as the cause of these peculiar sequestra.

Fig. 36.—(N. Y. Hospital Museum.)

Some cause must be found which will explain all the phenomena, and this cause, I think, it is not difficult to arrive at.

If we suppose that the nutritious artery of the bone is divided either by the saw while in its bony canal, or by the knife before it has entered it, then we have the vascular supply of the medulla temporarily suspended. The inner lamellæ of the bone, depending for their supply on the medulla, are also deprived of their circulation. The medulla itself, having vas- cular connections with the upper, spongy, and more vascular portion of the bone, gradually recovers its supply of blood by anastomosis, and probably never dies from this temporary cut- ting off of its circulation, but in the mean time its circulation is so enfeebled that it can supply nothing to the bone, and this has no resource but in its anastomosis with the outer lamellæ, nourished by the periosteum. The vessels of the outer lamellæ, anastomosing with those of the inner lamellæ by capillaries enclosed in unyielding walls, cannot dilate with sufficient rapidity to meet effectively the sudden demand upon them, and thus it happens that for a time the circulation of the inner lamellæ is entirely suspended, sometimes sufficiently long, I believe, to bring about its death. This will account for the necrosis presenting no symptoms until the presence of the dead bone begins to announce itself. It also explains why the ne- crosis limits itself to the inner lamellæ, and why the sequestrum is embraced between two tubes, one the outer periosteal por- tion, which has thickened itself gradually into an involucrum, and the other a thin cylinder of ossification of the surface of the medulla, which has recovered all its vitality after a temporary suspension of its circulation. It will also explain why it is that the upper end of the sequestrum grows thinner, and branches into slender terminal spiculæ of a very irregular and sometimes fantastic form. This is the outline of parts dead from loss of capillary circulation, a loss which is better and more quickly compensated above, by the greater facility of anastomotic sup- ply in the upper, spongy, than in the lower, compact portion of the bone. If this be accepted as a possible explanation of the phenomena before us, it remains to show that it is a probable one. This we arrive at by observing the course of the nutri- tious artery as it enters the bone. In examining forty-five femora contained in several museums in this city, I found that in twenty-three the nutritious foramen was situated about the junction of the upper and middle third, and in twenty-two it was at or near the middle of the bone. In several instances it was double. The direction of the canal, in every instance, was from below upward. The artery itself is given off from the middle perforating branch of the femoral, and runs upward a certain distance before it enters the canal, and thus we have a space of an inch, more or less in different individuals, in which if the knife or saw happen to fall it will divide the artery, and, when we consider that this dangerous inch is, in twenty-two cases out of forty-five, at the very middle of the bone, we can well believe that it will be traversed either by the knife or by the saw, in a considerable proportion of the amputations of the thigh, which are done through its middle third.

7. *Necrosis without Suppuration.*—The occurrence of suppuration in consequence of necrosis is so universal that its occasional failure to demonstrate its presence, by abscess and fistulæ leading to the surface, becomes worthy of special consideration. Mr. Stanley remarks: "Only a single exception to this has occurred within my own observation, which was in an instance of necrosis affecting portions of the inner lamellæ of the femur and of the tibia in the same individual. Here the perished inner lamellæ have completely separated from the living bone; yet there is no fistulous passage in the walls either of the femur or of the tibia." I have now under my care a case of a young gentleman, son of a medical friend, in whom all the symptoms of necrosis developed themselves more than a year ago, and yet, no abscess having formed, we have been in doubt as to the nature of the case, till within a few weeks, when a swelling occurred on the inside of the thigh, the femur being the bone supposed to be involved, which swelling gradually assumed the external form of abscess; that is to say, it was prominent from the surrounding surface, somewhat red on its apex, and gave an obscure feeling of fluctuation. After watching it for a number of weeks, hoping for more distinct evidences of matter, and finding no progress, we determined to make an explorative incision. This was done, and, after passing deeply down toward the bone, through brawny, thickened tissue, we came upon a cavity from which flowed a small quantity of pus, but which was mainly occupied by a soft, reddish-yellow substance,

of a jelly-like consistency, which could be scooped out of the
cavity in quantities, but seemed rather like imperfect granulation-substance than like any modification of pus. The cavity
being cleared, extensive necrosis of the posterior surface of the
femur was discovered. This delay or absence of the signs of
suppuration has occurred to me in one or two other instances,
and has led me to be cautious in positively deciding against
the existence of necrosis from the mere absence of the ordinary
manifestations of the formation of pus.

8. *Necrosis without Exfoliation.*—I have already spoken of
the indisposition to separation which is manifested by certain
cases of necrosis of the cranium, and also of the lower jaw.
The same hesitancy to cast off the dead bone is seen in other
cases, principally, I suspect, in those of a syphilitic character.
The following case is an example:

James Becket, aged thirty-eight, a seaman, was admitted
into the New York Hospital, March 25, 1857, with epilepsy
and amaurosis, supposed to be connected with an old injury of
the head, and for which he was trephined by Dr. Van Buren
on the 30th. He had, at the same time, an oval ulcer on his
left leg, which was about three inches long, and nearly two
inches wide, the bottom of which was entirely formed of dead,
black, and fetid bone. He said that he had had syphilis a great
many times, and that this sore formed on his leg about seven
months ago. For at least four months the bone had been lying
exposed and black on the bottom of the ulcer. It was an indolent sore, and but little thickening of the surrounding tissues
and no enlargement of the bone existed. On pressing rudely
on the bone it gave no pain, and it was observed to be entirely
immovable. It was thought best to remove the dead portion
of bone, and for this purpose the integuments were raised from
the anterior surface of the tibia, all around the blackened and
dead spot, which was found not to extend any farther than the
part which lay exposed in the ulcer. On clearing the surface,
no sign of a line of demarcation could be seen between the
dead and the living parts, and much less any furrow or other
indication of commencing separation. A slight irregular margin of new bony deposit existed at points near where the living
and dead bone joined, but the only way of distinguishing be-

tween the two was in the fact that one part bled when chiselled and the other did not. Taking this as our guide, the chisel was freely but carefully used, until the whole surface bled freely. In order to accomplish this, nearly the whole thickness of the anterior wall of the tibia was removed, and a considerable portion on each side, the necrosis having occupied, like a saddle, nearly the anterior half of the compact substance of the bone. There was no more indication of any commencing process of separation in the internal and deeper point of union between the living and dead bone, than had been observed at the surface. No serious accident occurred during the healing of the wound, the bone granulated sluggishly, but without any further necrosis, and the wound was nearly healed when he was discharged from the hospital, August 10, 1857.

Another instance of marked indisposition to separation occurred in a case of necrosis which presented features which, in many respects, were so peculiar that I venture to give the history in detail:

Charles Jones, aged twenty-three, by occupation a clerk, had suffered for many years with a diseased condition of the tibia, of which he gives the following account: At about the age of eight years he had an attack of inflammation of the left leg, which left the bone enlarged, and the seat of more or less constant tenderness, heat, and pain. About the age of thirteen an incision was made down through the thickened bone with a trephine and chisel, but no sequestrum was found nor any pus. This operation, however, was followed by some improvement in the condition of the limb, and, after the wound healed, it remained diminished in size, and less troublesome to him. For eight years the disease remained in a quiet condition, until about two years previous to my seeing him, when an abscess formed on the anterior face of the limb, which did not heal, but degenerated into an open ulcer, at the bottom of which could be felt exposed bone. This ulcer increased gradually until I saw him, in March, 1859. At this time it was five inches long, by one and a half broad, and the entire base of it was formed by the blackened, necrosed surface of the tibia. It gave him but little pain, but the discharge from it was considerable, and of so abominable and penetrating an odor that, with every attention to cleanliness, he could not keep himself free from it; and it was mainly this which made him anxious to have something done for the relief of his disease. Although there was no sign of loosening of the dead parts, yet the sequestrum was so superficial and so accessible that we had no hesitation in recommending an operation, which was performed by Dr. Buck. It consisted in still further exposing the front of the tibia, by dissecting back the integuments, and then, with chisels and gouges, removing the dead mass. We did not find merely death of bone, as we expected, but, as the chisel removed the most superficial blackened layer, it was found to be merely the exposed and dried surface of bone, which, at a line or two of depth, presented a condition of infiltrated suppuration. As cut by the chisel, the bone presented very much the appearance of a lung in the third stage of hepatization, though the pus was so concrete that none flowed out. As the gouge penetrated more deeply, the substance of the bone became more vascular and less infiltrated with pus. The diseased part was thoroughly and carefully removed, and was found to have penetrated at its central portions about an inch toward the centre of the bone, which, of course, was much thickened and consolidated by long-continued disease. The surface left on the completion of the operation seemed healthy, was fully vascular, and presented the appearance of bone the vessels of which have been enlarged by the proximity of long-continued inflammation. Great constitutional irritation followed the operation, and for a long time he remained in an exceedingly depressed, nervous, and feeble state. Gradually he rallied, and slowly convalesced. The wound granulated over a great part of its surface, but the margins of the excavated bone seemed to take on a condition very similar to that which existed previous to the operation. This striking difference, however, existed in the behavior before and after the operation, viz.: that after the operation the dead parts separated, and some exfoliated in a perfectly natural manner, in the course of a few weeks, while before the operation separation refused to commence, even after the lapse of years. His condition remained unsatisfactory, with every evidence of Bright's disease of the kidneys.

The wound was granulating languidly, and slowly improving, when he died August 17, 1868.

It is not easy to explain why it is that in these cases the failure to accomplish separation should be so marked a feature, even after the lapse of so long a period, but I think that in all the cases I have observed there has been some general cachexia which may stand for one step toward the solution of the problem. In the jaws it seems to be the poison of phosphorus or mercury; in many other cases it may be scrofula; but I am quite certain that much the larger number of cases are connected with syphilis; and it is reasonable to suppose that the peculiarities of the behavior of the disease are due to the peculiar constitutional conditions under which it is developed.

The general principles of treatment of necrosis may, it seems to me, be very easily and naturally deduced from the history of the disease as it has now been given. Three indications present themselves: 1. To prevent or relieve the inflammation upon which the necrosis depends, or which arises in consequence of it; 2. To promote the separation of the dead from the living bone; 3. To remove or to facilitate the removal of the sequestrum:

1. *To prevent or relieve Inflammation.*—So evident is the dependence of necrosis upon inflammation, that we might safely say that by preventing inflammation we can prevent the necrosis. It very rarely happens, however, that we can in reality prevent an inflammation, in the strict sense of the word; but the same principle is illustrated in those cases where, by the prompt abatement of the inflammation, we prevent its evil consequences. There are two ways in which this prompt abatement can be attained: the first by the very active use of antiphlogistic remedies locally applied; and, secondly, by removing the tension and pressure produced by accumulating effusions, by making free incisions down through the periosteum to the bone itself. The first plan is illustrated by the case of whitlow, where, by making free use of leeches and other antiphlogistics, in the earliest stages, we can often succeed in putting a prompt period to processes which we know, if not thus treated, are very sure to be followed by necrosis of the affected phalanx. The principle is applicable to all inflammations affecting the bones, of such acuteness and

severity as to lead us to apprehend necrosis. Of course, in a large bone, like the tibia, we should not expect to attain the same complete results that we often do in the finger, but by the active and energetic use of antiphlogistic treatment, in the earlier stages of inflammation, we may mitigate the severity, and, I believe, may materially abridge the destructive tendencies of the case.

The second mode of abating inflammation, that by making free incisions through the membranous covering of the bones, is useful at all periods of the disease, but, of course, as a preventive measure, most effective during the earlier stages. In the large bones, and particularly in the deeply-seated ones, it becomes so serious an operation, however, that, in the uncertainty of diagnosis which generally characterizes the earlier periods of necrosis, it may be doubtful whether it can often be available. I have known it to be employed in one case in this city, in a little boy, in whom a sudden inflammation attacking the shaft of the tibia, an incision was made by the late Dr. John Watson, along the whole anterior surface of the bone, dividing the periosteum down to the bone. In this case the inflammation had existed long enough to produce effusion between the bone and periosteum, for the latter membrane gaped open on being incised, exposing bone already bare, which soon became evidently dead. No good effect could be traced, in this instance, on the progress of the disease, for the whole shaft of the tibia necrosed, but our conviction at the time was that, if the incision could have been made early, it might have been more effectual, at least in limiting the extent, if not in preventing the occurrence of necrosis. The enormous wound made in this mode of operating, and the exposure of the bone to the air, are serious objections to it, and must very much curtail its application. In these respects the subcutaneous section offers advantages which I think entitle it to a more extended trial than it has yet had.

2. *To promote the Separation of the Dead from the Living Bone.*—And here, the first question which presents itself is, Can any thing be done to promote this separation? I am disposed to answer this question in the negative, as far as relates to the disease in its ordinary forms, and in tolerably

healthy constitutions. It may well be conceived, however, that there may be certain conditions, both of the part and of the general system, where sluggishness and inactivity characterize the morbid actions, and where stimulation, both local and general, would seem to be clearly indicated. . The local stimulants would be those which we would use in a corresponding case in the soft parts, such as a solution of some stimulating tinctures, or of the sulphates of zinc and copper, the balsams of Peru and of fir, either made into an ointment or applied pure, or a weak solution of the bichloride of mercury. Each of these classes of stimulants, in its appropriate case, either applied to the granulating surfaces, or injected into the suppurating cavities, may have, I do not doubt, a good effect in promoting the separation of the sequestrum, if Nature be dilatory in bringing the separation about. At the same time such general remedies as will improve the general vigor, and increase the tone of all the active functions of the body, will also assist in bringing about the desired result. But it seems to me that it is wise not to do too much in this direction, lest our stimulation excite new inflammation, believing that Nature will, in the large proportion of cases, do more and'better for us than we can do for her. And, as deduced from this same view of the case, I would object to any mechanical means being adopted, by instruments introduced either between the separating bones, or between the periosteum and the bone, in the view of expediting the separation, or of preserving the periosteum, believing that this instrumental interference will not do good, and will be liable to do much harm.

The Removal of the Sequestrum.—There are a few cases of this disease where the necrosis is slight, and where it is near the surface of the body, in which Nature is competent to cast off the sequestrum and remove it from the body without the assistance of art. In all cases, however, where the dead part has any considerable size, and particularly where it lies deeply from the surface of the body, some process of extrication is necessary, either from its encasement in the new bony formation, or from the soft parts which surround it, and these processes sometimes assume the proportions of a most formidable operation. Taking it for granted, then, that some operation will be required, two questions present themselves: first, as to the time when, and, second, as to the mode in which, the operation shall be performed. The time when an operation for the removal of a sequestrum shall be undertaken, other things being equal, will depend upon one thing only, namely, the fact of the separation of the dead from the living bone being so perfectly accomplished that, when the sequestrum is released from its surrounding entanglements, it can be easily and entirely removed. Any condition short of this is a contra-indication of the operation. And this for obvious reasons. If separation have not completely taken place, though we may be able to seize and bring away the bulk of the sequestrum, yet we run the risk of leaving behind some of the undetached portion, and this will usually happen at the deepest and most inaccessible portion of the wound, and thus the operation fails of its purpose, which is, the complete removal of all the dead mass. Again, if separation have not taken place, we may find ourselves unable to detach the sequestrum at all without risk of fracturing the bone whose integrity we are trying to save. This is an accident which has sometimes happened where surgeons have felt it necessary, for reasons peculiar to the case, to disregard the rule, and operate without waiting for complete loosening of the sequestrum; and it has this peculiar feature of disadvantage, that, if under such circumstances a fracture do occur, there is left between the fragments a portion of unremoved sequestrum, which makes a very serious complication of the case.

This rule of surgery, then, being accepted, the next point is to ascertain the fact of complete separation, as an indication that the time for operation has arrived. In many cases this can be done, with great ease, by the touch of the probe, which immediately reveals the fact that the dead piece is movable; but there are a number of cases which present themselves, where the ascertainment of actual separation is not so easy. The granulations which spring from the walls of the cavity in which the sequestrum lies, by pressing upon it from all sides, may hold it so firmly that no movement can be elicited by the mere pressure of the probe. Under these circumstances, if one probe be introduced at one opening, and another through another, some distance off, then, by making pressure alternately, with one and the other, a seesaw motion of the sequestrum may be perceived, which is sufficient to prove that it is entirely detached. Again, by introducing a straight steel sound down to the dead bone, and making forcible pressure for a moment, and then relaxing it, repeating the manœuvre frequently, and with considerable force, the loose piece will gradually be pressed down into the soft granulations, and make thus a space in which its movements can be readily appreciated. There remain, however, a certain number of cases in which no physical examination will entirely satisfy us that the bone is loose, and in these cases we have to trust to probabilities. If the death of bone have been ascertained to have existed for a certain time, if the discharge have been about uniform during this time, if the other symptoms have undergone no change, and if the orifice of the sinuses show the pouting, exuberant granulations, then we may believe that separation has occurred. The length of time required for the completion of the process has not been ascertained, nor is it supposed to be uniform, but I have been accustomed to think that in a healthy adult about three months would be a safe period to adopt, varying of course somewhat in individual cases. In children separation takes place much sooner.

Having ascertained that the sequestrum is loose, it is then the duty of the surgeon to remove it. As a general rule, nothing is to be gained by delay, and the presence of the dead mass is always a source of suffering and danger. Two conditions of the sequestrum present themselves in reference to an operation: one where it is covered in and imprisoned only, or mainly by the soft parts; and one where it is so encased in involucral formation that it cannot be extricated except by cutting away some of the newly-formed bone which encloses it. In the first condition but little is required except, by incision of the soft parts, to liberate the bone; but sometimes, when the sequestrum is small, and when it lies very deep from the surface, its liberation is not thus immediately effected. This is often an embarrassment which we encounter in trying to get rid of those small sequestra which form on the ends of the fragments in compound fractures. These, sometimes, without being enclosed in any bony casing, are so inaccessible, from their depth, and perhaps their concealed position between the fragments, that an incision of the soft parts does not help us much in their removal. In these cases the use of the sponge-tent, by dilating the wound, gives us a better access to the foreign body, and enables the forceps to open more readily, and thus to seize more firmly the presenting part. It is important, in such cases, to use repeated tents until the wound is largely dilated, and to thrust them well down to dead bone, so that the thorough dilatation shall reach the imprisoned sequestrum.

Where the dead bone is closely encased in the involucrum, then a more serious and well-considered procedure becomes necessary. The first step of these operations should consist in exposing the most accessible surface of the involucrum, so as to bring it under the reach of the trephine and the chisel. In the tibia this is of course the anterior surface, but in some of the deeper-seated bones, as the femur, it is a matter of nice consideration as to the side on which to approach the sequestrum. As a general rule, that side on which the fistulous openings exist will present the sequestrum most superficial; but this may not be the most favorable direction for the incisions by reason of important vessels and nerves, as is often felt by the surgeon to be the case in those common cases of necrosis of the posterior surface of the femur near the knee-joint. Here, the presence of the artery and nerves is an embarrassment which is to be avoided by a circuitous rather than a direct approach to the diseased bone; and as a general rule this approach is usually made from the outer side of the thigh, passing down between the vastus externus and the biceps, more safely and more conveniently than from any other direction. In each case this point must be determined for the case itself, but it seems to me very important that this preparatory step should be so taken that the surface of the involucrum can be freely exposed. By so doing, not only does the surgeon give himself freedom in the use of his instruments, but he has the opportunity to judge as to the best places and the best manner of applying them.

Having exposed the involucral surface, it will generally be found best to enlarge some of the cloacæ, which such an exposure reveals, by chiselling or trephining the shell of new bone. For my own part, I prefer the gouge to the trephine, which

14

latter instrument I rarely use in operations for necrosis. My
gouge is made large, with the cutting edge only slightly curved,
and terminating at right angles with the side of the instrument,

FIG. 37.

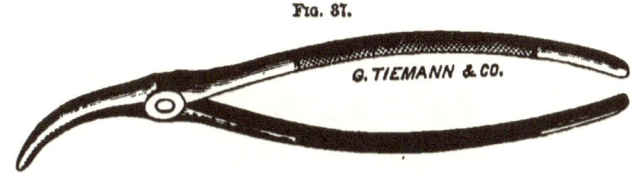

which right angle is slightly rounded (Fig. 40), thus giving me a
very delicate corner to work with, where delicacy is required,
and a powerful instrument where heavy cutting is to be done.

FIG. 38.

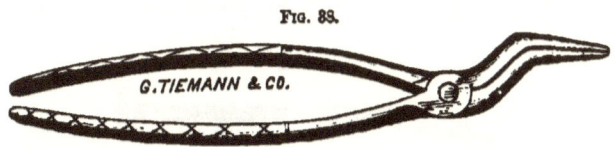

It is well to have several different sizes, and I have found one
small gouge, with a rounded cutting edge and a curved shaft
(Fig. 42), very useful in deep cavities. Fig. 41 represents a

FIG. 39.

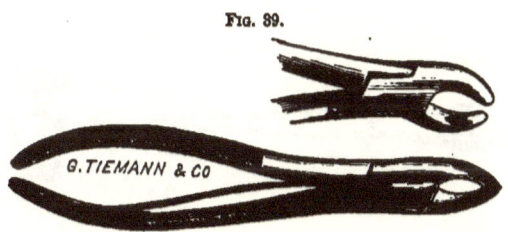

straight-edged chisel, which is very useful in splitting or cut-
ing a firm bridge of bone, and is often the only instrument
whereby the sequestrum itself, when it is necessary, can be

FIG. 40..

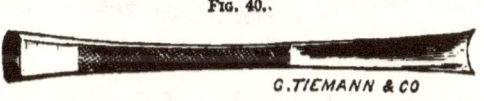

divided. Fig. 43 represents a metallic hammer, with its head
loaded with lead, which makes less jar in striking on the chisel

than an ordinary hammer, and is much more compact and
portable than any form of mallet. Fig. 44 represents a strong
elevator, which is used to great advantage in separating the
tough, thickened periosteum from the bone, and also in loosen-

FIG. 41.

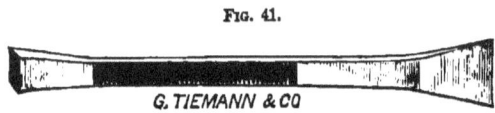

G. TIEMANN & CO

ing and dislodging deep sequestra. Fig. 39 represents the
rongeur, or gnawing forceps, by which small pieces of bone
can be cut away at each bite of the instrument, and thus the
involucral covering can be removed piecemeal in any direction

FIG. 42.

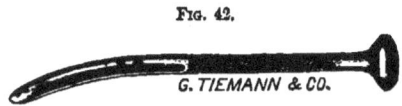

G. TIEMANN & CO.

and to any extent. Figs. 37 and 38 represent convenient
forms of strong, long-beaked forceps for removing sequestra
from deep cavities, or through small openings in the involucrum.

FIG. 43.

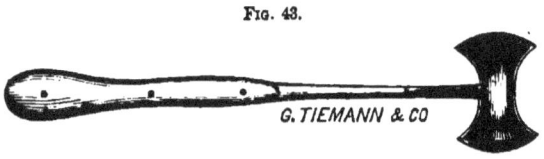

G. TIEMANN & CO

These instruments are made, some of them expressly for
me, by Messrs. Tiemann & Co., to whom I am indebted for
the illustrations presented.

FIG. 44.

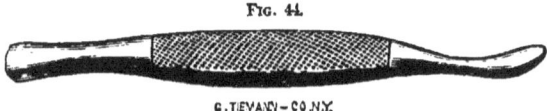

G. TIEMANN – CO. N.Y.

By these instruments sufficient of the shell is removed to
expose the sequestrum, and now an examination may be made
by moving it in various directions, to ascertain in which di-

rection the further cuttings of the involucrum can most advantageously be made. These are then to be continued, only so far as is necessary to liberate the dead bone, and no more, for I believe it is a pathological fact, well ascertained, that very little restoration of removed involucrum takes place, particularly in those past the earliest youth. In this same view, therefore, we should be particularly careful not to weaken the bone in its transverse diameter by unnecessary removal, gaining the required space, as far as may be, by longitudinal rather than by transverse chisellings. Having thus exposed the sequestrum, it may be seized by forceps, and, if it be loose, it can usually be drawn from its bed through the opening made by the chisel. If it be too long, or otherwise too large to be thus extricated, the chiselling of the involucrum may be continued until it is released, or by Liston's bone-forceps the sequestrum may be divided so as to be removed in two or more pieces. All these details must be left to the discretion of the surgeon, he bearing in mind, as cardinal principles of the operation, not to remove any more involucrum than is necessary, and not to mutilate the sequestrum in any such manner as may prevent its entire removal. And here it may be well to put in a word of caution. No one who has examined many sequestra can fail to have observed how irregular their extremities are, and how apt they are to terminate in fine, delicate spiculæ, and sometimes lamellæ, which extend some distance beyond the main mass of the sequestrum. These delicate prolongations may, by careless manipulation, be easily broken off, and thus may be left behind in the most inaccessible part of the cavity, an accident carefully to be avoided, by making as little twisting or angular movement of the sequestrum as possible, the surgeon aiming to draw it directly from its bed rather than to twist or pry it out. After the sequestrum is thus removed, a careful examination should be made with the finger and with the probe, to make sure that no fragments of dead bone be left behind. Occasionally we find some small piece thus remaining deep in the wound which our forceps will not reach, and which can only be approached by so serious an extension of our incisions that we hesitate to undertake to search for it. In such cases it is better to leave the dead piece, after making sure that there is opening in the bone sufficient for its passage, trusting that it will gradually be extruded by the granulations so as either to be cast out or brought within easy reach of the forceps. This power of the granulations to push a sequestrum from its bed is seen not merely in this disposition of small fragments, but also in the movements whereby extensive sequestra are sometimes moved toward the surface, and are sometimes cast out altogether. This is in obedience to what seems to be a general law, that all foreign bodies shall find their way to the surface of the body, a law which we see abundantly illustrated in small and superficial exfoliations, and the execution of which is only obstructed in the larger sequestra by the circumstance of their being imprisoned within an unyielding case of bone.

The wound should be dressed lightly, and allowed to granulate. It is rarely worth while to do more than loosely to approximate the edges of the incised integument, above and below the wound, so as to diminish the amount of granulating surface. If, as is the practice with some surgeons, the wound be stuffed full of lint, some of it is apt to get entangled in the bony granulations as they begin to spring up, and to be difficult to remove. Some of the lint also gets caught on the rough edges or surfaces of the chiselled bone, and thus becomes difficult of removal. No advantage comes of this packing of lint into the wound, and my own habit is to spread three or four pieces of thin patent lint with cerate, and lay them lightly just within the edges of the wound, pressing them downward into the cavity, and then laying charpie lightly over them, as much as may be necessary to fill out the vacuity. In this way no dry surface of lint comes in contact either with bone-granulations or with chiselled bone, and no annoying adhesion of the dressing will take place. When suppuration fairly begins, the dressings loosen easily, and are removed without pain, to be renewed in a similar manner as often as the discharge makes it necessary, making them lighter and smaller as the granulations diminish the suppurating cavity. The wound usually shows great activity in healing, and in a few weeks is reduced down to a narrow granulating line; but we must not be deceived. The cavity of the involucrum is very loosely filled with soft granulations, and a probe can still be passed deeply

into the bone.   Indeed, the final filling up of the involucral
cavity is a very slow process, and so, therefore, is the final
healing of the wound.   I have watched some of my cases for
months, and one case of the tibia for
years, before the cavity was entirely closed
and the wound healed.

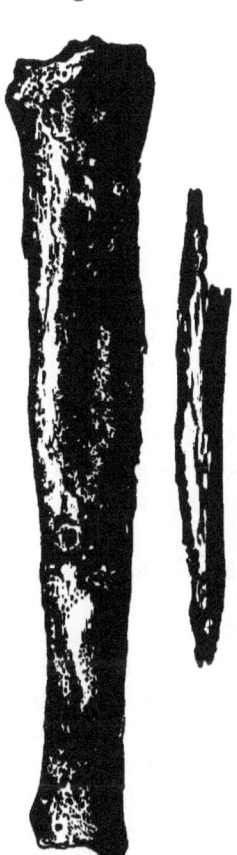

After cicatrization is complete, a mod-
elling process is instituted, which slowly
diminishes the deformities caused by the
disease, and gives the affected bone as
much shapeliness as it can receive after
so extensive destruction.   The involucral
enlargement gradually diminishes, the
roughnesses and irregularities are smoothed off, while the cavities left by the fall
of the sequestrum are, to a certain extent,
filled up by the granulations.   Usually,
however, this filling up is far from complete, and a groove or depression, more or
less considerable, marks the situation of
the cavities, into which depression the
cicatrix sinks.   As has been before stated,
these depressions, which are moderate in
the living subject, are much deeper in the
macerated bone, which then shows that
very little bony restoration has taken
place, what has been poured out serving
rather to smooth over the irregularities
of the wound in the bone-tissue than in

Fig. 45.—(From Billroth.)   any considerable degree to fill it up.   Of
course in young persons, and particularly
in children, the reparation is more perfect.   Fig. 45, taken
from Billroth, shows these changes two years after the removal
of the sequestrum.

PART II.

TUMORS OF BONE.

THE acknowledged difficulty of classifying diseases is met with in full force in attempting the study of tumors. The characters, indeed, of well-marked specimens are sufficiently distinct to make it very easy to distribute them according to their easily-recognized features; but so many tumors present uncertain, irregular, or mixed appearances and behavior, that it becomes an extremely difficult task to arrange them in such a way as that they shall fall naturally into classes sufficiently well characterized to be of use in our observations on the individual. The method adopted by modern pathologists, of arranging tumors by their anatomical structure, is doubtless the best and most convenient; but the difficulty is only mitigated, not removed, and the very accuracy and perfection of the microscopic diagnosis show us shades of difference which, while they enlarge our knowledge of the individual, may seriously interfere with our arrangement of the class. Thus the main features of the cartilaginous tumors of bone are sufficiently distinct to be easily appreciated, yet the microscope shows that the cartilaginous element puts on so great a variety of forms that it is at times hard to recognize, and often so uncertain in its signification that we sometimes feel as if the physical qualities of a tumor, as perceived by the unaided eye, were a more reliable test of its character than the minute dissection of the microscope. Again, the anatomical characters are not always the same in all parts of the same tumor. We may have cartilage in one part, bone in another, and unequivocal cancer in another, in tumors which present nothing, in their history or appearance to the eye, that indicates the reason of the difference in their several parts. Still further, their constituent elements undergo, in some instances, changes so distinct and so complete that it is fair to say that a fibrous or cartilaginous tumor is converted into a bony tumor; a cyst, by proliferation, is changed into a solid tumor; or either of them may be converted into a malignant form, and, after perhaps years of slow, benignant growth, may put on the rapidly-destructive features of the encephaloid. It is evident that these considerations must make a strict classification impossible, if we expect from it an arrangement by which every tumor shall be assigned to its proper position, and each division shall have its exact and proper limits, into which each individual shall, by virtue of its anatomical construction, be received. We must perforce be content, therefore, with using such classification as we may adopt, only with a view to the convenience and assistance it may afford us in describing and studying individual cases, without relying too much upon it as stamping each specimen with marks which shall be so unmistakable that we can at once assign to it its place in the catalogue, and thereby be saved the necessity of investigating its individual peculiarities and dispositions. Used in this way, we shall find the classification now commonly adopted, by which tumors are arranged according to their anatomical structure, to be the best and most convenient we can use, and one which will perhaps serve us better than any other in our study of individual specimens.

The arrangement usually adopted by writers is a division into—

1. Cartilaginous tumors.
2. Osseous tumors.
3. Fibrous and fibroid tumors.
4. Myeloid tumors.
5. Vascular and pulsating tumors.
6. Cystic tumors.
7. Malignant tumors.

These principal classes embrace many subdivisions, and in treating of them I shall not always strictly adhere to the order in which they are here placed, departing from that order, however, only when, for the sake of clearness, it seems more convenient to arrange them into somewhat different groups.

CHAPTER I.

CARTILAGINOUS TUMORS.

CARTILAGINOUS tumors are characterized, as a class, by their possessing the anatomical elements of cartilage. In a very large proportion of these tumors, the microscopical elements are identical with those of the normal cartilage; in some, however, they depart from the normal type, presenting many varieties, sometimes leaving much doubt as to their nature. One chief circumstance, which may be noticed as characteristic of this tumor, is the great diversity of microscopic forms which each specimen, in its different portions, may present. Mr. Paget, on this point, remarks: "This diversity of microscopic forms is enough to baffle any attempt to describe them briefly, or to associate them with any corresponding external characters in the tumors. The most diverse forms may even be seen side by side in the field of the microscope. But this diversity is important. It has its parallel, so far as I know, in no other innocent tumor; and the cartilaginous tumors form, perhaps, the single exception to a very generally true rule, enunciated by Bruch, namely, that it is a characteristic of the cancerous tumors, and distinctive between them and others, that they present, even in one part, a multiformity of elementary shapes." Mr. Paget, in his excellent chapter on cartilaginous tumors, from which the above extract is taken, gives a full account of the varieties he noticed in the careful microscopic examination of fifteen specimens. His general conclusions are, that the variations are shown in the basis or intercellular substance, in the cartilaginous cells, and in their nuclei. First, in the intercellular substance, he remarks that it varies in quantity, sometimes being largely in excess, with very few cells scattered through, and sometimes in small quantity, with a great pre-

ponderance of cells, which seem to make up the whole mass
of the tumor. It varies also in consistence, sometimes firm,
and sometimes very soft; and in texture, some specimens having a transparent, almost structureless basis, while the most
present more or less distinct evidence of a fibrous plan, the
fibres differing not a little among themselves, in their shape,
size, distinctness, and arrangement about the cells. The carti-

FIG. 46.—(From Paget.)   FIG. 47.—(From Paget.)

lage cells themselves vary also very greatly. Sometimes they
are large and abundant, sometimes few and small; some have
the rounded shape of the normal cartilage-cell, and some differ widely from them. Sometimes their outline is dark and

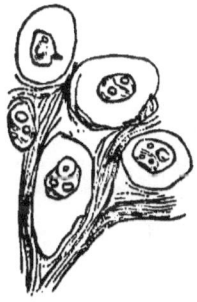

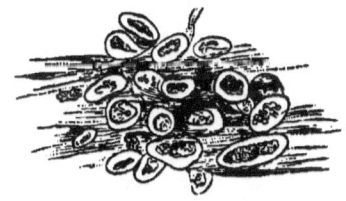

FIG. 48.—(From Paget.)   FIG. 49.—(From Paget.)

distinct, sometimes so faint as to be almost imperceptible, and
occasionally there seems to be no cell-wall at all, the nuclei
being embedded in the hyaline substance without any cell-en-
closure. The nuclei also present many varieties. Sometimes

they are single, sometimes two or more are seen, and these apparently acquiring for themselves the character of primary cells. Sometimes they show nucleoli, often they do not (Figs. 46, 47, 48, 49). Some are small, round, and clear in outline,

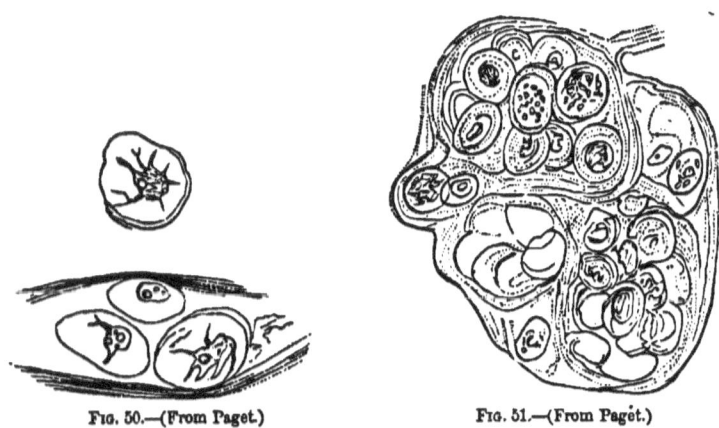

FIG. 50.—(From Paget.)   FIG. 51.—(From Paget.)

others are large, pale, and indistinct ; some are granular, and some show globules of oil in their interior. The most marked deviation from the usual appearance of the nuclei is that in which they present an irregular branching outline very much

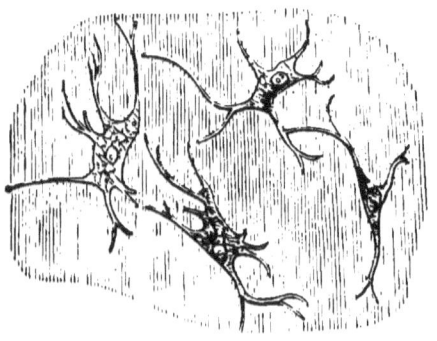

FIG. 52.—(From Cornil and Ranvier.)

resembling the shape of the bone-corpuscle (Figs. 50, 51, 52). This is so common that Mr. Paget noticed it in seven of his cases ; and although he does not admit that it is any indication of a commencement of a process of ossification, yet, in view of

the well-known fact that these tumors have a great propensity
to ossify, it would seem reasonable to suppose that this striking
change was one of its earliest manifestations, and not unphilo-
sophical to assume that it was so, in the absence of positive
evidence that it was not. In fact, Mr. Queckett, in his lectures on histology, adopts this view of their nature. Making
all due allowances, however, for these various deviations, the
fact still remains that this class of tumors is characterized by
anatomical features which are, in the main, identical with
those of normal cartilage; an identity which their clinical history very strongly confirms.

The causes of these growths cannot often be discovered.
They do occasionally seem to arise from an injury, though not
more frequently than other forms of tumor. A case, recently
amputated at Bellevue Hospital, commenced in a finger, apparently in consequence of a bruise against the mantel-piece. They
commence their growth most commonly in childhood and early
youth, though instances are recorded where they have made their
first appearance in old age. Their growth is painless, and commonly quite slow, though in exceptional instances a rapid rate
of increase is observed. This more rapid development is usually
connected with softness of texture, and a great preponderance
of cell-formation, and is very constantly observed in the recurrent tumors after removal. In their usual demeanor they are
undoubtedly benign, and when once thoroughly removed they
are not likely to reappear. But here, again, as in fibrous and
certain other tumors, we find sometimes a disposition to return
after removal, and to involve new and distant parts, and finally,
to destroy life by their more and more extensive encroachments,
which gives them the malignant character which their histological examination cannot explain. On the other hand, if the
removal be not complete, the disease will certainly grow again,
though sometimes not till after a long interval. I removed the
finger of a man from whom Mr. Cusack, of Dublin, had, nearly
twenty years before, cut out a cartilaginous growth, which sprang
from the surface of the first phalanx, and which had remained
well for many years, and then gradually grew again to a size
greater than that of the original tumor; but yet which presented
no other anatomical characters than those of normal cartilage.

But there is another point in the pathological history of these tumors which is too well ascertained to be passed by without notice, that is, their relation to malignancy. It is difficult, in any case, to prove that, in a given growing tumor, a change comes over its anatomical constituents, whereby it assumes the character of malignancy which originally it had not; but is it certain that tumors which, in every mark and sign, gave evidence of being simple cartilaginous tumors, have, after a longer or shorter period of slow and painless increase, such as characterizes the development of benignant growths, taken on a more active, rapid, and destructive behavior, and terminated with all the indications of the most virulent malignancy? But, still more, the cartilaginous is sometimes mingled with the cancerous element in the same tumor. Of this Mr. Paget gives a well-marked example in a tumor of large size which was taken from the front of the lumbar vertebræ (Fig. 53). In this case the two elements

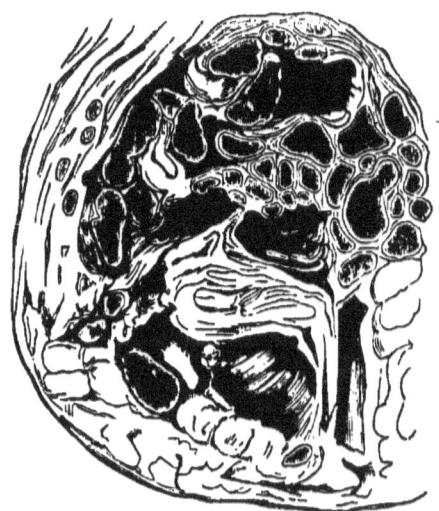

FIG. 53.—(From Paget.)

were mingled in an irregular manner, each lobule retaining its peculiar characteristics, and about in the proportion of half-and-half. This I suppose to be a rare specimen, but it illustrates, in a remarkable manner, the affiliation between cartilaginous growth and cancer, while at the same time it presents them as

essentially distinct formations, and maintaining that distinction
even when combined in a tumor which was far advanced in its
development. Mr. Paget also alludes to another case, where
cartilage and medullary cancer were associated in a tumor of
the testicle, which had been growing about eighteen months.
Virchow and several other writers have described similar com-
binations.

The size which these tumors sometimes attain is extraordinary, surpassing those of any other formation, if, perhaps, we
except the fibrous. Mr. Paget speaks of one which he saw in
St. Bartholomew's Hospital, in which, "within three months
of his first noticing it, a cartilaginous tumor increased to such

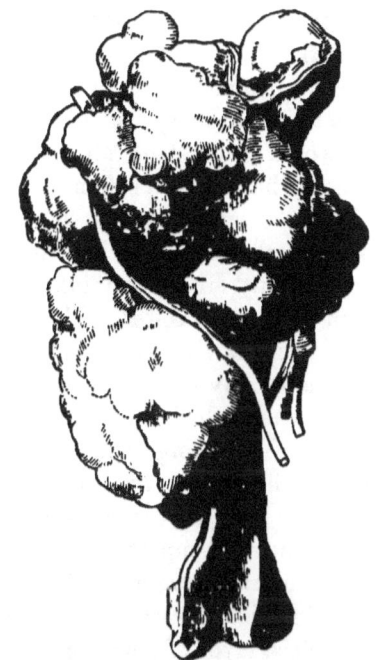

FIG. 54.—(From Paget)

an extent that it appeared to occupy nearly the whole length
of his thigh, and was as large round as my chest." He mentions another, amputated by Mr. Frogley, in which the tumor
extended from the knee-joint to within an inch of the trochan-
ters, and measured nearly three feet in circumference. Sir

Philip Crampton's case, however, surpasses all others that I have seen recorded. In this remarkable case, a cartilaginous tumor of the thigh was six feet and a half in circumference, being, therefore, a little more than two feet in diameter. Fig. 54, taken from Paget, gives a good idea of the general features of a large cartilaginous tumor growing from the upper part of the humerus. It was nearly thirty inches in circumference. The specimen is in the museum of the College of Surgeons.

The changes that cartilaginous tumors may undergo, form an important and characteristic part of their history. These changes can hardly be looked upon as representing a definite tendency which will be realized more or less completely in every specimen. Rather, they must be considered as exceptional and accidental, as the fact is, that unchangeableness is almost as characteristic of the cartilaginous as of the bony, or even the fibrous, or fatty tumor. But, nevertheless, changes are noticed so often as to require a special study both anatomical and clinical, if we would understand all that we should know about them. Thus we have first a softening. Sometimes the whole tumor, as it grows larger, grows softer; indeed, this is the usual fact, particularly where the increase in size is rapid, and has its parallel in many other hard tumors, which, as they grow larger, are apt to become softer. This change, however, does not seem to be necessarily connected with any alteration of structure, and perhaps may be explained by the greater succulence and looser texture which the growing mass assumes. There is another form of softening, where the alteration begins in the central parts of the tumors, and gradually involves their substance, until a large part of the mass has undergone the change, while perhaps the most superficial portions still maintain their original appearance and structure. This central softening is sometimes so complete that the whole tumor is involved, leaving only a thin superficial layer of unchanged material, and giving a cystic character to the tumor, which becomes more striking as the wall becomes thinner, and the central parts more fluid. In most cases, the softened portions of the tumor assume the appearance of greater translucency and clearness, so that they have been likened to fresh fish-flesh, or even to jelly. When they have become so soft as to be fluid, the appearance is often

likened to honey, and, when this honey-like material is distributed about the mass in many small cells or cysts, the appearances are strongly suggestive of colloid.

But there is another mode of softening, which is more serious, inasmuch as it commonly involves the commencement of a
process of destruction. This may begin with a process of inflammation, or may be a rapid softening, to which inflammation is
afterward superadded. Examined in the earlier stage, the part
shows broken-down tissue, degenerating fibrine, blood-corpuscles,
and pus-cells, variously intermingled. The products of inflammation collect in a focus, forming a sort of abscess which breaks
and discharges its contents. Ulceration now begins, sometimes
with sloughing, and we have imitated in all respects the behavior of the most malignant growths, an imitation which is carried
out, unfortunately, through all the worst and most destructive
phases of malignant disorganization. I do not pretend to say
that such a process may not in some cases terminate in simple
destruction of the growth and be followed by a proper healing
process, but it must be confessed that, when such action is observed in a cartilaginous tumor, the reasonable apprehension is,
that the ill behavior is indicative of ill character, and that the
originally benign tumor has assumed the nature as well as the
behavior of a malignant growth, and will probably vindicate its
claims to be so considered by ultimately destroying the patient.

Again, we have a change into bone. This change, from the
well-known relations of cartilage, might be considered as the
natural one, and might be expected to be frequent. Some degree of it is not rare, and yet it would not be correct to represent the ossific change as very common. It presents itself under two principal varieties: First, in a cartilaginous tumor
growing on a bone, we may have the ossification shooting out
from the original bone, and gradually encroaching upon the
tumor, until it is more or less largely converted into a bony
mass; or, secondly, we may have ossification commencing in
the centre of the tumor, or in many detached centres, and these
centres may gradually increase until they coalesce into one.
Many examples are seen of both these methods of ossification,
and it is not uncommon to find them combined in one specimen. Sometimes the process is limited and imperfect, and then

we have small bony-spiculæ shooting into the tumor, or small isolated masses scattered through it, or sometimes the process is more energetic and determined, and we have the whole mass converted into solid bone. The quality of the newly-formed bone varies much; sometimes being a mere amorphous calcareous infiltration, but often presenting every feature of the most perfectly-formed bone, so perfect that we cannot trace in its external features or in its microscopical characters any difference between the original and the morbid formations.

In a certain number of cases, the ossification of the tumor commences so early in its history, and proceeds so regularly as the tumor grows, as strongly to impress us with the idea that it is the normal progress of the disease, in which, after a certain period of cartilaginous existence is passed through, the structure is gradually replaced by bone, by virtue of a continuation of the same forces which formed the original tumor. The behavior of these tumors seems very much the same as the actions which take place in normal development in the cartilaginous extremities of the long bones in the child, the original layers of the new growth becoming ossified while new layers of cartilage are forming on their surface. So definite and orderly is this disposition, that it is not easy in every case to decide whether the tumor should be considered as a cartilaginous growth ossifying, or an osseous growth developed in cartilage. Hence, several of the older writers, and more lately Follin, have made a new class of these cases, and have studied them under the name of osteo-cartilaginous tumors. There seems to be some reason for this subdivision, and perhaps some practical advantages may arise out of it. The following case presents a striking example of these peculiar features. I publish it here by permission of my friend Dr. Van Buren, in whose practice it occurred, and by whose kindness I saw the patient at several periods of his history :

Elijah Vandenhoof, of New Jersey, of good constitution, aged forty-three, came under Dr. Van Buren's care in May, 1848, with an immense tumor, involving the lower half of the femur of the left side. About twenty years before, he had wrenched the left knee in wrestling, and some three months after this accident he first noticed a swelling about the knee-joint, which

15

has since slowly increased in size, gradually extending up the thigh. At this time, the tumor involved the whole circumference of the limb, extending from the knee-joint upward as far as the middle of the femur; it was immovably connected with the bone, and measured twenty-eight inches in circumference. On its anterior aspect it was generally spherical in shape, with very slight irregularities on its surface; posteriorly it was very irregular and craggy, presenting several hard, projecting, knobby eminences. It had everywhere the feel of bone covered with a thin layer of tissues. It was not tender to the touch, although there was a point where the skin had recently assumed a dusky-red appearance, which caused some complaint, apparently the result of simple tension of the integuments. There were no large veins observable on its surface. The tumor was more prominent on the posterior aspect of the limb than elsewhere, and seemed to terminate abruptly about six and a-half inches above the condyles of the femur; anteriorly it shelved off more gradually, and extended apparently some four inches farther upward. The knee-joint was but slightly movable, but its motions were not accompanied with pain. During the present year he had suffered almost constantly with a dull, aching pain in the tumor, which was invariably more severe at night and in damp weather. This pain seemed to be gradually increasing in intensity, and had of late deprived him of sleep and diminished his appetite. He was also losing flesh, and had a pulse more frequent than natural. The limb was amputated at about the middle of the femur, on the 20th of May, and the amputation was followed by a rapid recovery.

"The tumor, on examination, presented a magnificent specimen of true osteo-cartilaginous exostosis. Its periphery was everywhere covered by a layer of fibro-cartilaginous material, varying in thickness from a line to more than half an inch, filling up its anfractuosities, and giving it a much more uniform appearance than it has at present after maceration. It is now exceedingly irregular in outline, covered by rounded knobs and craggy, stalactiform projections. The condyles, it will be seen, participate in the alteration. The weight of the tumor, when recent, was thirteen pounds. The soft parts, covering the bony mass, were to all appearance perfectly healthy, with the exception of the alteration consequent upon the pressure of the tumor, and their change of position. The nervous trunks, particularly the popliteal and peroneal prolongations of the sciatic, were observed to be thicker than natural, and had evidently, by their elongation, been subjected to very considerable stretching."

In July, 1849, some signs of a return of the disease began to manifest themselves, in the shape of pain in the stump and an enlargement of the sawed end of the bone. These slowly increased, his health began to fail, and on the 21st of March, 1850, it was deemed best to endeavor to remove the whole disease by amputation at the hip-joint. This was done by Dr. Van Buren, by the method of the anterior and posterior flaps. The patient made a most satisfactory recovery.

" The specimen, previous to dissection, was successfully injected by my friend Dr. Isaacs, to whose kindness I am indebted for its preparation. It will be perceived that the appearance of the disease corresponds with the description given already of the tumor first removed. It is of a uniform bony hardness, and very irregular outline, involving the lower end of the bone, and extending upward toward the trochanter. One spicular prolongation, projecting toward the joint, on its anterior surface, was grazed by the knife in cutting out the anterior flap ; had this flap been half an inch longer, the knife would have been caught behind this bony projection, and the operation unavoidably delayed. This danger was partially recognized beforehand. As this specimen has been preserved in the wet state, the layer of the fibro-cartilage on the surface of the bone can be recognized. In removing the layer of muscles covering the disease, it was noticed that the sartorius and rectus, and most of the adductor group, were closely attached, by their cut extremities, to the enlarged bone ; the first-mentioned muscle was, in fact, inserted by a well-marked tendon, and was noticed before the operation to act strongly as a flexor of the stump. The muscles had preserved their volume fairly, although they had evidently undergone some degree of fatty atrophy. The femoral artery was pervious, and apparently of full size, up to a point about two inches from the extremity of the bone, where it became transformed into a fibrous cord. The sciatic nerve

was considerably enlarged, particularly at its extremity, where
it is closely adherent to the surface of the bone—occupying, as
it were, a valley between two projecting crags of bone, by the
growth of which it was constantly subjected to increasing pressure.   This was the spot upon the stump to which most of the
pain was attributed."

The patient, after his recovery from the amputation, returned to the country, where he enjoyed excellent health for
about two years.   He then began to suffer pain in the stump,
which increased for several months, and finally brought him to
town again for advice.   Dr. Van Buren recognized a return of
the bony growth in the os innominatum, of the side from which
the lower extremity had been removed, involving the acetabu-
lum and the neighboring parts.   This continued slowly to increase, causing pain similar in character to that formerly experienced.   Finally symptoms indicating pressure upon the rectum
and bladder gradually appeared, and increased in severity until
death followed, at the end of five years from the date of the last
operation, from intestinal obstruction, resulting from pressure
of the intra-pelvic growth upon the rectum.   The parts were
removed after death, and sent to the city for inspection.   "The
whole os innominatum was involved in an enormous outgrowth
similar in character to those already described, presenting no
new appearances which could be recognized as malignant."
The physician who made the autopsy reported that there were
no evidences of disease in any other organs of the body, the
immediate cause of death being peritonitis.

This case offers a good example of that semi-malignant
behavior in which, though no proper cancerous character is
assumed by the growth, and though no evidence is discovered
of generalization of the disease, yet, by its recurrence and extensive invasion of vital parts, it finally produces death, and
this after what seems to be the most complete removal.   Fig.
55 shows the appearance of both portions of the femur after
maceration.

Another quite interesting, and not very uncommon, form
of osteo-cartilaginous growth is that which affects the last phalanx of the great-toe.   It springs from the dorsal surface of the
phalanx, under the nail.   As it grows—and the growth seems

to be by cartilage which ossifies as it grows—it is pushed forward by the resistance of the nail, and makes its appearance just under the free portion of the nail, as a hard, wart-like growth, insensible to the touch, and usually painless, when not pressed upon, but giving rise to a great deal of pain and tenderness when pressed upon by the shoe in walking.

The first case of this curious affection that I saw was in the New York Hospital, in the service of my friend and preceptor, Dr. Buck. I give it in his own words :

"William Jewell, aged twenty, Norway, was admitted into the New York Hospital, September 25, 1839. Fourteen months ago, first felt pain in the great-toe of the right foot under the nail. Had walked about with a pair of new boots, which were rather small. Upon examination found a small, hard lump growing under the free edge of the nail ; this he kept pared close with his razor, which often caused it to bleed freely. Eight months ago it was partially removed with a portion of the nail, but soon after the wound healed it grew out again. September 25th it presented the following appearances : The edge of the nail was pared short, so that a small tumor protruded anterior to it, of about the size of a split pea, of a grayish rose-color, tough and dense, though not having the feeling of an osseous growth, free from pain. He always took the pre-

Fig. 55.—(From Van Buren's Collection.)

caution to wear an easy boot, otherwise he felt uneasiness.
From its apparent situation, anterior to the nail, I aimed to
save the nail, and passed a bistoury down through the nail, a
little behind its middle, in a transverse direction, to the bone,
then directed its edge forward, grazing the bone so as to remove the tumor at its origin, where it was evidently of an osseous character, requiring much force to cut through it. This
incision, I found, split down through the middle of the excrescence. I therefore determined to remove the entire nail; and,
in the same manner as above, commenced a new incision, two
lines posterior to the union of the nail and cuticle, going down
to the bone, and grazing its upper surface as before, where the
tumor grew from the bone. I pared away the surface as close as
possible. The hæmorrhage was trifling, color of bone healthy.
The resistance of the nail had given a direction forward to the
excrescence, and thus deceived me as to its point of origin,
which was beneath the middle of the nail. Simple dressings
to the wound.

"*October* 21st.—The wound gradually cicatrized under the
application of light dressings, with the occasional application
of nitrate of silver to repress the exuberant granulations. It
had diminished to the size of a split pea, without any appearance of reproduction, when at his urgent request he was discharged. A small portion of nail grew out of the posterior
corner, which had escaped the knife."

Some years after, another case presented itself to me, in
private practice, which I had the opportunity of watching after
the cure. Mr. George H. P., aged about thirty, showed me in
December, 1855, a small corn-like projection, under the nail of
the great-toe of his left foot, which had made its appearance
some five months previously, after having worn for some time
a boot which was too short for his foot. It had given him a
good deal of trouble whenever he walked far, and particularly
if he wore a boot in the least degree too tight; and whenever
he stubbed his toe, or received any blow upon it, the pain was
excessive. The projection was a little to the inside of the
median line of the toe, and was only partly covered by the nail,
from under which it protruded, and by which it was evidently
compressed. On feeling it, I recognized a hardness about the

base of the little tumor, which, taken in connection with its seat and history, induced me to regard it as a subungual exostosis. Unwilling to inflict an operation for so slight an affection, I tried for some weeks the effect of removing all pressure of the boot, and at the same time I destroyed, with liquor potassæ, the thickened, wart-like cuticle which covered the deeper-seated tumor of the bone. As the flakes of altered cuticle separated, and were drawn out from under the nail, some temporary relief would be obtained, from the pressure being, by so much, diminished. They formed again rapidly, however, and, as the tumor itself was all the time slowly increasing and becoming more sensitive, it was deemed best to remove it. The operation was performed on the 22d of March, 1856. An incision was made around the whole nail, about a line distant from its margins, taking care to go far enough back to include the whole matrix, and far enough forward to include the tumor. By this incision the whole nail and the soft parts under it were raised from the upper surface of the phalanx, and the tumor of course fully exposed. It was found to spring from the bone near its extremity, and sufficient sound bone remained to warrant me in cutting off the anterior half of the phalanx only. This was easily done by the bone-nippers. A flap was thus left which was a little longer than was necessary to cover the end of the bone. This flap was simply drawn a little up toward the top of the phalanx, and the gap thus left was allowed to heal by granulation. The healing process went on most favorably, and was entirely completed at the end of four weeks, leaving a shortened but very good-looking and useful toe, with plenty of soft parts covering the end of the bone. On examination, the tumor was found to consist of bone in three fourths of its extent, the other fourth being formed of cartilage which covered its most superficial surface. It had a decided neck, considerably narrower than the prominent portion of the tumor. The adjoining bone seemed sound. The tumor was about as large as a medium-sized pea.

This gentleman has been under my observation up to the present time. Of course, there has been no return of the disease. His toe has been perfectly well, and useful in every respect. One slight drawback to his entire comfort, however, exists in the fact that at one corner of the wound a small, irregular growth of nail exists—the evidence that some portion of the matrix escaped the knife. This, it will be observed, occurred also in Dr. Buck's case, though we both took much pains to avoid it. The accident arises from the fact that the corners of the nail are sometimes longer, and more deeply implanted in their matrix, than the central portions, and that, therefore, the root of the nail has a straight edge terminating in right angles with the sides. Any incision, therefore, which is to remove the matrix entire, must not curve round the root of the nail, but must extend straight across the dorsum of the finger or toe, at least a line beyond the lateral edges, and fully two lines back of the apparent root. This is a matter of much importance, for a growth of nail from a small remaining portion of matrix is usually a deformed and irregular growth, and gives as much trouble, when it gets long, as the disease for which the operation was performed. In Mr. P.'s case he was so much annoyed by the growth, while the cicatrix was still recent and tender, that I proposed to destroy the remaining matrix with nitric acid. As, however, the cicatrix got firm, and he learned, too, how to trim the nail-growth with a sharp knife, it became less troublesome, and he has never had any thing done for its removal.

Another well-marked case of this exostosis occurred to me in the person of Miss E., aged nineteen, who showed me in July, 1866, a hard swelling under the nail of the right big-toe. This had been growing gradually for several months, and she could attribute it to no evident cause. At first it gave her no pain or inconvenience, but as it grew more prominent it gave rise to pain in walking, particularly with a new or tight shoe. About two months before I saw it she had showed it to a surgeon, who called it an encysted tumor, and performed an operation for its relief. This operation must have been merely the paring off of the superficial portion of the tumor, for it was followed by no benefit.

The nail was found to be raised by a firm, solid tumor, evidently springing from the bone. The superficial portion which projected from under the nail was covered by a flaky, horny epidermis like that covering an ordinary corn. It projected to one side of the median line of the nail, and, as the nail had been cut away on one side to relieve the pressure, the whole development toward the surface had taken place quite on the side of the nail. Mr. Paget states that this is the usual fact with regard to these tumors, and that they rarely grow from exactly the middle of the dorsum of the phalanx. Feeling the tumor deeply and firmly, left no doubt that it was an exostosis.

Removal being the only remedy I had to propose, the operation was done on the 17th. I proceeded as in the last case, being careful to remove the whole matrix, in which, this time, I succeeded. The stump healed soundly and quickly, leaving a very comfortable though somewhat shortened toe.

FIG. 56.—(N. Y. Hospital Museum.)

The bone removed showed the usual osseous base, with very little cartilaginous tip. This was doubtless due to the operation which had preceded mine. The whole exostosis was about the size of a large pea, and, having a somewhat narrow base, and an expanded, flattened top, presented a decided mushroom shape (Fig. 56).

The seat of cartilaginous tumors is, by preference, in or upon the bones. Many, however, are found in other tissues, as the mamma, the testicle, and some of the internal organs, where they seem to have no relation whatever to any bone. The parotid region is a favorite seat of these growths; indeed, Mr. Paget remarks that the greater part of the solid tumors of this region have more or less cartilage in their composition. When originating from bone, the tumor may grow either upon and apparently from the surface, or it may be developed within the cavities of the bone, which in its growth it expands. Mr. Stanley thinks that this difference is connected with the size of the bone; thus he says: "In the instances of its occurrence in any of the larger bones, as the humerus, femur, or tibia, it usually grows from the outside of the bone, rarely within it. But in the instances of its occurrence in any of the smaller bones, especially of the hand or foot, it usually originates within the bone." The explanation of this peculiarity he does not give, and probably, in the present state of our knowledge, it cannot be given. As a pathological law, however, it is not without

its practical importance, and would certainly have a bearing on
the decision of the question of amputating the limb or removing the tumor.   Mr. Stanley also thinks that the origin of these
tumors can be discriminated by the character of the external
surface.   He says : "When the cartilaginous tumor originates
within a metacarpal or digital bone, the morbid deposit commencing in the cancellous texture is in some cases diffused
through it, unaccompanied by pain or any change in the cover-
ings of the bone indicative of the disease within it.   At length,
in one part, and it may be on one side only, or in the entire
circumference of the bone, its walls expand into a globular tumor, consisting of a thin, osseous shell, enclosing the cartilaginous substance.   The tumor in some instances remains small,
in others it increases to the size of an orange.   But, however
large the tumor may be, it retains the osseous shell, which
grows with the increase of the cartilage within it ; and, even
when of largest size, the tumor is unaccompanied by pain or
change in the surrounding tissues."

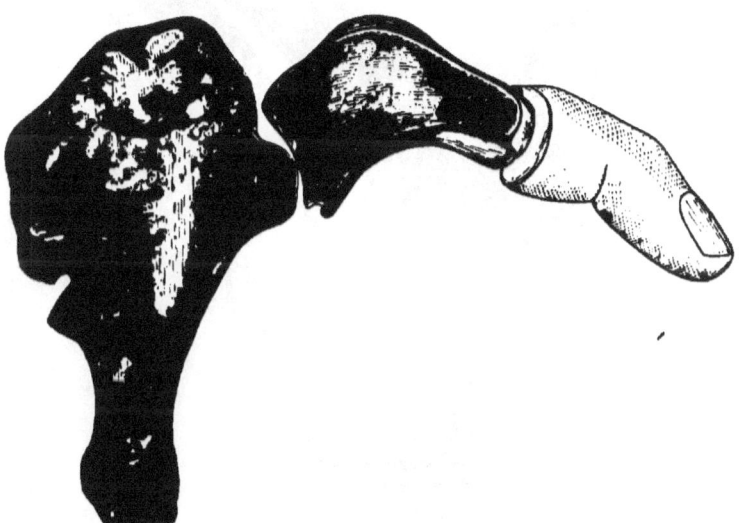

Fig. 57.—(From Cornil and Ranvier.)

"In the instances of the cartilaginous tumors growing from
the outside of a bone, the exterior of the tumor is usually nod-
uled, its cartilaginous substance is disposed in lobes united by

fibrous septa, through which the blood-vessels ramify, and a fibrous capsule encloses the tumor."

I believe that this may be an important diagnostic mark between the two forms of these tumors, and as such be ex-tremely useful; but that it is unvarying, or that the osseous shell is maintained, when the tumors grow very large, is, I

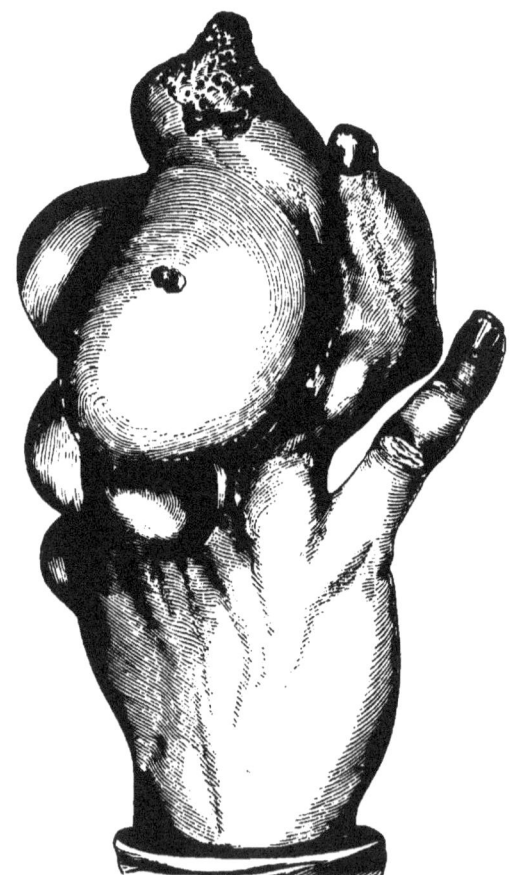

Fig. 58.—(From Billroth.)

think, scarcely ascertained with certainty. On this point of diagnosis Mr. Stanley makes the further remark that, when a single tumor occurs on the finger or toe, it is usually found to grow from the outside; but, when several fingers or toes are affected with these growths, they usually originate within the bone.

A favorite seat of the cartilaginous tumor is the hand, and less commonly the foot (Figs. 57, 58, 59). On the hand, they often affect several fingers, the tumors not all appearing at once, but following one another at longer or shorter intervals. Here, as elsewhere, the growth is very slow and painless, and the tumors are troublesome mainly from their bulk interfering with the use of the fingers. They usually show themselves first in early childhood, though occasional cases are noticed where they have begun in advanced life. The rate of growth,

FIG. 59.—(N. Y. Hospital Museum.)

usually slow, is sometimes quite rapid, and the rate of increase is not by any means the same for every tumor of the same hand; indeed, it is most often seen that one or more tumors, where there are many, take the precedence and go on rapidly increasing in size, and perhaps may pass through the stages of ulceration and destruction; while others of the same hand, perhaps on the same finger, quietly maintain themselves without increase or other apparent change. In these tumors, as well as in those developed in the larger long bones, it is often observed that the growth has commenced both within and without the bone, and that the two masses of cartilage thus growing have encroached upon the bone both from within and from without, until it has been entirely absorbed, and the external and internal tumors have coalesced into one, the continuity of the bone being entirely interrupted at its middle portion. In this condition a slight cause will produce a fracture, and the destruction of the bone occasionally advances so far that only traces of its central portion can be discovered in the mass, while the articular ends retain their integrity. This disappearance of the original bone is sometimes carried still further, as in the case of single tumor of hand above alluded to. This case was in the first phalanx of the middle finger of a patient in Bellevue Hospital—John Shannon, aged sixty, an Irish laborer, who was admitted September 29, 1869. The tumor had been growing about three months, and, as he thought, had originated from a blow against a mantel-piece about three weeks before the appearance of the tumor. The tumor was soft, and gave such evidences of fluctuation that on the 2d of October an exploratory incision was made about three inches long. A cavity was opened containing a soft, semi-fluid mass, which easily broke down under handling. This was mingled with portions which were firmer in consistence, and in particular the portion at the end of the phalanx was distinct in its appearance and presented a sort of cauliflower growth of tolerable firmness. The metacarpo-phalangeal joint was encroached on. The finger was amputated at this joint, and the wound did well. The tumor, examined microscopically, showed all the elements of enchondroma. Pretty rapidly the tumor grew again, now involving the metacarpal bone, and soon reaching a size greater than before. On the 12th of November the hand was amputated. The wound cicatrized without accident, and the man was discharged well, November 29th.

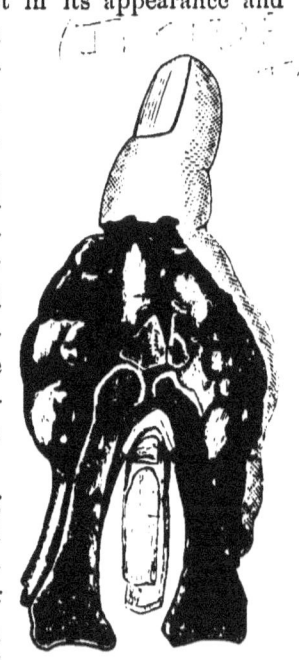

Dr. Delafield makes the following report on the tumor: "The carpal and metacarpal bones are almost entirely replaced by a tumor. This tumor is enclosed by the skin, except on the back of the hand, near the base of the middle finger, which had been removed. When the tumor is cut into, it is found to consist of a soft, partly-gelatinous, grayish, semi-translucent substance, traversed in different directions by fibrous bands. Microscopically examined, it consists of bands of fibrous tissue, mixed with small, round, and fusiform cells running in various directions. Enclosed and separated by these bands are more trans-

Fig. 60.—(From Cornil and Ranvier.)

parent portions of tissue. These portions consist of a basement-substance, either homogeneous or finely granular, or faintly fibrillated. Embedded in this basement substance, in some places are well-formed cartilage-cells; in other places the cells are of more irregular shape, are mixed with small, round, and fusiform cells, and are in such numbers as almost entirely to obscure the basement-substance. In other places nothing but small, round cells can be seen, and here the basement-substance is distinctly fibrous, and is arranged in small, regular alveoli. In other places the basement-substance is faintly fibrillated, contains only a few oval and fusiform cells, and resembles mucous tissue."

In cases where the growth is from the outside only of the bone, there seems to be less tendency to its destruction (Fig. 60).

CHAPTER II.

OSSEOUS TUMORS.

TUMORS, composed entirely of bone, are found almost exclusively in or upon the bones, though some rare cases are reported of perfect tumors of this sort being found in the soft parts entirely disconnected with any bone. In no case of growth, from any part of the body, is the homology of the new formation more absolute than it is in many of these tumors; they presenting, in most cases, not only an exact identity in intimate microscopical structure with true bone, but being arranged into compact and cancellous tissue with as much regularity and perfection as are the original bones of the skeleton. What is true of the structure of these tumors is also true of their chemical composition, which by numerous observers has been shown to be precisely that of normal bone, and most of the variations which the chemical composition of these tumors present are not greater than those which we find in the original bones, under the varying conditions of age, sex, and disease. Of the mode of development of these perfect osseous tumors, it is perhaps difficult to speak positively, because it frequently happens that no trace of any cartilaginous or fibrous matrix is found in any part of the tumor; but the analogy is so clear and so strong, with the development of ordinary bone, and is borne out so distinctly by those tumors when we do trace the ossific process in its progress, that there can hardly be any reasonable doubt that they are formed in a soft matrix, which is sometimes cartilaginous and sometimes fibrous, in this obeying, probably, the same general laws as those which determine this difference in the original development of the skeleton.

Osseous tumors present themselves under two forms, according as the cancellous or compact tissue prevails in their substance. By far the larger number present a well-formed cancellous arrangement in their interior, and an equally well-formed, compact shell surrounding them on the outside. In some, however, very little if any cancellous substance is found to exist, the whole tumor being formed of solid, very dense, compact substance, giving it much the appearance and the weight of ivory. Hence we have the distinction into the ordinary cancellous bony tumor, and the ivory-like tumor, two classes which differ not merely in the facts above recited as to their structure, but also in many points of their history, as well as of their practical relations. These two classes, therefore, may advantageously be studied separately; and first for the more common, the cancellous class.

The cancellous bony tumors occur in almost every possible situation, sometimes within and sometimes upon the surface of the bones. Their history is usually that of a slow, painless growth, though sometimes, when they appear to have been provoked by an injury, some pain and soreness accompany their early development. When they grow from within a bone, the external shell of the bone is usually distended by the growing tumor, and most commonly itself forms the outer shell of the tumor. Indeed, it should be remarked that, in these cases, as well as in those which grow from the surface, the line of distinction between the tumor and the original bone is not clear, and perhaps most commonly the tissues of the original bone are simply continuous with the tissues of the new growth, so that they belong to the class which Mr. Paget has denominated outgrowths. So strikingly is this the case, that, if a section be made of some of these which grow from the outside of the long bones, for instance, a continuity will be found, not only of the outer fibres of compact tissue, but also of the cancellous interior which will communicate with, and be continuous with, the cancellous interior of the bone upon which the tumor is developed. These tumors are usually round or oval in shape, and present a smooth, even surface; in exceptional cases they are irregularly lobed. Those which spring up from the surface of a bone, to

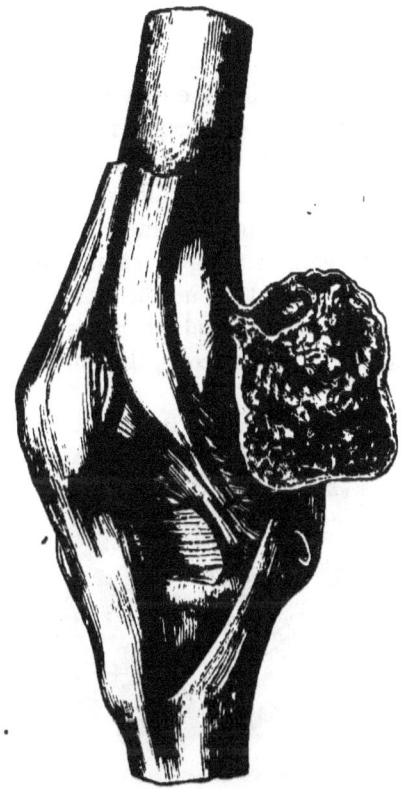

Fig. 61.—(From Billroth.)

which the term exostosis is more properly applied, have usually a narrow neck by which they are attached to the bone from which they grow (Fig. 61), and Mr. Stanley makes the statement that in the increase of the tumors this neck does not enlarge, all the growth taking place in the body of the tumor beyond the neck. Mr. Stanley does not give the observations upon which this idea is founded, and it can, therefore, not be accepted as proved; but, even if it be a fact of common occurrence, it would have some valuable practical bearings on the questions of the time for, and the mode of, effecting the removal of the tumor. Some of these exostoses, however, have not the narrow neck, but are themselves flat, and attached by a broad surface to the bone from which they grow. And here it is often difficult to decide as to the real nature of the disease; whether it is a proper tumor, or whether it is a thickening of the original bone-tissues, by inflammation of the bone, or its periosteal covering. Happily, the diagnosis is not of practical importance, for the question of removal is not often entertained, where the large base of attachment makes the removal of the whole morbid mass uncertain and difficult.

With regard to the seat of the cancellous exostoses, scarcely any bone in the skeleton is entirely exempt from them. Perhaps the most frequent seat is in the epiphysary ends of the long bones, where of course development is going on most actively, and where, in young persons, they may be considered as

FIG. 62.—(From Heath.)

due to a morbid excess of formative activity. Next to these points in frequency are the jawbones, both upper and lower. Fig. 62, taken from Heath, is a good example of the cancellous exostosis of the upper jaw. It originated in the left superior maxilla, projected downward, displacing and deforming the lower jaw, and largely encroaching on the mouth.

16

I have now a lady under my care who has an exostosis, of the shape and size of a small cherry, projecting into the mouth, and growing from about the middle of the under surface of the bony palate. It has been growing slowly for about twelve years. It is covered with healthy mucous membrane, is without pain, and gives no trouble except from its mechanical presence. It has a narrow neck, and could be very easily removed.

I have seen recently, with my friend Dr. E. Krakowitzer, of this city, a young lady in whom a tumor is slowly growing on the right parietal bone, and has now reached a size of about an inch and a quarter in its long diameter. It appeared, without cause, about ten years previous, at the age of eleven. It has the shape of a section of the blunt end of an egg, and rises about half an inch from the level of the surrounding bone. It seems to be immovably fixed to the bone, though occasionally we thought some movement could be developed in it by very strong pressure from side to side, as if to slide it on the parietal bone. A needle passed down to its surface indicates that it is

FIG. 63.—(From Billroth.)

entirely bone. It is painless and free from any tenderness, and the scalp over it is perfectly healthy. We advised that for the present no operation should be thought of. Fig. 63 represents a series of smaller growths of this kind scattered over the surface of the cranium.

An interesting variety of exostosis is that which has its seat in the larger tendons just at their point of attachment into the bone. These are quite common, and scarcely a museum can be found which has not one or more of these growths. They seem to be developed in the tendinous tissue, with which the growth is so intimately confounded that it is difficult to decide whether the bony growth has taken place in the tendon-substance as a matrix, or whether it has replaced the tendon by absorption of its fibres. They usually have a base of attachment to the bone no larger than that occupied by the tendon, and sometimes extend a considerable distance up into the muscular substance, the direction of whose fibres the increase of tumor always follows (Fig. 64.) According to my observation, these exostoses are always found in strong, well-developed men, in whom the muscles and tendons are large and vigorous, and the bony processes of attachment largely developed; and, if this be so, it may be fair to consider these also as a result of an excess of formative power irregularly exercised, rather than properly a disease. A fine specimen of this exists in the cabinet of the New York Hospital, which was found growing from the femur of an athletic negro, "in whom it had caused no symptoms, and about the origin of which nothing was known. It consists of a mass of bone, six inches long, springing by a large pyramidal base from the shaft below the trochanter minor, and passing downward as a slender, tapering process, parallel with the femur. The whole resembles very much in shape a snipe's head and bill, the head representing the base, and the bill the prolongation downward." Fig. 65 shows a flat exostosis on the anterior surface of the tibia.

The osseous tumor usually gives rise to no symptoms excepting such as may be due to its size, or to its pressure upon neighboring organs. Thus Mr. Stanley speaks of a case where a man had an exostosis growing from the posterior surface of the clavicle, in whom no pain was experienced while the arm was at rest, "but directly it was moved he suffered acute pain in the direction of the axillary plexus of nerves and its branches;" and also of another "in whom an aneurism was supposed to have arisen from the subclavian artery; but, upon more careful examination, an exostosis was discovered growing from the first rib, pushing the artery forward, and flattening it. Upon the front of the swelling the pulsation was strong, and extended over a large space; but at its sides no pulsation could be felt. The pulsation of the artery in the axilla was feeble. In the

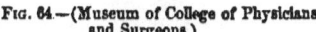

Fig. 64.—(Museum of College of Physicians and Surgeons.)   Fig. 65.—(Museum of College of Physicians and Surgeons.)

brachial, radial, and ulnar arteries no pulsation could be felt. Mr. Stanley also refers to several other curious localities in which exostoses have been found. Thus he alludes to one where the œsophagus was compressed by an exostosis growing from the body of one of the vertebræ. Another is recorded, where a conical exostosis, growing from the posterior part of the odontoid process of the second cervical vertebra, caused fatal compression and softening of the spinal cord. He mentions also a case where an exostosis grew from the os pubis and compressed the neck of the bladder, so that a catheter could not be introduced; and another very curious case in which " M. Jules Cloquet, in examining the body of an aged female, found the symphysis pubis ossified, and a bony growth projecting from its posterior surface into the cavity of the bladder. The pressure of the tumor had caused the absorption of the coats of the bladder; hence, on opening its cavity, the bony tumor was seen projecting into it, covered only by a thin layer of fibro-cellular tissue, which, at the base of the tumor, was continuous with the

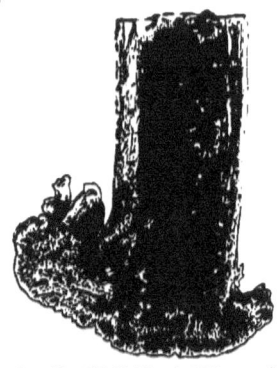

FIG. 66.—(N. Y. Hospital Museum.)

mucous membrane of the bladder." Fig. 66 shows a very common form of exostosis springing from the sawed end of a femur after amputation.

The exostoses which grow from the inner surface of the dura mater, and from the internal surface of the cranium, are sometimes the cause of various cerebral symptoms, and sometimes their presence has not been suspected from any sign of their existence during life. Thus, we have one in the New York Hospital Museum, which is developed in the falx cerebri, and has attained a size and thickness sufficient to make a very decided depression in the cerebral substance, against which it lay, and yet the patient, who was a man of about one hundred years of age, never had shown any sign or mark of cerebral disturbance. On the other hand, Mr. Stanley alludes to the case of a boy who was "admitted into St. Thomas's Hospital on account of epileptic fits," in whom "a spot was discovered where pressure gave much uneasiness. Here the trephine was applied. At the instant of raising the circlet of bone, he had a sharp epileptic fit; but this was the last. From the inner table of the portion of bone removed, a spiculum a quarter of an inch long projected, pressing upon the dura mater." Why this difference should exist between tumors which seem to have precisely the same physical relations to the cerebral substance, has not, as far as I know, been particularly investigated.

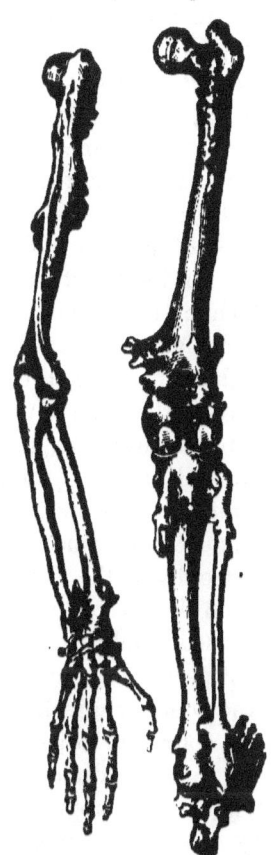

A feature of much interest in these cancellous exostoses is that, sometimes, they are quite numerous, affecting a number of bones of the skeleton (Fig. 67). Instances of this kind are related by several authors. One presented itself at the clinique of the College of Physicians and Surgeons, in which at least twenty of these bony tumors existed at various points, and usually the seat of the tumor corresponded on the two sides of the body. Thus there was one on each clavicle, one on the upper end of each ulna, one on each acromion process of the scapula, one on each internal malleolus, besides several others in which the correspondence was not quite so

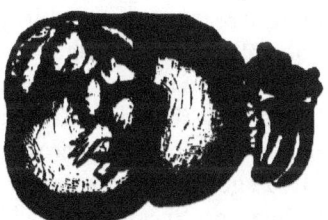

Fig. 67.—(From Billroth.)   Fig. 68.—(From Heath.)

perfect. They were of a size varying from that of a pea to that of a walnut, were without pain, and had grown slowly without assignable cause.

An interesting variety of exostosis is that which we occasionally find developed from the fangs of teeth, and which consists entirely of hypertrophy of the osseous tissue (cementum) of the tooth. Fig. 68, from Heath, gives a view of one of these exostoses attached to the side of a molar tooth. It was as large as a pigeon's egg, and came away with the tooth when it was extracted. "Under the microscope the specimen was seen to contain no dentine, but to consist exclusively of osseous tissue (cementum)."

The second form of exostosis, in which the growth consists principally, and sometimes entirely, of compact bone-substance, is a much more rare, but a much more formidable disease. It usually assumes the form of a single tumor, and its favorite seat is in the bones of the face and skull. It sometimes presents a narrow pedicle or base, but this is rare; the most common mode of development being between the layers composing the bone, as in the diploë of the supra-ciliary ridge, a point which these tumors very commonly affect. In its growth the tumor disparts the two layers of bone, which are extended over it at first, and afterward disappear, or are confounded with the growth which gradually pushes its encroachments in all directions, pressing upon the cavities of the orbit, or the nose, or the mouth, extruding the eye, displacing the brain-substance, and finally producing death after the most fearful suffering, and with the most repulsive features of deformity. Cases are also sometimes observed where no distinct tumor can be traced at any time, but a slow enlargement or hypertrophy of the affected bones takes place, which gradually develop themselves into a hard, irregular mass, which, in its fully-formed condition, cannot well be distinguished from the tumor proper. These hypertrophic growths are principally found in the superior maxillary bones, but the disease has a disposition to spread to adjacent bones, pushing its encroachments in every possible direction. Mr. Paget gives an account of a specimen in the museum of the College of Surgeons, in which "two large masses of bone, of almost exactly symmetrical form and arrangement, project from the upper jaw and orbits, and have partially coalesced in the median line. They are rounded, deeply-lobed, and nodular; nearly as hard and as heavy as ivory; perforated with numerous apertures, apparently for blood-vessels. They project more than three inches in front of the face, and an inch on each side beyond the malar bones; they fill both orbits, the nasal cavities, and probably the antra, and they extend backward to the pterygoid plates. Part of the septum of the nose, and the alveolar border of the jaw, are almost the only remaining indication of a face. The disease appears to have begun in the superior maxillary bones, and thence to have spread over the bones of the face; similar disease, in a less degree, existing in the bones adjacent to the chief outgrowths. The patient, who was sixty years old, believed the disease had been eighteen years in progress, and ascribed it to repeated blows on the face.

He suffered much pain in the face, eyes, and head. His eyes projected from the orbits : the right, after suppuration and sloughing of the cornea, shrivelled; the left was accidentally burst by a blow. During the last two years of his life he occasionally showed symptoms of insanity, and at last he died with apoplexy of the cerebral membranes." (Fig 69.)

In all these cases, however, the chief feature, and the one of most practical import, is the gradual increase of the osseous mass, until, by its sheer intrusion upon the surrounding organs, it produces so much injury and disturbance as finally, after long months of suffering, to destroy the patient. And this tendency to steady increase seems to be characteristic of this form of bony growth. It is a well-known fact that the cancellous exostosis is apt, after it has reached a certain size, to increase very slowly, or to remain stationary during indefinite periods, perhaps for life. These ivory exostoses, on the contrary, seem to have an inherent tendency to increase, which nothing can arrest, save the death of the sufferer.

Fig. 60.—(From Heath.)

The anatomical character of these ivory exostoses is generally that of pure and perfect, but very hard, bone-tissue. The hardest parts of these tumors present sometimes an irregular distribution of, and sometimes an absence of, the usual anatomical elements of bone, as in the case Mr. Paget alludes to in the museum of the University of Cambridge. It is also occasionally noticed that the elements of bone are not arranged in the usual orderly manner, but are irregularly distributed about the mass, varying somewhat in their arrangement at various points of the same tumor. Usually, however, the bone-tissue is perfect in every respect, and cannot by the microscope be distinguished from bone of original formation. Many of these tumors contain nothing but the hard, ivory-like bone-tissue, but in many again it is mingled at points with some cancellous tissue, and some tumors are recorded which present a thick outside shell of hard bone, enclosing cancellous tissue within, of perfect formation.

Their seat is most commonly the bones of the skull and face, and, as stated above, a predilection is shown for the orbital region, in or about which a large proportion of these growths originate. Fig. 70 gives a section of a cranium where one of

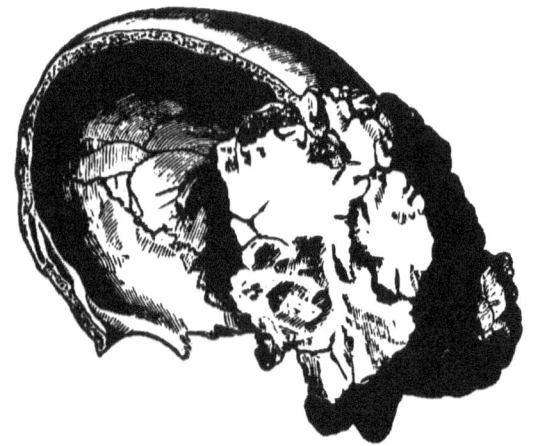

FIG. 70.—(From Paget.)

these tumors, apparently developed in the supra-ciliary region, has grown to an immense size, displacing all the bones of the face, and projecting backward into the cranial cavity. The specimen is in the museum of the University of Cambridge, and Mr. Paget, from whose work the plate is copied, says of it: "It is the largest and best specimen of the kind I have ever seen, and its osseous structure is distinct; only, as Prof. Clark has informed me, it is irregular; in the hardest parts there are neither Haversian canals nor lacunæ; in the less hard parts the canals are very large, and the lacunæ are not arranged in circles about them; and everywhere the lacunæ are of irregular or distorted forms." They are occasionally found in other parts of the skull and face, and sometimes, though rarely, there is more than one, as in the specimen in the Musée Dupuytren, alluded to by Follin, and of which he gives a drawing. Here two distinct osseous masses existed, one on the anterior and one on the posterior part of the vault of the cranium, each projecting about equally from the outer and inner surfaces of the bone, the inner projection largely encroaching upon the cerebral cavity. These tumors are occasionally developed in the lower jaw, and very rarely in other bones. It is curious to observe that, sometimes, the hypertrophic outgrowth that we find as the result of periosteal inflammation puts on this ivory-like character, and sometimes vies in solidity with the hardest of the tumors. Thus, in a specimen in the New York Hospital Museum, which presents an enlargement of the anterior half of the tibia, evidently from periosteal irritation, the new material which has been deposited, to the thickness of more than half an inch, is shown by the section to be of the hardest and most solid kind of bone, in which no cancelli and no vascular canals can be seen, by the naked eye. The immense weight of the bone confirms its solidity. This specimen seems to mark the dividing line between the ivory tumors proper and those enlargements, above alluded to, which are so general, and involve in their progress so large a part of the affected bone that they more naturally suggest the idea of an hypertrophy than of a simple tumor.

Of the cases in which the tumor character is the most marked, a number of examples are on record. One classical case is given by Mr. Heath, which was under the care of Sir William Fergusson, in King's College Hospital. The patient was twenty-one years of age, and the tumor had appeared twelve years before. It was the size of an apple, and occupied the situation of the orbit from which it projected, carrying out with it the eyeball. The tumor, after removal, was found to consist, "in all its anterior part, of nodulated bone as hard as ivory, and posteriorly of very dense ordinary bone, mixed with a small amount of cartilage. The tumor sprang apparently, as in the former case, from the upper parts of the maxilla, and had invaded the antrum, orbit, and nostril."

Mr. Heath also alludes to Michou's case, in which the tumor occupied the cavity of the antrum, springing from its upper or orbital wall, and distending it in all directions. "It weighed eighteen hundred grains, and was deeply lobulated, particularly on its posterior aspect. A section showed concentric markings upon a surface of ivory, and microscopic examination demonstrated the lacunæ and canaliculi of true bone."

Dr. Duka's case ("Pathological Society Reports," vol. xvii.) was still more remarkable, "and occurred in a female native of Bengal, aged twenty-six, on the right side of the face, which was not much deformed. There was a discharge from the right nostril, which was obstructed, and on examination a hard tumor was found within it, *which was movable*, but could not be extracted, and which had existed six years." It was removed with much difficulty, and the specimen is in St. George's Hospital Museum. "It has an oblong shape, and is not unlike a middle-sized potato, with depressions and elevations passing irregularly over it. The upper part, which is believed to have been in contact with the cribriform plate of the ethmoid bone, exhibits corresponding delicate depressions, with other deeper sulci in front, behind, and on the side, probably for the passage of blood-vessels. . . . The whole bony mass weighs one thousand and sixty grains; its long diameter is nearly three inches, the short one an inch and two lines, and the longest circumference seven inches. There are no distinct Haversian systems, but abundance of lacunæ arranged around vascular canals. In some parts of the tumor the characters are very much like those of simple ossified cartilage."

Fig. 71, from Heath, is a good example of the ivory exostosis growing from the angle of the lower jaw. The tumor projects both downward and on each side of the jaw, and measures nearly three inches in its longest diameter. It is composed throughout of bone, uniform in texture, and as hard and heavy as ivory.

Two accidents are apt to happen to these tumors, which present some points of pathological interest. I allude to necrosis and fracture. In several instances it has been noticed that inflammation has attacked these growths, and that after its subsidence abscess has been formed, communicating with and

exposing the surface of the bone, which has gradually fallen
into the condition of a sequestrum, which sequestrum has finally
separated from the surrounding bone, and become detached,
leaving a granulating cavity, which in several recorded instances has perfectly healed.   In Mr. Hilton's case, the process

Fig. 71.—(From Heath.)

of separation was going on for six years before it was finally
completed.   Acting upon this hint, Sir Astley Cooper made
the suggestion that an incision should be made down upon
such a tumor, exposing its surface, and detaching it from the
surrounding soft parts, in the hope that, by such exposure, necrosis would take place, and a spontaneous separation occur.
Whether any such expectation has ever been realized, I am not
informed.

　　With regard to fracture, the only instance that I know of in
which the ivory exostosis has been separated in this way is Dr.
Duka's case, before mentioned, in which the tumor growing in
the antrum had separated from its bony attachments, and was
lying loose in the cavity.   The cancellous exostoses, however,
and particularly where they have acquired a narrow base of attachment, are not unfrequently broken off.   Several examples
are recorded of this accident, and the suggestion has been made
to break them off, with a view to arrest their growth, as, in the

instances known, no growth has occurred after the base of attachment has been broken through.

In all these different forms of tumors situated on bones, the question of operative interference is liable to present itself. It may be asserted as a general fact that, in any case in which the tumor can be completely removed, the operation will be likely to be successful. It must be remembered, however, that in only a small proportion of bone-tumors is the base so distinct and so small that the surgeon's saw or chisel can reach the whole of its attachment with ease and certainty; and that, therefore, in these cases the removal is apt to be imperfect and partial. I do not mean to say that, in all cases in which the whole diseased tissue is not removed, a recurrence will take place, but that incomplete removal leaves a disposition to recurrence I suppose no surgeon will deny, and that, therefore, the possibility of complete removal becomes an important element in deciding upon the propriety of an operation. In many exostoses which have a narrow and accessible neck, the mere removal of the mass by incision through this neck is sufficient, for, as above stated, the stump thus left shows very little inclination to grow; but, in many others, when the base of attachment is large, and the tumor situated deeply, the operation of removal is among the most difficult, tedious, and troublesome, in surgery. These difficulties were experienced in the fullest degree by my colleague, Dr. John Watson, in a case of exostosis of the middle of the femur, which he was engaged in removing. The depth of the wound, though a liberal one, and the unyielding nature of the tendinous and aponeurotic tissues near the bone, prevented very seriously the oblique application of the chisels and forceps, which was necessary to get at the base, and which would have been so easy, could the soft parts have been removed. After a long and laborious operation, conducted with much patience, in his usual thorough manner, he succeeded in removing the whole growth, and the wound was brought together. Severe, deep-seated inflammation followed rapidly, and spread up and down the thigh, terminating in unhealthy suppuration, and bringing the patient so rapidly down that he sank and died about a week from the operation. It seemed as if the violence done to the tissues about the tumor, by the necessary manipulation, had provoked an inflammation which the injured parts were not able to resist, and hence the fatal extension of its ravages.

Nevertheless, if the tumor be growing rapidly; if it involve parts where its pressure may become dangerous, or painful, or even inconvenient; if it be situated where it is a deformity; in short, if there be any good reason for desiring its removal, the operation may be undertaken with a good prospect of perfect success; if, as above stated, the mechanical conditions of the tumor and its surroundings be such as will permit of its easy and complete removal. As to the mode of accomplishing the removal, so much will depend on the nature and seat of the growth that specific rules can hardly be laid down. The first step will be to expose the tumor by an incision, which should be a liberal one, and in deep tumors, in fleshy parts, Mr. Stanley gives direction to cut the muscular fibres transversely, both because it exposes the seat of disease more thoroughly, by the retraction of the fibres, and because it leaves the wound better open for the discharge of matter during the healing process. The bone is to be attacked by saws, chisels, or bone-forceps, according to circumstances, and the whole diseased tissue, with a liberal portion of the surrounding sound bone, should be removed, if it can with safety be done. In my own hands, the chisel (and particularly a moderate-sized gouge with rounded cutting edge) is the most effective and most generally useful instrument I employ. It is, however, in the ivory exostosis, about the face and head, that the most formidable operative difficulties present themselves. In the following case the manipulations are not stated to have been difficult:

Dr. Alexander B. Mott, of this city, was the operator, and the patient, a Scotchman, thirty-three years of age, of good constitution and health, had noticed for seven years an enlargement about the inner canthus of the left eye. It commenced without obvious cause, and gradually became the seat of great pain as it grew larger. Its growth, at first, was toward the nasal cavities, and afterward toward the orbit, projecting also from the surface of the cheek and side of the nose. Lately an abscess had formed and discharged near the inner canthus. On passing a probe through the opening of this abscess, bare bone could be felt. The deformity was still further increased by the left eye being pressed by the tumor very much from its proper position, a consequence of which pressure was a very great impairment of vision, amounting finally almost to a total loss. Dr. Mott exposed the surface of the tumor by making four flaps, and dissecting them up from their attachments. "This being done, I found the bony tumor was firmly impacted in the orbit and nasal cavity. I consequently separated the nasal bone of the left side from its fellow of the opposite side by means of a strong pair of Liston's bone-forceps, and, with a fine, straight, flexible saw, detached it from its frontal attachment. By a little manipulation I was thus enabled to remove the portion represented in Fig. 72, and, on accomplishing this, I next, by

Fig. 72.—(From Dr. A. B. Mott's Collection.)

means of a delicate chisel and hammer, gradually detached the other bony mass from the orbital plate of the frontal bone, and also from the orbital plate of the superior maxillary. The os unguis was so thoroughly incorporated with the tumor that I was obliged to remove it along with the mass; and the whole being now somewhat movable, I made slight traction by means of a pair of strong forceps. A few more cuts of the chisel enabled me to withdraw it." The tumor was found to be of dense osseous structure, and is represented in the plate of natural size. Its weight was three ounces and one drachm. The patient made a very good recovery, and has since remained entirely free from any symptom of return of the affection, a period of about thirteen years.

Sir William Fergusson, M. Michou, Dr. Duka, M. Demarquay, and others, have published full accounts of their operations on these tumors, and, though the number of operations is too few to be of any statistical value, the general result seems to be, for so serious an operation, quite encouraging. Sir William Fergusson's case died, but the three other surgeons named above were successful in curing their patients.

CHAPTER III.

FIBROUS TUMORS.

THE pure fibrous tumor is not rare in the bones; most commonly connected with the periosteum, of which, as in some forms of epulis, it seems to be an outgrowth; but sometimes found—as in the upper and lower jaws—developed in the substance of the bone itself. These tumors are commonly typical specimens of their class, being composed entirely of the white fibrous tissue, containing scarcely any other element, and with no trace of stroma or basement-substance, in which the fibres are embedded. Some differences in structure, however, are found. Thus, some are harder and drier, others softer and more juicy; some show the fibres cleanly defined and distinct, others show merely a general fibrous character, in which it is not always quite easy to distinguish, and quite impossible to isolate, separate fibres. Some show a distinct basement-substance, hard, firm, and white, almost like cartilage, in which fibres are variously interlaced, sometimes in comparatively small numbers; others, again, particularly the harder specimens, are so compact and condensed in their structure that nothing but careful microscopical examination will reveal the fact that they are composed of nothing but fibres. Elastic fibres are sometimes scattered through the tumor in considerable abundance, though in a large proportion of cases they are entirely absent. Nuclei are also found in young fibrous tumors, and in those which are growing rapidly, while in the older and more stationary examples they may be entirely absent. Again, cartilage and bone are not unfrequently met with in apparently accidental association with the fibrous tissue, though true bone is not often found in large amount in this form of tumor. It is true that there is a change in many of them, wherein, by a process of slow degeneration, the chemical elements of bone are so largely infiltrated through the tumor that it finally becomes a hard, solid mass, as heavy and as solid as bone, which to the naked eye it sometimes resembles; but this is calcification, not ossification, and the elements are seen, under the microscope, not to have assumed any of the characters of true bone. Cysts also are developed in fibrous tumors, sometimes many being scattered through their substance, while it sometimes happens that one large cyst so displaces and replaces the original structure that its character as a primary fibrous growth is difficult or impossible to recognize.

The external features of these tumors are somewhat constant. They have a distinct and usually smooth boundary-line, which separates them from the surrounding tissues, from which they can, by enucleation, be readily removed. This is true of those portions whereby they come in contact with parts other than the bone or periosteum, from which they spring. In their mode of connection with these latter, considerable differences present themselves. Thus, from the periosteum they often have the character of outgrowths, in which no boundary-line exists between the tumor and the tissue from which it is developed, and in some cases not even the microscope can discriminate between the new growth and its parent-tissue. In other cases a line of separation can be traced through the whole contour of the new growth, and even in some instances the tumor has no contact with the fibrous structures near which it grows, but is at every point separated from them by a loose areolar interspace. This is occasionally noticed in fibrous tumors growing about the metatarsus and metacarpus. The external surface of these tumors is usually rounded and smooth, sometimes lobed, rarely bosselated or botryoidal. Their consistence is very hard; their specific gravity, as a class, greater than any

17

other but the osseous. Their vascularity is generally slight, though some of the softer forms receive a large number of vessels.

They are, in the bones, usually single, their growth is very slow and painless, and they sometimes attain a very great size. With regard to their constitutional character they are, by general consent, considered to be uniformly benign. Their tendency, however, to local reproduction, particularly if imperfectly removed, is well marked, and in operating must not be lost sight of. The malignant history of some "fibroid tumors" must not lead us to the unjust imputation of evil character to any of those which, under the microscope as well as to the naked eye, deserve the name of "fibrous tumors." In short, it may be stated, as the expression of a general law, to which there are very few exceptions, that the benignity of these tumors is in direct proportion to the perfection which the fibrous element has attained — those which represent perfect fibrous tissue being absolutely benign, and those which present it in a less perfect state, and particularly in its embryonal form, are always to be looked upon with a certain amount of suspicion.

The seat of these tumors is sometimes on the surface of the bone, and then they may fairly be supposed to originate in the periosteum, with which they are commonly continuous, or it is in the central parts that they are developed, and then they usually distend, in their growth, the compact outer shell of the bone, which often, even in tumors of the largest size, forms a thin, uniform covering, sometimes not thicker than an eggshell, which gives them, on a slight touch, the feel of a bony tumor, but which, by firmer pressure, yields, and sometimes crackles under the finger like a broken egg-shell. They have been found in or upon most of the larger bones, usually near their cancellous rather then the compact portions. They have been noticed of very large size in the femur, humerus, and scapula. We have one very marked example of one of these tumors in the museum of the New York Hospital, developed in the lower part of the femur, which had been six years growing, and which, at the time of amputation, measured thirty-seven inches in circumference. Mr. Stanley speaks of one, in the museum of St. Bartholomew's, which grew from the humerus, and which measured three feet in circumference. Others of very large size have been recorded in the scapula. It is, however, in the maxillæ, both upper and lower, that the fibrous tumors are most commonly found, and have been most carefully studied. For many reasons the tumors of the jaws can be most conveniently considered together, and I therefore postpone any more particular account of fibrous tumors of the bone, till we come to the chapter devoted to the study of the various tumors which affect the jaws.

SPINDLE-CELLED FIBROIDS.

A considerable number of bone-tumors present themselves, of which the histological character is given, by the presence of spindle-shaped or oat-shaped cells, which compose the mass of the tumor, often to the exclusion of any other element. From the distinctness of their anatomical characters, and the facility with which these characters may be recognized, these tumors have long been known, and have been described by all modern writers. But, some controversy having arisen with regard to their histogenesis, different names have been given to them by different observers, in accordance with their different views, as to the signification of the microscopical elements of which they are composed.

Lebert first drew attention to them as a class worthy of separate consideration, and, as he adopted very confidently the idea that the elongated cells, of which they were composed, were nothing more than fibre-cells arrested in a certain stage of development, he named them, very appropriately, if his view were correct, fibro-plastic tumors. Billroth, Virchow, and others of the modern German school, have protested against this view, and have shown that in the formation of fibrous tissue in the embryo there is no stage or condition which presents the spindle-shaped cells, and that, therefore, Lebert's view being incorrect, the name he uses is inappropriate. Billroth insists that, if these peculiar cells represent a stage of incomplete development of any tissue, it is the muscular fibre, and not the fibrous tissue, to which they belong, and that therefore they ought to be included under the myomata, or tumors composed

of muscular fibres, rather than under the fibromata, with which
they have no proved relation. Virchow pronounces the spindle-shaped cells, which are often found in uterine fibroid, as
imperfectly-developed muscle-cells, and gives these tumors the
name of "*myoma læve cellulare.*" In comparing the views of
the best microscopists, it seems doubtful whether white fibrous
tissue is ever developed from cells at all, and even Virchow,
the great advocate of the doctrine "*omnia ex cellula,*" acknowledges that in the formation of fibrous tissue it is the intercellular substance and not the cells which are concerned in its
development. The yellow elastic tissue, it is true, seems to be
developed from cells, but this element is comparatively uncommon in fibrous tumors, and has, therefore, but little signification
as far as histogenesis is concerned. It is not without reason,
therefore, that pathologists have rejected Lebert's term, "fibro-
plastic," as conveying an incorrect idea ; but still it is necessary
to remember that, though his theory of formation is unsound,
and his nomenclature therefore faulty, his observations are nevertheless clear and admirable, and that from his labors, and
from the contributions made by numerous other observers, we
have a fair ground for including in one class all those tumors
that are mainly composed of these peculiar and easily-recognized cells. This class would include all those cases so well
described by Lebert, as well as those described by Mr. Paget
under the title of recurring fibroid tumors, those called by
Billroth spindle-shaped sarcomata, and those which Virchow
denominates sarcomata with fusiform cells. It will perhaps be
convenient for us to denominate them the *spindle-celled fibroids,*
as an appellation which embraces the facts in the case, without
the suggestion of any theory.

These tumors, as their name imports, have a nearer resemblance, in their naked-eye characteristics, to the fibrous than to
any other tumors. Indeed, the firmer specimens cannot in any
way be distinguished from the fibrous growth, except by the
aid of the microscope. They are usually tolerably firm, of a
whitish homogeneous section, from which but little juice can
be scraped, not very liberally supplied with blood-vessels, and
usually uniform in their appearance throughout their whole
substance. When they recur after removal, their appearance

is often much changed to the naked eye; they are softer, like the flesh of fish; they are more juicy and more vascular, in each recurrence departing more widely from the fibrous appearance, but showing under the microscope the same peculiar anatomical constituents. In shape these growths affect the spherical, but in or upon the bones they are of course much influenced by the pressure which they encounter as they spread; whereever, however, they escape into the softer tissues, they usually show a rounded mass which is limited by a pretty firm capsule, and which, like the fibrous tumors, can be easily enucleated from the bed in which it lies. After several recurrences, they are apt to involve more extensively the surrounding parts, penetrating between the muscles, adhering to the bones, and deporting themselves more and more like a malignant mass each time they return. Whether this form of tumor ever really invades and involves in its substance the tissues with which it is in contact, I do not know, but that the contrary is generally the fact, is well illustrated by one of Syme's cases, in which a large tumor on the chest, which was the last of five or six recurrences *in loco*, lay, at the time of death, among the muscles so loosely attached that it might have been removed without dividing any important part, "as a common fatty tumor might be."

The microscopic characters of these tumors are those of very closely-packed, spindle-shaped cells, often without any, and sometimes with a considerable amount of homogeneous, transparent, intercellular substance (Fig. 73). The cells contain a nucleus, which is situated at the thickest or bulging portion of the cell, and they terminate at each extremity in an elongated point, sometimes branched, which varies very much in its length and tenuity. These cells are most commonly arranged with some regard to order, so that in well-developed specimens a laminated or fasciculated tissue results, the lines running parallel with the surface of the tumor, thus increasing its likeness to the structure of a proper fibrous tumor. Virchow also notices the resemblance to epithelial growth which is assumed by some of these tumors where the cells are large, and where the intercellular substance is absent or in very small quantity. With the elements thus enumerated, we have often a number of free nuclei scattered through the tissue. Of these isolated nuclei, considered by many as an original and essential element of the formation, Virchow speaks very emphatically,

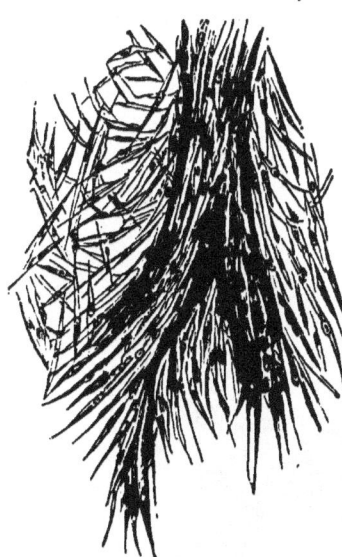

in denying to them any histo-genetic value, he considering them in all cases as the result of destruction of the original cell with liberation of the nucleus, most commonly occasioned by the violence done in the preparation for the microscope. In many of these tumors we have also, associated with the specific cell-formation, a certain amount of well-formed connective tissue, and this is usually arranged so as to form a capsule covering the mass, and partitions within separating it into lobes or lobules more or less distinct, or at least forming compartments in the internal arrangement of the

Fig. 73.—(From Billroth.)

growth, the contents of which compartments sometimes differ considerably from one another in their naked-eye and microscopic characters.

In the bones, these tumors are found almost exclusively in the face and head. Of the large number of cases collected by Lebert, only thirteen were on the bones, and, of these, one was developed in the cranium, four in the superior maxillary bone, two in the inferior maxillary bone, and five were connected with the alveolar portion of these bones in the shape of epulis. He gives no case developed in any other bone of the skeleton — which is also true of several of the principal writers on this subject—from which the fair inference is that they are, in a very large degree, confined to the bones above mentioned. Some exceptions, however, do present themselves to this general law. I shall give, farther on, two cases, in one of which the disease commenced in the malleoli, and another in which the growth sprang from the transverse process of a cervical vertebra. In their general characters, as to mode of growth, progress, and changes, much that has been said of fibrous tumors might be repeated, and their histories, up to a certain point, are not markedly different. Fig. 74 gives a very good idea of the external appearances of one of these tumors developed in the lower jawbone. The case was under the care of Mr. Heath, from whose work the figure is copied. It was of slow growth in a man aged thirty-two, and made a fungous protrusion into

Fig. 74.—(From Heath.)

the mouth and also through the integuments externally. It was removed by Mr. Heath, but the patient died exhausted on the sixth day. The weight of the mass was four pounds six ounces. Mr. Heath gives an elaborate account of the minute structure of the tumor, which terminates with this statement: "The general structure of the tumor is that usually described under the head of osteo-sarcoma, and it belongs evidently to the group of simple fibro-plastic tumors, but differs from the myeloid fibro-plastics in the equal proportion existing between the cellular and fibrous elements."

But, in their final tendencies, the tumors belonging to this class present a very much less satisfactory history than that we have given of the fibrous tumor. Their evil dispositions are manifested in three ways: 1. In a tendency to reproduction *in loco*, after the most thorough extirpation. 2. In a disposition to reappear in neighboring parts. 3. In generalization of the disease, allowing of its extension to other and distant parts, after the most malignant fashion of true cancer.

Of the first two facts in the history of these tumors, viz., a disposition to recurrence, both in the original spot and in its neighborhood, but little needs to be said. They are the striking facts which first drew attention to the semi-malignity, as it is called, of this class of diseases, and they are illustrated, most unhappily, in every collection of cases which are reported. With regard to the third evil feature sometimes observed in these tumors, viz., their generalization, it is happily exceptional and rare. Paget speaks of no case; Virchow describes three very interesting and well-marked examples; and Lebert mentions seven as having been seen by himself and by others, but of these only two were tumors of bone. In these cases we have, either after the removal of the original growth, or during its progress, new tumors appearing at a distance from the primary tumor, which may multiply at various points and in various organs; these secondary or metastatic growths assuming the prominent importance, and finally destroying the patient by the extent of their involvement of organs necessary to life. These metastatic growths sometimes take place along the course of the absorbent vessels, involving the glands in their progress, but sometimes, also, they appear in distant organs, when we can conceive of but one mode of infection, viz., through the blood. It is very remarkable that in almost every case in which an autopsy has been made, where any internal organ has been found infected, the lungs have been either the exclusive or the principal seat of the morbid deposit. One example, taken from Virchow, will be a sufficient illustration of the disastrous and malignant behavior which occasionally characterizes this disease:

A morocco manufacturer, aged thirty-one, shortly after a severe attack of pleurisy, observed, growing on the dorsum of his left foot, a tumor which appeared to be connected only with the fibrous structures of that region, and soon after a second tumor developed itself on the external malleolus of the same foot. These tumors grew rapidly, and about two months after their appearance another attack of pleurisy came on, attended with extreme oppression of breathing, without cough or expectoration, and which rapidly proved fatal. The tumors of the foot were found to involve the malleolus, and some of the bones of the tarsus, in some of which scarcely any thing remained of the original bone but the periosteum and cartilage. The tumors showed a very soft, almost diffluent consistence, much like encephaloid, in some points of a brownish-green color, in others reddish from infiltration of blood. Externally they showed numerous lobes, more or less distinctly separated. In the popliteal space was found a gland, enlarged and medullary in appearance, and the same was true of several of the lower chain of inguinal glands. In the anterior mediastinum was found a series of tumors of the same medullary appearance. The right pleura contained a large sanguinolent effusion, and over its whole surface, soft, very delicate, and very vascular growths were seen, which formed almost a complete layer, covering it entirely. The same appearance in a less degree presented itself in the left pleura. In the lung itself, several medullary nodules of a gelatinous consistence were found, mostly near the base of the left lung, while near its summit was a single tumor, the size of an apple, and easily enucleable from the tissues in which it lay. The right lung was simply compressed by the pleuritic effusion. All these masses had the same microscopic structure. They were everywhere composed of the spindle-cells of small size, with an intercellular substance, showing very little trace of fibres, and of great numbers and very large vessels. The arrangement of the cells was fasciculated.

The statement, thus presented, of the malignant behavior of some of these tumors, is not by any means to be received as their usual history. The fact is—and it is in this fact, now well ascertained, that the importance of the anatomical distinction consists—that the larger part of these spindle-celled tumors do not show any evil dispositions, and, if removed early and thoroughly, do not return, either in their original seat, or in any other part of the body. This brings these, like the myeloid tumors, fairly into the class of benign affections; and, while we recognize the fact that some exceptional instances may occur, in which a semi-malignant or even a malignant history may be realized, we may, with good warrant, hold out to our patients the hope and expectation that a thorough extirpation will be followed by a perfect and permanent cure. Even the local recurrence is not necessarily utterly discouraging. Many cases are on record where several operations were required for successive returns of the disease, and where finally the disposition to the recurrence of the disease seemed to be exhausted, and the patients have maintained for many years perfect health. In one singular case of Mr. Stanley's, mentioned by Mr. Paget, after four extirpations by Mr. Stanley, a fifth tumor appeared and grew to a certain size, and then remained stationary, in which condition it had remained at the time of the report, "a long time without in any way interfering with the patient's health." Another very striking case is reported by Mr. Paget as occurring under the care of Dr. Douglas Maclagan, in which, "after four recurrences and four operations, the patient has remained five years well, and, at the present time (November, 1862, thirty years after the removal of the first tumor), she is in perfect health, and daily follows her avocation as a laundress. Since 1857 there has been no recurrence of the tumor." Similar cases are recorded by other observers.

The following case of spindle-celled fibroid, attached to the transverse process of the fourth cervical vertebra, illustrates many of the points to which we have referred, and is in itself so wonderful a surgical story, and terminated in such a complete and surprising success, that I feel warranted in giving it in full detail:

Mrs. I. N. E., then about the age of twenty-three, consulted me first, March 26, 1866, about a tumor on the right side of her neck, which had been growing for several months, and which was attended by a great deal of neuralgic pain. The tumor was about the size of a large hickory-nut, pretty firm to the feel, situated about the middle of the neck, a little behind the sterno-cleido-mastoid muscle, by the posterior fibres of which it seemed to be overlapped. It had grown slowly, and without apparent cause, and, although there was no history of any other glandular enlargement in any other part of the neck, I felt no hesitation in pronouncing it an hypertrophied lymphatic gland, and in recommending its removal. The patient's general health and condition were perfect.

The operation was performed May 1, 1866. The tumor presented itself with a smooth, enucleable surface, on all but its deepest parts, and there it was attached so closely to the transverse process of the fourth cervical vertebra that, in trying to separate it, it broke and discharged a whitish-yellow, cheesy, semifluid substance, leaving a pretty thick but not very tough sac still attached to the bone from which it appeared to grow. This sac was, as thoroughly as possible, snipped with the scissors, or dissected with the knife, from its attachments, and the cheesy matter carefully wiped from the wound. Things did not go well after this operation. The wound inflamed, and matter formed, burrowing down the neck toward the clavicle. The whole region became extremely sensitive, and the subject of severe, apparently neuralgic pains. She lost courage as well as strength, and nothing seemed to bring her up until she went into the country, when the wound healed, and she regained some of her former excellent health.

Microscopic examination of the tumor was reported by Dr. Delafield, as follows: "Tumor was broken during the operation, and a quantity of thin fluid escaped. The fragments consisted of a grayish tissue, resembling that of a lymphatic gland, and of portions of cheesy material. The firmer portions consist of fusiform cells and oval nuclei packed closely together in bands. Here and there are groups of rounded, nucleolated cells, some resembling gland-cells, and four times as large. In other places, round cells were mixed with large fusiform cells. There was hardly any stroma. The cheesy portions consisted of the same elements, degenerated."

After her return from the country, she still complained of a great deal of pain in the neck, about the scar, and affecting all the muscles of the region. She was particularly distressed at night, and after sleeping found it exceedingly painful to move the head. Some fulness remained about the scar, slowly increasing, so that within a few months it seemed as if the tumor were forming again. Hoping that it might be merely a tumefaction of the scar, we applied leeches, and used all sorts of dis-

cutient applications, but without effect. It grew gradually, until, in the spring of 1869, it seemed as large as, if not larger than,
before. In April, 1867, about a year after the first operation,
she had borne a healthy, vigorous child, her first, and had been
very well, except the local complaints about the neck, during
all her gestation and in her recovery from childbed. During
a great part of the interval, as well as for months before the
first operation, she had used iodine very largely, both locally
and internally, without any perceptible effect.

During the latter part of the winter, and in the spring of
1869, she complained of numbness of the right arm and side,
without any marked impairment of motion, and this seemed to
be slightly on the increase up to the time of the second operation, which was performed on the 10th of April, 1869. In this
operation, which exposed a tumor very similar in size and shape
to the one previously removed, we experienced more difficulty
in detaching the deepest parts of the mass from the transverse
process. Indeed, the morbid growth seemed to penetrate between the transverse processes of the two adjacent vertebræ,
where we followed it as thoroughly as we dared. The sac had
broken as before, and in so deep a wound it was very difficult
to distinguish the morbid from the healthy tissue, and still more
difficult to remove it. Great pains were taken to remove every
thing that seemed diseased, but it was impossible not to feel
that some might have been left behind. The actual cautery so
near the spinal cord was not to be thought of. From this operation she recovered rapidly, and without accident. The numbness of the arm disappeared, and she felt freer from pain, and
more hopeful of entire recovery than she had been at any time
since the first appearance of the disease.

The microscopic report of the tumor was : "It was composed
of a soft, gelatinous material, with some cheesy portions enclosed
in a fibrous capsule. It was broken in its removal. The softer
portion consisted of a gelatinous, finely-granular basement-
substance, in which were embedded large numbers of round
and oval nuclei."

In the fall of 1869 she began to notice a return of the old
numbness, now in both hands, and in the right foot. This
slowly increased until she found she was obliged to give up

sewing altogether. In January, 1870, she could no longer arrange her own hair. In March her second child was born, after an easy and rapid labor. By this time she had become very helpless, but improved a little as she recovered from her confinement. Still, she was very clumsy in handling the baby, though through the summer she managed to nurse it, and maintained her health in a remarkable degree. She suffered, however, a great deal from a fissure of the anus, which a very costive habit tended much to increase. Until September, she was still able to walk about, though with some difficulty, especially in the right leg and foot, and she could use her hands in serving herself at table, the right better than the left. Early in September she had, without apparent cause, an attack of severe pain in the muscles of the neck, with great difficulty in moving the head. This pain continued more or less at intervals for several weeks. Coincident with these increased pains, the paralysis increased more rapidly. By the latter part of November she had lost entirely the power of walking, and soon the power of supporting herself upright, even for a few moments. Her helplessness now became complete, and by the middle of January she was entirely paralyzed in all parts of the body below the neck. By the time of the last operation, the only movements she could make were, to raise the right hand a few inches in the direction of flexion, and to raise the legs a similar distance by drawing up the thighs. These movements were executed very slowly and painfully. Every movement of the body, in lifting her from her bed or sofa, or even in slightly changing her position, gave her great pain. With the paralysis of motion there was a paralysis of sensation, which could be recognized by the dividers over the whole body, but more markedly in the hands than in the feet. The bowels now became more obstinately costive than ever, and, as she had entirely lost the control of the sphincter, the operation of medicine was attended with great trouble and inconvenience, so that we finally fell into the way of giving her a dose of castor-oil once a week. In the mean time her appetite had continued pretty good, and the general nutrition not so much impaired as might have been anticipated. She was, however, very despondent about herself, and life was a weary burden. By this time the tumor had again

slowly developed, and was nearly as prominent, and presented
very much the same feel that it had done previous to the last
operation.

Dr. Wm. H. Van Buren now saw her in consultation with
me, and the question presented itself, Could any thing be done
to relieve her by another operation? The evidences of pressure on the cord, probably produced by an extension of the disease within the spinal canal, were so unmistakable; the probabilities, derived from the fact that the left side was most
affected, that the pressure was from a growth which had developed itself most on the left side, were so great, that I myself
felt hopeless of any good result from an operation. In view,
however, of a partial relief being possible from a partial removal of the compressing cause, and taking into consideration
the utter hopelessness of her present state, it was, after much
hesitation, decided to try what could be done by another attempt at removal.

The third operation was performed on the 25th of January,
1871, Dr. Van Buren and Dr. H. B. Sands assisting me. We
had determined that it would be justifiable to remove as much
of the transverse process, and the edge of the lamina of the
vertebræ, as would give access to the point of pressure, in case
this point seemed at all accessible, and for this I was prepared.
A longer incision was made than on former occasions, parallel
to the sterno-mastoid muscle. The surface of the tumor was
exposed, and then, to gain more freedom in the deeper manipulations, another incision was made directly backward, at right
angles to the first, commencing at about its middle point. The
more superficial portions of the tumor presented very much the
same appearances as on former occasions, and were quite readily
separable by enucleation from the surrounding parts. We were,
of course, extremely anxious not to break the sac if it could be
helped, and succeeded in keeping it whole, until we arrived at
its deepest parts, which we found to dip down by a sort of pedicle, between the transverse processes, and to reach quite down
to the foramen of exit of the cervical nerve. No trace of that
nerve could be discovered coming out alongside of the pedicle
of the tumor, nor any sign of the vertebral artery, whose track
from one transverse process to another we had now crossed.

All this space was pretty closely filled by the root of the tumor, which, as we carefully isolated it from surrounding parts, could be distinctly seen to enter the spinal canal. At this moment the tumor broke, and its soft contents were evacuated, making it, of course, more difficult to identify its outline, and to discriminate between the morbid growth and the normal tissues. Proceeding very carefully, however, we found that the bony canal had been much enlarged by absorption, from the pressure of the tumor, and it soon became evident that through this opening, as large as would easily admit the end of the finger, the external tumor communicated with a growth within which lay in contact with, and pressed upon, the spinal dura mater. As far as could be reached, the growth, which was of a soft, gummy consistence, easily friable in the forceps, was removed piecemeal as thoroughly as possible. After all was got away that could be reached, the surface of the dura mater of the cord was left bare and clean, and not visibly depressed below its proper level. We could still perceive, under the edge of the bony opening, that some of the morbid material existed, but it was impossible to remove any more through the opening in the bone, and the great depth of the wound seemed to make any enlargement of the bony opening an undertaking so formidable that we shrunk from undertaking it. We had, moreover, good ground for believing that the great mass of the tumor had been removed, and that the thin remaining edge which lay under the bone was so much lacerated and contused by the forceps, that it would probably be destroyed by the suppuration. The wound was therefore closed by fine sutures, leaving a small portion at the junction of the two incisions open; into this a tent of silk thread was passed fairly down to the bone, with the view of keeping this part of the wound open. This was done partly to give free exit to any fluids forming in the wound, but mainly to give a chance to any new growth, that might form, to develop itself toward the surface rather than into the spinal canal.

The microscopic report of the tumor is: "It has the same gross appearances as at the first occurrence. The basement-membrane is still soft and hyaline, but contains blood-vessels. The nuclei are larger and more numerous, and the structure is that of a myxo-sarcoma."

January 26th.—Had tolerably good rest during the night, but complains of severe headache. It should have been mentioned that before the operation she suffered from severe pains, quite irregular in their recurrence, in the thighs, and legs, and back, sometimes very severe, and sometimes slight. These pains were, at night, accompanied often with sudden and violent contractions of the muscles, flexing up the thighs on the body, and the legs on the thighs, the spasm of the muscles very severely increasing the pain, and often entirely depriving her of sleep. She complained this day of increased pain on the outside of the left thigh, and in the right leg. No contractions of muscles. She was sensible of greater power over the whole body, and found she could move the toes a little, and slightly raise the right hand.

January 27th.—Severe pain in left arm, and distressing headache. Improvement in the use of limbs; can raise left arm.

January 28th.—Good night's rest, and has very little pain. She begins to feel hungry. Toward evening complained of numbness all over the body, with increase of pain in the left thigh. No contractions of limbs.

January 29th.—Sleepless night. Complains of dark objects flitting before her eyes, and seems to herself to be carrying on both sides of a conversation. Has severe headache and burning sensation in the eyes. Pulse slightly accelerated, skin natural. She feels her body very hot while the feet are cold. Gave a full dose of morphine at bedtime.

January 30th.—Not much relief from anodyne. Great pain to-day down the spine and left leg. Any bending of the spine in changing her pillow or position gives dreadful pain, as if the back were being broken. In making any change of position the hips and head must be raised on the same level. Wound doing well; has healed mainly by the first intention, the central portion discharging a watery pus. By drawing up her knees, she finds that she can raise her hips from the bed for the first time in about four months. Toward evening, severe pain in side and back, from changing her position, continuing most of the night.

January 31st.—Chloral substituted for morphine, but without producing any satisfactory sleep. She is much reduced in flesh, pulse feeble, and about 100. The skin sometimes hot and dry, and sometimes relaxed; the feet generally cold. The thin discharge from the wound is in great abundance, and, on examination, is found to be a pure, white, transparent water, which trickles from the opening in such quantities as to soak through the sheets and pillows, and to keep her bed constantly wet. This can only be the cerebro-spinal fluid, and its point of exit must be the prolongation of the dura mater which covered the spinal nerve as it left the canal, and which sheath must have been opened in the operation. It is probably increased in quantity by the spinal meningitis, from which she is evidently suffering. She suffers greatly from pain, constant in the head, migratory in the trunk and limbs, and also from great soreness and sensitiveness of the surface, sometimes in one region and sometimes in another, which makes it very painful and difficult for her to move, or to be moved. She was now kept systematically under the full influence of morphine, of which she took, however, only a moderate quantity, say five to ten drops every four hours.

February 2d.—Still suffering greatly. Complains of a constant sensation of fatigue; cannot bear any light or noise. This evening, in consequence of changing her position, violent contractions of the left leg, with excessive pain, were produced, recurring at intervals during the night. The watery discharge very abundant.

February 4th.—A better night, and general improvement. Can use all her limbs more freely, and can almost turn over in bed alone. Cannot raise the head and shoulders, by bending the spine, without giving severe pain in left leg. From this time improvement went on steadily for a few days, and was then interrupted by a severe attack of headache, and pain in the back and limbs, with some fever. This subsided in a few days, and similar attacks recurred several times, at intervals of a week or ten days, each attack becoming less severe, and in the interval a greater improvement being attained. The cerebro-spinal fluid continued to trickle away till toward the end of February, when it ceased for a few days, to begin again as freely as ever. About the first of March it ceased again, and finally.

18

No apparent connection could be traced between the flow and any of her symptoms.

By the first of March the paralysis had pretty much disappeared in every part of the body. There was still some stiffness in moving the fingers, and some want of precision in taking hold of small objects, but hardly more than could be accounted for by the long disuse of the muscles. On the 11th of March she was carried down-stairs to dinner, and on the 13th took a drive of three-quarters of an hour. She is quite thin, but free from pain, eats well, and sleeps with the help of a grain-pill of opium.

May 1st.—Mrs. E. called at my office to say that the wound had entirely healed over the tent, which on examination I found to be the case. There is no swelling or tenderness about the cicatrix, and I advised that the tent be left undisturbed. She is perfectly well, gaining flesh and appearance, no symptom of paralysis remaining, excepting that the limbs get asleep more easily than in health. She walks, rides, sews, and does every thing that she ever did with a rapidly-increasing facility and perfection. Menstruation is regular, as also the action of the bowels. The old symptoms of fissure give her but little inconvenience. Appetite and digestion perfect.

January, 1872.—Mrs. E. continues perfectly well.

The proportion of cases in which recurrence takes place after operation has been carefully studied by Lebert. He gives an account of sixty-three cases, situated in all parts of the body, in which operation had been performed, of which thirteen cases were followed by one or more recurrences. Of these thirteen, six were instances in which the operation had been imperfect from the situation of the tumor, or from its extent, and in which, therefore, it might be inferred that the return of the growth was only a continuation of its former existence, rather than a new formation. Of the remainder, two were somewhat mixed in their character, or doubtful as to their nature; leaving, out of sixty-three cases operated on, only five frank, unequivocal relapses after complete ablation of the original tumor. None of these five, however, were tumors of the bone. Of course, such statistics as these can be of little value in settling the actual proportion of recurrences to permanent cures, because the element of time is necessarily imperfectly stated in the calculation. How many of these patients would have had a return of the disease, if longer time had been given to the observation, cannot of course be ascertained. But, nevertheless, the statement is of interest, as giving a general idea of how frequent recurrence is within a few years of the time of operation, and it is fair to hope that a relapse so long delayed indicates a permanent cure in a good proportion of cases—this hope strengthening with every year of freedom from the signs of return. Some of Lebert's cases had been under observation for a long period after operation. Three patients he speaks of whom he had watched for periods varying from twelve to fifteen years. He also gives the duration of thirty-five cases where the disease had been observed from its 'beginning to its termination, either in operation or death, which he thus tabulates:

Existing from	1	to	2	years in	5	cases.
"	"	2	to	3	"	in	5	"
"	"	3	to	4	"	in	5	"
"	"	4	to	5	"	in	4	"
"	"	5	to	6	"	in	4	"
"	for	9	years			in 1 case.
"	"	10	"			in 3 cases.
"	"	12	"			in 1 case.
"	"	15	"			in 2 cases.
"	"	18	"			in 1 case.
"	"	20	"			in 3 cases.
"	over 20	"				in 1 case.

35

With regard to the comparative frequency of generalization of the disease, he does not attempt any statistical statement, and I have met with none in any other writer. He simply states that he has known of seven cases, of which he gives more or less full details, from his own observation, and that of others. Of these seven, only two were bone-tumors, one of the bones of the knee, and one of the bones of the tarsus.

CHAPTER IV.

MYELOID TUMORS.

THE name of myeloid (marrow-like) was given by Mr. Paget to a class of tumors which present as their principal anatomical constituents the elements of the medulla or marrow of the bones. The English writers generally accept this name for a class of diseases which has a most unequivocal character, and which seems to be as well marked and as distinctive as the cartilaginous or the bony class of tumors. The French writers, following M. Eugene Nélaton, prefer the clumsy term of *tumeur myeloplaxique*, or *tumeur à myeloplaxes*. To Robin seems to be due the credit of having first made the distinction of a certain class of tumors whose principal elements consist of the elements of the normal medulla. In the Comptes Rendus of the Société de Biologie for October, 1849, M. Robin, after giving an account of certain anatomical elements of the normal medulla, goes on to state that these elements are sometimes found to be the sole constituents of certain tumors; of which tumors he then proceeds to give some description, and ends his communication by again calling attention to the fact that these tumors are composed essentially of an aggregation of these peculiar elements of the marrow, which he now for the first time brings to the notice of the society. M. Lebert had already noticed that certain tumors, heretofore deemed cancerous, did not show the clinical history of cancer, and these he had placed in a new class, calling them, from their histological elements, fibro-plastic tumors. Among these were many which had the peculiar marrow-like cells in great abundance, but these Lebert does not allude to as distinctive; and it was not till Robin described them as the constituent elements of the normal marrow, that their significance was understood. Robin immediately recognized these new elements as the same found in the tumors which he and Lebert, it would seem, had seen together; and to him, therefore, and not at all to Lebert, belongs the credit of the discovery. Some confusion has thus arisen, and a proper discrimination has not always been made between the two classes of diseases, viz., the tumors composed of fibro-plastic cells, and those composed of marrow-like cells. Mr. Paget, usually so accurate, has fallen somewhat into this confusion, and describes the myeloid tumor and the fibro-plastic as if they were one, while the fact is, they are as different in their anatomical constitution as bone and cartilage or any other two classes of tumors. It is true that the fibro-plastic elements are sometimes mingled with the true myeloid, but this is true of all other classes of tumors, and does not forbid a discrimination where one or other element very greatly predominates.

And here, perhaps, the interest which at the present time attaches to the subject may justify a sketch of the normal constituent of the marrow, the presence of which, in greater or less abundance, gives the character to the class of tumors which we are describing. I know of no description so minute and complete as that of M. E. Nélaton, who has published an elaborate thesis on this subject, founded on the careful observation and study of forty-seven cases, nine of which came under his own eye. He says, in speaking of the normal marrow-cells (myeloplaxes), that they exist in all the vertebrata and at all ages; but they form only a small part of the whole medullary substance. They are found more easily in the fœtus, and in very young subjects, because they are not obscured by the adipose development which predominates in later years. Their favorite situation is close to the bone-surfaces rather than in the midst of the marrow, and they are also sometimes seen in the Haversian canals. Their form is variable. They may be round, oval, triangular, elongated, hour-glass-shaped, or curved on themselves. Their almost uniform tendency is to be flat; so much so as to give them the character of plates (*plaques*) rather than of masses. Their dimensions are as variable as their forms, extending from $0''''''$ 03 to $0''''''$ 08 or $0''''''$ 10. Their thickness is from one-quarter to one-half their breadth, and some are seen no larger than blood-globules. Their color is grayish, sometimes a little yellowish.

With regard to their structure, they seem to be composed of a homogeneous mass without color, uniformly pervaded by very fine grayish granules, soluble in acetic acid, and mingled sometimes with granules of a yellow tint. In the thickness of this stroma exists a number of nuclei, ovoid and transparent, and containing one and sometimes two nucleoli. The number of nuclei varies from five to fifteen ordinarily, in exceptional cases from one to sixty. They are irregularly distributed through the mass of the plate, but are usually accumulated at or near the centre.

A second variety of these medullary bodies differs from that described, in several particulars. They are smaller, more regular in size and shape, not flat, but round or oval. They have one or two and sometimes no nuclei, which, when they exist, are ovoid in shape, and have a distinct nucleolus. They are usually less numerous than the larger flat plates, and, being smaller, are less easily found. In other respects their structure corresponds with the large plates.

These anatomical elements had been seen by several observers in certain tumors which they were engaged in studying, but their character was misinterpreted, simply because the key to their explanation had not been supplied, as it afterward was by Robin's discovery of these peculiar bodies as normal elements of the marrow. Thus M. Lebert, seeing these myeloplaxes scattered through some of the tumors he had named fibro-plastic, embraced the notion that they were parent-cells out of which were generated the fibro-plastic cells of which the tumor was essentially composed. Under this view he gave them the name of *fibro-plastic mother-cells*, thus ranging them very easily under his favorite theory of the formation of the fibro-plastic elements. Such erroneous views of the significance of these bodies are now happily corrected by M. Robin's discovery, and all the authorities agree in accepting it as the satisfactory solution of the vexed problem. It will readily be perceived how much importance this study of the microscopic characters of these tumors has in settling the important question of their homologous or heterologous character; and it is eminently satisfactory to find that, in tumors of a manifestly benign character, the elements which heretofore have been considered at least doubtful, have now been ranged positively under the head of the normal constituents of the body. Still further, it seems very much in accordance with the regularity of true science that this discovery completes our catalogue of

the homologous bone-diseases, giving us the tumors composed
of the elements of cartilage, of bone, of the fibrous tissue of
the periosteum, and of the medulla, all of which we might expect to belong, and all of which we find to belong, to the class
of benign affections.

On this point, which, after all, is the most interesting and
important one connected with the study of the disease, the
testimony of the best observers is unhesitating and uniform.
Mr. Paget's whole chapter on Myeloid Tumors is devoted to
show that, as a general rule, they are benign in their nature,
and that, if thoroughly removed, the likelihood of their return
is extremely small. Nélaton says: "The 'tumeurs à myeloplaxes' (especially those of the typical variety) deserve, in
virtue of their habitual localization, and almost to the same
degree as the lipomas, the fibromas, and the enchondromas, to
.be classed among the benign tumors." Virchow, while he is
not willing to acknowledge the myeloid as generally benignant,
gives no case of his own in which well-marked myeloid disease
has been accompanied with generalization, and says in discuss-
ing the value of the different anatomical elements of sarcoma:
"The size of the cells is not without importance. All the
sarcomata with small cells are more dangerous than those with
large cells. The soft sarcomata with the gigantic multinuclear
cells give even a prognostic comparatively very favorable." If
to this be added his avowal of the almost uniform benignity of
the myeloid epulis, and of the tumors of the jaws in general,
we may accept him as an unwilling but a strong witness to the
general pathological law that myeloid tumors are essentially
benignant. Billroth says: "Central osteo-sarcomata (myeloid
tumors) are usually solitary, very rarely generally infectious."
Cornil and Ranvier say: "Among the myeloid sarcomata those
which resemble absolutely the marrow of the bones are more
benign than those in which we find parts representing the tissue of the encephaloid or fasciculated sarcoma. It is essential
to note these complications and their value in prognosis, which
will explain why, for example, the tumors, which some authors
still call 'tumeur à myeloplaxes,' may not be always regarded
as benign."

The occasional malignity of myeloid growths has been

frankly admitted, both by Mr. Paget and Eugène Nélaton; and it is unfortunately illustrated in the experience of every surgeon who deals with many of these interesting tumors. Nélaton seems to be the special apologist for benignity of the myeloid disease, while Virchow, though hardly acknowledging the fact of its usual benignity, alludes to several examples in which the disease has terminated life, with all the malignant characters which we generally regard as characterizing the worst forms of cancer. He gives no case of his own, however. One of the earliest cases reported in New York was one of a tumor of the lower end of the humerus, in which the microscopical appearances were carefully observed by Dr. H. B. Sands, and were unequivocally myeloid. This patient was amputated by Dr. Sands, and made a very satisfactory and apparently perfect cure. He remained well for at least two years, and then a return of the affection occurred, of which he finally died. I regret that I am not able to get any particulars of the relapse. Mr. Paget recounts two cases, one by Mr. Stanley, and one by Mr. Laurence, in which after removal the disease returned in distant parts, and proved fatal. Mr. Mitchill Henry, Mr. Cooper Foster, Drs. Cock and Wilkes, have each given a record of one or more cases in which fatal metastasis has occurred after removal, and in which the recurrent tumor has been shown by the microscope to be of the same nature as the original growth. If to these cases we add those in which, after complete extirpation, the disease is reproduced *in loco*, we are forced to acknowledge that the myeloid tumor shows, in certain cases, a character of inveteracy and malignancy which must always be taken into the account in making our prognosis. Nevertheless, we are warranted, from the more kindly behavior of the great proportion of the cases, in regarding the myeloid as an essentially benignant affection—one in which, as stated above, a thorough extirpation, if performed early, gives a good hope of a perfect cure, and one in which the evil course and malignant termination are rare and exceptional, thus bringing, by the bad behavior of a few members, a certain amount of discredit on an otherwise well-behaved and reputable family.

A fact which seems to stand alone in connection with these tumors is their occasional spontaneous disappearance. Mr. Paget, in giving an account of one of Mr. Stanley's cases, mentions that the patient, from whom the right upper jaw was removed for myeloid disease, had a similar tumor on the left jaw and on the parietal bones. He says: "The patient recovered perfectly from the effects of the operation; and, to every one's surprise, the tumor on the left upper jaw, which had been in all respects like that removed from the right side, gradually disappeared. It underwent no change of texture, but simply subsided. The swellings on the parietal bones, also, the nature of which was not ascertained, cleared away; and when the patient was last seen, a few months ago, she appeared completely well, and no swelling could be observed." This disappearance, by spontaneous subsidence, has been occasionally observed in tumors of the soft parts; and even cancerous disease has, in rare instances, been apparently absorbed and removed, as illustrated in a case alluded to under the malignant diseases of bone; but this disappearance of tumors formed in the bones is, I believe, extremely uncommon.

The myeloid tumors, like the osseous and cartilaginous, most commonly affect the bones, yet, like them, occasionally are found growing independent of them. The alveolar portions of the upper and lower jaw seem to be their favorite seat, but they also occur in the head of the tibia, in the condyles of the femur, and more rarely in other bones which contain a large proportion of medullary or cancellous tissue. Fig. 75 is taken from Paget, and represents a myeloid tumor of which he gives a very interesting history. It shows the growth of the mass both externally and internally from the bones of the vault of the cranium. It produced death by pressure on the brain. They sometimes grow from the surface, often from the interior of the bones, not unfrequently in the medullary canal itself, when it sometimes happens that the line of demarcation between the sound medulla and the morbid growth cannot be at first sight recognized. These tumors are usually single, occasionally multiple on the same bone, with a smooth, rounded surface, projecting equally in all directions from their base of attachment, when they grow from the surface of the bone. Their substance varies from a firm, almost cartilaginous consistence, down to a softness equal to that of fresh granulations. Their color is remarkable.

Sometimes the whole cut surface presents a deep, ruddy hue; often even a darkish brown. Perhaps more commonly a pinkish or a greenish tint pervades the whole mass, though varying in depth at different points. Interspersed through the tumor are spots or blotches of deep red or brown color, looking as if ex-

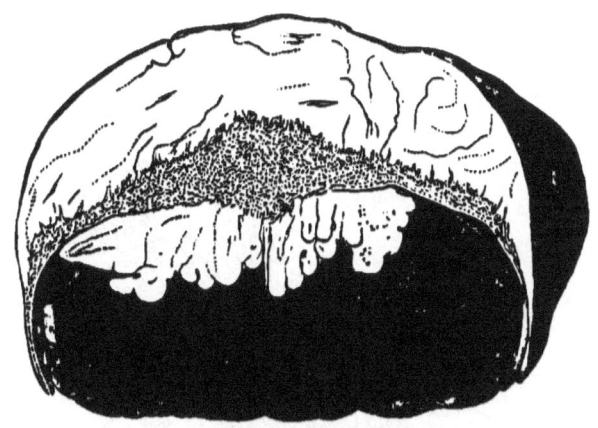

Fig. 75.—(From Paget)

travasation of blood had taken place from small ruptured vessels. These colorations of the tumor are the most striking and characteristic features to the naked eye, but the microscopical examination gives still more distinctive characters.

Thus we find the whole tumor made up of the elements which normally exist in the medulla. Mr. Paget thus describes them: 1. "Cells of oval, lanceolate, or angular shapes, or elongated and attenuated like fibre-cells, or caudate cells, having dimly-dotted contents, with single nuclei or nucleoli. 2. Free nuclei, such as may have escaped from the cells; and among these some that appear enlarged and elliptical, or variously angular, or are elongated toward the same shapes as the lanceolate and caudate cells, and seem as if they were assuming the characters of cells. 3. The most peculiar form: large, round, oval, or flask-shaped, or irregular cells and cell-like masses or thin disks, of clear or dimly-granular substance, measuring from $\frac{1}{300}$ to $\frac{1}{1000}$ of an inch in diameter, and containing from two to ten or more oval, clear, and nucleolated nuclei. Corpuscles such as these, irregularly, and in diverse proportions, embedded in a dimly-granular substance, make up the mass of a myeloid tumor. They may be mingled with molecular, fatty matter; or the mass they compose may be traversed with filaments, or with bundles of connective tissue and blood-vessels; but their essential features (and especially those of the many-nucleated corpuscles) are rarely obscured." Figs. 76, 77 show the appearance of these various cells.

M. E. Nélaton, in describing the microscopic characters of these tumors, says they are composed—" 1. Of a great quantity

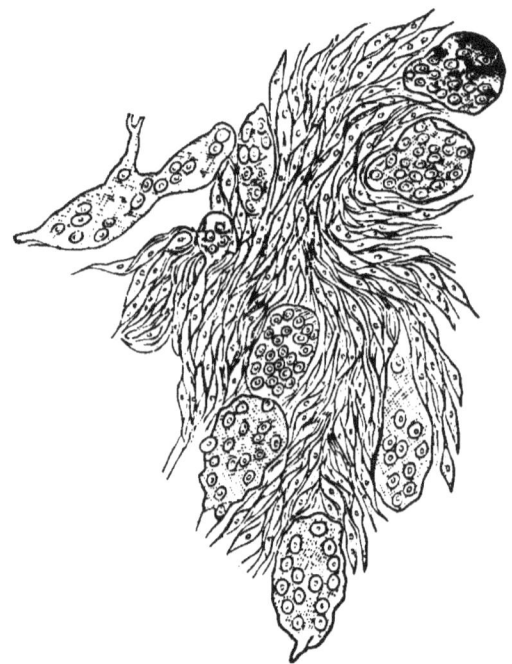

FIG. 76.—(From Cornil and Ranvier, after Virchow.)

of myeloplaxes, the fundamental elements which, by their predominance, characterize the tissue. 2. Of certain accessory elements, such as fibrous or fibro-plastic cells, amorphous matter, molecular granules, fatty granules, free nuclei, some medullocelles, some capillary blood-vessels; besides these the microscope can distinguish in the preparation a certain number of blood-globules, sometimes coloring-matter in a free state, and sometimes also a small amount of osseous substance. It will be observed that these are almost the same elements as those which compose the tissue of the medulla of the bones, but with this difference—a difference of capital importance in histological study—that the accessory element has here become the principal, and conversely."

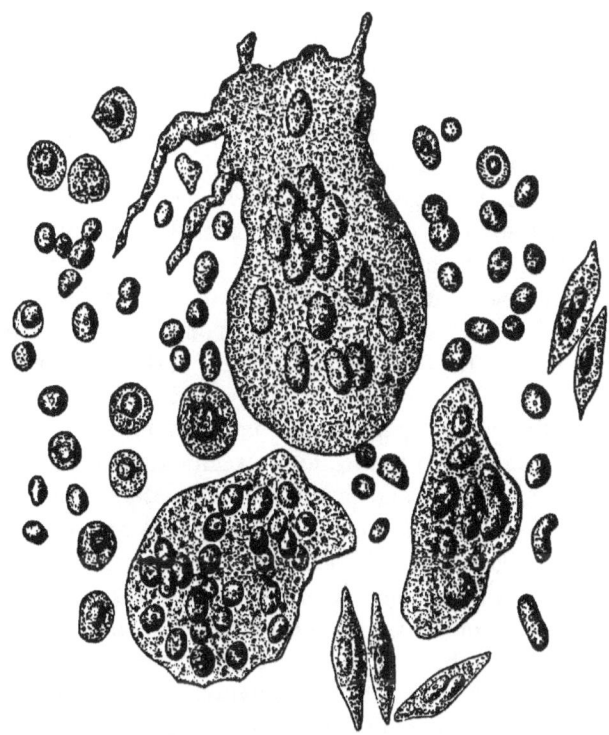

FIG. 77.—(From Cornil and Ranvier.)

It would seem as if there existed a pretty well-marked relation between the varying proportion of these elements and the physical qualities of the tumor. Thus, in those specimens where the fibrous or fibro-plastic elements abound, the parenchyma of the tumor is firmer; where the marrow-cells are greatly predominant, the tumor is softer; so soft as sometimes to be almost a diffluent pulp. In the same way the color seems, from the observations of Eugène Nélaton, to depend upon the proportion of the marrow-cells to the other constituents; these marrow-cells, according to him, possessing the peculiar intrinsic color which marks these tumors, and this entirely independent of blood either contained in the vessels, or extravasated.

The history of myeloid tumors is generally one of slow and painless growth. Most commonly originating from no appreciable cause, their increase is regulated somewhat by their situation, those within the bones developing more slowly, those on the surface, like the myeloid epulis, having a more rapid course. They are far more common in youth and early life than after middle age. They show comparatively little disposition to ulcerate, even when injured, or when very large. The most interesting feature in their history is their almost uniform benignancy. It is true, several cases have been observed of tumors in which myeloid elements have existed, sometimes pretty largely, which have proved fatal, and many have occurred in which the myeloid and cancerous elements have been found intermingled in the same tumor. It is also true, as stated at page 280, that some instances have been observed, in which a true metastasis and generalization of myeloid disease have taken place; but the general pathological fact remains incontestable, that myeloid tumors, as a class, have usually none of the characteristics of malignancy, and that, when completely removed, we may with confidence pronounce that they will not return. A partial or imperfect removal is certain to be followed by a reproduction of the disease, and hence it becomes a study of much importance to ascertain the physical relation of these tumors to the parts within which or upon which they grow. Unfortunately, it is found, by careful examination, that these growths have a great propensity to push themselves in every direction, and often, by prolongations, so slender as to escape notice, to invade the surrounding areolar bone-spaces, or cavities, stretching themselves like roots, some distance from the original mass. This is markedly the case with those developed in the alveolar tissue of the jaws, where several successive alveoli have been found to contain small outgrowths from a tumor, whose general mass was apparently entirely independent of and at some distance from them. Again, small outlying tumors have been noticed immediately in the neighborhood of the principal mass, some so small as scarcely to be identified, certain to be overlooked during an

operation, and only to be found by a careful anatomical examination. Once more: though these tumors have generally an
outline so distinct, and a surface so lightly adherent to the surrounding parts, that they are in fact readily enucleable, yet certain ones are so disseminated through the tissue in which they
form that they might almost be classed among the infiltrations,
rather than as tumors properly so called, and therefore have an
outline which cannot be accurately followed by the eye, much
less by the knife of the operator. All these are considerations
which, while they do not affect the real benignity of the disease,
make it a matter of prime importance that no operation should
be undertaken, or deemed satisfactory, which does not absolutely
secure the entire ablation of the disease.

The development of cysts in these tumors is a fact so frequently noticed as to entitle it to belong to the history of the
disease. This feature is most prominently brought forward
by Mr. Henry Gray, in his paper on "Myeloid and Myelocystic
Tumors of Bone," in the thirty-ninth volume of the "Medico-
Chirurgical Transactions;" but Nélaton, and indeed all the
writers, acknowledge their very great frequency. These cysts
are of various forms and sizes, sometimes as large as a hen's egg,
with very distinct, smooth, polished walls, as if lined by serous
membrane; often so small as scarcely to be discerned by the
naked eye. Sometimes they have no clearly-marked wall, but
seem to be mere cavities, hollowed out in the substance of the
tumor, and all conditions intermediate between these have been
seen in the same growth. Their contents are usually reddish
or brownish serum, sometimes transparent, often muddy, and
sometimes mere fluid or semifluid blood, and this particularly
in those irregular and ill-defined cavities which hardly ought to
be called cysts, and yet which form a very important feature of
the disease.

There seems to be no very marked tendency in these tumors
toward ossification, and yet a certain amount of bone is often
produced in the progress of their growth. This bone is sometimes found in irregular plates of various sizes, but not unfrequently it pervades the mass, with some uniformity, in the shape
of a delicate framework, more or less perfect, giving a certain
feeling of firmness and solidity to the tumor when lightly han-

dled, but giving way with a peculiar crackling feel when firmer pressure is made. The shell of thin bone, in which these tumors are often enclosed, belongs entirely to the original bone, and has no other relation to the tumor than that of enclosing it.

As an illustration of the history, both pathological and clinical, of these tumors, I know of none more complete and more carefully observed than the following, which I condense from Nélaton's paper:

Pierre Bossuge, aged twenty, came under M. Nélaton's care in April, 1856. He had noticed, about seven months previous, a small, indolent tumor, deeply situated on the face, just at the side of the nose. This had gradually increased, pressing upward toward the orbit, and inward toward the nasal cavity. At the time of admission, the tumor had gained the size of a pigeon's egg, hard at its base, which was evidently in the substance of the lower jaw, and more yielding at its more prominent surface. It had been punctured with a lancet some time previous, but only a few drops of blood had flowed out. The integuments and surrounding tissues were sound, and the man was in a good condition of general health.

M. Nélaton operated on the tumor on the 23d. He made an incision into the tumor through the mouth, and then broke up and removed piecemeal all of the diseased mass which he could get away in this manner; and then with the hot iron burned very thoroughly in every direction the cavity which he had thus left. A moderate suppuration followed, and a gradual healing, so that the cure appeared to be complete. On the 20th of November, however, the man again presented himself with a reproduction of the tumor, which had now attained a greater size than before. It pressed far in upon the nostril, and extended back so as to be felt in the fauces. The tumor also now for the first time gave him some pain.

On the 3d of December, the whole superior maxillary bone was removed on the left side, embracing, as was thought, every portion of the tumor. The case went on favorably, and he was discharged cured early in January.

The examination of the pieces removed in the first operation showed a reddish, friable substance, much like the substance of the kidney or like a lung in a state of red hepatiza-

tion. M. Robin made the microscopic examination, and found
it almost entirely formed of myeloplaxes, with some amorphous
granular matter, some fibro-plastic cells, and a very slight
fibrous net-work, with a few blood-vessels. The tumor examined, after the removal of the jaw, was about the size of a large
hen's egg. It was situated in the substance of the jaw, encroaching upon and almost obliterating the antrum. A section
displayed a firm elastic substance, resembling the tissue of the
heart, or of the foetal liver, or of a kidney in a state of active
congestion. Its color, therefore, was a reddish brown, pretty
uniform in all of its parts. In making the section, the scalpel
encountered some slender osseous fibres penetrating the mass
in various directions. Several small cysts were scattered
through its substance, containing only bloody serum. The
microscopical constitution of the diseased tissue was again
studied by M. Robin. He found it "an exaggerated multiplication of the special elements of the marrow of the bones, that
is to say, plates with many nuclei, i. e., myeloplaxes bound together by very delicate fibro-plastic elements, a few laminated
fibres, a certain amount of amorphous matter, and some capillary vessels ; these last elements appeared in rather larger proportion than in the first pieces examined. The vascular element, however, plays evidently a very secondary part, for it is
less developed than in certain whitish or slightly rose-tinted
tumors, considered as types of encephaloid, which were examined by way of comparison." The cure after this second operation was rapid and satisfactory. More than three years after,
the patient was seen and examined by M. Nélaton, and found
free from any suspicion of a return of the malady.

CHAPTER V.

PULSATING TUMORS OF BONE.

A DISTINCT pulsation is noticed in some tumors of bone,
the cause of which is, in different cases, to be traced to different pathological conditions. Thus some of these pulsating
tumors lie in such relations to a large artery that its pulsations

are communicated to the tumor. In other cases there is either such an abundant or such a peculiar vascular arrangement through the substance of a tumor, that its own circulation gives it an evident and sensible pulsation. It is clear, therefore, that the mere fact of pulsation existing in a tumor cannot give it any specific anatomical character, or really entitle it to be considered as belonging to a class of its own. The symptom is so striking, however, its discrimination so important, and its bearing upon practice so direct, that most writers on the subject have given the tumors which are characterized by it a separate place in their catalogue. It seems strange that so striking a feature had not earlier attracted attention, but the first distinct account of a pulsating tumor of bone was one published by Pearson, of London, in 1790. Since attention has been called to it, numerous cases have been published, and we are now quite familiar with the general facts which characterize these pulsating growths.

There are three conditions recognized as producing pulsation in bone-tumors. These are: 1. The proximity of a large artery which imparts its own pulsation to the swelling; 2. The disproportionate development and activity of the vessels of the tumor itself; 3. A peculiar arrangement of blood-cavities or blood-spaces in the tumor, which communicate with the vessels, and which give the structure a close resemblance to the natural structure of the corpus cavernosum penis.

Of the first variety, numerous instances are recorded. Mr. Stanley gives the following: "A man, aged sixty-eight, suffered two severe falls upon the shoulder. Subsequently an enlargement of the part ensued, with pulsation in it. The tumor was considered to be an aneurism, and the subclavian artery was tied. Three weeks after the operation the patient sank. The tumor was found to be a mass of medullary substance, to which the axillary artery firmly adhered, the vessel itself being perfectly sound." Mr. Stanley alludes to six other cases which had come to his knowledge. Of these six cases two were in the upper part of the humerus, one in the lower part of the femur, one in the head of the tibia, and two in the lower extremity of the tibia. In all the disease had been supposed to be aneurism.

19 .

Of the second form, those in which the pulsation is dependent upon unusual development of vessels in the part, we have perhaps the best examples in the very vascular encephaloid tumors which are sometimes developed on or in the spongy extremities of the long bones. Other forms of soft and rapidly-growing tumors may be accompanied with pulsation, but no class of tumors is so abundantly supplied with vessels as the encephaloid, and none so often present this particular symptom. Indeed, so decided is this association, that pulsation in a bone-tumor has come to be looked upon with much suspicion, as being extremely likely to depend upon the existence of encephaloid disease. Mr. Paget remarks: "I think that, in many of the cases which have gained for erectile tumors their ill repute, a clearer examination would have proved that they were, from the beginning, very vascular medullary cancers, or else medullary cancers in which blood-cysts were abundantly formed." The vessels in these cases are sometimes excessive, merely in number and size, not in other respects differing from the healthy formation; while in others they are enlarged irregularly, tortuous, varicose, thinned in their coats, or thickened at points; in short, they may be in various ways and degrees diseased, as well as excessively developed. The amount and distinctness of the pulsation will of course depend upon these anatomical conditions of the vessels. If they be merely increased in number and size, still continuing healthy in their structure, I can hardly suppose that the pulsation can ever be more than an increase of the ordinary arterial throbbing, that can be observed in every very vascular part, when it is compressed slightly by the hand. If, on the other hand, the vessels be very much dilated in the tumor, over the calibre of the parent trunk from which its circulation is derived, and particularly if this dilatation be irregular and pouch-like at many points, then we have, in obedience to well-known hydraulic laws, the conditions of a pulsation, which is sometimes so distinct and so powerful as very naturally to lead to the suspicion that our bone-tumor is an aneurism—a mistake which has been made in a number of instances by excellent and careful surgeons.

The third form of pulsating tumor of bone, viz., that in which something like a true, cavernous, erectile tissue is formed through the mass of the growth, is much more rare. MM. Cornil and Ranvier, in their admirable *Manuel d' Histologie Patholo-gique,* give the following description of this formation: "The tissue is hollowed out into alveoli, communicating in a very irregular manner with each other, very much in the same way as do the alveoli of carcinoma. The blood circulates in this cavernous system, which occupies the place of the capillary system, situated as it is between the arteries and the veins. The circulation through these cavities is extremely active." They further describe the walls of the alveoli as composed of a well-marked fibrous tissue, and lined internally by a pavement epithelium, similar to that which lines the veins. A curious fact is also noted by these observers—that the blood in these cavernous spaces contains very few of the colorless blood-globules. As these are known, by their adhesiveness to the walls of the vessels, to present a certain amount of impediment to the natural circulation of the blood, it is argued that their comparative fewness makes the circulation more active, and the pulsation therefore more marked than it would be under the ordinary circumstances of the circulation. The reasoning seems good, if the facts are accurate; and that they are so would seem very probable from the mode which these gentlemen adopted in their investigation. The mass after removal was immediately placed in alcohol, by which all the blood in the tumor was coagulated. It was then cut into thin slices and brushed over with carmine, which adheres to the white but not to the red globules, and then soaked in glycerine. This rendered it very easy to count the number of white globules, which

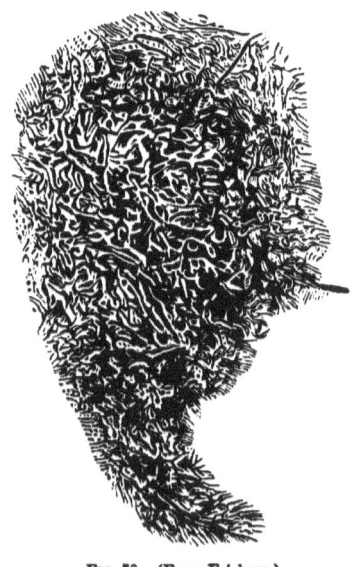

FIG. 78.—(From Erichsen.)

was done, with the result above stated. Billroth gives almost precisely the same anatomical description of this form of tumor as that presented by the French writers quoted. Fig. 78, taken from Erichsen, is a representation of what he calls aneurism by anastomosis of the parietal bone. It corresponds tolerably well with the description of the disease here given.

The clinical history of these different forms of pulsating tumors of bone, of course, depends upon the nature of the tumor itself. They are mostly found in the extremities of the long bones, the position in which all bone-growths are most likely to appear. The pulsation is sometimes an early and constant, sometimes a late, and occasionally an intermittent symptom. It may be accompanied with a thrill, sometimes with a distinct *bruit de soufflet*, and is sometimes so distinctly and strongly expansive as to puzzle the most careful and experienced examiner. The diagnosis, however, can usually be made from proper aneurism, by the location of the tumor, by its evident connection with and continuity with the bone from which it grows, by its usually presenting at some period a thin shell of bone on its surface, and most commonly by the feebleness and want of expansiveness of the pulsation.

The following case, for which I am indebted to my friend Dr. Charles D. Smith, and which I saw with him on several occasions, illustrates extremely well some of the usual clinical features of the disease. I take the account of the case from the report published in the *New York Journal of Medicine* for March, 1853:

"Miss C., twenty-four years of age, unmarried, of nervous temperament, and of previous good health, came under my care in the month of March last for a painful swelling of the left ankle, which came on without any apparent cause a month or two before. The skin was reddened, and painful to the touch, particularly over the internal malleolus. There was also a creaking sensation about the joint when handled. She walked with difficulty, increasing thereby the pain and tension. The pain would occasionally leave her, and the swelling subside. It had the complexion of a scrofulous disease of the joint, but, there being no evidence of struma in the system, I was at a loss to what to attribute it. Local means as well as constitutional remedies were resorted to without avail. The disease remained about the same until the month of May, when I detected something like fluctuation over the internal malleolus, which in two weeks became distinct. The skin was not changed in color, neither did it have the feel nor present the appearances of an abscess.

"In the early part of June I noticed in this situation a pulsation which, from day to day, became more evident, and was synchronous with the arterial pulse. Pressure on the posterior tibial artery arrested the pulsation in the tumor. At this time Dr. Van Buren was called in consultation, who confirmed my diagnosis, viz., aneurism of the posterior tibial artery, and at the same time suggested that possibly the bone might be involved. She readily consented to our proposition, to tie the posterior tibial; and, with a view of cutting off the recurrent circulation, it was also deemed advisable to put a ligature upon the anterior tibial, where it passes over the dorsum of the foot. On the 2d of July the posterior tibial first was tied, about an inch and a half above the tumor. The pulsation ceased only for a short time, and the size of the tumor was not at all diminished. The same result followed deligation of the anterior tibial. On visiting my patient the morning following the operation, the pulsation had returned with full force, and was plainly felt through the bandages. During the month of July the disease steadily increased. The skin in the neighborhood assumed a transparent appearance. The tumor grew larger, more firm and resisting to the touch, and the pulsation became decided. Pressure upon the femoral as well as popliteal artery arrested it. Its true character was determined by the crackling sensation, and breaking down of something like an osseous shell, under the fingers. The wound from the operation did not heal kindly. It was seven weeks before she recovered, yet her general health was not materially injured, either by the progress of the disease or her long confinement. About the middle of July Dr. Mott was called in to decide the question of amputation. His opinion was that, inasmuch as pressure over the femoral artery completely controlled the pulsation in the tumor, deligation of that artery might be tried. He was also of opinion that the ligature was preferable to compression in this particular case.

"On the 23d of August, Miss C., having entirely recovered

from the first operation, in the presence of Drs. Mott, Van Buren, Stone, and others, I placed a ligature around the femoral artery, immediately below Poupart's ligament, and above the profunda. Pulsation in the tumor instantly ceased, but it did not collapse, as in ordinary aneurisms, neither did it diminish in size. From this operation my patient rapidly recovered, without any unpleasant symptoms. The ligature came away on the twenty-second day, and the wound healed readily. The tumor subsided about half an inch in the course of the week following the operation, but it soon increased to its former dimensions.

"On the 12th of September I felt a gentle pulsation in the femoral artery in Scarpa's space, and at the same time in the tumor, since which period it has been noticed only occasionally, and then exceedingly feeble. Suffice it to say the disease steadily progressed. The tibia expanding, stretched the anterior tibial nerve, causing great pain. Her health, too, began to feel the influence of the disease, and rendered amputation necessary. Another consultation was held. She was advised to lose the leg, to which she unhesitatingly consented, and on the 20th of November I removed it at the place of election. A day or two after its removal, my friend Dr. C. E. Isaacs injected the limb, through the posterior tibial artery, with a preparation of chromate of lead dissolved in ether. The skin and fascia were then removed, and exposed the periosteum thickened. The shell of bone under it was broken down, and in some points partly absorbed. When cut into, there was presented a soft, brain-like mass, of a reddish-brown color, mixed with the injecting material. Upon turning this out, it was discovered that the lower end of the tibia was absorbed for about half an inch. The cartilage lining the surface articulating with the astragalus was preserved. The bone was expanded into a thin shell, the cancellated structure gone, and its place occupied by the matter described. No vessels were found entering the tumor, although the bone and neighboring parts were exceedingly vascular. The other tissues were healthy."

Another case was under the care of my friend and colleague, Dr. Willard Parker, about the same time, and was published in the same journal in the number for May, 1853. It gives so many features of interest in the history and progress of the disease that I give it almost entire, as related by the patient himself, who was an intelligent physician :

"In the summer of 1842, while jumping for recreation, I struck my left heel upon a round stick about an inch in diameter ; it gave me severe pain at the time, which, however, lasted but a few minutes, and I thought no more of it. Several days after, upon rising from my bed in the morning, I experienced a sharp pain darting through my heel, which quickly passed off, but recurred again on the following morning in the same manner. This transient pain continued to return every morning on assuming the erect position, until the summer of 1847, without the occurrence of any other symptom, such as swelling or tenderness, to indicate the nature or seat of the difficulty. This pain invariably returned on rising to my feet, after resting some time in the horizontal position, but never continued to exceed one or two minutes. During this period, my heel gave me no uneasiness, my general health was good, with the exception of some dyspeptic symptoms for two or three years after the injury, which I attributed to sedentary habits, being then a student, and which passed off after engaging in practice.

"In the summer of 1847 I began, for the first time, to experience a tenderness about the heel whenever it came in contact with solid substances with more than ordinary force, as in stamping or making a false step. This tenderness gradually increased, until I began to suffer some pain in walking at my usual pace, unless I was careful to slide my foot along without raising it much from the ground. There was no appreciable swelling until December of that year, when, upon drawing on my boot one morning, I suffered so much pain that I was obliged to withdraw it immediately. During the day the heel swelled considerably, and, being hot and painful at night, I scarified it deeply, and held it in hot water to favor the bleeding. On the following day I was disappointed at finding my foot still worse, and was obliged to use a crutch in walking. Leeches and poultices were applied, and subsequently iodine and other medicinal applications were employed, but without even palliating the symptoms. Nothing but cold water and snow gave me even temporary relief ; these were very grateful, and I resorted to

them often, as the relief they afforded enabled me to attend to
my business, though I suffered much pain night and day.

"I continued to grow gradually worse until some time in
February, 1848, when I determined to consult Dr. Parker. At
this time there seemed to be thickening of all the tissues about
the os calcis, with a deep-seated, constant pain, as if the fibrous
tissue was put upon the stretch; occasionally the pain was lancinating.

"Dr. Parker advised an incision down to the bone, which
he accordingly made, dividing the periosteum of the os calcis
about an inch and a half on its inferior surface; the wound
bled freely, and gave a little relief to the severity of the pain,
but of short duration. I kept the wound discharging four or
five weeks, but, finding no material benefit, allowed it to heal.
Soon after this I applied moxas, by the advice of Dr. Ticknor,
U. S. Navy, but with no benefit. The pain continued to increase in severity, being worse at night than during the day.
I resorted to large doses of morphine to obtain sleep, and often
two grains at a dose would produce only a short nap, from
which I would be awakened by the most excruciating lancinating pains in the heel. I finally began the use of quinine in
the summer of 1848, as I was beginning to emaciate and to
lose my appetite, taking eight grains a day, with cold applications to the affected part. Under this treatment my appetite
and general health improved, and also the local difficulty; the
pain was much less severe, and in a short time I threw aside
my crutch, still continuing my practice, and got around very
comfortably with a cane. This improvement lasted until December, 1848, when I had an attack of acute bronchitis, for
which I was bled, and took antimony, and of course omitted
the quinine. I was confined to my bed about ten days, and in
this time the pain in my heel became worse. On getting up
I discovered, for the first time, a tumor on the outer aspect of
the heel, just below the external malleolus, which had a spongy,
elastic, and pulsating feel, and was painful on pressure; the
veins were much enlarged about the heel. I again resorted to
the quinine, from which I had derived so much benefit, but it
now gave me no relief.

"I grew worse so rapidly that I again visited New York with

the intention of submitting to amputation, if this course was deemed advisable. I had come to the conclusion that I could not much longer survive such indescribable agony (I will not call it by so soft a name as pain). Dr. Parker advised immediate amputation, to which I cheerfully assented. He performed the operation on the 24th of January, 1849, after administering a mixture of chloroform and ether. I resumed the practice of my profession about three months after the operation, and have continued actively engaged since, in the enjoyment of good health. I have supplied my deficient extremity with an artificial limb, which answers its purpose admirably."

. On examination, it was found "the bone expanded into a thin shell, the cancellated structure absorbed, and in its place a material answering the character of carcinoma."

Both these cases seem to have been instances of the softer variety either of cartilaginous or myeloid or possibly of the spindle-celled growth, which, from the excessive development of their vessels, received the pulsating character. Their general appearance was that of encephaloid disease, but that they were not truly cancerous affections is proved by their after-history. The last case, the tumor of the heel, was alive and well four years after the amputation, and Dr. Smith has recently informed me that his patient was entirely free from any symptom of recurrence of her malady two years ago, being about sixteen years after her limb was removed.

Practically speaking, the main interest which attaches to these tumors is the question of treatment. The pulsation, particularly where it is well marked, very naturally suggests itself as a prime factor in the problem, and the question of cutting off the circulation by ligature almost necessarily presents itself to the mind. It has been put to the test of experiment in quite a number of instances. Dr. Smith, in the paper above quoted, refers to Dupuytren as the first surgeon who tried the ligature. "His case occurred just below the knee, at the inner side of the tibia, in a man aged thirty-two. He tied the femoral, the pulsation ceased, and the tumor disappeared. Seven years after, it returned and acquired a large size ; he amputated, and the patient recovered. It proved to be composed of numerous cysts, some filled with gelatinous matter, and others with coagulated blood. A fine membrane lined these cysts, through which vessels were seen distributed in the form of a close network." This seems to be the most satisfactory result that has been attained. Lallemand, Roux, Velpeau, Guthrie, Luke, Hargreaves, and Teale, have each operated by ligature, with a partial or negative result; in the best cases the growth of the tumor being arrested only for a few weeks or months, the disease then resuming its original rate of progress, until death or amputation relieved the patient of his sufferings.

A certain and sometimes very great mitigation of pain is occasionally gained by cutting off the circulation in these tumors, evidently by relieving the tension of the growing mass on the unyielding tissues by which it is imprisoned. This I have experienced in two cases of malignant disease of superior maxillary bone, where the disease had extended so far as to preclude any idea of extirpation. In one of these cases I applied a ligature to the common carotid, in hope of arresting the progress of the malady. The patient died a few days after the operation, too soon to judge of any effect on the growth of the mass, but not too soon to demonstrate that the operation had brought immediate and complete relief to the excessive pain which he had been suffering. In the other case, for a similar but more desperate condition of the superior maxillary, malar, and temporal bones, in the hope of alleviating dreadful and constant pain, and perhaps arresting somewhat the progress of the growth, I tied the common and internal carotids; the former half an inch below, and the latter half an inch above, the bifurcation. I did this with a view of more completely controlling the recurrent circulation through the common carotid from the other side, which so quickly reëstablishes itself through the circle of Willis. The man, who was old and feeble, died about a week after the operation, but during that time was entirely freed from pain, so as not even to require an anodyne to procure sleep at night. In 1854, Dr. John Neill, of Philadelphia, tied both occipitals for the cure of a large pulsating tumor of the occipital bone. It had been growing slowly for many years, but more recently its increase had been more rapid. "It had a pulsation distinctly perceptible both to the eye and touch, accompanied by a marked aneurismal bruit. The pulsation was not a simple rising and falling of the tumor, but an expansion in all directions. The right occipital artery could be felt beating strongly, and with a distinct thrill. Pressure upon it sensibly diminished the pulsation of the tumor, and pressure upon both occipitals almost entirely destroyed pulsation." The effect of the ligature of these arteries was to check in some degree the progress of the disease. The patient lived four or five months after the operation, no change taking place in the tumor, except a diminution of pulsation and bruit. *Post-mortem* examination showed the tumor to be of an encephaloid nature, and encroaching largely on the cerebral cavity.

Dr. E. D. Mapother reported to the Surgical Society of Ireland, January 23, 1863, a case of pulsating tumor on the left tibia, in which, after trying a variety of remedies, he finally determined to use the actual cautery. There did not seem to be much encouragement to attempt the ligature, as he found that pressure upon the femoral did not control the pulsation. He says, in his report in the Dublin *Free Press*, February 4, 1863: "We resolved to try the effect of actual cautery, and having chloroformized the patient, we pressed an iron button of the diameter of a shilling, heated to a white heat, deep into the tumor; a good deal of hæmorrhage followed, but was repressed by muriated tincture of iron. In seven days the slough separated in small gritty pieces, and then was disclosed a mass of hard, pulsating substance, of the shape of large granulations, but of a pale color. Seeing that it was necessary to reapply the cautery, we did it this time with a sharp conical iron, which was thrust five times into the tumor, and thus it burnt its way for an inch and a half from the surface of the tibia. In ten days a thick and somewhat conical slough came away, leaving a cavity filled with small, healthy granulations at its sides, but with a small spot of rough bone at the bottom. This gradually became covered in, and the ulcer assumed the healthiest character." At the end of two months, Dr. Mapother reports the ulcers healed, and the tumor entirely removed. At the end of a year the patient was still perfectly well.

Of course, if the tumor be favorably situated, there may be cases in which extirpation can be performed by the gouge and saw. Here the result will depend on the nature of the tumor;

but, as far as I know, the mere fact of the vascular character of the tumor need not discourage the resort to the usual operations in similar non-pulsating growths. In the limbs, amputation has been, in by far the larger number of cases, the only method of ridding the patient of his alarming and very commonly fatal disease.

CHAPTER VI.

TUMORS OF THE JAWS.

THE enlargements and tumors which we encounter on the jawbones present so many features which are peculiar to the bones in which they occur, that it is convenient, in studying these affections, to place them under one head, and thus bring together many points which are, in other parts of the skeleton, differently classified. This arises partly from the anatomical peculiarities of the jaws, such as the large mucous cavity of the antrum, the spongy substance of the alveoli, the implantation of the teeth, the close connection of the gingival membrane with the bone, the large proportion of the bone which is covered by mucous membrane; and partly certain pathological peculiarities, such as the fact that cystic disease of bone is almost· exclusively found in this region, and that the myeloid tumor is so habitually found in these bones, rather than in the other bones of the skeleton, that its whole history might be written from its development in this part alone. Besides, the very superficial position of both upper and lower jaws makes some important modification in the facility and completeness of the diagnosis of their diseases, while their accessibility gives peculiar advantages to the surgeon in seeking their cure or extirpation. Most of the writers on diseases of the bones have found it convenient, for these reasons, to discuss the affections of the jaws under a division by themselves. I shall follow so good an example, and present what I have to say on this division of the subject under the following heads;

1. Inflammatory distention of antrum.
2. Cysts and cystic growths in the jaws.
3. Tumors connected with the gums.
4. Solid tumors of the jawbones.

INFLAMMATORY DISTENTION OF ANTRUM.

Inflammation, attacking the mucous membrane lining the antrum, may, by retention of the inflammatory products, from a closure of the small opening into the nostril, cause a distention of the cavity, which even in acute cases may reach a considerable size, and in the chronic form may give rise to doubts and mistakes as to the nature of the swelling which is thus produced. Inflammation of this cavity may be an extension of catarrhal disease from the nasal cavity, or it may originate from some diseased condition of the roots of the first and second molar teeth which project upon its floor, sometimes slightly, and sometimes quite considerably. External injury, particularly that of extraction of the molar tooth, is a frequent cause of this affection. The symptoms can usually be easily recognized by the dull, aching pain localized in the centre of the upper jaw, and, after a very short time, the general inflammatory swelling of the face is seen to be connected with an enlargement of the jawbone itself, which, in the region of the antrum, is extremely sensitive to the touch. As the distention increases, the sufferings of the patient become more severe, and the deformity of the face more and more marked. The bony wall of the antrum, as it yields to the accumulating fluids within, becomes thinned, and gives the yielding, crackling, broken egg-shell sensation, so characteristic of distended bone. If the attack be very acute, the matter finds its way pretty early through the nostril, or under the cheek anteriorly, or through the floor of the antrum, into the mouth. If a tooth has been recently extracted, its socket often affords a ready outlet for the matter, and suggests the most direct mode of reaching it with the surgeon's trocar.

If, however, as is perhaps more commonly the case, the acute symptoms abate, and a subacute or chronic course is assumed by the disease, then the external evidences of inflammation gradually subside, while the distention of the antrum as gradually increases, and the affection often presents itself in a shape that leaves it very doubtful whether the tumor is one depending upon accumulation of pus, or whether it be a cystic growth in the antrum. Indeed, it is recorded that surgeons have undertaken the removal of the upper jaw, under such circumstances, and have not discovered their mistake until their hands have been covered with pus from the ruptured abscess. Liston and Stanley both mention such occurrences ; and the facility with which even a good surgeon might fall into such an error will perhaps be appreciated, when we remember that, in many of these cases, the early history of inflammation has been unnoticed or forgotten, and that, in those instances where the actions are very slow and deliberate, a thickening and induration of the distending wall of the antrum take place, instead of a thinning of it, which thickening conceals the fact of the existence of a fluid within, and thereby makes the diagnosis sometimes extremely difficult.

The consequences of these inflammatory distentions of the antrum are often serious. Necrosis of the bone is sometimes produced, as in a case related by Mr. Christopher Heath, where " the front part of the floor of the orbit, the upper cheek-portion of the superior maxilla, and the infra-orbital, and a large plate of bone from the inner (nasal) wall of the antrum," were involved and removed as sequestra. In this case, the eyeball had been encroached upon by the swelling, and, from the pressure, the sight had been utterly destroyed. Other instances are recorded where amaurosis followed this disease, and one in which convulsions and death in sixteen days were produced by it. At all times it is, in its acute form, a painful and deforming disease, in which the assistance of art should be invoked as soon as possible. An opening may be made into the antrum in one of two ways : Either the socket of the first molar tooth may be perforated by a trocar, or the lower part of the anterior wall of the antrum, just above the gum, may easily be penetrated, and a portion of the thin shell removed sufficient to allow a free and permanent opening into the antral cavity. If the molar tooth be sound, the second will probably be the best method. Of course, after such an inflammation, the cavity does not immediately return to a healthy condition, its mucous membrane continuing for an indefinite time to secrete muco-pus, which, if the opening, made by the surgeon, be not kept free, will accumulate and give rise to a return of pain, and perhaps a renewal of the inflammatory disease. The opening through the bone, in whichever situation it is made, should be free, and it will, in most cases, be necessary to dilate it at stated intervals, to prevent its contraction. In doing this, I prefer a conical steel bougie, introduced and allowed to remain a few minutes, at appropriate intervals, as giving less pain and being less liable to do mischief than the sponge-tent. The cavity should also be frequently injected with warm water or some slightly stimulating or corrective lotion, such as sulphate of zinc, carbolic acid, or chloride of soda, or, what I like better than all, a weak solution of common salt. I have under my care a gentleman, aged thirty-six, who noticed about six years ago a painless swelling, just above the root of the right first molar tooth. It gradually grew larger and larger, and soon began to make a decided prominence of the cheek. It was then it came under my notice. I found the anterior wall of the antrum bulged forward into a prominent tumor, which was covered by the thinned bone, and crackled under the finger, giving a distinct feeling of fluctuation. The swelling was now somewhat tender and painful, and was gradually becoming more so. I recommended that the first molar, which he suspected was the cause of the trouble, should be removed, and as it was drawn from its socket, matter flowed freely, and the tumor partly collapsed. This was about two years from the time when he first noticed the swelling. Since the opening, the cavity has been kept free by injections of water or salt and water, or a solution of sulphate of zinc. Occasionally I have introduced a probe, or a conical bougie. If this is neglected, and accumulation is allowed, he immediately begins to suffer pain, and the whole jaw feels inflamed. By constant care of this kind, the antral cavity has now shrunk so as to contain much less injected fluid than it formerly did; it discharges but little, the prominence is no longer visible; in short, it is gradually and very slowly regaining a healthy, natural condition.

Some remarkable cases of extreme distention are on record from the accumulation of fluids within the antrum. A very

striking case is spoken of by Mr. Heath as having occurred to
Sir William Fergusson, the preparation from which is preserved
in the King's College Museum: "It was taken, many years
ago, from a subject in the dissecting-room, and from the person
of an old woman. The tumor, which was of very large size,
had burst shortly before death, leaving the remarkable deformity, shown in Fig. 79, which is due to the complete absorption
of the front wall of the antrum, and its collapse, by which a
prominent horizontal ridge of bone, formed by the upper wall
of the antrum, has been left immediately below the orbit. The
preparation shows great distention of the antrum, the diameter

of which varies in different parts
from two to two and a half
inches, and bony wall so thinned
out as to resemble parchment.
The gums are edentulous. There
is no communication between
the nose or mouth and the cavity, which is lined by a membrane
covered with laminated deposit.
Whether this was originally a
case of cystic growth or a chronic
abscess, it is impossible now to
decide; but it is, so far as I am
aware, a unique *post-mortem*
specimen of this distention."

Fig. 79.—(From Heath.)

Besides this case of simple
distention of the antrum by the
accumulation of fluids within it, there are other cases in which
a true cystic formation occurs within this cavity. Sometimes a
single cyst is found growing in the antrum, to some part of
whose mucous membrane it is attached. These have been detected in all stages of their growth, from the smallest noticeable
size up to the point of completely filling and distending the
antrum. Their walls are usually thin, and their contents are
described as most commonly of a transparent viscid character,
but in the older tumors becoming flaky from the presence of
cholesterine, and occasionally thick and opaque like butter or the
caseous fluid found in sebaceous cysts. Sometimes, instead of

being single, there are several cysts, and Mr. Heath gives one instance, taken from M. Giraldès's prize essay on this subject, where the whole of both antra were packed full of cysts of varying size, but of great numbers, and in every stage of development. These cases, of course, during life, present no features by which they can be distinguished from the other forms of chronic antral distention. As to their management, particularly where many of them exist, it is evident that an operation, more thorough and more extensive than mere puncture, would be necessary for their perfect removal.

CYSTS AND CYSTIC GROWTHS IN THE JAWS.

Cysts may occur in the substance of either jawbone, and present themselves sometimes in connection with the teeth, and sometimes entirely independent of them. Of those connected with the teeth, some are attached to the fangs of perfectly developed teeth, and others are found to be connected with teeth either imperfectly developed or abnormally placed in the jaw, which wrongly-developed teeth are commonly considered to be the cause of the formation of the cystic tumor, by reason of the local irritation which they produce.

Of cysts connected with the roots of sound and well-developed teeth, Mr. Heath gives three examples as coming under his observation. They are stated to be quite small, and, judging from the drawings, not larger than a pea, except one of them, which is the size of a hazel-nut. One of them has quite a long pedicle by which it is attached to the end of the fang. They may, however, grow to a large size, and several cases are on record where they have intruded into the antrum, which cavity they have more or less completely occupied. Of course, the discrimination between such a case and one originating in the antrum could hardly be made, except by a careful dissection of the parts after death or removal.

Of cysts connected with undeveloped or misplaced teeth, dentigerous cysts, examples have now been recorded by many observers. Most commonly it is the permanent teeth which, by their abnormal condition, give rise to the cystic growth, but it has been occasionally found in connection with the temporary

20

teeth, and, in at least one instance, with a supernumerary tooth. The explanation of the mode in which these cysts are formed about the impacted tooth is given by Mr. Salter as follows: "When a tooth is thus situated, its fang is enclosed in a bony socket, lined by periosteum, as in ordinary circumstances, while the crown of the tooth is free in a little bony loculus, lined by that which was the so-called 'enamel-pulp.' This structure is clothed with a sort of epithelium, which is apt to assume the function of secreting fluid. After the enamel is completely formed, the soft membrane, which rests upon the surface of the crown of the tooth, frequently separates from it, the interval being occupied by a sort of serum. This is generally the result of some irritation or difficulty in tooth-cutting; and where the irritation runs on to acute inflammation, as in some cases of tedious eruption of wisdom-teeth, the secretion may become purulent. In the deep-seated cases of impaction of teeth, the action is, I believe, always slow, and the secretion almost always serous."

Mr. Salter gives two instances of his own, one of which I will relate, as a type of this class of cases: "A girl, eighteen years of age, had an elastic fluid-containing tumor in the substance of the incisive bone, extending up to the base of the nose on the left side. She had been seen by two or three surgeons, but the nature of the malady was not ascertained. She had the normal number of teeth in the jaw, though the character of one of them was abnormal for her age. When the patient was sent to me for my opinion, I perceived that the left central incisor was a temporary tooth; and this circumstance was a key to the correct diagnosis of the case. The left temporary central incisor occupied a position which its permanent successor should have held; the absence of the tooth, under such circumstances, suggested the almost inevitable position which it must occupy above and behind its temporary predecessor, that is, in the axis of the serous cyst. The temporary tooth was removed, and the cyst explored, to discover the succeeding tooth. The permanent central incisor was found deep in the bone, in an upright and natural direction; its crown bare within the cyst; but, upon its removal, it was observed that the fang was aborted, and had only grown to one-fifth of its

natural length. This circumstance it was which had prevented
its extruding its temporary predecessor, and establishing itself
in its normal position. The retention of the tooth in its
epithelioid sac furnished the anatomical grounds from which,
under favoring circumstances of irritation, the serous secretion
arose, and the bone-expansion followed."

Fig. 80, taken from Mr. Heath's work, represents a lower
jaw distended by a cystic growth, in the lowest part of which
is seen a canine tooth, the irritation of whose presence probably
had given rise to the development of the cystic disease.

FIG. 80.—(From Heath.)   FIG. 81.—(From Heath.)

The affection is stated to be more common in the upper jaw
than in the lower, but all the teeth in either jaw seem to be
liable to give rise to the disease. The symptoms of this form
of tumor can be no different from those of other expansions of
the jawbone by cystic formations, but a very reasonable ground
of suspicion that the case is one of dentigerous cyst may sometimes be found in the fact that the teeth are not normal in
number or in character. This point is not one of mere pathological curiosity, for it has a direct and most important bearing
on treatment, as it must be evident that, if the disease depends
upon the presence of a misplaced tooth, it will not be effectu-
ally cured until that tooth is found and removed.

Cystic growths not directly connected with the teeth are not uncommon in both upper and lower jaws; though, from Mr. Heath's account of them, I infer that they are more frequent in the lower. They may be spontaneous in their origin, as in one case reported by Mr. Coote, where the disease was congenital; or they may have their origin in some injury of the alveolar substance; or, as is perhaps most commonly the case, they may originate from the irritation of defective teeth, or stumps, which are allowed to remain in sockets which, perhaps for years, have been more or less constantly in an inflamed condition. They may be unilocular, which is by far the most common form (Fig. 81); or they may be multilocular, and occasionally proliferous. This was the fact in Mr. Coote's congenital case, and on opening the tumor it was found to "be filled with a regular nest of cysts, one placed within the other." Another case, of Dr. Robert Adams, quoted by Heath, was composed of numerous small cysts arranged side by side: "The mucous membrane covering it was here and there raised into rounded eminences of the size of peas, though some were larger, and of a purple color. The tumor was composed of bony cells, of a texture as fine as the ethmoid bone. The cells generally were of such a size that each might be capable of receiving within it a garden-pea. They communicated with each other, and amounted to no less than twenty-six in number. They were all lined by a pulpy, very red, vascular membrane, and contained an albuminous fluid tinged of a reddish color, apparently from blood dissolved in it."

This polycystic form of growth is well illustrated in Fig. 82, which is given by Heath from a case of M. Giraldès.

These cysts sometimes attain a very great size, expanding the whole bone into a great tumor, which is a mere bony shell with fluid contents. In many cases, particularly in the multilocular form, the disease extends to the ramus of the lower jaw, quite up to the condyle, and even into the coronoid process. The fluid is commonly a glairy, transparent, albuminous material, sometimes so thick as to flow with difficulty, sometimes a serous fluid, containing flocculi of fibrinous matter, and occasionally some blood. Their growth is usually slow and painless, and patients are apt to be urged to apply for relief more on account of the growing deformity, than from increasing suffering.

The treatment of all these forms of cystic development in the jawbones is nearly the same. The cyst must be evacuated, and the cavity kept open, and then by tents or plugs of lint, or by stimulating injections, a healthy action must be promoted in

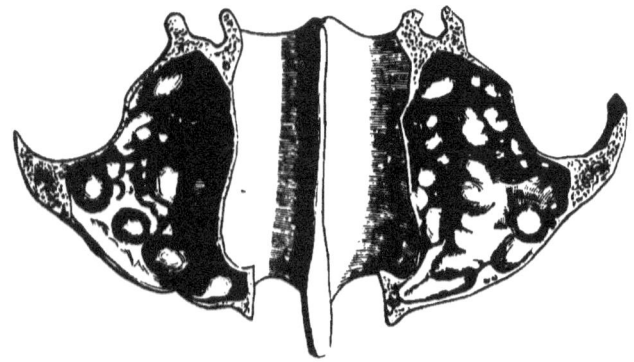

FIG. 82.—(From Heath.)

the lining of the wall of the cyst. This, happily, can generally be accomplished, and when aided by the crushing together of the expanded bony shell, so as to obliterate, as far as may be, the abnormal cavity, very perfect restoration of the shape of the deformed bone may be hoped for. Some writers, as Mr. Butcher, of Dublin, recommend the free removal of the anterior bony wall, and the scooping out of all the contents of the cavity; but most of the later operators have found that they secure success quite as surely by a more moderate procedure. Dr. John Mason Warren, of Boston, very strongly advocates this less severe treatment of these cases, and I cannot better illustrate what seems to be the received opinion on this point, than by relating one of his cases: "A young woman, aged twenty-five, with light hair and blue eyes, and delicate skin, applied to me in the spring of 1862, on account of a large tumor involving the whole right side of the lower jaw above its angle. The tumor was of a globular shape, extended back under the lobe of the ear, forward so as to encroach upon the cavity of the mouth, and upward so as to press upon and somewhat to overlap the zygoma. The external surface of the tumor was smooth and shining, slightly œdematous, and she suffered from its pressure upon the surrounding organs. It had commenced, some years before, by a swelling at the root of the wisdom-tooth of the right side; and the inconveniences caused by the pressure had become so great as to lead her to take measures for its removal.

"Upon consultation, it was decided that a portion of the jaw would require removal; the tumor having been first exposed by an incision made inside of the mouth, to verify its character. The following operation was performed under the influence of ether. An incision was made in the most prominent part of the tumor in the mouth, upon which a large quantity of glairy fluid escaped. Upon passing the finger into the opening, it was found that the whole jaw at this point, with the articulating and coronoid processes, was expanded into a mere shell, at some parts as thin as parchment, and destitute of osseous substance. It was without solid contents. Under these circumstances, and considering the good health and youth of the patient, it was determined to make the attempt to save the jaw. A portion was therefore removed from the sac; and with the fingers the sides of the cavity were made to collapse, so as to come in contact with each other. In order to excite still further irritation, a bit of cotton cloth was forced into the interior, and the end left projecting into the mouth. A moderate degree of irritation followed; and at the end of a day or two the pledget was removed, suppuration having commenced in the sac. The aperture was dilated from time to time, by the introduction either of the finger or of a bougie, and the sac injected with tincture of iodine. At the end of two or three weeks she left the hospital with the tumor reduced to about one-half its original size. From that time until the present, she has occasionally visited me at my house, and by keeping the external opening free, and occasionally irritating the interior of the sac, a solid mass of bone has been deposited anew, and the jaw has resumed somewhat of its original shape.

"In November, 1863, I again saw the patient, who came to consult me, not about herself, but about a friend. All signs of the tumor had disappeared, and the jaw had regained almost its natural shape; but a small aperture still existed, at the site of the former opening into the mouth; and a glairy fluid was occasionally discharged from it. She was quite well, and all the functions of the jaw were perfectly performed."

In order to secure the more perfect obliteration of the cyst, pressure by pads acting externally by the force of springs, as in the ordinary truss, has been found to be occasionally of great assistance. It need hardly be repeated that, in all cases which depend upon the irritation of misplaced teeth, the offending cause must be carefully searched for and removed.

TUMORS CONNECTED WITH THE GUMS.

These tumors have commonly been all included under one head, and described by the name of epulis, from two Greek words, signifying *upon the gum*. Much difference exists among these tumors, however, both in their seat and nature. Thus, some of them are mere hypertrophies of the gum-membrane, and reach a formidable size, spreading above the teeth, which sometimes they almost entirely conceal, projecting from the mouth, very vascular, liable to ulceration, and producing all the inconvenience and distress of the most malignant form of disease. One such case is described by Dr. Gross in his "System of Surgery," and another, quite similar, is fully described by Dr. Salter, in his article on "Diseases connected with the Teeth," before referred to. These cases seem to have been simple hypertrophy of the tissue of the gum of both jaws, and also, in some degree, of the alveoli, which it covers. The mucous membrane participated very largely in the hypertrophic changes, both papillæ and epithelium becoming enormously exaggerated in their anatomical characters.

Again, some of these growths are polypoid in their form. These often spring from the gum at the side of or between two carious teeth, and grow quite large, with a pedicle which is often entirely concealed by the mushroom-shape of the growth. Several of these projections are sometimes found in the same individual, all depending upon one cause, namely, an irritated condition of the gums, mostly connected with defective or neglected teeth.

The true epulis (Fig. 83) is a firm fibrous tumor, developed in the substance of the gum, usually springing from that part of the membrane which is close to or between the teeth. It

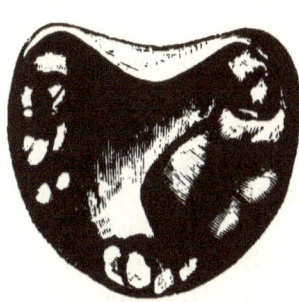

Fig. 83.—(From Heath.)

grows slowly, without pain, and often, in its earliest stages, without tenderness, and it extends in all directions nearly equally, so that, as it projects from the mucous surface, it extends in a nearly equal degree on that surface. The membrane covering it is of a natural appearance, and rarely becomes the seat of ulceration. As the epulis enlarges it commonly displaces one or more of the teeth, and sometimes grows so as to fill up and obliterate the sockets of the teeth that have thus been removed. After a time the bone begins to participate in the action, becoming vascularized, spongy, and sending prolongations, in the shape of delicate spiculæ, into the fibrous substance of the tumor. In the older and larger specimens, some detached masses of bone are occasionally found through the growth, but never in such a degree as to give a true bony consistence or character to the tumor. The course seems rather, that the tumor invades and displaces the bone, than that bony formation pervades the softer growth. Their naked-eye features vary according to the consistence of the growth. In the harder varieties we have the firm, glistening, pearly-white appearance of the ordinary fibrous tumor, while in the softer forms we have the ruddy, brown, or greenish yellow of the myeloid tissue. The microscopical appearances correspond to the outward features, and in the firm varieties we have in general the simple fibrous tissue, more or less perfectly formed, while in the softer forms we have an abundance of those peculiar elements which so distinctly characterize the myeloid growth. Mr. Salter says: "Epulis tumors are always, I believe, a form of 'fibro-plastic;' a combination of fibrous tissue and myeloid cells, the proportion of the two constituents varying indefinitely. In general, the main bulk of the tumor consists of fibrous tissue; but sometimes the myeloid-cell element preponderates, and may form the major part of the growth."

In their clinical history these tumors present the course which their histological characters would indicate. They are never malignant in the true sense of the word, and yet pertinaciously recurrent under partial extirpation. They are therefore regarded by all as in their nature benign. Even Virchow, while he insists upon absorbing these tumors all in his immense class of "sarcoma," does not deny that, as a general fact, epulis does not assume any malignant features.

As a general rule, these tumors are single; they affect the upper jaw rather more frequently than the lower; they never occur in jaws which have no teeth, or in parts of jaws where the teeth have long been removed. Mr. Salter gives a case which, at first sight, seemed an exception to this rule: "One of the most severe examples of this malady which I have seen, consisted of a bilobular mass, the size of a large walnut, extending on the left side of the lower jaw from the dens sapientiæ to the canine teeth, the four intermediate teeth having been removed. The excision of the tumor had been repeatedly performed, but it always returned. Its removal, on this occasion, disclosed the remains of one fang of the first molar tooth in its very axis; this was extracted, and the disease did not again make its appearance."

The treatment is extirpation, as thorough and as early as possible. If removed while small, the operation may be effective without touching the bone; though, in all cases, the teeth immediately involved should be extracted. If, however, the disease has been of long standing, and has therefore involved the underlying bone, then any thing short of a thorough removal, not only of the tumor, but of the altered bone which forms part of the growth, will be attended with disappointment. With the gouge, or the gnawing-forceps, or the sharp curved bone-nippers, the whole of the soft, spongy, alveolar bone, which is implicated, can easily be removed, without leaving any deformity which the dentist's art cannot repair, and without at all diminishing the strength of the jawbone.

SOLID TUMORS OF THE JAWBONES.

All the forms of bone-tumor which are found in any part of the skeleton are found in the jaws. Some, however, such as the

cartilaginous, and the cancellous exostosis, occur no more frequently in this situation than in other parts of the skeleton;
while others, such as the fibrous tumor, the myeloid tumor, and
the ivory exostosis, are rarely found in any other bones. These
tumors may develop themselves by growth into the antrum,
their base springing from its walls, or they may originate in the
bone outside of the antrum, which by their growth is more or
less completely obliterated. In all these cases, if the tumor
grow from within the bone, the striking feature is, that the
outer compact tissue of the jaw, both upper and lower, is distended by the increasing growth, and forms a thin shell which,
during all the early periods of the tumor, entirely encloses it,
and gives rise, if the tumor within be tolerably soft, to the sensation of crackling when pressed upon by the finger, which we
have seen to be so characteristic of the distention of the antrum
by fluid accumulation. This thin, yielding shell of bone is retained to a late stage in the growth of benign tumors, though
sometimes, if the increase be rapid, the bony covering is pierced
by the growth, and the peculiar feature is thenceforward lost.
This symptom is sometimes only discernible at one or more
points, the shell at other places being still so thick as not to
yield to ordinary pressure. In a case I have recently seen at
the Strangers' Hospital, of myeloid tumor of both upper jaws,
I found the crackling at only two points, viz., just above the
roots of the molar teeth on both sides in the upper jaw.

Many of the growths into the cavity of the antrum arise
from a comparatively small base, and distend without otherwise implicating its walls. This peculiarity sometimes enables
the surgeon to remove completely and thoroughly, by a very
simple operation, tumors which, from their formidable size
and extensive encroachments, seemed to demand the removal
of the whole of the affected jaw. Sir William Fergusson, in
his late volume on the "Progress of Anatomy and Surgery,"
insists very strongly on this point. In speaking of it he says:
"In operations on this bone, as on the lower jaw, and as with
bones in other parts of the body, I take the liberty to protest
against the doctrine that the whole bone must be taken away
when there is tumor present. Indeed, it is largely in consequence of what I have seen in the maxillæ, that I have come to

the practical conclusion, that total excision is not always needful in the case of tumors."

The encroachment of these tumors upon the surrounding regions is an interesting feature, both as to diagnosis and as to the necessities and indications of operative interference. Most commonly the tendency of growth seems to be principally in one direction. Thus, we have the tumor expanding the anterior wall of the bone, and appearing prominent on the face. This is the direction most frequently noticed, and in many instances the extension is only in that direction. In others the tumor invades the nasal cavities, sometimes the orbit, sometimes the roof of the mouth, and sometimes the posterior fauces; very rarely all are successively and nearly equally encroached on. The case above alluded to, of double tumor of both upper jawbones, is a striking example of this uniform distention. The tu-

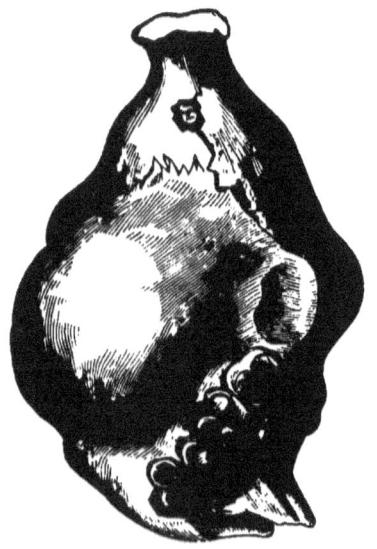

Fig. 84.—(From Heath.)

mor makes a moderate projection forward on the face, it bulges down the palatine plate on both sides into the mouth, it has begun to push up the eye, and can be felt deep in the orbit, and, by passing the finger behind the velum, a rounded edge of the growth can be felt very distinctly pressing into the poste-

rior fauces. These encroachments take place to a very distressing extent as the tumor increases, and the inconvenience they
cause is often the warrant for operation, while the tumor itself
is perhaps neither painful nor externally deforming in any very
urgent degree. The encroachment upon the orbit is of course
mainly important in regard to the implication of the eye, which
by the pressure is dislocated, and often disorganized, after repeated and distressing attacks of inflammation ; and yet some
remarkable instances are reported of very great displacement,
causing frightful deformity, without loss of sight. In one of
Mr. Fergusson's cases the eyeball was thrust forward more than
an inch from its natural position in the orbit, and yet the sight
remained unaffected. In most cases the sight is lost very early.
The projection into the mouth is very distressing, by interfering
with the action of mastication, and indeed by preventing the
comfortable introduction of any kind of food. When to the
mere bulk is added the fact of excoriation, and in some instances
severe and painful ulceration, with bleeding on the slightest
injury, then, indeed, we have in some of these jaw-tumors, growing principally into the mouth, the most distressing and exhausting of all the growths which are not essentially of a malignant character. The encroachments on the nasal cavity and
on the posterior fauces are, on the whole, less serious in their
consequences.

Of the general characters of the fibrous tumors of bone we
have already given an account at page 256. In the jaws, where
these tumors are most commonly situated, they may be found
growing either from the outside of the bone, and then they are
usually confounded with the periosteum, from which, rather
than the bone, they seem to be an outgrowth, or, in other cases,
the growth is from the central part of the bone outward, and
in the increase of the tumor the outer compact shell of the
bone is often distended to an enormous extent over the mass.
The practical difference between these two methods of growth
seems to be that, in the periosteal outgrowth, the diseased mass
cannot be cleanly separated from the bone, which is gradually
more and more implicated in the tumor; while, in the growth
from within, the bone covering the tumor is merely in contact
with it, and the mass can readily be enucleated from its bony

connections, except at the point from which it springs. This anatomical difference is illustrated in Figs. 85 and 86, taken from Mr. Paget's "Surgical Pathology."

Fig. 84, from Heath, gives the external appearance of the bone as its walls yield before the growth of these tumors.

Of all the tumors, however, which affect the jaws, the myeloid is that which has attracted most the attention of recent

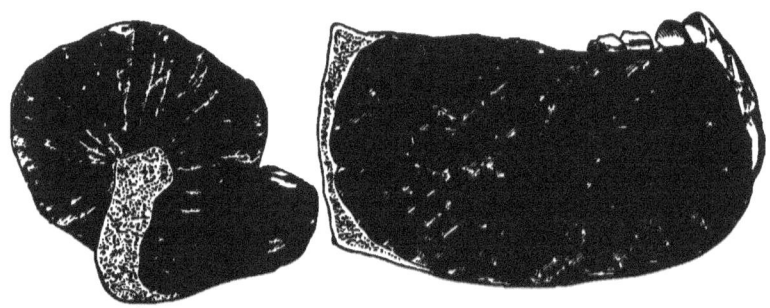

FIG. 85.—(From Paget.)   FIG. 86.—(From Paget.)

surgical writers. Though occasionally found in other bones, yet it is so much more common in the jaws as to entitle it to be considered the peculiar tumor of this region. We have already, in a previous chapter, given the general history of this form of tumor; there only remains to say a few words of some of its features as affecting the jaws. First, they almost uniformly grow from the inner parts of the bone, either the cancellous tissue or the antrum, and hence they are almost invariably covered with the thin shell of bone so often alluded to. It is true that some even very large myeloid tumors are connected with the gums, and secondarily involve the jaw. The history of these cases clears up their nature, and shows that they have commenced as true epulis. Their growth in the jaws is very slow, sometimes occupying years in their development—contrasting, I think, somewhat with their more rapid career in other bones. A very striking exception to this general fact occurred in a case recently treated by my friend Dr. Henry B. Sands, the notes of which he has kindly placed at my disposal:

"*August* 14, 1870.—Operated to-day on Emma K., aged thirteen, for the removal of a tumor of the right superior maxilla, which was first noticed two months ago, and was then mistaken by the parents for a gum-boil. When examined a short time afterward, by Dr. Sampson, it was thought to be confined to the alveolar process, and involved the sockets of the first and second molar teeth, which, though sound, were loosened. Dr. Sampson extracted the teeth, and excised the tumor. Shortly after this operation, the growth reappeared, and an attempt was made to remove the diseased parts by means of the knife and actual cautery. The second operation, performed a fortnight ago, does not appear to have checked the growth, and it is probable that in neither operation was extirpation thoroughly accomplished. When the patient came to me, a few days since, I discerned a soft, elastic, fleshy-looking swelling, occupying the right half of the roof of the mouth, and evidently involving the alveolar process of the upper jaw. Its surface was convex and slightly ulcerated. It extended from the curve of the dental arch inward nearly to the median line, and backward as far as the posterior edge of the palate process of the maxillary bone. Whether it occupied the antrum I could not determine previous to the operation, which I performed this morning."

The operation consisted in the careful and thorough removal of all tissue that appeared diseased, leaving the orbital plate. The operation showed that the mass sprung from the alveolar floor of the antrum, into which it had protruded without any attachment to its sides or roof. It was, therefore, essentially alveolar in its origin, and pretty certainly epuloid in its earliest stages. Posteriorly the limits of the tumor were ill defined; it was followed back to the pterygoid process of the sphenoid bone.

"No cause could be assigned for the disease. The patient is a healthy-looking country girl, and inherits no morbid tendencies. Her parents are alive and well, and have nine living children." Three months after the operation she was heard from, quite well.

Dr. Delafield makes the following report of the microscopical characters of the tumor: "The tumor has a peculiar loose, spongy consistence. It consists of a basement stroma, partly fibrous, but mostly composed of small, round cells. In the stroma are numerous alveoli, either rounded or oval. The alveoli are single, or a number of them are found close together like the section of a racemose gland. They are filled with small polygonal cells." These represent the myeloid element, and are present in great numbers. "Most of them also contain large hyaline bodies of globular shape. These bodies, when isolated, consist of a homogeneous hyaline substance, sometimes wrinkled, sometimes on a pedicle of the same material, sometimes strung together on a broad band of the same material." Most of the hyaline bodies in the specimen shown to me were oval instead of round.

Another case, which I saw at various times with Dr. Sands, illustrates the more common course of this disease, and its very great tendency to be reproduced *in loco*. I condense from Dr. Sands's notes:

Asa Hill, aged thirty-eight, presented himself, December 12, 1863, with a tumor of the superior maxilla which had been growing for about eighteen months. The right cheek showed a well-marked prominence over the body of the superior maxillary bone. On looking into the mouth a large tumor is seen projecting into its cavity, occupying the whole of the jaw, and extending a little beyond the median line. Tumor firm, elastic, not tender, not ulcerated. Right nostril somewhat obstructed. No pressure into orbit. The upper jaw was entirely removed by Dr. W. Parker, and the patient made a good recovery.

May 17, 1866.—The disease has returned, occupying the walls of the cavity from which it had been removed, filling the nostril, and involving the pterygoid plate of the sphenoid. It was again removed as far as it could be reached, and, to the points where the knife could not safely be carried, the actual cautery was freely applied. The wounds healed kindly.

January 27, 1870.—The disease, doubtless imperfectly removed in the last operation, has returned, and now involves the left antrum, while a large projecting mass presses down into the pharynx, and seriously interferes with deglutition. It involves the entire left superior maxilla. It has also invaded the right tonsil. The whole left superior maxilla was removed, and every particle of the diseased tissue was extirpated as far as could be reached, and, as before, the actual cautery was thoroughly applied on all doubtful spots. He recovered from this severe operation, though the wounds in the mouth were not all healed when he died of pneumonia on the 23d of July, 1870. His health until his last attack had been very well maintained.

The microscopical examination of the last tumor removed was made by Dr. Delafield: "The portion of the tumor which was examined was of uniform consistence, of a white color, mottled with brown (after preservation in alcohol). The minute structure of the tumor is a fibrous stroma containing cells. The stroma forms in some places a very delicate net-work, in others thick bands of fibrous tissue. The cells which are embedded in the stroma are round, oval, fusiform, and stellate connective-issue cells, with great numbers of the large, irregular, finely-granular masses, filled with nuclei, usually called myeloplaxes."

Many years ago, while curator of the New York Hospital Museum, we received a donation of a specimen of upper jaw, which had been removed several years before, and which was presented to us by the operator, Dr. A. H. Stevens, then one of the surgeons of the hospital. He had removed it from a private patient, and had preserved it in his own cabinet until the formation of the hospital collection began, when his was one of the first contributions. It is No. 48 in the catalogue. Mr. G., the gentleman from whom it was taken, was a man in the prime of life, about thirty-three years of age, one of our most prominent lawyers, active in his habits, and in other respects perfectly healthy. He consulted Dr. Stevens in August, 1823, "on account of a swelling and a livid redness of the gum from the root of the first left incisor tooth to the penultimate molar of the upper jaw. The membrane lining the roof of the mouth between these same points exhibited the same appearances. Externally, the cheek, under the orbit of the eye, was projected forward, so as to fill up the angle between the nose and the cheek." The tumor, with a considerable portion of the jaw, was removed August 14, 1823. The operation has an historical interest, as being the first one of its kind performed in this city, and one of the first anywhere attempted, Dr. Jameson's operation, which is recognized as the first, having been performed in 1820. Dr. David L. Rodgers's operation, which was more extensive than either, involving nearly the whole of both upper jaws, was done in 1824. The operation was done mainly with a fine saw made out of a watch-spring, and did not embrace the orbital plate of the maxillary bone. " The examination of the removed jaw showed a fungous tumor occupying the whole antrum, and arising by a broad base from the lower portion of it."

Mr. G. recovered without any drawback from the operation, and an ingenious dentist of that day fitted to the gap in the jawbone an ivory plate, with the proper teeth, which answered a very good purpose, entirely concealing the deformity. I became acquainted with Mr. G. in 1848, and, though much with him, I never suspected that he had lost any portion of the bones of his face until he told me of the fact, and showed me the seat of the operation, which presented a perfectly sound and healthy appearance. He died of pneumonia in 1850, then approaching sixty years of age. He lived, therefore, twenty-seven years entirely free from any symptom of recurrence of the disease.

Dr. Delafield made a careful examination of the tumor after it had lain in the museum of Dr. Stevens's private collection, and afterward in that of the New York Hospital for forty-seven years. His report of his examination, made in 1870, is as follows:

"*Adenoma of the Antrum. New York Hospital Museum, No. 48.*—A tumor fills the antrum, and replaces the superior maxilla and hard palate; the orbital plate is absent from the specimen. The incisor teeth remain in place. The superior maxilla retains its normal shape, but the bone is replaced by the new growth. The tumor, after preservation in alcohol for many years, is mostly of a loose, spongy consistence, though some parts are hard and fibrous. A few spiculæ of bone are scattered irregularly through it. The minute structure is that of follicles, which appear round, oval, or long, in different sections. These follicles are, for the most part, very regular in shape and arrangement, resembling the section of a racemose gland. The walls of the follicles are of fibrous tissue. The follicles are filled with an amorphous mass, probably epithelial cells destroyed by the long preservation of the specimen. In some places, however, these follicles do not have the same

21

regular shape and arrangement, but are found very large, or small and isolated in fibrous tissue."

This case seems to me a very interesting example of an extremely rare affection. Adenoma is unknown in the bones, and its existence is only rendered possible in the jaws by their extensive connection with the mucous membrane, in the numerous glands of which it seems quite reasonable to suppose it may have had its origin. The microscopical appearances are, it must be acknowledged, somewhat obscured by the lengthened maceration of this specimen, but enough remains to make its characters unmistakable. The regular alveoli, enclosed with well-formed fibrous tissue, can hardly be mistaken for any thing but the alveoli of epithelial cancer, and this idea of its nature seems to be refuted by the manifest and well-proved benignity of its course. This very benignity, attested by twenty-seven years of non-recurrence, coincides very accurately with the acknowledged good character of the adenomatous tumors wherever found.

The operations necessary for the removal of these solid tumors of the jaws are of two kinds, viz., those which involve a partial, and those which demand an entire, resection of the bone. In a considerable number of cases, particularly where the tumor is mainly confined to the alveolar arch or to the antrum, a partial resection is all that is required to secure the final conditions of success. This partial operation, involving only such parts of the bone as are manifestly diseased, is always to be preferred to the more severe and extensive resection of the whole jaw, not merely because it is a less serious surgical operation, though that consideration should have great weight, but because the resulting deformity is so much less; and the inconveniences of the loss of support to the fauces and velum, as well as of the wide exposure of the different mucous cavities, are not so disagreeably experienced by the patient. The dentist's art has reached so great perfection that he is able to supply extensive deficiencies, if only he has a base to work upon; but the mutilation caused by the removal of the whole of the upper or lower jaw is a serious evil to which the patient, if he recover, is condemned for life, and for which the most skilful dental mechanist can offer but an imperfect compensation. It becomes, therefore, the duty of the surgeon to measure with great care the amount of destruction he inflicts on the bone diseased, and limit, with scrupulous precision, this destruction to the degree necessary to secure him against leaving behind any portion of the diseased growth.

To this point the emphatic cautions of Sir William Fergusson strongly tend, and I think it has been in this direction that the mind of the best surgeons has inclined, ever since the operation of excision of the jaws has been introduced. Most of the operations, of which I have had any knowledge during the past few years, have been of this partial character. Sir William Fergusson's advice is, in all cases, to begin the operation by attacking the tumor at its central points, extending the area of excision as the parts may be found diseased; and in this way we have proceeded at the New York Hospital with very satisfactory success, in a number of instances. What difference there may be in the ultimate result of partial and entire exsection, only extensive and careful statistical comparison can discover, but it seems to me that only the ascertained fact, that recurrences *in loco* are more common after well-conducted partial than after complete removals, would justify us in inflicting the greater injury, provided there seems good evidence that in the lesser operation we have entirely removed the disease. It can only be in reference to the benign class of tumors that this question has any interest, for it is well understood that many of this class have that local inveteracy by which, if any portion be left behind, they are sure to be reproduced; assuming thus a character of semi-malignancy, as some express it, or local malignancy, as I think it is better described, which makes the point of complete removal one of prime importance. In the true cancerous affections, any operation short of complete removal would rarely be justifiable.

But, while we give full weight to these considerations, the other side of the question must not be overlooked. Modern pathology explains the growth of some tumors by an infection of the surrounding parts with the juices of the original diseased mass, in such a way that there is supposed to be, at all times, in the immediate neighborhood of the morbid growth, a zone or district of tissue which, while not yet manifestly altered in

its physical appearances, is already poisoned by the infecting
fluids which issue from the growing tumor. This view is pretty
certainly correct for some cancers, and it seems reasonable and
even probable for some other tumors not so essentially malignant in their nature. If this be so, it must be acknowledged
that the risk of reproduction is very considerably diminished
by taking away the whole limb or organ containing the focus
of disease, and modern clinical observation has abundantly
proved the fact. In operating, therefore, upon some cases of a
doubtful nature, it is the surgeon's duty to consider whether his
anxiety to save the patient from the more extensive mutilation
of the removal of the whole jawbone may not lead him to sacrifice the prospect of a perfect ultimate recovery ; for it must
not be forgotten that a morbid growth, which has reappeared
after a partial removal of either the upper or lower jaw, does
not present so easy or so favorable a subject for complete extirpation as did the original tumor.

Again, it must be borne in mind that some tumors, particularly the myeloid, often extend themselves by minute prolongations, or even detached nodules, so small as not easily to be
detected by the surgeon at the moment of operation, and yet
sufficient to insure a reproduction of the mischief, even before
the wounds made by the partial excision have entirely healed.
This insidious encroachment of the myeloid tumor on surrounding healthy parts has already been mentioned in the chapter devoted to the general study of these growths, and it is nowhere
more strikingly illustrated than in the spongy and alveolar
structure of the jawbones, where frequently the area of real
disease is found to be much greater than the apparent tumor
indicated. In all such cases it seems very certain that the only
safety for the patient must consist in a very thorough operation,
if not in a complete amputation of the whole infected bone. No
general rule, therefore, as it seems to me, can be laid down on
this point of the extent of operation which shall be performed.
Each case must be judged of by itself; but I think no judicious
surgeon will venture to decide on his course without carefully
considering both the views of the question which have been
above presented.

The details of the operation will necessarily vary with the

case. This is hardly the occasion to enter into the various modifications of procedure which have been adopted, or which may be necessary. I confine myself, therefore, to a few suggestions of general practical interest. And first, with regard to incisions. Many of the partial operations can be conveniently and easily accomplished without any incision of the skin. The tissue of the lip is so extensible, that with proper assistants, and with suitable spatulæ, very extensive excisions, and, even in small tumors, complete extirpation of the upper jaw might be accomplished. If incisions are required, then, in the upper jaw, the most useful and least deforming is one commencing in the median line of the upper lip, extending round the ala of the nose, and up along its side to the inner canthus of the eye. Mr. Fergusson strongly recommends this incision. He says: "By these incisions through the lip, up the side of the nose, and along the lower eyelid as far out as may be useful, say even to the zygoma, all the room required for the removal of a large tumor may be secured, and the most conspicuous part of the cheek left untouched. Another great advantage which I claim for these incisions is, that the chief vessels of the surface are all divided at their narrowest points, and thus hæmorrhage is less severe than when the facial artery is divided in the middle of the cheek, as in the common incision." Of course, it will happen, in particular instances, that more extensive or differently-planned incisions may better answer the surgeon's purpose; but there must be very few cases in which the incision given by Sir William Fergusson will not be the best, both as regards convenience of operating and subsequent deformity. When the flap thus marked out is carefully raised from the bone, the next step in the operation, if the entire maxilla is to be removed, is to separate the median attachments of the two bones at the line of junction along the palate. This is best accomplished by a fine saw, which is passed into the nostril, and by it the hard palate is divided from above downward as far back as the palate-bone. Much is not said by writers on this operation, about saving the palate-bone, thereby leaving a support for the velum, and preserving the shape and usefulness of the isthmus faucium. In persons past middle life it cannot easily be done, as the palate processes of the superior maxillary

and palate-bone are so firmly welded together as not to be easily
separated; but in young people, if the nature of the tumor will
admit of it, the attempt should be made, and will often be successful.   This incision had better be completed with the saw,
and will be much facilitated by the previous removal of the incisor tooth.   The malar bone is next to be cut through, and this
is perhaps best accomplished by cutting the compact tissue of
the surface with the saw, and completing the section, across to
the anterior end of the spheno-maxillary fissure, by the strong
cutting-forceps.   Then, by the same forceps, passed into the
nostril and orbit, the nasal process of the maxillary bone is
divided, and we have only remaining the attachments to the
palate-bone, and through it to the sphenoid behind, and to the
lower edge of ethmoid in the orbit.   These attachments are
easily broken by a slight rocking motion of the nearly-severed
jaw, and this can very conveniently be imparted to it by seizing
it with the double-toothed "lion-forceps," first suggested by
Sir William Fergusson for this purpose.   These motions should
be cautious and gentle at first, so as to secure, if possible, a
loosening at the natural junctions, and afterward more forcible
and extensive, as may be necessary to detach the mass.   The
soft parts which hold it must be severed with the scalpel, or
strong curved scissors, care being taken not to wander away
from the surfaces of the bone which is being removed, lest important nerves and vessels be unnecessarily injured.   The infra-
orbital nerve should be treated with especial consideration, and
no violent tractions should be made upon it before it is cut.
This caution as to the early careful movement of the loosening
mass is of special interest where it is desired to save the palate-
bone from coming away with the maxillary.

Commonly, no large vessels are wounded, if the surgeon
have been careful in hugging the bone while using his scissors.
The space left by the removal is so large and open that the vessels can easily be secured.   I have once seen the trunk of the
internal maxillary opened just as the jaw was about to be detached from its bed.   The bleeding was profuse, but it was
easily controlled by the sponge, and without much trouble safely
secured by the ligature.   I have never seen the carotid ligatured
before the operation, nor has it ever seemed to me to be at all

necessary. The wide-open character of the wound makes it easy to apply the actual cautery with precision to any points which may have a doubtful look after the main disease is removed; and with us it has been a common practice to resort to it freely.

The removal of both upper jaws has now been several times performed with success, and with less deformity than might be expected from so extensive a mutilation. Dr. David L. Rogers, of this city, was the first surgeon to attempt this operation, which he did in 1824. His case is recorded in a volume of surgical essays, published by himself, in 1849. It was a man, aged thirty-four, who came to Dr. Rogers with a tumor occupying all the front of the upper jawbone, and extending into the right nostril, with the loss of all the upper incisors. It was growing rapidly, and had only existed about six weeks. His operation was performed May 10, 1824, and was published in the third volume of the *Physico-Medical Journal* of that year. From his own book, published fifteen years afterward, I take the following account of the operative procedure: "An incision was made first through the filtrum of the upper lip, which was dissected from the tumor and alæ of the nose, so as to turn both portions of the lip over upon the cheek. The second incision was to detach the cartilaginous portion of the septum narium from the top of the tumor. After extracting the first two molar teeth on each side, a fine saw was used which readily divided the superior maxillary bone including the palatine process, the two incisions meeting at the palatine suture. After sawing through the principal bones, the tumor was easily removed, although it extended much farther back than was at first anticipated. It was found necessary, during the operation, to remove the two inferior turbinated bones, a part of the septum narium, the vomer, and a part of the right antrum." The man recovered well, with a moderate amount of deformity. The record of the operation is lacking in anatomical precision, and the extent of the excision is left somewhat doubtful. It can hardly claim, however, to have been a complete extirpation of both upper jaws, while to it must nevertheless be accorded the honor of being a pioneer effort in the field, since so happily cultivated, and deserving of all the credit to which its boldness, originality, and success are, in all fairness, entitled. In operating on the lower jaw, much may be done without any external incision. Small portions, and indeed the entire half of the bone, can be excised through the mouth without cutting the lip. If, however, the tumor be large, and particularly if it involve the ramus, as in some instances of cystic growth, then external incision is indispensable. The incision usually practised is one parallel with the base of the bone, and thrown back as much as possible, that the scar may be out of sight. This incision, by being prolonged on the cheek, gives ample room even for the removal of the entire bone; and some writers recommend to incise the lower lip, in the median line, as far as the vermilion border, if more room is required. The simple vertical incision of the lower lip, prolonged well backward, is said to give all the space necessary for any of these

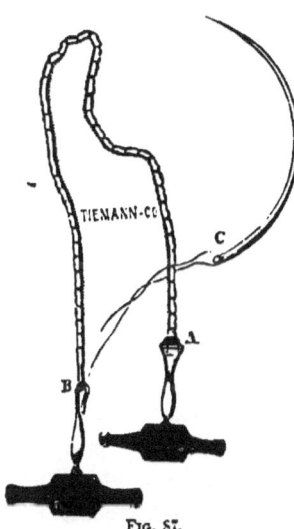

FIG. 87.

operations, though I have not used it nor seen it employed. After separating the bone carefully from the soft parts at the chin, both before and behind, and extracting a central incisor of the side on which the disease exists, a chain-saw (Fig. 87) may be passed round the bone, and its division accomplished at or near the symphysis. Then, with a sharp and strong scalpel, closely hugging the bone, the attachments are to be divided, an assistant at the same time managing the loosening bone, so as to keep the remaining attachments in a state of tension. This part of the procedure is sufficiently simple and easy, but becomes difficult as we approach the condyle, where from the depth of the part it is not easy to sever the ligaments of the joint. This difficulty becomes serious when the ramus and coronoid process are distended by the morbid growth, and it sometimes is simply impossible to finish the removal without cutting off the mass as near the joint as possible, and then with sharp, curved forceps, and the *rongeur*, removing the detached condyle piecemeal. Fergusson's lion-forceps (Fig. 88) is the best instrument for this purpose, giving the holder perfect control of the movements of the fragment, and enabling him to change the tension of the attachments to meet the operator's knife. The facial artery is the principal vessel usually cut

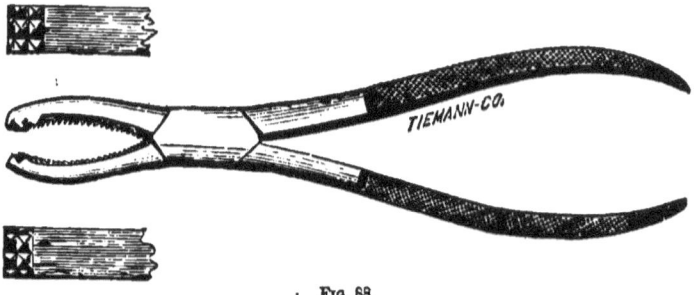

FIG. 88.

in this operation, and this is cut and tied at the time of making the first incision. When the entire jaw is to be removed, it is well to secure the tongue from falling back into the pharynx and choking the patient, as in several of the earlier recorded operations it threatened to do. This is easily accomplished by passing a strong double silk thread through the substance of the tongue about an inch from the tip, which is given to a careful assistant, whose duty it is to watch for this particular danger and obviate it by drawing the tongue firmly forward. After the wound is brought together, and the muscles have become accustomed to the loss of balanced action, there is but little danger from the swallowing of the tongue.

The wounds made in these operations should be lightly stuffed with soft, well-picked lint, and the incised integument brought together with the most careful accuracy. Some surgeons prefer the silver sutures. We have, at the New York Hospital, used the fine annealed iron wire with great satisfaction; but, in my later operations on the face, I have been much pleased with the very fine silk suture, made with an ordinary round cambric needle. From its extreme pliability, the silk adapts the edges more perfectly to each other than any metallic wire can do, and the cambric needle, though not quite so easily thrust through the skin, makes less of a wound than the ordi-

nary surgical needles, and leaves much less of a scar. If the
flaps are loose, and not well supported by the parts beneath,
then the harelip pins, at intervals among the other sutures,
maintain the parts more perfectly in coaptation, and steady the
whole line of suture. No adhesive plasters are usually necessary.

Considering the magnitude of these operations, and the extent and importance of the parts involved, they are very successful in their result. In the *Medical Times and Gazette*
for September 3, 1859, is found a table of seventeen cases of
resection of the upper jaw for various diseases, and by various
operators, and of the seventeen only three died. The rest recovered entirely from the operation, though several suffered of
course from a return of the malignant disease which had rendered an operation necessary. I think our own operations in
New York would show a not less satisfactory result. A similar
table in the same journal shows a mortality of three in eleven
cases of the lower jaw operated on in several of the London
hospitals. These tables of course do not claim to represent the
exact mortality after these operations. They are sufficient, however, to indicate that, under favorable circumstances, the operation is a safe and successful one.

The following case I saw with much interest with my friend
Dr. Goodwillie, and I give it in his own words. It is an interesting account of a very neat and successful operation, and at
the same time a good, and I think quite a rare, example of the
hard form of osseous growth of the cancellous variety in the
alveolar border of the superior maxillary bone. The microscopical appearances, of which a drawing is given, were reported
by Dr. J. W. S. Arnold:

"Mrs. B., aged forty-four years, has always enjoyed very good
health. Some six years ago she first noticed that the alveolus
of the right superior maxillary began to enlarge, and has gradually increased to the present time.

"She has experienced no pain, and desired to have it removed, as from its large size it has become a source of great
annoyance to her. In size and shape it very much resembles
a hen's egg, the large end presenting posteriorly. It extends
antero-posteriorly from the right superior canine to the internal

pterygoid process; laterally from near the centre of the palate to the maxillo-malar fossa forward to the canine fossa. The floor of the antrum of Highmore was encroached on to a slight degree. The mucous membrane over the surface of the tumor appeared a little lighter in color than is common to the alveolus; this was no doubt due to the tension on it by the parts below; otherwise it was in a normal condition. In the surface of the tumor could be seen the fangs of the first and second molars. The canine and bicuspids were not decayed. Canine and first bicuspid retained their normal position in the jaw. All the crown of the latter was buried in the tumor, except the cusps. The crown of the second bicuspid could all be seen, but the whole tooth was raised out of its normal position, and thrown inward about one-half of an inch (Fig. 89).

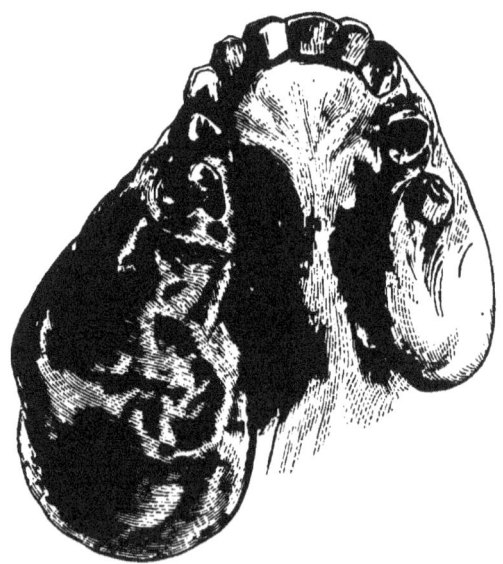

FIG. 89.—(From Dr. D. H. Goodwillie's Collection.)

"There being no pain or discharge from the mouth or nose during the long period of its growth—its apparent firm texture with no crepitation—together with the excellent health the patient has always enjoyed, there appeared no doubt of its benign character.

"The following cut (Fig. 90) represents an oral saw that I devised to be used in operations on the maxillary bones.

"To a handle (*a*) is firmly fastened a U shank (*b*) to take in the cheek or lip, and thus do away with making external incisions. On the other extremity of the shank is a square socket to which are fitted saws (or knives) of different sizes, these being firmly fastened by a thumb-screw (*c*). The socket being square, allows the saw (or knife) to be turned and worked in four directions. It is only necessary to unscrew the fastening a short distance, to turn the saw in the desired direction.

Fig. 90.

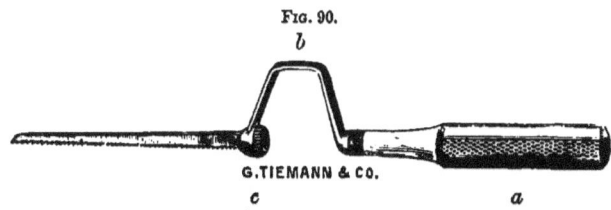

G. TIEMANN & CO.

"The saw, being in direct line with the handle, can be very easily guided. The backs of the saws are thin, while the teeth are broad, thus giving free action.

"On June 20, 1871, the patient was placed in an operating-chair, and, when she was fully under the anæsthetic, the head was thrown back, and the mouth kept open by a gag between the molar teeth of the opposite side. Taking my position to the back and over the head of the patient, I placed a sponge cut to completely fill up the passage to the throat, and held in position on the soft palate by a sponge-holder to prevent the blood passing into the throat during the first part of the operation. The patient was only allowed to breath through the nose, which she could very well do. No external incision of the face was made. The two internal incisions were made from behind on the posterior prominence of the tumor, one-half inch on each side of the fangs of the molars forward to the left central incisor. The bone was now laid bare by stripping the soft parts with periosteal denuders; the latter part of this operation was to tear the palatal muscles from the posterior part of the hard palate without injuring the palatal vessels and nerve that passes over on to the hard palate at this point. There being no further use for the sponge on the soft palate, it was removed. The right lateral incisor was now extracted, and, by its socket through a little to the right of the centre of the hard palate, so as to save the vomer, a section was made with the oral saw, thus dividing the superior maxillary bones. This saw was now removed from the socket and replaced by another one, half as long (one and a half inch), the teeth of which were changed to a different angle, so as to allow the cheek to go into the U-shank, and let the saw play freely. This section was made up between the tumor and the internal pterygoid process to the malar bone, then forward through the canine fossa, dividing also the inferior turbinated bone, to meet the other section at the right ala nasi. After the saw had entered the antrum, the handle of the saw was more rapidly advanced th n the point; this prevented the

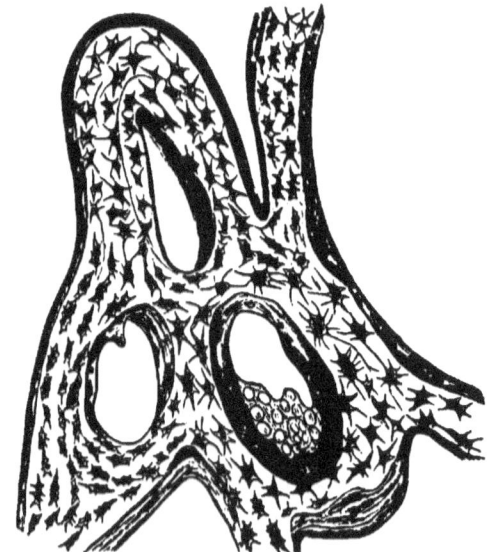

Fig. 91.—(Osseous tumor from Dr. D. H. Goodwillie. magnified 850 diameters.)
Drawn by J. W. S. Arnold, M. D.

point of the saw from piercing the vomer which I desired to save. By these two sections the tumor with the adjacent bone was removed clean. After hæmorrhage had stopped, the soft parts were closed by seven silk sutures. On the fifth day four of the sutures were removed, and the remainder on the following day, the wound having healed by first intention. Four months after the operation, there appears every indication of a new formation of bone.

"Pathological examination of the tumor shows it to be osseous. On making a section of the tumor through the line of the teeth, the following was observed:

"At the apex of the root of the second molar tooth there was a small, soft cyst containing pus, and for a short distance surrounding this bone appeared quite cancellated, but the rest of the tumor was quite dense. The pulps of the canine and first bicuspid teeth had still some vitality, but that of the second bicuspid was dead. The pulp-chambers were decreased in size by a deposit of osteo-dentine to their walls. The cementum on the fangs of the teeth was hypertrophied. A large nerve entered the tumor on its buccal side.

"*Microscopical Character.*—Composed of cancellated tissue almost entirely; the outer rim or edge of a thin layer of more compact bony tissue; in the spongy part a small amount of soft marrow, containing the usual constituents of fœtal marrow, that is, medullo cells and myeloplaxes, with oil-globules." (Fig. 91.)

PART III.

MALIGNANT DISEASES OF BONE.

In the light of recent microscopical and clinical studies, it is not easy exactly to define the meaning of the term malignant as applied to morbid growths. The difficulty does not arise so much from any want of precision in the term itself, or any want of appropriateness when applied to typical and well-marked cases, as it does from the varying degree in which the qualities it expresses are manifested in the different tumors in which we study it, and the want of constant correspondence between their anatomical structure and their clinical history. It is pretty well agreed among pathologists that the chief clinical features of malignity are: 1. A tendency to soften and ulcerate. 2. A tendency to return after extirpation, even the most complete. 3. A disposition to appear in many places successively in the same individual, invading many tissues in the region originally affected, and developing itself in many distant organs, where it seems to have no connection with the original disease. These clinical features have been sought to be associated with certain physical forms, which pathologists have hoped would prove characteristic. This hope has not been fully realized. No anatomical form has yet been found, which, of itself, is distinctive of cancer, and without which malignancy cannot exist. No association or grouping of histological elements can be said to be absolutely characteristic of malignancy; and much as has been done by Virchow, Weber, Waldeyer, Beale, and Huxley, in unravelling the laws of histogenesis, no mode of development, whether as to source, forms, rate, progress, or irregularities, can be invoked to solve the question of the clinical history of every morbid growth. There will still remain some obstinate exceptions, where structure and history do not correspond, exceptions which at present we must accept as indicating to us how superficial is our knowledge of the deepest laws of vital organization.

With this acknowledgment, enough remains upon which we may build our classification with sufficient precision for many practical purposes; and as we may accept those above given as the most striking and constant features of what we call malignancy, so we have certain histological and histogenetic characters which commonly accompany these clinical ones, which we may with practical utility and safety consider as the physical condition with which they are commonly associated, and upon which they usually depend. Thus malignant growths are usually unlike the tissues from which they spring, and many present features which are unlike those of any tissue found in the normal structures of the body. Again, malignant growths have usually their elements scattered through and intermixed with the normal tissues, so as to entangle these normal tissues with them in their progress, and to involve them in the destruction to which they are so certainly hastening. These two features, heterology and infiltration, are well marked and characteristic in a vast proportion of cases of malignant disease, and therefore may be considered the general anatomical features of these affections. Accepting them as simply the general characters of the disease, we may, for more particular study, divide the great class of malignant, or cancerous, or carcinomatous diseases, for these terms are generally received as synonymous, into the subclasses of scirrhous, medullary, epithelial, colloid, and melanoid. Some other subdivisions are sometimes made, but, in reference to the bones, I believe these will be sufficient.

CHAPTER I.

SCIRRHUS, OR HARD CANCER OF THE BONES.

As a primary disease of the bones, scirrhus is extremely rare. Several authors allude to the possibility of its occurrence; but I have not myself seen, nor have I met in any published account, any such details of an unequivocal case as would warrant my presenting it as an example. As a secondary development, it is not so uncommon. It usually has been found in persons in whom the cancerous cachexia is far advanced; in many instances, the patients have been bedridden. In one case which occurred a few years ago in this city, the patient, an old lady, dying slowly from the disease, primarily developed in the breast, had been confined for some time to her bed, when, on one occasion, on attempting to turn or to raise herself in bed, one of her thigh-bones gave way, and some days after, on a similar trifling exertion, the other also broke. In her case the skeleton was very extensively infiltrated with true scirrhous cancer. The femora, the ribs, the humeri, the pelvic bones, and I believe all of the bones which were examined, showed traces, more or less considerable, of the disease, in some more advanced than in others. The specimens were presented to the Pathological Society, and, in particular, I remember that the ribs were so soft as to be flexible, and capable of being cut by a scalpel. In this case, as in the other reported cases, the morbid material has all the appearances of the disease when it is developed in the soft parts, both to the naked eye and under the microscope. It is sometimes seen in large, more or less rounded tumors, as in Mr. Paget's case, delineated Fig. 92, but more frequently, as in the specimens I saw, disseminated in small nodules through the cancellous tissue, after the manner of an infiltration. The bone-substance becomes gradually dis-placed, or rather, probably absorbed, so that

Fig. 92.—(From Paget.)

fracture from slight causes is extremely likely to occur; and, indeed, it has been noticed, in certain rare instances, that the whole bone has disappeared, leaving the periosteum unchanged in size or form, but filled with cancerous material instead of the original osseous tissue. Mr. Paget speaks of a case in which

22

"a cancerous femur was broken eight months before death, and the new bone with which it was repaired was infiltrated with cancer as well as the original textures."

To the naked eye the morbid material presents, on section, the usual bluish-white, pearly, shining, semi-transparent appearance of hard cancer elsewhere. Under the microscope, the cells present the same appearances which are characteristic of the disease in other parts. Their irregularity of form, their dim, pellucid cell-wall, their large nuclei, commonly single, with large, distinct nucleoli, are features well marked; while the semi-fluid substance in which these cells lie enclosed, as in a stroma, can be squeezed out or scraped out in considerable abundance. There is some difference of view among pathologists as to whether the fibrous element, so commonly found in this form of cancer, be one of new formation, or whether it be only the original tissues, distended by, and enclosed in, the growing cancerous mass. This question, it seems to me, receives some light from the fact that this fibrous structure is sometimes almost completely absent in hard cancer of the bones. In some of the firmest and most fibrous-looking of these cases there is no fibrous tissue to be discovered.

Dr. Delafield made a careful examination of some of the bones removed after death from a patient of Dr. Sprague, of Fordham, who had died of cancer of the breast of the scirrhous form. "All the long bones were diseased; had become bent during life, especially one femur. Specimens are femur, first, and tibia, last affected. Femur is much bent, and tibia not. Periosteum and cartilages not involved. Nearly the entire bone and medulla changed into a firm, white, lardaceous substance; a little of bone of shaft and cancellous tissue left. New tissue consists of dense bands of white, fibrous tissue, crossing and interlacing and forming round and oval interspaces. These spaces are mostly empty, but, in the youngest part of tissue, are filled with polygonal, nucleated cells. The mamma was a small, contracted, hard lump. Only fibrous tissue could be found; no cells."

In another case, brought into Bellevue Hospital November 25, 1867, fracture had occurred of the right femur by a fall in the street the day before her admission. The patient was a very old woman, eighty-seven years of age, and had an ulcerating carcinoma of the breast of unknown duration. An attempt was made to treat the broken limb, but she rapidly failed, and died December 8th.

Autopsy.—"Body very much emaciated. The right mamma is the seat of a large ulcer, with indurated edges; the axillary glands are much enlarged; several small tubers in the skin near the ulcer. *Head.*—In the vault of the cranium are three rounded places where the bone is replaced by a structure resembling fibrous tissue; the periosteum and dura mater are adherent to these places, but there is no tumor. In the bone surrounding these places, the diploë is filled with new tissue, and the bones thinned. All the bones of the skull are softer than natural. Brain is normal. *Lungs.*—There are a few old adhesions over both lungs. Both lungs are more than usually pigmented. The upper lobe of the right lung is hepatized. The liver has hardly any left lobe. There are gall-stones in the bladder and ductus communis; the latter is dilated so as to admit my finger up to one quarter of an inch of the intestine, where it is obstructed. Spleen small. A few nodules in the capsule. Peritonæum throughout studded with small white tumors. Kidneys, in both pelves and calyces, dilated and containing pus, especially the left. Large intestine, its walls containing many small tumors, over which the epithelium has ulcerated. *Bones.*—The right femur is fractured at its middle, the fractured ends much displaced, and bathed in pus. At the point of fracture the shaft of the bone is thinned, and the medullary cavity filled with a new growth. The left femur, both tibiæ, both humeri, the sacrum, and one os innominatum, contain similar deposits of new tissue in their medullary cavities. The scapulæ, ulnæ, radii, clavicles, and metacarpal bones, contain no such deposit.

" *Minute Examination.*—The new tissue in the mamma and in the tubers in the skin presents the same appearance, viz., polygonal, nucleated, epithelial cells, .018 to .025 in diameter, contained in round and oval alveoli, the proportion between cells and framework varying in different parts. The tumors in the peritonæum differ from these in their greater number of cells. In the long bones, the tumors are situated either next to the shaft of the bone or in the cancellous tissue, and are surrounded by red, indurated medulla. This red medulla is composed largely of 'medullocelles.' The new tissue consists of a pretty dense fibrous framework, forming alveoli which contain cells. The cells are the same as those found in the breast. There are also found numbers of nuclei adhering together and surrounded by protoplasma, *not* myeloplaxes. In some places only cells are seen. In the cranium the cells are the same, but their arrangement is somewhat different. The fibrous tissue is more abundant, and the alveoli small; some only containing two or three cells, others much larger; and these small alveoli may be close together, so that it looks like fibro-cartilage. The character of the cells and the examination of a sufficient number of specimens destroy the possibility of this."

CHAPTER II.

MEDULLARY, OR SOFT CANCER OF THE BONES.

By far the most common form of cancerous disease of bones is the medullary, or soft cancer. Indeed, of all the cases of medullary cancer, the bones furnish a very considerable fraction. Mr. Paget gives a table of 103 cases of external medullary cancer, omitting those of the uterus and other internal organs, and of these 21 were in the bones. Lebert gives a table of 447 cancers, of all kinds, of which 35 were in the bones. M. Tanchou's extensive tables, embracing 9,118 cases of all kinds, give only 38 to the bones. This small fraction might probably be increased somewhat by adding something for those cases which he includes under the head of thigh, shoulder, leg, arm, etc., some of which were doubtless affections of the bones. Mr. Sibley's tables give, of 520 cases, 15 of the bones, and Mr. Baker, in 500 cases, records 23 as occurring in the bones. None of these are to be relied on as giving an accurate statement of the relative frequency of cancer in bones, but they may serve to convey some general idea on the subject; and, when we take into account the fact that by far the larger proportion of all are medullary, we have arrived at some rough estimate of the proportion in which each form presents itself in the bones as compared with the soft parts.

These statistical statements have reference to cancer in all its forms and all its conditions. As a primary disease, however, cancer in the bones is, almost without exception, of the soft variety. The primary tumors present themselves in all parts of the skeleton—Mr. Paget thinks most frequently in the thigh-bone—and usually affect the cancellous tissue in the first instance; often, however, extending their encroachments to the compact substance, which is gradually incorporated with the growing mass, losing always its compact character, and becoming either altogether absorbed, or spread out into a spongy mass, pervading the new growth, in which finally no trace of the original compact structure can be discovered. This is particularly the case with the arm and thigh bones, and it is in cancer in these situations that we most often have fractures occurring from the most trivial degrees of violence. Most commonly the primary cancer is single, and in the shape of a rounded tumor, which distends before it the outer shell of the bone, which shell, growing thinner and thinner, as the tumor enlarges, it sometimes retains until it has attained a great size, when finally the cancerous mass breaks through its covering, and soon all traces of it disappear. The tumor may either be an isolated mass of medullary substance displacing the surrounding bone-tissues, or, as is most frequently the case, it is an infiltration from the first; and grows as such, gradually appropriating to itself, and enclosing within its growing mass, whatever bony material, whether compact or cancellous, it comes in contact with.

In this way the most various shapes are assumed, and the most various conditions of the growth itself are found. The tumor usually projects from the surface of the bone on one side; sometimes it projects unequally on both sides, as in the cranial bones. Sometimes, as in the heads of the long bones, the whole spongy extremity expands nearly equally, and often reaches an immense size, with a somewhat symmetrical form (Figs. 93, 94). On the cranium these tumors very commonly project from the surface of the vault in the form of evenly-rounded domes or hemispheres, and where several are growing close to one another the head presents a most extraordinary appearance. The figures 99 and 100 are taken from patients who died of the disease developing itself internally, while the tumors seen on the head were slowly increasing.

FIG. 98.—(From Billroth.)

The cut surface of these growths presents a whitish, pearly section, in which an arrangement into lobules can be more or less distinctly seen; the lobules varying much in size, and still more in consistence and color; some are quite hard and white, others are softer, and reddish or brownish in color. Others are so soft as to flicker almost like jelly, and have a deep-red or modena color, as if stained deeply with blood. In other points actual extravasations of blood, some apparently contained within cyst-walls of a sort of fibrous tissue, are found, giving the appearances which were formerly spoken of as fungus hæmatodes. The tumor is usually contained within a capsule formed from the periosteum, often much thickened, which capsule is, during the earlier periods of the growth of the tumor, fortified, as men-

tioned above, with the thin shell of compact bone upon which
the periosteum lies, the two layers at first expanding together;
then, as the tumor increases, the bony shell giving way first; and
afterward, as the mass softens and ulcerates, the periosteum
disappearing at the point of greatest prominence; and the soft
growing mass, now released from the support of its hitherto

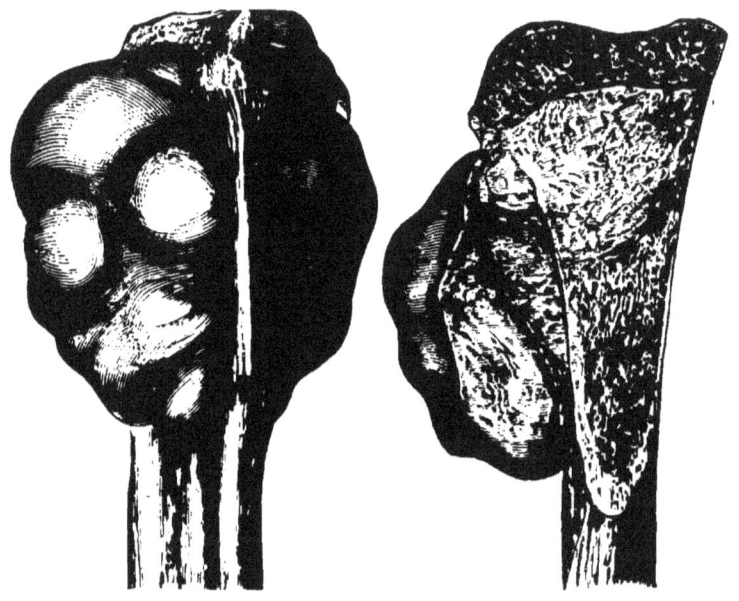

FIG. 94.—(From Billroth.)   FIG. 95.—(From Billroth.)

firm envelope, sprouts without restraint in whatever direction
it is least opposed by surrounding tissues.   If the tumor have
not yet reached the surface, when it has escaped from its fibrous
incasement, then we find it invading and appropriating to
itself all the softer materials which it encounters, which, becoming incorporated with the growing mass, lose all identity; or,
pushing itself in and among the various interspaces where pressure is the least, it reaches out its finger-like processes, extending
often much deeper and much farther than its external appearance would lead one to expect.   At the same time it often
seems limited by encountering a firm aponeurotic layer, against
which it spreads laterally, and adheres to it without involving

it, at least for a considerable period. If, on the other hand, the mass has reached the surface when the fibrous envelope gives way, then we have the proper fungous character assumed, with the rapid growth, and almost as rapid destruction of the protruding cancerous material.

The relations of the original bone to the growing cancer have already been alluded to. Here the processes are invariably those of destruction and disappearance, more or less complete, of both cancellous and compact bone-tissue. This disappearance is irregular, however—at some points being further advanced than in others, so that at different parts of the tumor we may have either much or very little of the disappearing original bone remaining. With these irregular remains of the skeleton of the part we have a certain amount of disposition on the part of the tumor itself to generate new bone. I think this is rarely observed to any great extent in the medullary cancers of the long bones, but in those affecting the skull it is often very marked. In the maceration of the head, Fig. 100, we found, on clearing off the soft parts, and drying the bones, a most extraordinary and beautiful framework of delicate spicular bone springing from the surface of the skull, which was itself eroded and partially absorbed wherever the tumor had grown from its surface. These slender spiculæ and thin laminæ of newly-formed bone were, almost all, at right angles with the surface of the bone from which they grew, and from their delicate formation, varying form, and beautiful feathery terminations, made a most beautiful preparation. This we kept, carefully protected under glass, in the New York Hospital Cabinet for some years, but it gradually disintegrated and fell to pieces, so that now none but the rougher and stronger foundations remain of the light and delicate structure, showing by its destruction how imperfect and feeble it was in its organization. This form of radiating skeleton, as found in the soft cancer of the skull, is spoken of by several writers, but nothing so marked is often found in other bones. In some rare cases an increase of bone-substance is found from the beginning of the disease, giving a hardness to the growth which makes it quite difficult to pronounce, without microscopical examination, whether we have to deal with a cancer or an exostosis.

The vascularity of these cancers is usually very great, and new vessels are formed with surprising rapidity. These vessels are generally very large in size, thin in their walls, tortuous and often varicose in their course, and in such abundance as to be out of all proportion to their amount in any normal tissue. It is on account of this disproportionate development of vessels, large and small, arterial and venous, that we have, in many of these tumors, so active a circulation that the pulsation of the arterial vessels often gives rise to the suspicion of aneurism— a suspicion which is sometimes strengthened by the fact that they do diminish in size when pressure is made upon the main trunk above the tumor. This diminution, so much like the subsidence of an aneurismal swelling, under the same manipulation, is simply due to the fact that the bulk of the tumor is so largely made up of vessels that a diminution in the amount of blood they contain is sufficient to produce an evident decrease in the size of the tumor itself. Hence, also, we have the frequent extravasations of blood into the substance of the medullary mass, and, when ulceration has taken place, the same abundance of large and thin-walled vessels explains the facility with which hæmorrhage occurs, and the alarming extent to which it sometimes reaches.

In the softer cancers, a large quantity of juice can be scraped or squeezed from the cut surface, and indeed, by moderate and repeated squeezings, the whole solid mass of the tumor may be emptied of its fluid and semifluid contents, and then appears as a flaccid, whitish, shreddy, wet, tow-like mass, which bears a surprisingly small proportion to its original size. This large proportion of fluid matter, retained in the meshes of a comparatively small amount of weakly solid stroma, explains very readily the deceptive feeling of fluctuation which medullary cancers in the soft parts so often present, and which feeling is not by any means rare in the advanced stages of the disease as it occurs in the bones.

The microscopical study of these tumors gives us nothing different from their well-known features in other parts of the body. Of cells, we have the characteristic multiformity. Thus, we have the ordinary cell, with its single, rarely double nucleus, and bright, sometimes multiple nucleolus; these cells presenting every variety of shape, sometimes round, sometimes flattened, sometimes elongated into processes of most irregular outline.   These are mingled with a large proportion of what are considered as free nuclei, though Mr. Beale's researches would lead us to regard these as cells as much as the other forms, these free nuclei having shapes as various as the cells, and often presenting a close approximation to the spindle-shaped cell, of which we have seen that the bulk of some non-malignant tumors is composed.   The true elongated, spindle-shaped cell, with nucleus and nucleolus, is not uncommon, but never, so far as I know, makes up any considerable portion of the mass.   Cells also occur in which no nuclei can be seen, and sometimes we have the large cells with many nuclei, resembling the peculiar cell of the myeloid growth.   The intercellular substance is softer than in the case of scirrhus, and a good deal of the cell-growth seems to take place in a substance which is nearly fluid.   Here, however, much difference prevails in different specimens, the intercellular substance in some examples being quite firm, and in extremely small amount, whereas in others it forms the bulk of the growth, is almost liquid, and has the cells floating in it, much as pus-cells float in the liquor puris.   It is somewhat characteristic of this form of disease, that all these varieties, both of cell-formation and of intercellular substance, are constantly found in the same tumor, and often in the same lobule.

Much has been said, of late years, of the fibrous stroma or framework in which the cancerous material proper is contained. The alveolar character has been considered by many able observers as the one characteristic anatomical feature of cancer, by which a ground of distinction from all other tumors may be maintained.   I do not feel prepared to accept this as a universally applicable anatomical distinction, yet it has much evidence in its favor.   Rokitansky, as long ago as 1852, published a description of the development of the stroma or skeleton of cancers, accompanied with beautiful plates, giving his ideas with great distinctness and minuteness.   He describes the stroma of cancer as composed of two distinct elements; one somewhat of a fibrous character, and the other made up of cells closely packed without any distinct fibrillar arrangement.   These two

substances are arranged in the form of bands of a tolerably
regular size, which interlace among themselves, leaving spaces
of various sizes and shapes, in which are contained the true
cancerous cells, and their proper intercellular substance. This
stroma he considers as the real basis-substance of the cancer,
as much a part of it as the cells themselves, and, pervading all
parts of the diseased mass like a skeleton, is one of its essential anatomical features (Fig. 96). Many of the most eminent

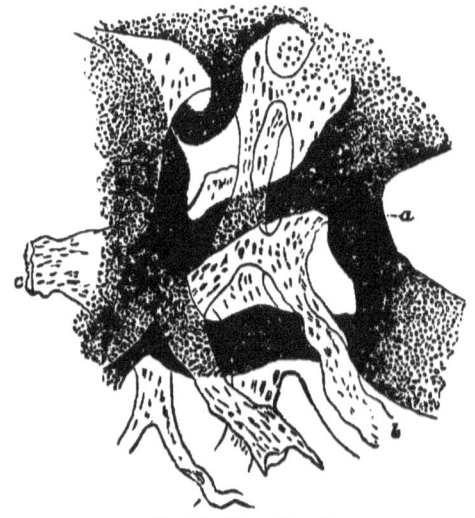

Fig. 96.—(From Paget.)

pathological anatomists since Rokitansky have given a description of an alveolar arrangement of the stroma of cancer varying somewhat from, but in the main confirmatory of, his views.
Thus, in Cornil and Ranvier's manual, carcinoma is defined to
be "a tumor composed of a fibrous stroma arranged in alveoli,
which form, by their communication, a cavernous system; these
alveoli are filled with free cells contained in a liquid more or
less abundant." Billroth entertains views, with regard to the
tumors which should be included under the term cancer, in
which he differs somewhat from other recent writers, but he
evidently recognizes as an anatomical fact the alveolar character of the cancerous tumors which he describes, as his plate, of
which Fig. 97 is a copy, very evidently shows. He does not,

however, seem disposed to admit the alveolar arrangement as
an absolutely characteristic feature of cancer.

The clinical history of soft cancer of bones presents many
variations from a typical case. Most frequently the disease
commences without any or with very little pain, and without

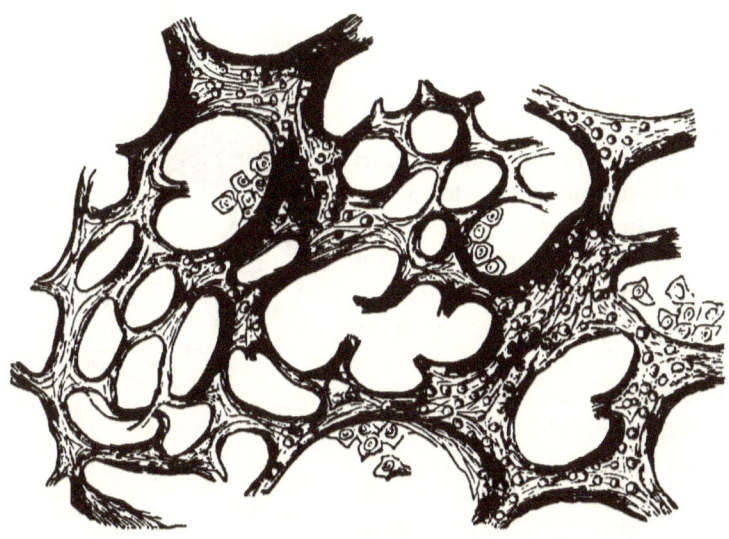

Fig. 97.—(From Billroth.)

any very evident assignable cause. Without being confined to
any age, it is most common at a much earlier period of life
than either the scirrhous or epithelial form of the disease. In
my observation, most of the very rapid-growing cases have
been in young adults. In one very remarkable case which occurred in the New York Hospital, and of which we have the
specimen in the pathological cabinet, a cancerous tumor of the
clavicle and scapula proved fatal in six weeks from the day of
its first appearance, by which time it had attained a size of one
foot in diameter. This tumor occurred in a young man of
eighteen years of age. Another enormous and very rapidly-
developed tumor was the one presented in Fig. 98. This was
developed from the clavicle in a girl aged fourteen, and reached
its gigantic size within a few months. It was of the softer
medullary character, and to the last showed but little tendency

to ulcerate. She died, worn out by the disease, and cancerous deposits of a similar character to those of the large tumor were found in the lungs. She had also, as seen in the woodcut, a very singular-looking redundan-
cy of the skin, with hypertrophy of its tissue, on the right arm, making a hanging sort of bag of thickened, discolored skin, with numerous strong hairs growing upon it. It was for this curious formation, which had been grow-ing for several years, that I pre-sented her to the Pathological Society, about a year before her death, when the tumor of the clavicle had scarcely begun to show itself. The tumors shown in Figs. 99 and 100 were both young men, one eighteen, the other nineteen years old.

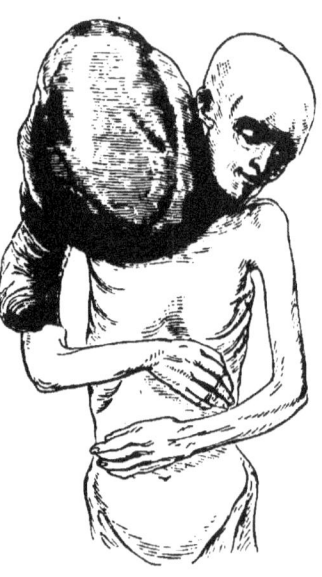

Fig. 98.—(N. Y. Hospital Museum.)

The cause of these growths cannot generally be ascertained. Sometimes an injury, as a blow, is the starting-point of the dis-ease, and one case in our collection followed a fracture. No. 107 is a picture of this case, which was briefly this: A man, twenty-two years old, broke his arm in the act of throwing a snowball. "No union took place, and at the end of six months he entered the hospital, where the limb was removed at the shoulder-joint; an encephaloid deposit having meanwhile taken place upon the fractured humerus, so abundant as to form a large fusiform swelling, involving the greater part of the arm, and measur-ing at least twenty inches in circumference." Some cases are spoken of where encephaloid disease has attacked carious joints, where the products of old inflammation may be supposed to have been the nidus in which the cancer originated. In by far the larger number of cases, however, no distinct cause can be ascertained. As the tumor grows, the patients suffer pain from its distention of and pressure upon the surrounding soft parts, the tumor itself remaining free from pain or tenderness. In

some exceptional cases great pain is experienced from the earliest to the latest stages. The tendency to ulceration does not
seem to be so marked in medullary cancer of the bones as it is
in cancers of other parts and of other forms. Many of the largest
tumors I have seen were not ulcerated at all, and those which
were open at any point of their surface seemed to have become
so from some abrasion, or pressure, or some other accident
which had determined an ulceration where it would not otherwise have occurred. The great tumor of the shoulder had a
very small surface of ulceration upon its summit, which only
appeared in the last weeks of life. The tendency of most of
these tumors is rather toward rapid proliferation of the cell-
growths, of which they are composed, than to ulcerative destruction. This ulceration, however, does occur in some cases, usually
preceded by a bulging of the tumor at one or more points, which
become very vascular in their external appearance, and often
very tender to the touch as the ulceration is about to take place.
This bulging and apparent inflammation is the accompaniment
of a process of rapid softening which is going on at that point;
and, when the surface does give way, we have an ulceration followed by fungous sprouting forth of enormous, soft, spongy
granulations, rapidly increasing in size and prominence, bleeding fiercely on the slightest injury, and discharging a copious,
thin, bloody ichor, which very rapidly exhaust the remaining
powers of life. The condition which precedes this ulceration,
viz., the soft, bulging, very vascular prominence of a certain
part of the surface of the growth, very closely simulates the
process of suppuration in its external features; and, when combined with the fact that a pretty rapid and quite considerable
softening of the mass occurs at the protruding point, it is not
wonderful that many good surgeons have been deceived, and
have plunged a bistoury into the suspected spot, expecting a
free escape of matter to follow their incision. The feeling of
fluctuation is so perfect in these cases that I know not how to
discriminate between it and the fluctuation of real pus. The
mistake is an unfortunate one, for ulceration and fungus are very
apt to follow the incision; and yet, in several instances, I have
known such a cut to heal as quickly and as soundly as if it had
been made in a perfectly healthy part.

During all the earlier part of this disease, particularly if the patient do not suffer much pain, the constitution does not seem to experience much deterioration. Some of these patients, with rapidly-growing and large tumors on the arm or leg, will keep about their ordinary avocations, and, among the lower classes, seem sometimes to feel very little anxiety about their disease. One of the largest tumors of this kind that I have ever seen, occupying two-thirds of the whole thigh-bone, and of enormous diameter, walked to our college clinique, and up to the third story, with no more inconvenience than was occasioned by the excessive weight she had to carry. In the later stages, after softening begins, and particularly after fungus has protruded, the system gives way rapidly, and the true cancerous cachexia occurs, if the patient live long enough for its peculiar features to be developed. Secondary deposits, of the same nature as the original tumor, are found in the liver, the lungs, and various other internal organs, sometimes in immense masses, and sometimes very extensively diffused over various organs and regions of the body. Specimens No. 557 and 558, in our collection, are instances of secondary cancerous developments in the lungs and pleura, in a man from whom the thigh had been removed a few months before for a large medullary tumor. About three months after the amputation he began to suffer from pectoral symptoms, of which he finally died. "A growth of fungus hematodes was found to have involved a large portion of the lung, while, between the lower surface of that organ and the upper surface of the diaphragm, which is pushed down, a cavity was found containing nearly a gallon of brownish-red serous fluid, with coagula and shreds of lymph floating through it." This cavity was that of the pleura, whose surface was studded all over with "numerous rounded and flattened masses, soft, and of a white color," which were evidently of the same nature as the tumor originally removed from the thigh. No. 556 is an immense secondary medullary tumor, developed in the mediastinum, and compressing the lungs and other thoracic organs into a very small space. This specimen was also taken from a man who, about a year before his death, had had his thigh amputated for a large encephaloid tumor of the femur. Secondary deposits of all the forms of cancer are quite common in the bones.

It is well known that all of the forms of cancer are capable, under certain circumstances, of undergoing a change for the better. This change may be shown by the tumor, heretofore progressive, remaining stationary; the bulk of the tumor, in other cases, may actually diminish, even sometimes to the extent of the disappearance of all signs of the disease; the surface, previously deeply ulcerated, may fill up with healthy granulations, and cicatrize; or, lastly, these favorable changes may be consequent upon a process of inflammation and sloughing, whereby, the whole tumor being destroyed, a sound cicatrix may be secured. These flattering phases of cancerous life are perhaps best and certainly most frequently seen in the form of the disease we are now studying; but, it has so happened, that I have never seen any good exemplification of it in any form of cancer of the bones. It doubtless does sometimes occur in medullary tumors of the bones; but I must believe it to be more rare than in any of the forms of cancer affecting the soft parts. A very slow growth of the tumor is sometimes seen, as, in one instance, where a woman presented herself at the New York Hospital, with a large tumor of the tibia, which, she assured us, had not grown at all for twenty years, and which, only within a short time, had given her any uneasiness. The limb was amputated, and the tumor, which sprang from the anterior face of the tibia, gave the most unmistakable evidence of encephaloid cancer.

The following cases illustrate so well the chief clinical features of the disease we have been considering as to justify me in introducing here a brief outline of their history. The first case was under my care as resident surgeon of the New York Hospital, Dr. Gurdon Buck having the responsible management of it as attending surgeon, and, from his very full and careful notes, dictated at the time, I draw my material:

Albert Milderberger, a boatman, aged nineteen, was admitted into the New York Hospital, December 14, 1839, with a tumor of the size of a large orange covering the parietal and temporal regions. "In the month of May last preceding, while at work on board a vessel, he struck his head against the boom, as he was in the act of lifting a stove; but, having on a fur cap at the time, he perceived no unpleasant effects from the blow, and continued his work. The same evening he noticed a soft tumor, under the scalp, of the size of a walnut, on the spot where he had received the blow. In a fortnight it increased to the size of a Madeira-nut, and was pronounced a wen by a physician who examined it. In July it was as large as a hen's egg, and, on being punctured, it discharged a pint of florid blood in a jet that was easily arrested. The puncture healed in two days, and the size of the tumor was diminished. The loss of blood relieved a headache from which he was suffering at the time. Pressure was now applied, during four or five weeks, by means of a piece of lead, but had no other effect than to flatten the shape of the tumor, which continued increasing in size. For four weeks preceding his admission, very powerful pressure was kept up by means of a piece of lead, weighing two pounds, flattened out and adapted to its surface, and bound firmly to the head. This caused the tumor to spread at its base, particularly along the lower side, toward the orbit and zygoma. Five days before admission it was punctured a second time, and a pint of bright-red blood flowed rapidly in a jet, without diminishing its size. The blood was easily arrested, and the puncture healed kindly.

"At the time of his admission, the tumor had attained a formidable size, and presented the following characters (Fig. 99): It rose two inches above the surface of the cranium, standing off in an oblique direction outward. Its base was of an oblong form, and extended upward to within two fingers' breadth of the median line; backward to the lambdoidal suture; downward to within an inch of the ear, and forward to within three fingers' breadth of the outer margin of the orbit. Its limits were abrupt and well defined, except about one fourth of its circumference that expanded out over the temple in a superficial soft swelling that was gradually lost near the outer canthus, and along the zygoma. This portion appeared after pressure was applied the second time. The tumor measured, in an oblique direction, forward and downward over the summit, seven inches and a half. The surface was of the color of the rest of the scalp, and sparsely covered with hair. Numerous veins ramified under the skin, and, when pressure was made on the internal jugular vein, they became swollen and prominent. A

23

small congeries of purple arborescent capillary vessels existed
at one point on the surface.   There was a softened spot, of the
size of a split-pea, and of a dirty-yellowish color, at the point
where the last puncture had been made, apparently from the
formation of a superficial abscess.   The tumor was tense and
elastic in every point, rather softer and more supple in front

Fig. 99.—(From N. Y. Hospital Museum.)

than elsewhere.   No fluctuation could be felt, nor could any
diminution of its size be produced by pressure.   The pulsation
of the branches of the temporal and occipital arteries was perceptible on applying the hand, but there was no pulsation of
the mass.   On applying the cheek, however, I thought I perceived a slight movement of elevation and subsidence.   A distinct *bruit de soufflet* and thrill could be perceived in the temporal artery above the zygoma.   A solid, roundish lump was felt
within the tumor at its posterior part; the patient himself had
noticed it, and sometimes had noticed two lumps.   That portion of the tumor that spread upon the temple, after pressure
was applied the second time, was soft and doughy, except at its
anterior part, where there was a circumscribed portion of almost
bony hardness that seemed movable on the cranium, and con-
veyed to the touch a sensation of crepitus.   Pressure on the

carotid had no other effect than to stop the pulsation in the branches of the temporal and occipital arteries. Patient had no pain in the tumor itself, but had been subject to pain across the forehead for six years previous, which came on at intervals." His general condition was good; pulse sixty-eight; appetite good, and bowels regular.

From the evident vascularity of this tumor, it was thought best to try the effect of cutting off its arterial supply. This was done by Dr. Buck, on the 21st of December, by applying a ligature to the common carotid artery, and afterward, by circumscribing the tumor, by an incision through the scalp, about an inch from its base, which encircled the whole tumor except about two inches in the temporal region. The vessels had of course ceased to pulsate when the carotid was tied, but each was carefully ligatured as the incision was made. The ligature came away from the carotid on the 13th day, and the incision round the tumor rapidly cicatrized. No change was produced in the tumor, by this thorough operation, except the arrest of all pulsation.

January 4, 1840.—"The tumor was again punctured; blood flowed freely, and a probe passed in moved easily about in the substance of the tumor, as if its substance were of the consistence of brain. An attack of erysipelatous inflammation followed this manipulation, and the wound remained open, discharging bloody fluid."

January 11th.—"The punctured opening has taken on a circular form of the size of a split-pea. Pressure around it does not force out any discharge. The anterior half of the tumor is softer, and its covering thinner, having much the feel of an abscess near the surface; it has subsided and is less prominent." The last two punctures were open and discharging, and a probe could be passed from one to the other. A bistoury was therefore passed, and the communicating sinus laid open, thus largely exposing the centre of the tumor. This exposure of the mass of the tumor was followed by a gradual softening and disintegration of the exposed portion, pieces sometimes coming away as putrid sloughs. This process gradually destroyed the more prominent part of the tumor, but it nevertheless extended at its base until it became converted into an immense promi-

nent, but not fungous, cancerous ulcer, the level of which was
not more than an inch above the surface of the skull. At one
or two points the bone was exposed. Granulations covered the
surface, and at times healthy-looking pus was discharged from
it. Occasionally, severe hæmorrhage now began to be produced by slight causes, which, with severe epistaxis now and
then occurring, reduced his strength rapidly.

In May he left the hospital, and went to reside at his sister's house in the city. The disease continued to spread over
a greater area, but did not assume at any time the fungous
character. He died, worn out by frequent hæmorrhage, in November, 1840.

Post-mortem examination showed that " the tumor extended from the middle of the superciliary arch to within two fingers' breadth of the median line, in the occipital region, and
from the sagittal suture above to the angle of the jaw below,
so as to hide the right ear, the cheek, and outer half of the eye,
the lids being drawn down with it. The margin of the tumor,
along the sagittal suture and as far forward as the orbit, presents an irregular bony ridge, as though the external table were
pushed outward. The suppurating surface of the tumor was
coated with dry pus. At the upper part, a mass of dry lint,
impregnated with blood, adhered to the surface, where it had
been applied several months since to arrest hæmorrhage, and
had not been removed for fear of its return. The circumference of the tumor measured twenty-five inches. Bony spiculæ
could be felt in the substance of the tumor. The inner table
of the cranium, as well as the outer, was very extensively absorbed, and the tumor had pushed before it the dura mater, so
as to encroach very much on the brain. A prolongation of the
diseased mass extended into the sphenoid fissure and zygomatic
fossa. The surface in contact with the dura mater was of a
grayish color, and of a firm, jelly-like consistence. The margin
of the opening in the inner table was thin and sharp, and not
pushed inward, while that of the outer table was elevated and
uneven. Besides the aponeurosis that invested it, the tumor
seemed to be contained in a strong, fibrous envelope, that divided it into lobes. These consisted of a substance of firm,
fleshy consistence, and of various colors—portions resembling

coagulated blood, while others were of a grayish color. The dura mater and other membranes, as well as the brain itself, were apparently healthy.

"The left kidney was six times larger than the right, and formed an irregular nodulated mass of the same morbid structure as the tumor. The outline of the organ could be recognized upon the anterior surface of the mass, the morbid changes having mostly invaded the posterior half of the kidney."

Both specimens are preserved in the hospital cabinet. The microscopical appearances are not noted in the record.

The next case was that of a man, nineteen years of age, who was admitted into the New York Hospital in June, 1856, with an enormous tumor of the thigh, which had been growing about four months. It occupied the lower half of the femur, and the limb, at its largest part, measured twenty-six inches in circumference. The thigh was amputated on the 24th of June, and the tumor found to be encephaloid cancer. He did well after the operation, and the stump healed slowly. On the 26th of December following, a sudden attack of œdema of the face called attention to a soft lump on the side of the head, at the junction of the frontal and parietal bones, near the sagittal suture. Stated that he had noticed it about three weeks before, but, as it gave him no pain, he said nothing about it. It is of the size of the fist, has a soft, fluctuating feel, and is not movable on the skull. Has also a small tumor on the right clavicle, which gives him some burning pain, and is tender to the touch. Has a good deal of headache, especially on the left side of the head. The œdema of the face soon subsided, and he seemed as well as usual. Small periosteal swellings were noted on the third and fourth ribs, on the right side, near their middle.

January 4, 1857.—The swelling on the clavicle has disappeared. The large tumor of the head is also subsiding, and his headache is much relieved. He has been taking iodide of potassa in increasing doses since December 28th. In the latter part of January another attack of œdema of the face came on, without chill or fever, and without any evident cause, and passed away as before in a few days.

January 24th.—The tumors are beginning to grow again,

though he is taking eighty grains of potassa daily. The medicine seemed to disorder his stomach, and was reduced to five grains three times a day.

February 20th.—Another tumor has sprung up over the occiput. The original tumors are increasing. About the 1st of March another tumor showed itself on the right side, over the parietal bone. He has been using cod-liver oil, and a general tonic and invigorating regimen. He now suffers great pain running down the left arm, requiring large anodynes for its relief. In April a swelling without distinct tumor appeared over right lower jawbone. The tumors of the head are gaining a formidable size. That on the clavicle at one time again almost entirely disappeared, which was also the case with the swellings on the ribs. The tumors on the head, after their first partial subsidence, steadily but slowly increased.

May 12th.—Tumor of jaw diminishing. From this time general cancerous cachexia made pretty rapid progress.

June 22d.—He is noted as delirious, and his eyesight failing; still his appetite is wonderful. He gradually wasted away, and died, July 27th, with no other cerebral symptoms than occasional delirium and gradual but not complete loss of sight.

Autopsy.—The weight of the head was $21\frac{1}{2}$ pounds. Its circumference, measuring horizontally round the most prominent points, was $27\frac{1}{2}$ inches. The perpendicular prominence of the largest tumor from the surface of the skull was about 8 inches (Fig. 100). The tumors, of varying heights, but mostly of a rounded, dome-like form, covered nearly the whole surface of the vault of the cranium, several of them merging, at their bases, into one another. All gave the feeling of fluctuation, and when cut open were soft, brain-like, very vascular, with bony spiculæ and solid bone-masses scattered about through the growth. The skull was perforated, and the tumors pressed down upon the brain. The lungs and pleuræ were studded with firm, white, tumor-like masses, varying from the size of a hazel-nut to that of a walnut. An encephaloid mass, as large as a child's head, was found in the right iliac fossa, developed from the bone upward into the pelvis, and downward so as to surround the head and neck of the amputated femur in a sort of cancerous capsule. The other tumors, on the clavicle and ribs, noticed before death, were found to be of the same medullary character, and besides these several small tubera were developed upon the bodies of some of the vertebræ.

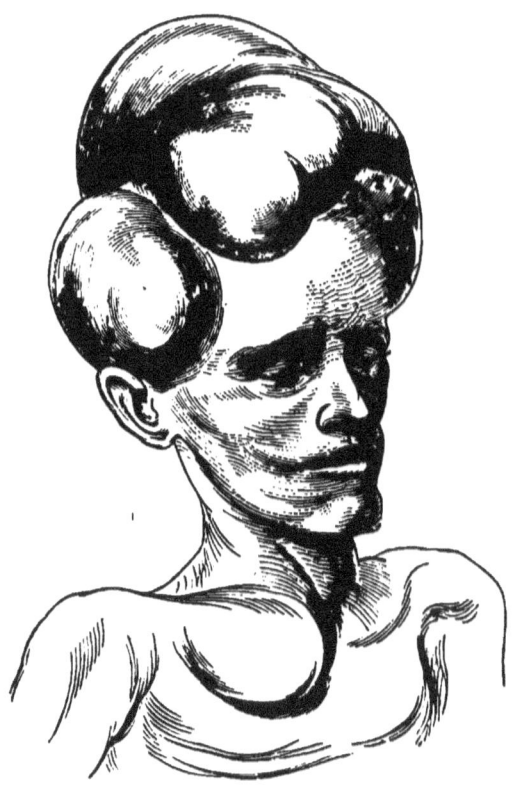

Fig. 100.—(N. Y. Hospital Museum.)

These tumors, after maceration, gave the beautiful, radiated, feathery skeleton of soft, friable bone-tissue, described at page 344.

CHAPTER III.

EPITHELIAL CANCER OF BONE.

MUCH less common than the medullary, and considerably more so than the scirrhous cancers, the epitheliomata of bone occur sufficiently often to have been carefully observed by several writers. As a primary affection it is rare; I have never encountered one which was recognized. The most clearly-marked case I find recorded is one which was admitted into Guy's Hospital, under the care of Mr. Cock, in May, 1858. The patient was a man forty-five years old, pale and cachectic-looking, but his general health was good and his habits regular. "Twenty-six years ago he noticed a swelling in the right knee, which continued to increase for some time, till at last he was unable to walk. This swelling then burst, and he was much relieved. The wound, however, never healed, and was sometimes worse than at others. About two years ago he fell down and struck the part; the wound then became rapidly larger, the bone died, and at last he came to this hospital. When admitted, the right leg presented over the surface of the tibia a large, sprouting, epithelial growth, involving nearly the whole bone; in the centre was a deep hollow, which excavated the bone, and at the bottom some dark, carious, and necrosed bone was visible."

Mr. Cock amputated the limb, through the lower third of the thigh, and soon after the man left the hospital cured.

"On examining the limb, it was clear that both the tibia and the integument over it were involved in one mass of epithelial disease. The bone was for the most part dead, and infiltrated with the elements which characterize epithelial cancer, or epithelioma. The sprouting cauliflower-growths from the integument presented the same characteristics; but the cells in the bone were very well marked, and proved remarkably beautiful microscopical objects."

Another case is given by Mr. Bryant, of the same hospital, of a man who had an epithelial cancer in his heel, involving the os calcis. It seems very probable, however, that in this case, the disease began in the scar of an old injury of the integuments of the heel, and only spread secondarily to the bone. The same suspicion, it must be confessed, attaches to Mr. Cock's case, though nothing is said about any development of the disease in the skin before the bone became affected. Billroth, who makes all carcinomata to consist of epithelial elements, says: "According to my whole histogenetic view, I must regard it as impossible for an epithelial cancer to occur primarily in a bone or lymphatic gland. The observations that I know, to this effect (in the lower jaw, on the anterior surface of the tibia, in the lymphatic glands of the neck), do not seem to me sufficient proof, because the skin and mucous membrane are so near; there may have been an insignificant carcinomatous disease of the skin or mucous membrane as a starting-point of the disease, without its having been noticed."

Secondary developments of this form of cancer in the bones are not extremely rare. Lebert says, without specifying as to the primary or secondary character of the disease, that, in ninety cases of cancerous disease of bones, he found it six times of the epithelial variety. Of these, four were in the lower jaw, probably secondary after cancer of the lip, one was in the upper jaw, and one was in the os calcis.

The anatomical characters of the disease are well marked. Microscopically they consist essentially of epithelial cells in varying conditions of perfection, and very variously arranged in their relations to one another. Sometimes the epithelium is contained in tubes and rounded cavities, on the internal surfaces of which it makes a distinct, well-arranged layer, so regular and orderly in its appearance as to make it difficult to be sure we are not dealing with true gland-structure (Fig. 101.) At other times, the epithelial elements are massed confusedly without any apparent order, and for no useful end. Often they are rolled upon themselves into roundish masses, in which the successive layers of flattened epithelium are arranged somewhat like the layers of an onion (Fig. 102). In short, every possible variety of arrangement and disarrangement of these cells may be found, and upon these varieties some writers have founded numerous subdivisions of the disease. It is sufficient for us, as students of bone-pathology, to be aware of the great variety of forms into which the epithelial elements are in different cases arranged.

Besides these typical cells, many other cells are often found which are differently described by different authors. Paget speaks of them as free nuclei. He says: "Nuclei, either free, or embedded in a dimly molecular or granular basis, are

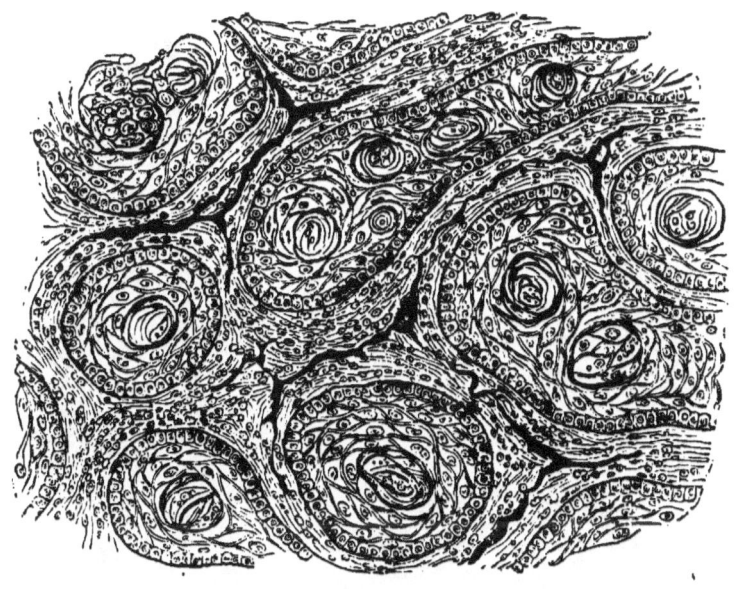

FIG. 101.—(From Billroth.)

commonly found mingled with the (epithelial) cells. I believe they occur in the greatest abundance in the most acute cases. They may be just like the nuclei of the cells; but usually, among those that are free, many are larger than those in the cells ; and these, reaching a diameter of more than $\frac{1}{3000}$ of an inch, at the same time that they appear more vesicular, and have larger and brighter nucleoli, approximate very closely to the characters of the nuclei of scirrhous and medullary cancer-cells." Billroth says : "But we must here state that, in cancer-tumors, besides the epitheliums, there are usually numerous young, small, round cells which, infiltrated in the connective-tissue portion of the tumor, form an important part of it. This small-celled, connective-tissue infiltration, which exists in varying quantities, whenever epithelial proliferations grow into the tissue, appears to be caused by a sort of reaction, and to be the result of the penetration of the epithelial new formations into the tissue, according to the number of infiltrated cells and their future fate,

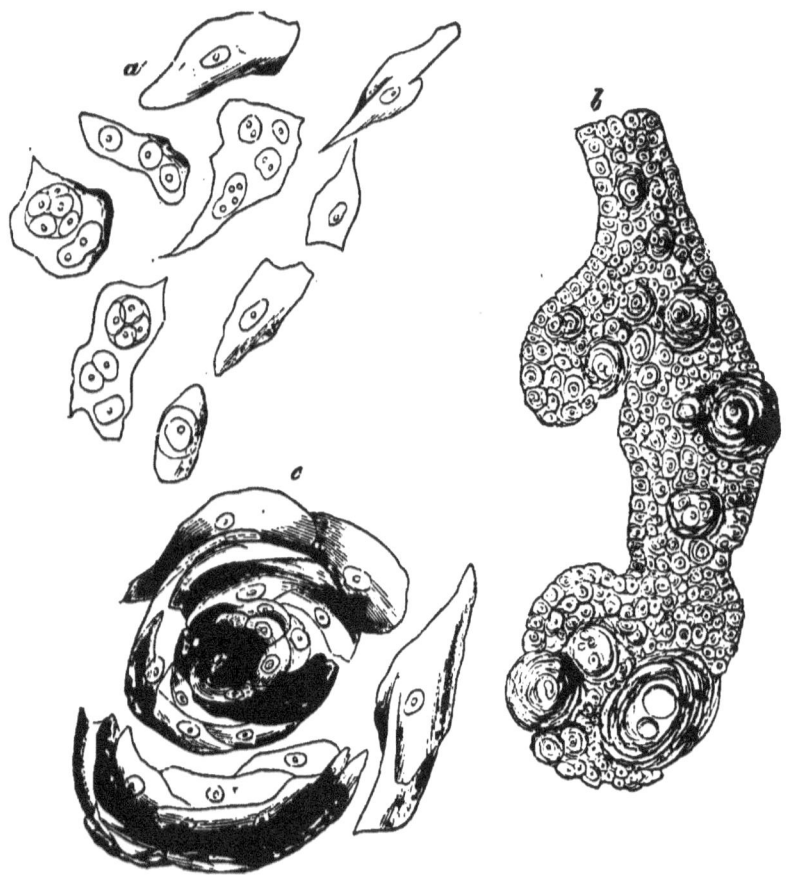

Fig. 102.—(From Billroth.)

as well as the degree of vascularity, just as, in inflammation, it sometimes leads to softening, to atrophy, and cicatricial thickening of the tissue. In some cases, this small-celled infiltration is so considerable as almost entirely to hide the epithelial new formation, from which it may be very difficult to distinguish it, if the latter be small."

The stroma of epithelial growths does not seem to be constant or always well defined. In many cases, and I think always in bone, no proper alveolar stroma, such as has been described in connection with medullary cancer, exists. The tissues are merely displaced for the reception of the new deposit, and what fibrous structures we find traversing the morbid mass are probably derived from modifications of preëxistent normal tissues. In the tubular and follicular forms, the substance of the tube or follicle, which is lined by epithelium, may be supposed to be a direct derivative from the normal tissue, of which it is usually only an exaggeration.

These tumors are permeated with a certain amount of fluid, "cancer-juice," as it is called; and, as the cells have but little cohesion among themselves, there is easily scraped off, from the cut surface, a milky fluid, which is made so by containing great numbers of the epithelial cells floating through it, suspended, as in an emulsion.

The clinical features of epithelioma, wherever situated, are mainly those of ulceration. Most epithelial cancers are really cancerous ulcers from their commencement. In and about the base of these ulcers, the cancerous deposit is constantly taking place, so that, as the ulcer grows, the cancer increases; and it is rather uncommon for an epithelioma to gain any great size as a tumor, on account of its constant tendency to ulcerative destruction. In the bones these features are somewhat modified, according as the deposit reaches the osseous tissue from an ulcerated cutaneous surface, or by infection from a distant tumor. Of cases travelling subcutaneously, and infecting bones deep-seated and distant from the focus of disease, Virchow gives one instance, in a man aged fifty-nine, who had an ulcerating epithelial cancer of the left breast. On the 5th of February, 1853, the left breast and several enlarged axillary glands were removed by operation. The man died with symptoms of pyæmia, February 21st. At the autopsy, marked lesions, characteristic of pyæmia, were found. The ribs, from the third to the sixth on the right side, were infiltrated with epithelial cancer. The vertebral end of the first rib on the left side was also similarly infiltrated. In the upper part of the left mediastinum were found several small nodules of epithelial growth. There seemed to be no direct communication between the tumor of the breast and the axillary glands, or with the infiltrated ribs. In such cases as this there could be no chance for ulceration, and I take it for granted these tumors, if the man had lived, would have comported themselves much as other deep-seated cancers do.

In by far the larger proportion of cases, the epithelial disease is merely an extension of a similar affection from the mucous membrane or skin which covers it, and hence, as far as the bone-disease is concerned, it may be said to commence as an ulceration, in the same sense that this statement may be made of superficial epithelioma elsewhere. Mr. Stanley, in his admirable book on "Diseases of Bones," gives a number of cases which he calls instances of phagedenic ulceration of bone. These cases, very graphically described, are characterized "by successive abscesses and ulcerations of the soft parts spreading to the periosteum, and thence the ulceration extended through the bone. Hard, wart-like granulations arose from the ulcerated surfaces of the soft parts and of the bone, but these granulations had no disposition to cicatrize, and they discharged very profusely a thin, fetid fluid. In this state I have known the disease to continue many years without the slightest effort of reparation." His cases were all in the tibia, and followed some injury which had produced abscess or ulcer over the bone.

I cannot help thinking that these cases were in reality epithelial in their character, and I am the more strongly led to that belief from the following case, which I watched with great interest, and which, in all its clinical features, corresponded very accurately with his descriptions :

John O'Brien, aged thirty-two, was admitted into the New-York Hospital, September 10, 1854, with an ulcer on the front of the tibia, connected with enlargement and disease of the bone. At the age of twelve years he had received a severe, contused, and lacerated wound of the leg, by the fall upon it of a heavy piece of machinery. The laceration was mostly on the front part of the leg, and never healed entirely, but contracted down to a small ulcer, which gave him little trouble. Several times, during the twenty years of its existence, the ulcer had become enlarged, and covered with proud flesh, and given him a great deal of pain, particularly in soft weather and at night. After such an outbreak, it has slowly returned to its usual quiet condition. The last of these attacks, under which he was suffering when admitted to the hospital, began about twelve weeks ago. While thus enlarged and ulcerating, it has often bled freely. No bone has been discharged, and he denies ever having had syphilis. The ulcer was upon the middle of the tibia, which was much thickened above and below, as was also the lower part of the fibula. The surface of the ulcer, half the size of the palm of the hand, irregular and prominent, was formed of large, hard, wart-like granulations, giving issue to a thin, fetid, watery fluid. The probe, on being pressed down among these granulations, entered at several points half an inch into the substance of the bone, and encountered rough spiculæ, particularly round the margin of the sore, where there seemed to be a border of sharp, irregularly-ulcerated bone, from which the granulations sprouted. There was no great tenderness or inflammatory appearance about the limb, and his general condition was good. On the 23d of September, finding no improvement under treatment, Dr. Buck cut down and exposed the whole surface of the tibia, and found that the wart-like granulations sprung from the bone, which was hypertrophied above and below. With a chisel, the whole ulcerated portion was gouged out to the depth of about half an inch, leaving spongy and hypertrophied bone below, which, however, seemed otherwise sound. At one point the gouge opened the medullary artery, which bled very freely, and which was only arrested by pressing a plug of wax against the bleeding orifice. The wound was left open and dressed lightly. *November* 29*th.*— No improvement followed the operation. The wound did not assume a healing action, but produced anew the peculiar wart-like granulations, bleeding freely from the slightest injury. Several large pieces of bone came away, and the ulcerative actions were progressive in the centre of the sore. His general condition was rapidly deteriorating, and, at his own request, the leg was amputated just below the knee.

On examination, the lower two-thirds of both bones were found very greatly hypertrophied. At the point of ulcer there was a loss of substance of the bone equal to more than one-third of its diameter. This excavation was covered and partly filled up with cauliflower-like granulations containing no bone. The bone-substance seemed to be irregularly excavated, and worm-eaten, but without any reparative formation of new bone. The posterior surface of the tibia showed that the diseased action was penetrating throughout its whole structure. It was prominent, with irregular nodules of bony deposit on its surface, and the substance of the bone gave the idea of being infiltrated throughout with the same material as that composing the granulations. The same substance seemed to form the basis of the skin-granulation, and was, in several places, infiltrated into the muscles. My friend Dr. John T. Metcalfe made the microscopic examination of the tumor for me, and found the mass composed mainly of cells. In the fluid pressed from the bone-granulations these cells were of various characters. There were many small, round cells, with well-marked, sometimes double, nuclei; others larger, with branching processes; others spindle-shaped, but among them a considerable proportion of large, flat, single nucleated cells which were manifestly epithelial.

The patient made a good recovery, and when the stump was healed he left the hospital; but already some enlarged lymphatics in the groin looked suspicious. On the 11th of March I was sent for to see him, and found him greatly changed. The swellings in the glands of the groin had grown to be immense tumors, which had broken out into foul and fungous ulceration, which were rapidly destroying their surface, while their base was being as rapidly increased. The pain, and discharge of matter and blood, were rapidly bringing on true cancerous cachexia. I heard from him occasionally till his death, which took place a few weeks after I saw him. I heard that the autopsy showed large cancerous masses developed in the pelvis, and in some of the internal organs, but I got no authentic report of the appearances.

Mr. Stanley considers the disease as a local malady, and I am not prepared to deny that it is so in some cases. He does not give, however, the after-history of any of his patients, but I think there is good ground for believing that the malignant history of my case was repeated in at least some of his.

Dr. Delafield gives me the following account of a knee-joint, which was the seat of a large tumor which had been growing for some years, the knee having been in a condition of disease for about sixteen years. The limb was removed by Dr. James R. Wood. "The articulating extremities of the femur and tibia, the patella, and the soft tissues around the joint, are softened, ulcerated, and partly replaced by new tissue. There are several fistulous openings into the joint. The new tissue consists of cells of various size and shape, mostly of an epithelial character. Round and polygonal nucleated cells, and large, flat, pavement epithelial cells predominate." *Stachelzellen* "are also found in considerable numbers. The characteristic mark of the tissue is the nests of epithelial cells packed together. The cancroid structure is most complete in the tissue replacing the bone, least so in the tendons. In the latter are found portions consisting of round granulation-cells."

CHAPTER IV.

MELANOID CANCER IN BONE.

PATHOLOGISTS are hardly yet agreed as to whether this form of cancer can lay claim to any other anatomical peculiarity than the existence of the black pigment through the structures of which it is composed. Mr. Paget is very emphatic on this point. He says: "I have not seen or read of any example of melanosis, or melanotic tumor in the human subject, which might not be regarded as a medullary cancer with black pigment. In the horse and dog, I believe, black tumors occur which have no cancerous character; but none such are recorded in human pathology." In the main, this view prevails with the best writers on the subject, who generally agree that melanotic tumors are, in the human subject, medullary cancers into which the melanotic material has been introduced, without in any other way altering the anatomical features of the structures in which it is found. It exists mainly in the shape of black or brown granules which are sometimes found in the cells, sometimes in the nucleus, and, often enough, entirely independent of cells or fibres, merely disseminated through the intercellular substance of the tissue. In this distribution it is extremely irregular, sometimes affecting single cells, and not their neighbors, generally more abundant in some cells than in others, often found plentifully infiltrated through one lobule, while those around it may be of a natural color, sometimes all in the cells, and sometimes mainly outside of them, and not unfrequently affecting one or more tumors in a very marked degree, while several others may be entirely free from it. What the source of the black material may be, whether it be essential black pigment, like that of the choroid or lungs, or whether it be altered hematoidin, is not by any means positively ascertained, but this much is certain, that in the eye and in the integuments it is more common than in regions which naturally contain no pigment, or but small quantities of it. The disease itself is one of the rarer forms of cancer. Mr. Paget gives a table in which he found, out of 365 cases of cancer of all kinds, 25 were of the melanoid variety; of these 14 were in the skin, 9 in the eye and orbit, 1 in the testicle, and 1 in the vagina. He alludes to none in the bones.

In the bones it is mostly found as a secondary deposit, and in this respect the disease shows one feature which may be said to be, at least in its extent, peculiar. I mean the very remarkable disposition it has to generalization; so marked that in some instances no tissue—almost no organ, and scarcely a single bone in the whole body—can be found which does not show some trace of the black deposit. And here a question suggests itself, whether, with all this constitutional propensity to the formation and deposit of the melanotic substance, it may not sometimes be found accumulated in the healthy tissues independent of any cancerous formation whatever. This question I cannot answer, but, from analogy in the inferior animals, from the extremely general and abundant manner in which it is often distributed over all parts of the human body, and from the absence of all appearance of any other change, as far as the naked eye can discern, of many of the spots, as seen particularly in the cancellous structure of bone, I am disposed to expect that the microscope will show us that these secondary black-pigment infiltrations are sometimes projected into tissues otherwise perfectly normal, and entirely independent of any cancerous forma-

24

tion. These views were suggested to me, and, I think, confirmed to a great extent, by the observation of the following case, which, perhaps, will afford us a study of the most important clinical features of melanoid disease :

Peter Ries, aged thirty-three years, applied at the German Dispensary of this city, April 27, 1869, on account of several black tumors on different parts of the surface of his body. The patient stated that he had had, from his earliest childhood, a pigmentary nævus of the size of a small bean, situated over the angle of the left scapula, which, without any known cause, began to grow larger about two months before, and had then attained the size of an egg. The first melanotic tumors developed in the immediate vicinity of this mole. From the first day when he applied for treatment, up to the very last day of his being under observation (a period of about eight months), not a day passed without new tumors being discovered, either on the surface of the body or inside of the cavities of the mouth, larynx, or ear. From close observation of hundreds of these melanotic tumors of the skin, Dr. Simrock, under whose care the patient was during almost the entire course of the disease, states that they all took their origin from the subcutaneous tissue, and encroached upon the cutis only after they had attained a certain size, until finally they reached the surface of the skin, by thinning its elements by pressure from below. As soon as the growths reached the surface, they began to undergo marked retrogressive metamorphosis, and, shrivelling up and decaying, they gradually disappeared, and left only a black mark as indicating their former presence. In some cases even this last dark pigmentary discoloration was observed to fade away, leaving the skin only of a somewhat darker hue than in the surrounding parts.

In some instances the surface of the tumors became ulcerated, and a scab formed over them which finally desquamated, leaving only a discolored surface beneath. A few tumors were observed, which showed no pigmentation. About two months after he first came under observation, he began to complain of his eyesight, and especially of soreness of the left eye, when the existence of a melanotic tumor of the size of a large pin's-head was detected in the inner and upper half of the iris. In a very short time—about fourteen days—the iritic tumor developed to its utmost size, about the diameter of a large pea, and then, in about the same length of time, it ran through its retrogressive course, until finally only some extremely slight discoloration of the affected spot could be observed. Vision was at first slightly interfered with, but, upon the subsidence of the tumor, it became normal. A similar growth appeared in the right eye, with much more severe impairment of vision.

The patient's general condition underwent no marked change for the worse, until some large tumors developed in the tongue, the painful condition of which materially interfered with mastication and deglutition, and this began to tell upon his nutrition. Up to the latter half of October the man continued to work at his trade, and had not lost a single day. About that time he had a slight attack of varioloid, from which he recovered without any untoward symptom, but he steadily failed in strength afterward. One of the melanotic tumors, on the right side of the tongue near its root, was very deeply ulcerated, and so painful that it was difficult for him to swallow. The surface of the body was covered with innumerable black tumors, varying in size from that of a small shot to that of a hickory-nut. He continued to fail in strength, and died, exhausted, January 13, 1870.

Dr. Simrock says: "The diagnosis of the character of all these metastatic tumors was based upon the microscopical examination of the primary one, and of several others which were taken out for the purpose. The primary tumor from the back proved to be true sarcoma, in the formation of which the fusiform and round cells equally participated. Pigmentary particles I was not able to see in any of the sarcomatous cells. The pigmentary part of the tumor was entirely intercellular, and appeared in the form of irregularly-shaped particles and cakes of different tinges, from blood red to deep black, in the formation of which the extravasated and stagnated blood may have had its part. One small tumor, the size of a bean, was extirpated from the inner side of the left humerus, and showed the same sarcomatous elements as the primary one, with pigmentary interspersion as the chief characteristic part of its constituents. Five particles were removed from tumors which afterward disappeared almost entirely, leaving only a discoloration of the skin, and in both the same characteristic elements of

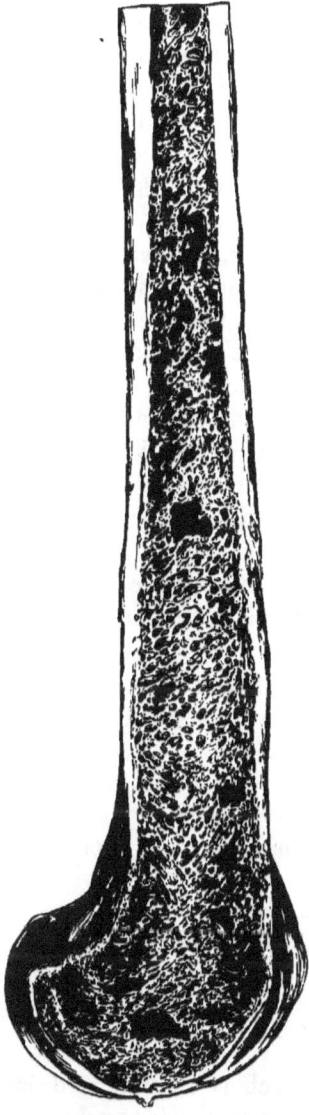

sarcoma were undoubtedly prevalent. If late microscopical examinations corroborate my diagnosis of true sarcoma, then its spontaneous disappearance will prove a precious experience to the pathologist. Virchow remarks, in his book on tumors, that 'up to this time he knows of no well-proved case of sarcoma having spontaneously disappeared. '

"On *post-mortem* examination, black tumors were found here and there on the membranes, and in the substance of the brain. The pleuræ, both parietal and visceral, and also the pericardium, were studded with small black masses. External surface of heart covered with pigment-spots, some projecting, others not. In the substance of the heart, the pigment seemed to follow the course of the muscular fibres. The columnæ carneæ, as well as all the internal surface of the organ, were mottled with similar masses. Both lungs were infiltrated with pigment-matter throughout. Mucous surface of larger bronchial tubes containing spots of pigment. Bronchial glands enlarged and black. The diaphragm contained melanotic tumors on both surfaces and in its substance, as did also the peritonæum, both visceral and parie-

Fig. 103.—(Museum, College of Physicians and Surgeons.)

tal, the omentum, the stomach, the intestines, large and small, the pancreas, the mesenteric glands, the liver, the spleen, the kidneys, the urethral mucous surface, the bladder, the prostate, the corpora cavernosa, the testicles, and the cord. The muscles everywhere were infiltrated with the same black pigment, which followed in a marked manner the course of the muscular fibres." Dr. Delafield made a careful examination of many of the localities mentioned, and his observations are of much interest. In all the situations where distinct tumors existed, the pigmentary matter was contained either in round or oval cells, or in their intercellular substance, in granules fine and coarse, or infiltrated into the neighboring tissues, thus forming, as it were, the outskirts or borders of the sarcomatous nodule. In several situations, however, it was distinctly made out that the deposit had taken place in the substance of, and in the interstices between, the elements of perfectly normal and unchanged original tissue. This was particularly the case in the bronchial mucous membrane, in the kidneys, in some parts of the skin, and in a portion of the fibrous structure of the dura mater. These observations were made with much care; and in reference to this very point, as to whether, in the human subject, pigmentary accumulations ever take place independent of cancerous disease, in any of the situations where pigment is not normally found. They seem to me quite conclusive.

Several of the bones were marked by black spots, and when sawed through the cancellous tissue presented numerous black dots, and irregularly-shaped spots, due to the infiltration of the melanoid matter into tissue otherwise perfectly healthy. Fig. 103 represents a section of the lower portion of the femur, which exhibits quite a number of the peculiar black spots.

CHAPTER V.

COLLOID CANCER OF BONE.

THAT form of cancerous disease which is characterized by numerous alveoli, containing a glue-like material, is occasionally seen in the bones. Mr. Stanley gives a very well-marked example, occurring in the phalangeal bone of a finger. The case was under the care of Mr. Lawrence, in St. Bartholomew's Hospital. " A man, sixty-five years old, had been healthy from birth, and both his parents had been healthy and long-lived. Rather more than a year ago, he noticed a swelling in the first phalanx of the right fore-finger; it was moderately firm, gave him little pain, but gradually increased. Six months ago a lancet was thrust into it, and some blood, with a watery fluid, was discharged, and ulceration of the opening ensued. A seton was afterward passed through the swelling, and immediately afterward it rapidly increased. The hand was amputated at the wrist-joint, and, in the examination of the diseased parts, the following particulars were observed: The tumor was of a globular form, soft and elastic, and about two inches and a half in diameter. It enveloped the first, with part of the second phalanx of the fore-finger; its interior consisted of a semifluid, jelly-like substance, contained within cells formed by dense, white, fibrous bands. The tumor closely surrounded the bone, which was rough in one situation, while, in another, part of its wall had disappeared. Within the bone, gelatinous substance was deposited, like that of which the tumor consisted. Mr. Paget submitted this substance to microscopic examination, and found that it possessed none of the characters of cartilage, but apparently consisted of a structureless, viscid jelly." He also remarks that there is in the museum of St. Bartholomew's Hospital an example of this same form of tumor growing from a rib.

In the museum of the New York Hospital there is a cast (No. 47) of the head of a patient with a huge tumor, involving one side of the face, which is stated to have sprung apparently from the antrum, and to have extended from that point in all directions, so as to fill the mouth and pharynx, pressing upward into the orbit, and causing absorption of the septum narium, extending up through the sphenoid bone to the base of the brain, and forming externally a large tumor upon the lateral and lower parts of the left side of the face (Fig. 104). The tumor was surrounded by an imperfect capsule, and consisted chiefly of cells filled with an amber-colored gelatinous fluid. The bones upon the outer parts of the growth were softened, and very much thinned by pressure, but did not seem to be infiltrated with any foreign material. The brain was not involved.

The patient was a man thirty-five years old, who had long suffered from symptoms resembling those of ozæna, but the tumor was not discovered in the fauces until within a year of his death, which took place chiefly from exhaustion, from continued ptyalism, and inability to swallow food.

Fig. 104.—(N. Y. Hospital Museum.)

Dr. Louis Bauer laid before the New York Pathological Society, at its meeting in January, 1857, a tumor of the size of a man's fist, which he had removed from the surface of the left femur just behind the great trochanter, which presented all the appearances of colloid disease. The tumor had been growing about two years. At one time, an abscess had formed, discharging a viscid substance with the pus. He had suffered much pain, and was greatly reduced by the disease. About six months previous to the time of presenting the specimen, Dr. Bauer had removed the tumor. After the portion presented had been taken away, the femur was found to be extensively carious. All diseased bone, as far as could be reached, was gouged off, but the whole of the tumor could not be got away. The wound healed, however, and, at the time of reporting, the man remained well.

Lebert gives the history of a case which was under the care

of Roux in 1846. A man, aged thirty-eight, had two moderate-sized tumors of the upper end of the tibia, one on either side of the knee-joint. They had been growing about three months without pain, and followed a strain. There was no heat nor red-ness about them, and no other feeling but a growing weakness of the limb. There was a slight pulsation felt on laying the hand gently over the surface of either swelling. Supposing them to be of a vascular nature, Roux tied the femoral artery. Secondary hæmorrhage occurred; a second ligature was applied higher up; but the man died from pyæmia. No change had been produced in the tumors by the operation. The upper part of the tibia was found occupied by an encephaloid mass, pro-jecting on either side into the two tumors noticed during life. This mass contained, in all parts, numerous gelatinous points. The bone-substance was displaced by the tumor, and had at that point entirely disappeared. In the inside of the mass the mor-bid deposit was of a yellowish, pale-rose color. "By micro-scopic examination, as well as by the naked eye, the colloid nature of the cancer can be seen, which is besides very vascular. There is everywhere a very abundant transparent substance, in which are a few fine, rare, divergent fibres. This substance everywhere contains fusiform cancerous elements, having a length of $\frac{1}{20}$ of a millimetre. Some of these were pointed, and some rounded at their ends. The nuclei are round or elliptical, and from $\frac{1}{80}$ to $\frac{1}{80}$ of a millimetre in diameter. Some are free. The nucleoli are about $\frac{1}{400}$ of a millimetre in diameter. There are almost no fatty elements in the cancer."

Cruveilhier figures a very beautiful case of alveolar cancer which grew in the bones of the face of a woman who died of it at the age of fifty-two. It occupied the ethmoid, nasal, and frontal bones, made a huge projection on the anterior and upper part of the face, and encroached back into the fauces, filling up the nasal cavities, and pressing backward upon the brain. It had grown slowly for about ten years, with great pain, though the patient, who was a painter of some merit, had continued at her work almost to the end. On section, the whole mass pre-sented the peculiar alveolar arrangement which characterizes colloid. The alveoli were large, and, though of different size, were nearly uniform in every part of the tumor. The peculiarity of the case was, that these alveoli, instead of being filled with a transparent, jelly-like material, contained a whitish-yellow substance, which Cruveilhier, in one place, likens to concrete pus, and in another speaks of as consisting of caseum. No cancerous disease was found in any other part of the body.

These cases all are instances of the primary form of the colloid disease, and of this they present a tolerable picture. From what we know of the tendency to generalization of this disease in the softer parts of the body, we can well suppose that it may sometimes appear as a secondary deposit in the bones; I think, however, it must in this form be rather rare. I have never seen an instance, nor have I encountered any statement of one, in any of the authors whose works I have had an opportunity of consulting.

CHAPTER VI.

OSTOID CANCER.

SEVERAL writers have insisted upon giving this name to a form of cancer containing a very large proportionate amount of bone; and yet in other parts and in other respects presenting all the characteristics of true cancer. These ostoid cancers are found most often in the lower end of the femur, and most commonly affect equally the inside and the outside of the bone. The softer parts of the growth do not exactly correspond either with the scirrhous or encephaloid material. Mr. Paget describes the substance as "usually exceedingly dense, firm, and tough, and may be incompressibly hard; its cut surface uprises like that of an intervertebral cartilage, or that of one of the toughest fibrous tumors of the uterus. It is pale grayish, or with a slight yellow or pink tint, marked with irregular short bars of a clearer white; rarely intersected as if lobed, but sometimes appearing banded with fibres set vertically on the bone."

The bony portion of the mass is still more peculiar. He says: "In the central parts it is, in the best-marked specimens, extremely compact, scarcely showing even any pores, white and dry. To cut it is nearly as hard as ivory, yet, like hard chalk, it may be rubbed or scraped into fine dry powder. At the periphery it is arranged in a knobbed and tuberous form, the knobs being often formed of close, thin, gray, or white lamellæ,

Fig. 105.—(From Paget.)

whose presenting edges give them a fibrous look, exactly like that of pumice-stone. In this part, also, the bone is very brittle, flaky, and pulverulent. In some specimens, the whole of the bone has this delicate lamellar and brittle texture; but, more generally, as I have said, the central part is very hard, and this, occupying the walls and cancellous tissue of the shaft, equally with the surrounding part of the tumor, makes of the whole such a compact, white, chalky mass as the sketch here represents." Fig. 105 is the picture Mr. Paget gives of the disease thus described.

Whatever may be thought of the expediency of erecting this form of disease into a separate class of cancers, its well-marked features evidently entitle it to a position as an important variety. It has already been remarked that, with most of the cancers of bone, the osseous tissue is displaced by the cancerous growth, and that very little and often no new growth of bone accompanies the destruction of the old bone-substance, at the expense of which the morbid growth is constantly increasing. Even in those cases where something like a bony skeleton is formed in the cancerous mass, this skeleton is usually composed of exceedingly slender spicula, and thin and delicate laminæ, which hold a very small proportion to the whole mass, and which are usually so imperfect in their construction, and so fragile in their consistence, that, when macerated and dried, it is exceedingly difficult to preserve them from falling to pieces almost by their own weight. To all this a very strong contrast is presented by the tumors now under consideration, whose most striking feature is a very great deposit of new bone as a basis of the growth—a deposit which seems to be a constant accompaniment of that growth, and to increase *pari passu* with its increase, so that, in some of the largest tumors of this kind which have been described, the proportion of bone in the growth was quite as great as in the smallest.

Another feature, equally striking and equally important as clearly marking the true cancerous character of the disease, is found in the tendency to generalization which these tumors so markedly display, in which the most distant and most unexpected organs are sometimes implicated. The secondary deposits preserve the character of the original growth, and hence we have the lymphatic glands, the uterus, the blood-vessels, and even the thoracic duct, filled up or infiltrated with bony substance so completely as in some instances to become unrecognizable.

Mr. Stanley gives three cases of this disease which he terms malignant osseous tumor of bone: "A man, aged thirty, was admitted into St. Bartholomew's Hospital under the care of Mr. Lawrence, with a swollen and painful state of the right knee-joint, consequent on a fall, for the removal of which antiphlogistic treatment was successfully employed; but, shortly afterward, a painful swelling arose immediately above the knee, and gradually extended around the lower third of the thigh. A softening of the swelling at one point being discovered, an incision was made into it, from which arterial blood flowed freely. Pulsation was now discovered in the swelling, and at the same time it was observed that the leg had become œdematous, and that the toes were colder than in the opposite limb. The femoral artery was then tied. Pulsation in the tumor ceased, and its size gradually diminished; but after some time it again enlarged, sloughing of the skin and central substance of the tumor ensued, but unaccompanied by hæmorrhage. The man gradually sank from exhaustion.

"On examining the limb, I found the tumor to consist of a compound, soft, fibrous, and dense osseous substance, the latter extending completely round the femur. The whole series of femoral, inguinal, and lumbar absorbent glands, were converted into osseous tumors. The femoral and popliteal vessels were sound. In this case the tumor of the femur, and the tumors of the absorbent glands, were identical in structure, both being composed almost wholly of a solid, dull-white, chalk-like, osseous substance, which, in the femur, was continuous with a similar deposit in the medullary and cancellous tissue of all that part of the bone which was surrounded by the tumor."

As a general rule, this form of cancer is rapid in its progress, and Mr. Paget reckons them about equal to the medullary in the length of life they allow to the patient. Some cases are spoken of in which life was prolonged for many years. Thus, Mr. Stanley mentions one where the disease was in progress for eighteen years. Mr. Paget alludes to two cases where death did not occur until in one instance twenty-four, and in another twenty-five years, had elapsed from the time of the first appearance of the affection. On the other hand, some cases are recorded in which the disease has run a course as rapidly destructive as the most rapid medullary cancers. Mr. Paget gives one case of this rapid progress of ostoid cancer in a girl of fifteen, who was admitted into St. Bartholomew's Hospital "with general feebleness and pains in her limbs, which had existed for two or three weeks. They had been ascribed to delayed menstruation, till the pain, becoming more severe, seemed to be concentrated about the lower part of the back and the left hip. A hard, deep-seated tumor was now felt, connected with the ala of the left ilium. This gradually increased, with constant and more wearing pain; it extended toward the pelvic and abdominal cavities; the patient became rapidly weaker and thinner; the left leg swelled; sloughing ensued over the right hip; and she died, cachetic and exhausted, only three and a half months from her first notice of the swelling.

"A hard, lobulated mass was found, completely filling the cavity of the pelvis, and extending across the lower part of the abdominal cavity. It was firmly connected with the sacrum, both ischia, and the left ilium; it held, as in one mass, all the pelvic organs; and the uterus was so embedded in it, and so infiltrated with a similar material, that it could scarcely be recognized. The general surface of this growth was unequal and nodular. It was composed of a pearly-white and exceedingly hard structure, in which points of yellow bony substance were embedded, and which had the characters of ostoid cancer perfectly marked. The ilium, where the tumor was connected with it, had the same half-fibrous, half-bony structure as the tumor itself. The common iliac veins, their main divisions, and others leading into them, passed through the tumor, and were all distended with hard substance like the mass around them. From the common iliac veins, a continuous growth of the same substance extended into the inferior cava, which, for nearly five inches, was distended and completely obstructed by a cylindrical mass of similar fibrous and osseous substance one and a quarter inch in diameter. At the upper part this mass, tapering, came to an end near the liver. The lower lobe of the right lung was hollowed out into a large sac, containing greenish pus, and traversed by hard, coral-like bands, which proved to be branches of the pulmonary artery plugged with firm white substance, intermingled with softer cancerous matter, and resembling the great mass of disease in the pelvis. The rest of the lung was healthy, with the exception of some scattered grayish tubercles; and so was the left lung, except in that there were a few small abscesses near its surface, with hard, bone-like masses in their centres, like those in the branches of the right pulmonary artery. The skull, brain, pericardium, heart, and all the abdominal organs, were healthy."

In the other aspects of its general pathology, the ostoid cancer differs in no material respect from other forms, except perhaps in the fact that it shows no particular tendency, under ordinary circumstances, toward ulceration, or any other form of rapid destruction. It is acknowledged, however, by those who have best studied the disease, that materials for the full story of its life and terminations have as yet hardly been accumulated.

CHAPTER VII.

TREATMENT OF MALIGNANT DISEASE OF BONE.

The cancerous tumors of bone present, as a matter of course, nothing more encouraging, as far as their treatment is concerned, than cancerous tumors in other parts. A large share

of the success which some of the older surgeons claimed as the
result of their several methods of treatment we can now explain, with great plausibility, by their want of accurate diagnosis; while the few instances in which the cure is unequivocal,
we are disposed to refer to the coincidence of a spontaneous
or natural retrogression, rather than to the result of the remedies employed.   It is somewhat disheartening to find that, as
our knowledge of these growths advances, our conviction of
their utterly intractable nature grows deeper; and that surgeons
of the present day, with all their increased light, and with their
greatly-improved means of diagnosis, are less sanguine and less
confident, as to the therapeutics of cancer, than were the men
of half a century ago.   The hopes which have been excited by
the various remedies lauded as curative of cancer have one by
one been sadly disappointed, the expectations roused by the
vaunted powers of compression, electricity, caustic *flèches*, galvano-cautery, acetic acid, etc., have sobered down to the simple
question, not whether these remedies are curative, but whether
they are in any degree beneficial to the sufferer.   Indeed, I think
it would not be too much to say that, in the minds of the best
men who are now occupying themselves with this study, the
question of cure has very much given place to the question of
palliation; and that the labors and hopes of such men centre
more upon alleviating suffering, and prolonging comfortable
life, than they do upon utopian projects for the fundamental
cure of the disease.   Much may be done short of a cure, for
the great benefit of our cancerous patients, and it seems very
clear to me that it is in this direction that our therapeutical
labors are likely to be most fruitful, and our efforts on behalf
of our patients most beneficial.

I am far from wishing to undervalue or to deny the usefulness of certain internal remedies, from some of which I think
I have myself derived benefit.   Indeed, I consider the subject
is worthy of our most serious attention.

The most recent statements I have seen on this subject are
those of Mr. T. Weeden Cooke, whose long experience as surgeon of the Cancer Hospital in London gives great weight to
his opinion.   In his work on " Cancer, and its Allies and Coun-
terfeits," he devotes much space to the subject of treatment,

and passes in review the various internal remedies which have been most used in the hope of curing cancer. His verdict upon all of them is unsparing and decisive. He has found no benefit from their use which is worth naming, and he dismisses them all as unworthy of confidence, as having any specific influence on the course or termination of the disease. Nevertheless, he is one of the most hopeful and encouraging of modern writers on the treatment of cancer. Viewing the disease as one in which the perverted cell-growth depends upon want of tone in the system, and believing that this tone can, in a certain degree, be imparted by appropriate treatment, he asserts most confidently that, by the judicious use of certain nutritive tonics, with proper local applications, much may be done in arresting the progress, relieving the suffering, and actually curing the disease. The internal remedies which he relies upon with most confidence are cod-liver oil, iron, hydrochloric acid, and cinchona-bark. The first two are the principal remedies he employs, the latter auxiliaries, to which he sometimes adds other tonics according to the condition of the digestive and nervous systems. Of the oil he says: "There is only one other medicine which has any large claim upon our attention, either as an assistant and rectifier of the digestive process, or as a direct alterative and tonic to the blood. In my hands cod-liver oil, administered in the occult stage of a scirrhus of the breast, has more nearly approached the character of a specific than any other agent. It seems to supply that aliment to the cells of new formations, for the want of which they droop from their rotund form, and lose the power of creating normal tissues." The results of his treatment are encouraging and surprising, for he gives an outline of fifteen cases in which manifest benefit was derived from the course adopted, of which cases, all under his personal observation, he says: "These are a few instances of arrest of scirrhus of the mamma by constitutional means, for ten, twelve, even sixteen years, and the patients are still living evidences of the conservative powers of Nature, when properly supported by art, to stem the destructive influences of this malignant disease, and reduce it to a more inert mass."

It will, however, be more in accordance with my plan to glance at a few of the local remedies, which have gained most

favor with the profession, as favorably modifying the progress
and result of cancer developed in the bones. Of these, five
are of chief interest: 1. Repeated local depletion by leeches;
2. Systematic compression; 3. Galvano-electricity; 4. Ligature
of artery leading to tumor; 5. Ablation.

1. *Repeated Local Depletion by Leeches.*—This method of
treating cancer is one of the oldest known. In former times,
when almost every swelling was regarded as a modified form
of inflammation, the idea very naturally suggested itself to
treat the cancerous form of inflammation by local abstraction
of blood. Something was found to be gained by this practice,
and it has maintained its popularity perhaps more steadily
down to the present day than any other remedy on the list.
The explanation of its good effects, according to our present
view, must be based upon its influence in abating local conges-
tions, and accidental inflammations in the tumor, to which local
actions modern pathology ascribes a certain considerable share
in the destructive agencies which are at work in any cancerous
growth. That any thing can be gained in modifying what may
be called the normal nutritive processes of such a tumor, by a
remedy which, like leeching, can only have an occasional application, does not seem to be likely; but that, by relieving fulness,
and averting or curing inflammation, it may do good in diseases
where the worst influences in operation are acknowledged to
be those of the inflammatory character, is, it seems to me, a
reasonable expectation. On this point Walshe, after alluding
to the long-continued popularity of the treatment, says:
"Modern experience has established the degree of utility of
local abstraction of blood. In the earliest stages of diseased
induration the application of leeches is strongly advisable; even
as a guide to the diagnosis of tumors of a doubtful character,
it is useful. The progress of growth of undoubtedly carcinomatous nature may be thus retarded, and incidental inflammatory
symptoms in the adjoining tissues successfully combated; but
beyond this capillary depletion has no power. The number of
leeches applied must be regulated by the size of the tumor; it
should vary between twelve and six; a smaller number causes
an afflux of fluids to the part without emptying the vessels
sufficiently. When the tumor is adherent to the skin, there is

danger in continuing the practice, as the bites have frequently been known to pass into persistent ulcerations."

Whatever may be the decision of a more rigorous statistical inquiry into the retarding influence of occasional leechings, there can be no doubt that in certain instances they do accomplish some good by the relief of pain. Much of the suffering inflicted by these dreadful diseases is caused by or aggravated by accidental inflammations, which are under the control of well-regulated local depletion; and, it is a wonderful fact, recognized by all who have much employed the remedy, that in some instances the immunity from pain procured by a single application of leeches will last much longer than can be explained by the relief of a simple attack of inflammation. It would seem as if the sedative effect of loss of blood sometimes remained after the immediate depressing effect had been apparently recovered from, and the vital actions of the affected parts seem to be modified for a certain indefinite period by a cause which we ordinarily consider to be of temporary and generally of brief influence. This relief of pain, and its accompanying soreness and tenderness, is an immense benefit to the sufferers with cancer; and we can hardly help associating with the means of procuring alleviation, the idea of at least a tendency toward a cure. The testimony of many writers is favorable to the use of this remedy, although it must be acknowledged that those who have spoken most eulogistically of its effects have been those who upheld most earnestly the inflammatory nature of all cancerous disease.

Much caution should be exercised in the use of this means, which is powerful for evil if used too freely. By too frequent or too liberal an employment of local depletion, it is very evident we may so reduce the vital power of the part affected as to favor rather than to check morbid action, and thus, by weakening the power of resistance, we may increase the evil tendencies of the disease by the very means we employ to relieve it. Again, as Mr. Stanley remarks, care should be used in applying leeches over a tumor which is already adherent to the skin, the leech-bites becoming sometimes the starting-point of ulceration, which might perhaps have been long postponed had the skin remained unwounded.

25

2. *Systematic Compression.*—This is not a new remedy for cancer. It was first brought to notice by Dr. Young in the earlier years of this century, and was tried very fully at the Middlesex Hospital in 1816, with so unsatisfactory results that but little more was heard of it till M. Récamier revived its use, and announced some wonderful successes. Unfortunately, the enthusiastic experimenter claimed a great deal too much for his pet plan, and accordingly the profession generally has discredited his results. He says: "Of one hundred patients, sixteen appeared to be incurable, and underwent only a palliative treatment; thirty were completely cured by compression alone, and twenty-one derived considerable benefit from it; fifteen were cured by extirpation alone, or chiefly by extirpation and pressure combined, and six by compression and cauterization; in the twelve remaining cases, the disease resisted all the means employed." Even the high character of M. Récamier can hardly give currency to such magnificent statements, and yet something must have been realized by the treatment to have formed a basis for such exaggerated praise. What this something was, we can glean from the reports of other, perhaps more candid, experimenters with the same method.

In the year 1859, my late venerable and esteemed friend Dr. J. P. Batchelder published, in the *New York Journal of Medicine*, an account of his experience in the treatment of various affections by pressure applied by compressed sponge. Among other things, he had tried the effect of the remedy in a number of cases of cancerous and other morbid growths, and the results he obtained are well worthy of attention. No one who knew him could doubt the truthfulness of his statements, certainly not the honesty of his convictions. His explanation of the *modus operandi* of his plan he thus states: "The pressure occasioned by the expansion of the compressed sponge disturbs the cancer-cells, and forces them out of place; affects their consistency, and causes them to be dissolved; and the tumor, thus freed of its malignant ingredients, may be more readily removed by absorption, if the process be continued, or, if not absolutely removed, it may be so divested of its malignity as to remain harmless for years, as happened in a case which will be related. Does this pressure, as the doctrine teaches, deprive the cancer-cells of their power to contaminate other parts, or the system in general ? The cancer-cell, like the pus-globule, is dissolved, and, being thus changed in its nature, is more readily absorbed, and of course, enters the circulation, not as a malignant, but as an innocuous substance; and, instead of contaminating the system, is eliminated therefrom, as are other disintegrations of tissues and structures, without harming any part. Cancerous affections, locally considered, seem to derive their nutriment from surrounding parts by a sort of imbibition or endosmosis, and not from any direct vascular medium. The sponge, by its peculiar mode of pressure on the diseased part, either destroys its texture, or prevents its being nourished, and continues to do so until its agency is fully resisted by the circumjacent parts which are in a healthy condition." In support of his views, he then goes on to relate a number of cases in which great benefit was gained by the use of the sponge; in one of them the tumor entirely disappearing in less than two months from the commencement of the treatment. Some of the cases were treated in private practice, and some in Bellevue Hospital, and all of them were watched more or less carefully by some of our best surgeons. I give the full history of one which is most to our purpose, inasmuch as the disease was seated in a bone :

"A lad, about eight or ten years old, from New Jersey, was brought by his mother to Dr. Mott's clinique, in 1847 or 1848, with a fungous tumor protruding from the lower jaw, situated in the space formerly occupied by the first and second molar teeth, on the left side. This morbid growth had made its appearance some months before, loosening the teeth, protruding on each side of them, and pushing away or involving the gums, previous to his coming to the clinique. The teeth had been extracted, and the tumor, with, I believe, a portion of the alveolar process, removed by a surgeon in the boy's immediate vicinity, which operation was now repeated by Dr. Mott. In a few weeks, the little fellow was brought again to the clinique, the disease having returned. Unable to lay my hand on the notes of the case, I have indeed forgotten, as well as Dr. Mott himself, whether another operation was performed. Whether it was, or was not, is quite immaterial to our purpose. The disease had returned ; and at my suggestion the compressed sponge

was to be tried; and he was assigned by Dr. Mott to my care
and management. I took him, with his mother, to my office,
and cut two or three pieces of thoroughly compressed sponge
sufficiently large to cover the whole tumor, and indeed extend
beyond it on the outer and inner sides of the alveolar process,
and rising higher than the upper surfaces of the adjacent teeth
before and behind it; and then bound the lower maxilla firmly
to the upper by means of a roller, leaving the pieces of sponge
to expand by the imbibition of saliva. The mother was supplied with several pieces of compressed sponge, and directed to
apply them in the same manner once or twice a day. She was
told by Dr. Mott that the disease was of a malignant character,
and would be very likely to destroy her son—certainly, if not
properly and faithfully attended to. The doctor's faith in a
favorable result was obviously not very strong; nor was any-
body's else, except my own. Notwithstanding, in the course
of five or six weeks the mother and lad again appeared at Dr.
Mott's clinique, not to ask advice, but to show the result, that
the boy was perfectly cured. The remedy had been entirely
successful. The location of the disease had been favorable to
the application and action of the sponge. The result in this
case was analogous to what I had witnessed in others."

The doctor then alludes to one other case in which a similar
tumor, situated on the lower jaw of a lady between fifty and
sixty years of age, was treated by the compressed sponge with
an equally perfect result.

The theoretical views expressed by the advocates of this
mode of practice are ingenious, and not improbable. That cell
life and growth may be modified and destroyed by pressure,
seems entirely likely, as the mere result of the action of mechanical force; that it is actually accomplished is demonstrated
by the cases published. Thus much is practically certain, that
tumors, even malignant tumors, can be entirely removed, under favorable circumstances, by the mere action of carefully-
regulated pressure; and this clinical fact adds just so much to
our means of contending with cancerous disease. That the
method has any power of modifying the local cancerous action
on the surrounding parts, or on the general system, is not only
not proved, but not rendered probable by any of the facts which
have as yet been made public.

3. *Galvano-Electricity.*—This agent has been employed in the treatment of cancerous diseases in two modes quite distinct from one another. One of these methods is that in which the circuit through which the electricity passes is so arranged that, at a certain point, the conducting material becomes intensely heated, and this heated portion, being in contact with the point of disease on which it is desired to act, produces the cauterizing effect of intense heat, and destroys the part exposed to its influence. This, is an exceedingly convenient method of employing electricity to produce the effect of the actual cautery, but it must be evident that the action is simply that of a caustic, not, so far as appears, specially modified by the fact of electricity having been used to produce the heat. There is no breach of contact, and therefore no passage of the electric fluid through any part of the tissues ; and, therefore, any specific effect of electricity, as such, in modifying the morbid actions in the parts through which the conductor passes, may, I think, be properly left out of consideration, and this form of electrical application may be considered, as it is commonly named, a mere galvano-cautery.

The other method is one in which the electrical current is caused to pass through the part to be acted upon—the mode of its passage, and the extent of its action upon the tissues, varying very much according to the manner of its employment. Either the Faradaic or the direct current may be used, and either may be applied externally on the unbroken skin, or either may be caused to act upon the deeper tissues through needles thrust into their substance. The use of electricity by external application is much the oldest method, but much the least effective ; indeed, the testimony we have of its usefulness, in the discussion of tumors of any kind, is confined to so few well-authenticated instances, that not many surgeons now employ it. The method which has of late attracted most attention is that in which the power of the current is so great that, when introduced into the tissues by properly-prepared needles, a decomposition of some of the textural elements takes place, by which such alteration in the mass is set up that absorption or alteration of the tumor is the immediate or ultimate consequence. What is the precise extent of this decomposition, and how precisely it affects the elements of the tissues, are points which are not yet fully explained. The method itself, from the decomposition which accompanies it, is called electrolysis.

Electrolysis has now been used in quite a large number of tumors of all kinds, and with a degree of success which leads us to hope that it is to be a positive addition to our means of dealing with these intractable and unpromising deformities. I do not know that any thing has yet been achieved in the direction of controlling the malignant features of these diseases, but, merely speaking of them as tumors, much has certainly been accomplished. I cannot better present the main features of this method of treating tumors than by giving an outline of a case recorded by Dr. R. P. Lincoln, in the *Medical Record* of this city, for December 15, 1870:

A gentleman, aged thirty-three, was the subject of a soft tumor in the supra-clavicular space of the left side. It had appeared, without known cause, about eighteen months before, and with slight interruptions had pretty steadily increased up to the time of his coming under Dr. Lincoln's care. The tumor was now the size of a large goose's-egg, moved to a certain degree with the trachea, was rounded in shape, two inches in diameter, and rising about five-eighths of an inch from the natural surface of the neck. The tumor was soft and compressible, but elastic, and when pressure was removed resumed its usual shape. There was no pulsation, but it grew turgid when the breath was held, or any straining effort made. Under excitement, as from public speaking, this turgid condition of the tumor would become constant, and was sometimes attended with very alarming symptoms of suffocation. The diagnosis was venous erectile tumor, and electrolysis was applied, September 30, 1870.

" The patient having been chloroformized, I introduced four gilded steel needles, insulated to one-half or three-fourths of an inch from their points, into the four quarters of the tumor, the two upper being one and one-fourth inch apart, and one inch above the lower, which were one inch apart. The two inner needles were connected with the subdivided anode, and the outer two with the subdivided cathode, and ten elements of the battery, which was working with a weak current, connected within a few moments, and gradually the power of the battery was increased to its maximum, and the number of elements increased to fifteen. At the expiration of fifteen minutes, the two lower needles were disengaged from the current, thus concentrating the whole force upon the two upper; at the expiration of fifteen minutes more, the needles were removed. During the operation all the prominences of the tumor disappeared, and a delicate examination detected a hard mass in its place. Not a drop of blood escaped on the removal of the needles. The skin over the tumor presented a bright flush, and the trachea had returned toward its normal position.

"*October* 10*th*.—Patient presented himself for examination. There was no tendency to a reappearance of the tumor; on the contrary, the induration in the neck was steadily diminishing in size.

"*October* 22*d*.—The following is an extract from a letter from the patient, who had already made several public addresses : 'I am feeling very well, and there is nothing to indicate any thing like a recurrence of my malady.' "

It is true that this case is probably one of an erectile tumor, and as such would be likely to be more easily affected by such local action as that of intense decomposing electricity than almost any other form of growth. It is nevertheless a fact of great interest as it stands on the record, and perhaps will be more encouraging when we reflect how large a portion of tumors, and particularly of malignant tumors, are made up of a very abundant reticulation of vessels.

But electrolysis has been tried on malignant tumors. Althaus, Von Bruns, and Gherini, have used it each in a number of cases. Althaus reports that he has gained some advantages in the treatment both of scirrhus and encephaloid, and particularly speaks of the relief which he has obtained from the severe lancinating pains which are so distressing a feature of many cases of cancer. Von Bruns is not so sanguine, and says that electrolysis rarely, if ever, disperses or even materially diminishes a malignant tumor.

The most surprising case on record, however, is one published by Dr. William B. Neftel, of this city, in the *Medical Record* of September 1, 1869. It is substantially as follows :

A gentleman, fifty-eight years old, had a tumor of the left mamma, which by several good surgeons was pronounced cancerous. It was successfully removed by the knife, and the wound healed favorably. The axillary glands of that side began to enlarge soon after the healing of the wound, and formed a large tumor which also was successfully removed. This wound healed slowly, and upon its cicatrix a new tumor grew, which soon attained the size of an orange. The general system had by this time become seriously impaired. To this third tumor electrolysis was applied by Dr. Neftel, at three sittings, on the 27th of April, and on the 4th and 7th of May, 1869. He used the "large apparatus of Krüger and Hirschmann, with elements of Siemens, subdividing, at the second and third operation, the cathode into three or four branches, connected with the needles by serres-fines. The latest improvements of the apparatus afforded the possibility of gradually increasing the quantity of the current without interrupting the circuit, and of diminishing it in the same way, so that the circuit was broken only by the extraction of the last needle. Not a drop of blood escaped. The first operation lasted two minutes, using ten elements; the second five minutes, with twenty elements; and the third ten minutes, with thirty elements. After the operation the tumor increased considerably in size, but became softer and more elastic. No febrile or other local or constitutional symptoms followed. On the contrary, the patient, who before was weak, anæmic, and cachectic, began to gain flesh and strength, the tumor at the same time diminishing slowly but constantly. A month after the first sitting the tumor was found a great deal softer and smaller; at the end of the second month it had almost disappeared, and a fortnight later no trace of it remained. The general condition of the patient is now in all respects excellent, and new deposits can nowhere be detected. In his last letter he writes to me as follows: 'I am not able to discover any new deposits anywhere, nor would the tumor in the right breast be detected by any ordinary observer.'" A year and a half after this date Dr. Neftel reports this gentleman as doing well.

It is of course unsatisfactory, certainly unwise, to attempt to generalize from a single case like the above. We must wait for more light. When we remember the natural tendency to retrogression of some cancers—a tendency which, under improved general and local management, has been certainly very much more prominently recognized during the last few years; when we recollect that under all reasonable modes of treatment some cases have appeared to be benefited; and when, still further, we make allowance for the natural disposition for all men to believe what they wish to be true—we shall, I think, be disposed to receive these confident and sanguine statements with some grains of hesitation, and, instead of accepting them as decisive of any therapeutical result, we shall be disposed to lay them away for future comparison with other facts which are yet to be accumulated; satisfied with the encouraging hope that they are pointing us in the right direction.

4. *Ligature of Arteries.*—In a previous chapter some allusion has been made to the cutting off the vascular supply as a means of modifying the growth of certain very vascular or erectile benign tumors. The same idea has been applied to malignant growths, and particularly those in which great vascularity of the tumor is a prominent feature. The idea of starving malignant tumors by cutting off their circulation has been a popular one with surgeons, and confident hopes have been entertained that it would prove to be a valuable resource. Theoretically it has some considerable plausibility. Though all pathologists recognize a certain independent life, and independent function in all forms of cell, yet it is equally recognized that the continuance of this life, and the perfection of the function, depend directly upon the supply of appropriate material from the blood. The absolute stoppage of this supply involves death, the diminution of it certainly modifies activity: why may not this diminution, carried to a point extreme, but not fatal to the tissue involved, act so as to change the morbid actions, either by stopping them altogether, or reducing them within the limits of health? For the answer to this question we must of course turn to experience; and I think I may say that experience is ready with an answer—probably not a final and decisive answer, but one which I think will enable us, in some good degree, to appreciate the true value of the remedy proposed. .

The advocates of the operation claim for it three distinct points of benefit to the patients: 1. A relief of pain; 2. An arrest of progress; 3. A perfect cure. Of the first point, that of relief from pain, the claim seems to be pretty well sustained; a very large majority of all the cases operated on expressing themselves very greatly benefited, as far as relief from suffering is concerned. With regard to the second point, that of arrest of progress, it must be borne in mind that we have here a problem much more uncertain in its elements than the mere existence or non-existence of pain. What the rate of progress was before operation, and what it would have been if no operation had been performed, are questions which we cannot answer with precision; and hence it comes that we are very liable to be deceived in our estimate of what has been accomplished by the ligature in diminishing a rate of progress, which rate we have not the means of very accurately determining. Still, good observers have, in so many instances, felt warranted in recording such arrest of growth as one of the common results of the application of a ligature, that we are constrained to accept it as a fact. Of the third point—a perfect cure—the record is of course by no means promising. I must here, however, explain what is meant by perfect cure, as used in this connection. Certainly it does not mean that a perfect removal of local cancerous growth has been followed by an evident eradication of cancerous diathesis, and a restoration of the patient to perfect soundness, both local and constitutional. Indeed, so far as I understand the views of the reporters, it is not intended to imply that under this treatment there is necessarily any better chance of escaping secondary tumors, generalization, cachexia, and death, than in cases where other means of removal are employed. Some enthusiastic admirers of the ligature, encouraged by their theoretical views of its action, do evidently try to persuade themselves that these bright hopes are to be realized in the cases they give; but no high authorities that I have had access to claim any thing more than a local cure, leaving the question of final result unsettled, either by their opinions, or by the facts which they present. With this understanding, then, of the meaning of the words we use, we may say that, in a very small proportion of the reported cases, a perfect cure has resulted. I have not myself been so fortunate as to see one of these perfect cures, nor, indeed, have I met with any published case with full details. I give two cases, one of which I saw often with the gentleman who reports it, and the other occurred in the practice of one of my friends, though I am not sure that I ever saw the patient. These cases are not cures, but will perhaps represent the average benefit which results from the operation, and therefore are truer clinical examples than if they were more perfect in their results.

Madelaine Nichols, aged fifty-four, a married woman, was admitted to the New York Hospital, March 30, 1855, under the care of Dr. Halsted, with a large tumor of the antrum on the right side, the history of which she gave as follows : "Two years ago was first attacked with pain in the upper jaw of right side ; the pain constant and lancinating in character. During the next two months a swelling of the jaw showed itself, gradually increasing, projecting not only upon the external surface, but also upon the roof of the mouth, and in its growth pushing out the last two molar teeth. About two months before admission, the tumor having in the mean time greatly increased in size, it began to ulcerate, and, since it has presented an open sore, frequent hæmorrhages have taken place. Mastication of food is difficult, and deglutition much embarrassed. Since ulceration commenced, the increase of the tumor has been much more rapid. The general condition of the patient is pretty good.

"*March* 30th.—An attack of hæmorrhage came on, in which she lost about four ounces of blood. During the following night she lost about the same amount.

"*April* 2d.—On consultation it was determined, with a view of arresting temporarily the growth of the tumor, and preventing the frequent and exhausting hæmorrhage, to ligature the common carotid artery. This was accordingly done by Dr. Halsted, just below the point where the artery is crossed by the omo-hyoid muscle. The first effect of the operation was to produce some giddiness, with dimness of vision in right eye. This made us feel some anxiety for the brain ; but in a few days this passed away, and, with the exception of an attack of erysipelas, every thing went on favorably.

"*April 9th.*—The wound has not healed by first intention and is commencing to suppurate. She has had no hæmorrhage since the operation, and there has been a visible decrease in the size of the tumor. Deglutition is more easy.

"*May 3d.*—The ligature came away to-day. The tumor is now about one-quarter of its original size." From this point the improvement continued. She left the hospital on the 8th of May, the tumor continuing to diminish in size, until it is stated in the notes to have almost disappeared. The patient regained her general health and appearance, and remained well for seven months, when the tumor again began to grow. She died February, 1856, unwilling to submit herself to any further surgical treatment.

The other case occurred in Bellevue Hospital, under care of my friend Dr. Stephen Smith.

Alice Griffiths, aged fifty-three, a widow, of good habits, was admitted to the wards of Bellevue on the 13th October, 1856. She had a tumor of the left upper jaw, which had come on about seven months previously. She had had some sloughing of this tumor, leaving an open sore, which gave great distress on attempting to eat, and from which flowed a large and offensive discharge. She was then much broken down from suffering, and inability to masticate her food. She did not remain long in the hospital at that time, but was readmitted January 23, 1857. "The cheek was now much enlarged from the growth of the tumor. The fissure from the slough had nearly filled from new growth. The tumor now extended back along the mesian line as far as the soft palate (part of which had sloughed away), and both within and without the jaw, from the second incisor of the left side to the last molar. She had great difficulty in swallowing, owing to the size of the tumor, which was now as large as a hen's-egg, and also from the tenderness. There was a constant oozing of matter into the mouth, rendering her stomach very irritable, and also oozing of blood from time to time, on her attempting to masticate any food of unusual hardness. Her health had rapidly failed during the time she was out. The left naris was so perfectly occluded that she was unable to force air through it in blowing.

"*April 24th.*—The tumor, instead of diminishing by the

treatment which had been adopted, has increased. The discharge into the mouth and from the left naris is extremely offensive; her hearing is so much impaired on the left side, that it is with great difficulty that any conversation can be had, or the patient made to understand any thing. There is extreme tenderness in the roof of the mouth, and bleeding almost every time the patient attempts to take any food of greater consistency than fluids. Her general health is rapidly failing; the tumor now extends across the mesian line, back to the soft palate, and is of the size of a medium-sized lemon. The pains are of a lancinating character, and almost constant; the integuments over the tumor are tense, shining, and painful to the touch. The patient is willing to submit to any operation that will afford . her even temporary relief from the pain. The hæmorrhage averages from one ounce to two ounces per day from the roof of the mouth, which is so sensitive that the patient is unwilling to take her wine, from the pain it produces; the erysipelatous attacks have become more frequent; the breathing is so much interfered with that the patient is obliged to keep the mouth open in respiration; she is rapidly failing from repeated losses of blood."

In this condition the carotid was tied by Dr. Smith, April 24, 1857, in the usual situation. She bore the operation well. No evil consequences followed. The ligature came away on the 20th day, being the 14th of May.

" *May 28th.*—The wound is almost entirely healed; a small point remains where the ligature was removed, which is progressing favorably. The tumor remains about the same size; the integuments are much paler; the pain has almost disappeared; the integuments can be corrugated without complaint on the part of the patient; the hardness still remains; there has been no hæmorrhage from the mouth since the operation, except that mentioned as occurring on the second day, and that followed the attempt at vomiting. The breathing is still interfered with; patient unable to force air through the right naris; slight discharge from the nares and mouth continues; she has improved in health and strength; the pain has been alleviated; the comfort she has enjoyed since the operation, from the arrest of the disease, and improvement of the general health, are daily remarked by the patient."

The history taken from the records of the hospital goes no further, but Dr. Smith has recently informed me that this improvement lasted only a few months, when the disease again began to make progress, and soon destroyed her life.

In both these cases the arrest of the disease was manifest, and in both so great an improvement took place in the local and general conditions, from the time of the application of the ligature, that we are justified in regarding the remedy as having shown great power in modifying and retarding the progressive development of the cancerous affection. This same result, sometimes more and sometimes less pronounced, is stated to have occurred in quite a large proportion of the cases which are recorded.

In the July number of the *New York Journal of Medicine*, for 1857, Dr. James R. Wood has collected all the cases he could find of ligature of the common carotid artery by American surgeons. Of these cases, seventeen were performed for the relief of cancerous tumors, mostly of the jawbones. Of the seventeen, four are stated to have resulted in the apparent cure of the disease; ten were decidedly benefited, the growth of the tumor being for the time arrested; two died; one not noted. Looking at the operation merely as a palliative procedure, and it is only in this light that we have any warrant for regarding it, this certainly is an exceedingly satisfactory exhibit. To these statements I might add the recollections of Dr. Mott, contained in a letter to Dr. Wood, and published as part of the paper above referred to.

Dr. Mott says: "The conclusions I have come to are the following: that in malignant disease of the nares, antrum, sides of the head, posterior fauces, and orbit, the ligature of the common carotid of the side affected is, not only a safe, but proper operation. If the disease is not arrested by the tying of one carotid, the other ought also to be tied, as soon as the increase of the disease is in the slightest degree manifested. In several of each of these classes of cases, I have operated myself, and have seen it done by others, and never without manifest advantages to the patient, provided a recovery from the operation has followed. It is well known that some have only lived three to five days after tying the first carotid.

"I have seen a case lately, a malignant tumor in the posterior fauces, originating probably from the periosteum and bodies of two or more of the cervical vertebræ, closing one side of the posterior nares, obliterating the Eustachian tubes, and impeding deglutition, which was greatly benefited by tying the carotid of that side. The tumor obviously diminished in size, and all the unpleasant symptoms were assuaged. When he left for home, he promised to return and have the artery on the other side tied, as soon as there was a return of his suffering. In the first case of this frightful affection, in which the artery was tied, the tumor actually sloughed. In four instances of this disease which we had previously met with, and in which the artery was not tied, they all lingered out a most painful and distressing existence.

"I have seen and known more than one year elapse before it was deemed necessary to tie the second artery. During all this time the disease was not arrested, but atrophy was going on constantly; and, upon tying this second artery, the tumor, though malignant, has entirely disappeared. Two instances of this kind I can now refer to, in which the individuals have enjoyed good health for years without a vestige of the disease remaining."

It may fairly be deduced from the above statements, that ligature of the artery leading to the region affected by a cancerous growth does, in a certain quite large proportion of cases, favorably modify that growth in all the three ways claimed by its advocates. But the other side of the question is still to be considered: In how many cases does the operation involve the death of the patient? The answer to this question depends upon many inquiries, and the most important, perhaps, are as to the disease for which, and the artery on which the operation is performed. By far the largest number of cases have been growths about the jaws and head, and in these the carotid artery has been tied. The femoral and brachial have also been several times operated on for growths of the lower portion of each extremity. The larger trunks have very rarely been subjected to ligature for cancerous disease. The question, therefore, might be narrowed down to these three arteries, and even to the carotid alone, for I think few surgeons would be willing to risk the dangers of applying a ligature to the great trunks, where the expectation can only be one of palliation and temporary benefit.   It is not easy to get at the dangers of these operations, as separated from the diseases and injuries for which they were performed.

Dr. C. Pilz, assistant to the Physiological Institute of Breslau, has published, in Langenbeck's "Archives of Clinical Surgery" for 1868, a most elaborate and valuable table of all the cases in which the carotid artery was tied for all causes, in all countries, and by all surgeons.   This wonderful specimen of German industry and thoroughness contains 586 cases, and gives some details of the operation, the disease, and the result.   Of course, in such a vast table, the details must be very slight, and it is, therefore, only general results which can be obtained from its study.   He gives 142 cases in which the artery was tied for tumors of all kinds, and of these he reports 87 cures, 49 deaths, and 12 not stated. · The cases embrace all forms of tumors, erectile, malignant, etc., and it is evident that the term cure refers only to recovery from the operation, and not at all to recovery from disease.   How much the condition of disease had to do with death cannot be educed from this table; but this very striking fact appears: that, while in the cases where the ligature was applied for hæmorrhage, for aneurism, for tumors, the mortality was from forty to fifty per cent., when we come to operations performed for epilepsy and for neuralgia, we have the surprising statement that, out of 34 operations, in 33 the patient recovered, and in only one was death the result.   Still further, Dr. Pilz refers to some tables published on this very point by Velpeau, of Paris, and Norris, of Philadelphia, in which a better result still is given, viz., eight cases by Norris, in which the carotid was tied for the cure of some affection of the nerve centres, all of which recovered; and Velpeau, three cases and three recoveries.   This statement is all the more remarkable when we reflect that out of every hundred cases in which the carotid is ligatured for hæmorrhage, for aneurism, and for the cure of tumors, twenty-two patients die of cerebral symptoms, supervening after the operation, and manifestly depending on it as a cause.   That this should be the testimony of statistics on so large a scale, and collected by three independent and reliable observers, seems enough to convince us that the ligature of the carotid artery in itself is almost free from danger, and yet the statement is so·surprising, and so contrary to all our preconceived notions, that I am sure surgeons will be slow to accept it without qualification.   The fact stands on the record, however, and we are bound not to overlook it; but, at the same time, the careful surgeon will not be willing to act, in any given case, as if he knew that the ligature he was about to apply to the carotid artery could never be productive of injury.   The same statistics that show that the ligature of the carotid, in one class of cases, is never followed by death, show as clearly that, in another class, including the one in which we are now specially interested, the mortality after ligature is somewhere in the neighborhood of thirty-three per cent.   It is but just to make one class of cases rectify the results of the other; and to deduce our practical rules, not from the consideration of one, but from a fair comparison of both, and an honest recognition of the value of each.   My own feeling in the matter is that, in all suitable cases where the cancerous disease is making rapid progress, or is attended by excessively painful, or dangerous, or exhausting complications, the patient has a right to expect from us the mitigation of suffering, the rescue from immediate danger, and the hope of prolonged life, which we may with intelligent confidence promise him as the probable result of the·ligature of the artery from which the morbid growth derives its sustenance.   The patient should be fairly informed that death may be the effect of the operation to which he submits; but it is our privilege to say to him that he has a chance of a perfect cure, and a much better chance of an improvement in his condition, such as will fully warrant the risk he runs.

5. *Ablation.*—It can hardly be appropriate for me to discuss in this place the general subject of the propriety of operation in cancer.   The views of surgeons on this point are gradually assuming so much of positiveness in the light of recent studies, both in diagnosis and in the statistics of treatment; we know so nearly just what to expect, and just what we may promise; the result of our procedure is so nearly uniform in each class of cases—that it would seem as if the canon law of surgery

26

might almost now be recorded on this subject, with the hope that future revelations would not materially affect its provisions. Certain things seem to be definitely ascertained with regard to the effect of removing cancerous tumors: 1. No degree of thoroughness or promptitude in operation will, in any given class of cancers, secure an immunity from recurrence. This statement is one which most surgeons find it hard to accept. The idea that cancer is, in its earliest stages, merely a local disease which begins to affect the system only after it has gained a certain development, and the feeling that, if operated on at this period, it will be eradicated from the system, and that, therefore, the early extirpation should be insisted on with the hope of permanent cure, are so plausible, so much in analogy with many other pathological actions in our system, that even such men as Mr. Erichsen and Sir William Fergusson, fully informed as they are of all that has been done of late years in giving us precise information on this subject, cannot avoid clinging to it as one of the grounds upon which they base their advice for early operation. That nothing is to be gained by early as compared with late operations, I would not be understood to say. On the contrary, it seems quite certain that the local disease is, at all times, a centre of contamination, both to the neighboring parts and to the general system, a contamination some of the effects of which can undoubtedly be obviated by early operation. What I mean to assert is, that there is no period in the history of cancer where it is so unequivocally a local disease that its ablation will protect the system against its reappearance. I believe this to be, if not positively proved by the statistics of Mr. Sibley and Mr. Paget, so fairly deducible from their researches, that it may safely be accepted as a pathological fact, and that upon it we may wisely base our conceptions of the value of treatment.

2. Want of completeness in an operation for cancer, whereby any portion of the diseased mass is left behind, is injurious in its effect upon the progress of the disease, usually exciting it to a more rapid growth, and hurrying the disease more quickly through its worst and most distressing phases to an earlier death than would have occurred had it been left entirely untouched.

This proposition is so clearly demonstrated, both by reasoning and experience, that I think it will hardly be denied. Even in those recurrent tumors which have no other quality of malignancy than their tendency to return *in loco*, we have ample evidence of the evil effect of partial or imperfect operations, in provoking a more rapid development of the disease; and, in the most benign form of tumor, a portion of the growth, left behind, is almost sure to reproduce, in aggravated form, the original difficulty. The exceptions I have seen to this pathological law have been mainly in those softish fibrous polypi of the uterus where, after ligature, the stump left behind shrinks away and disappears; and in one instance of fatty growth, where no line of demarcation could be traced between the original and the morbid tissues, the operation whereby a large portion, but evidently not the whole of the mass, was removed, was followed by a perfect cure. These are so manifestly exceptional instances, that they do not invalidate the general law, applicable to all morbid growths of the tumor character, and especially and emphatically true of those belonging to the essentially malignant class.

3. The operation itself is an element of danger to the life of the patient so important, that it must not be overlooked. It is extremely difficult to separate this element entirely from the others which go to make up the problem of the value of life in these cases, taken as a class, and still more difficult to estimate its value in studying any single case; but it is not difficult to perceive that death, as a consequence of the operation, is sufficiently common to modify very seriously any statistical results we may wish to arrive at, and to be an important matter of consideration in estimating the propriety of operation in any individual case. Taking, however, the statistics of Mr. Sibley, we find that, of sixty-three operations for cancer of the breast, sixty recovered from the operation, and three died; giving a mortality of about five per cent. due to the operation itself. Mr. Paget states that out of two hundred and thirty-five operations which he collated, without selection, twenty-three died— a mortality of ten per cent., which he is willing to accept as probably not too high, at least for hospital cases. Of the operations likely to be required in cancer of the bones, we have

extirpation of the jaws and amputation of the limbs. The mortality, after removal of the upper jaw, taking Hutchinson's and Esmond's collections together, is, out of thirty-three cases, six deaths. The average mortality of the larger amputations, when performed for disease, is sixteen and one-half per cent. These statements, though not claiming to present the danger of the operation itself, separated from the effects of the disease for which it is performed, show very clearly that the risk to the life of the patient, from the operation itself, must enter as a large and a very important factor in the sum of the considerations against the operation, when deciding as to its performance in any given case.

These three considerations: 1. That operation does not cure, but merely palliates ; 2. That incomplete operation hastens the fatal termination; 3. That the operation itself adds largely to the dangers of the condition, seem to me to embrace the strongest points that can be made against an attempt at removal of a cancerous tumor. Let us look now at what should be said on the other side :

1. A certain number—very small, it is true—of those operated on do recover, and retain their health for such a number of years so perfectly, so far as cancerous symptoms are concerned, as almost to entitle them to be considered perfect cures. Most of the practical writers on this disease have noted examples of this unexpected success. Velpeau speaks of cases where fifteen and twenty years of health have followed an operation for cancer. Sir Benjamin Brodie speaks of two cases, one of thirteen years' and one of fourteen years' immunity from the disease after extirpation. Mr. Weeden Cooke gives a very interesting case of scirrhous breast removed sixteen years previous to his report, by Mr. Lawrence. It remained well for ten years. The disease reappeared, and was treated on two occasions by caustic, and three times afterward by extirpation, one of the operations embracing two enlarged axillary glands. At the time of the report, the patient was in good health; and, though the arm had become within a few months œdematous, there was no certain evidence of the reappearance of the original disorder. Mr. Cooke says that he has met with four instances in which, after operation, the patients have remained free from the disease

for a period of ten years. Mr. Paget alludes to a case where a patient died of cancer of the pelvis, twelve years after the removal of a cancerous testicle; and finally, Mr. Baker, in his statistical paper, gives a case in which a chimney-sweep had a soot-cancer removed from his scrotum, and remained well for thirty-five years, when the disease reappeared as an epithelial growth on the finger and hand. All authorities agree in considering these as only exceptions to a general law, but the practical surgeon, in estimating the chances of life in any given case, is fairly entitled to all the encouragement which can be derived from the knowledge that his patient may be one of the fortunate ones where, by the operation, life is prolonged almost indefinitely.

2. All the statistics which have been published on this subject go to show that some prolongation of life is gained by a complete extirpation of a cancerous tumor. The principal English writers, who have given their attention to the comparing of large numbers of cases of cancer, are Mr. S. W. Sibley, of the Middlesex Hospital, London, and Mr. William M. Baker, of St. Bartholomew's. These gentlemen, working each in a separate field, have collated more than one thousand cases of all forms of cancer—Mr. Sibley five hundred and twenty cases, all treated in the Middlesex, and about half of them observed by himself, and Mr. Baker five hundred cases, all of which were seen and diagnosticated by Mr. Paget, about two-fifths of them having occurred in St. Bartholomew's Hospital, and three-fifths in private practice. These numbers are sufficiently large to give value to the deductions made from them, and they bear internal evidence of having been carefully and conscientiously studied, besides having received the approval and indorsement of the highest surgical authorities. Mr. Baker's cases are the most valuable to us, as they were all external cancers, or such as come under the care of the surgeon, while Mr. Sibley's tables embrace both external and internal; the latter, however, in a very small proportion.

Both writers give special attention to the question we are now considering, viz., the length of life of the cancer-patient from the commencement to the termination of the disease, and the effect of extirpation of the cancer upon the duration of the

disease. Mr. Sibley gives for the average duration of life
for scirrhous and medullary cancer 32¼ months, and of epithelial cancer 53 months. These he considers the average times
of duration when no operation has been performed, the disease being allowed to run its course without any surgical
treatment other than palliative. Of the whole number there
were 63 operations, and no operation is admitted into this
table, or into Mr. Baker's, which was not supposed to be a
complete one. Of the 63 operations, three died and 60 recovered from the effects of the operation—33 of these cases were
kept in view, and the rest lost sight of. Of the 33, 27 had recurrence of the disease, in periods varying from a few days up
to 108 months, which was the longest period to which the local
return was in any case delayed; six cases remained under observation, being as yet free from the disease, the time since the
operation extending in four of them to 7, 29, 36, and 64 months
respectively. The average period of recurrence, in those where
it was known to have reappeared, was about 15 months.

Mr. Baker's results are founded on 111 cases in which operation was performed. He gives the average time of recurrence
in scirrhous about 14 months, in medullary 7⅓ months, in epithelial five months, some of them returning in a few days, others
being delayed to 42, 94, and one to 110 months. The very
small number of medullary and epithelial, as compared with
the large number of scirrhous cases, would raise the general
average very nearly to the rate given for scirrhous, the result as
stated by the two writers not differing more than one or two
months.

Now, comparing the length of life from the beginning to
the end of the disease, in those not operated on, and in those
on whom one or more operations had been performed, Mr.
Sibley says: "Taking the period at which death took place
after the operation, it is found to vary from five to 72 months,
the average duration of life, after operation, being 30½ months.
It is thus seen that the patients operated on lived 53 months,
while those upon whom no operation was performed lived only
32 months, showing that the cases operated on lived 21 months
longer than those left alone." In this estimate the three that
died from the immediate effects of the operation are included.

If they had been left out, the average length of life in those operated on would have stood at 56½ months.

Mr. Baker's results are not very different from Mr. Sibley's. He gives the average duration from the beginning to the end of the disease, for those not operated on, as, in scirrhus, 43 months, in medullary cancer 20 months, and in epithelial cancer 27 months; while, in those who have undergone extirpation, the length of life is stated to have been in scirrhus 55½ months, in medullary cancer 33½ months, and in the epithelial form 57½ months. He makes the average length of life in all cases not operated on as 30 months, in those operated on 48 months. Mr. Baker still further shows that the period at which the operation is performed makes a difference in the result which is quite far from what was commonly supposed, and that late operations usually give late recurrences, and a longer average life than where the cancer is extirpated early. This, however, he explains by the fact that late operations are usually upon chronic cancers, which maintain after operation the same slow progress which characterized them before, and he does not seem to consider that his statistical result militates in any way against the propriety of an early operation.

In applying the results obtained from these tables to cancer of the bones, we can only do so upon general principles. The number of cases of bone-cancer is so small that no reliable results can be obtained from their comparison. It seems pretty certain, however, that life is much more rapidly destroyed by primary cancer in the bones than by any other external or surgical form. Thus Mr. Sibley gives the duration of life in cancer of breast as 32¼ months, of the stomach 8¼ months, of the bone 10 months; and M. Lebert gives very nearly the same view of their comparatively rapid fatality, though he places the duration of life in cancer of breast at 42 months, and in cancer of the bones at 27 months. Due allowance being made for this more rapid mortality, there seems to be no good reason why the general results, obtained from the study of this large number of cases occurring in the soft parts, may not safely be applied to the bones. The sources of fallacy in such tables become more evident the more they are studied, and yet, making all abatements from their authority which the most fastidious may

require, there remains enough to indicate very clearly, if not
to prove the fact, that, as a general law, operations on cancerous
tumors, if performed in suitable cases, and thoroughly and faithfully done, promise, even including the risk to life of the operation itself, a prolongation of life, which, it is much to be hoped,
improved methods of constitutional and local management, and
a better knowledge of the appropriate hygiene of the cancer-
patient, will very materially increase.

3. When, after removal, the disease returns, it does so, either
entirely or mainly, in the internal organs, and the patients generally die from the gradual exhaustion of the cachexia accompanying secondary cancer, rather than from the direct and
dreadful effect of local disease. That this is a positive advantage on the side of operation, few will doubt who have carried
a case of external cancer through all its fearful stages of ulceration, sloughing, hæmorrhage, pain, and sickening fetor, to the
weary and distressing end, and have compared this dreadful
progress with the more quiet, more supportable, and infinitely
less offensive features which characterize the equally unrelent-
ing advances of cancer of the lungs, or of the liver.

In making the statement that the return of the disease is
apt to be in the internal organs, rather than in the original
spot, I wish to be understood as confining the remark to medullary cancer, which is the class to which almost all the cancers
of the bone belong. How it may be in other forms I do not
know, nor am I prepared to support the point by statistics, for
I know of none which bear on it that are sufficiently extensive
to be reliable. I give it merely from the recollections of my
own cases, many of them not recorded, a few typical examples
of each kind having left a strong impression on my memory.
Among the internal organs I include the lymphatic glands,
particularly those within the pelvis, where recurrent cancer
of the bones of the lower limbs is apt to expend its greatest
force.

4. If the patient recover from the operation, he has an interval of perfect freedom from the disease, varying, according
to the character of the case, from a few weeks to many months.
In estimating the blessing which this complete respite confers
upon one who has been long a sufferer under the steady ad-

vance of cancerous disease, we ought to take into our account the effect on the mind as well as on the body. This effect is one of elation, of hope, of confidence—a state of mind which, apart from the happiness which it confers, must necessarily be more favorable as to the progress of the constitutional disorder than the same number of months passed in the gloom and anxiety of steadily progressive local disease. Few patients, who find themselves perfectly well after the removal of a cancer, can resist the feeling that they are permanently well. Their judgment may not tell them so, and probably the most intelligent of them would not be willing to acknowledge it to themselves, but there is a certain feeling, which I think I have often recognized, which gives as much comfort, in certain dispositions, as if their own judgment and that of their surgeon combined to assure them that their cure was as certain and as permanent as it would be after the removal of a cystic or a fatty tumor. Of these patients Mr. Paget very justly remarks: "When they are no longer sensible of their disease, there are few cancerous patients who will not entertain and enjoy the hope of long immunity, though it be most unreasonable, and not encouraged."

In connection with this point, and in strong contrast, as far as the mental condition is concerned, let us remember that a refusal to operate is often a deadly blow not only to the hopes, but to the courage and endurance of the unfortunate patient. Many of them have only gradually brought their minds to consider the possibility of an operation, and have finally nerved themselves up to the point of consent. Many perhaps have come in this frame of mind from a distance, with much personal discomfort and pecuniary sacrifice, to consult a surgeon, ready to submit to any thing which he may deem necessary for their relief. After careful examination and mature deliberation, the refusal of an operation is to them the verdict of the jury, and the sentence of the judge, in the same breath, condemning them to death. It must sometimes be our painful duty to pronounce this fearful doom; the circumstances of the case, the condition of the disease, may require us not only to discourage, but absolutely to forbid any attempt at removal; but we should never forget that in so doing we are taking away the last human hope, and leaving our patient to the darkness and hopelessness of despair.

I have thus laid down, as fairly and as candidly as I am able, the considerations upon which we must base our advice, as to the propriety of an operation, in any given case. But no general application of these considerations can be made in dealing with individuals; each case must be studied by itself; and I know no more difficult problems, in all the practice of surgery, than some of these cases present; and no more delicate question than to decide how earnestly we may persuade our patient to, or dissuade him from the operation, which he either regards with terror, or looks to as his only human hope. Nevertheless, as our knowledge has assumed more precision, so may our advice become more unhesitating and more positive. Let us hope it is becoming more valuable as it becomes more emphatic.

Acting upon the principles we have now considered, I would refuse to operate:

1. In any case in which there was not a reasonable certainty that the whole of the diseased tissue could be removed.

2. In any case where there was clear evidence that secondary cancer had taken place. This requires some modification. The mere fact of internal cancer having begun to show itself might not, in all cases, forbid an operation. If the local disease presented unusually distressing or threatening appearances, we might sometimes be warranted in relieving the patient, by operation, of his immediate sufferings and dangers, though we might be sure that no prolongation of life could be gained by the operation. As a general rule, however, no operation should be performed where secondary disease has already developed itself.

3. In any case in which cancerous cachexia was already well marked. It is to be presumed, in this case, that the general system is already poisoned by the disease, and that the powers of reparation are materially reduced. If the removal of the local cause could be relied on as a removal of the whole disorder, then we might hope, as in other cases in surgery, that the constitutional disturbance would abate on the removal of the source of irritation; but this is not to be expected in cancer. The constitutional impairment is not the mere reflection of a central irritation with which all parts suffer, but it is the effect, and at

the same time the sign, of a change in the actions of the whole economy, which is as much a part of the disease as the ulcerated tumor itself, and which will not be arrested in its progress by the most successful extirpation of the primary disease.

4. In any case where the operation required was so formidable in its extent or character as to add materially to the dangers of the patient's condition. We would not hesitate to amputate a forearm, where we might refuse to exarticulate at the hip-joint, and generally a trifling and safe operation would be more readily resorted to by the surgeon than one of great magnitude and danger. Our hopes of benefit do not warrant the running of greatly increased risk of life.

5. Where the patient was very old, and the cancer chronic in its course. The slow progress of the disease is likely to continue if it is left alone; the operation would be very likely to hasten a fatal termination in advanced age.

6. Where the patient was not a good subject for any operation by reason of bad habits, excessive fat, great feebleness, or any organic disease impairing nutrition or reparative power. I think, too, that unconquerable fear of an operation, or unreasonable dread of its consequences, should be a contraindication not to be overlooked.

On the other hand, I would advise an operation:

1. In all cases where the disease could be easily and entirely removed, and particularly if, as in the case of amputating a cancerous bone, I could be sure of removing, not only the disease, but the whole organ affected by it. This, I think, is a very important practical point; and I believe that the cases in which any other operation than amputation should be performed on one of the long bones affected with cancer must be very rare indeed.

2. Where there was no suspicion of any secondary disease in any internal organ, and no extensive affection of the lymphatic glands. The mere enlargement of a few of these glands by local infection is no contraindication of an operation, statistics not showing that this condition adds materially to the unfavorable prognosis, particularly if they admit of complete removal.

3. Where the true cancerous cachexia was not as yet devel-

oped in any marked degree. It is not always possible to discriminate between the constitutional effects of cancer, as such,
and those depending on the ordinary causes of failing health
and strength, such as pain, hæmorrhage, excessive discharge,
and the like. In many cases, however, it can be arrived at,
and, where there seems to be no failing of the powers of life
but what can be accounted for by the effects of the local actions,
we have a right to recommend an operation, in the hope that,
for this form of constitutional impairment, the removal of the
local cause will prove a remedy.

4. If the operation required for the thorough removal of
the disease be not one seriously imperilling life. In cancer of
the bones this question is brought down to the comparison of a
very few operations; mainly, amputations and excision of the
upper or lower jaws. All these are serious operations, and
should not be lightly determined upon; but, for most of them,
the precise grade of danger is almost mathematically proved by
reliable statistics; and, inasmuch as in these operations we are
cutting through perfectly sound parts, we may almost say that
we can announce the precise amount of risk we are recommending our patient to assume, in undergoing any given amputation. Of course this risk will be modified by the condition of the patient in other respects than the cancer for which
the operation is to be performed, but this condition presents
nothing which we are not accustomed to deal with in the ordinary problems of surgery, and is to be appreciated in accordance with its well-known laws.

5. If the cancer be of slow growth, and the patient not old,
we have very good reason for believing that the recurrence will
be long delayed, and the period of exemption from the disease
will be a long, perhaps a very long one. It is from this class
of cases that most of the so-called cures are derived, and, though
I cannot assert that statistics prove the fact, yet I think their
results render it highly probable, that the slower a cancerous
growth is in passing through its earlier stages, the longer is it
delayed after operation, and the slower its progress when it
does return. Very acute cancers are generally unfavorable
cases for operation.

6. The good general health of the patient is a strong point

in favor of an operation, deemed proper for other reasons, as well as an earnest of its success. I cannot help feeling, too, that in all cases a strong desire for the operation, and strong conviction that it will be successful, on the part of the patient, may be accepted by the surgeon, not only as a good omen, but, so far as it goes, a positive indication.

Lastly : though it may not flatter our scientific vanity, yet it is but honest to confess that the uncertainty of our diagnosis may give some encouragement to operation, as, in removing what we believe to be a cancer, we may perhaps be extirpating a perfectly benign growth, and, instead of giving our patient a brief respite from death, our mistake may secure for him an uncontaminated and a healthy life.